Drafted Luck

TWISTED LUCK BOOK 5

TERNION UNIVERSE

Mel Todd

BAD ASH PUBLISHING

Bad Ash Publishing
86 Desmond Court
Powder Springs, GA 30127
www.badashpublishing.com

Publisher's Note: This is a work of fiction. Names, characters, places, and incidents are a product of the author's imagination. Locales and public names are sometimes used for atmospheric purposes. Any resemblance to actual people, living or dead, or to businesses, companies, events, institutions, or locales is completely coincidental.

Book Layout © 2015 BookDesignTemplates.com

Drafted Luck/ Mel Todd -- 1st ed.
Paper ISBN 978-1-950287-16-1

Dedication –
To all the people that helped make this book a
reality: Doug, Ginger, Cisca, Michelle, Marcus,
Marguerite, Monika, Marcia, and so many others.
Thank you.

CONTENTS

Mandatory Mage Registration & Service Act
Section 1.1 -

All mages are required to be tested and ranked by
their 27th birthday. At that time they will be assigned
a rank of: Hedgemage, Magician, Wizard, Archmage, or
Merlin. Hedgemages are regarded as normal in most
cases and are not faced with the burden placed on
other mages.

SPIRIT

I wheeled my suitcase down the dingy hallway on
the third floor. The linoleum looked older than me. Each
side of the hallway had small doors leering at me, some
with a name written on a sticky pad stuck to them. My
fellow draftee mates I assumed.

All mages were required to serve in the draft, and
being a merlin, my service was a decade long. Odds
were most of the others would only have a four-year
draft.

Lucky them.

I kept walking the interminable hall, searching for
my name, Corisande Munroe, as I went, the dim
fluorescent lights and lack of windows doing nothing to
assist me. Gauging the distance between the doors I
figured each room would be about the size of my closet.

Well, the size of Sable and Jo's closet.

Jo, my best friend in the world, and her spouse Sable
wouldn't be able to get all their clothes in something this
small. Good thing that wasn't one of my foibles. And I

missed them already, which seemed vaguely silly. I might be gone for the next decade; why was I missing them barely hours into the next act in my life?

Because you are Joined and miss them?

I twisted the ring on my right ring finger at the thought, the magical stone brighter than it had any right to be.

~I do not understand why we must stay here,~ Carelian protested as he walked by my side. ~Sable and Jo did not need to leave their home for their orientation, why do you?~

I fought back a sigh. My familiar was a Cath, a species of intelligent cat-like beings that lived in the Chaos realm. Cath did not believe human rules applied to them. Carelian often refused to understand why I had to follow laws or rules or orders or a myriad of other restrictions when he had a much simpler solution. Usually kill them, eat them, or do it anyway. Caths were the ultimate example of "that can't possibly apply to me" creatures.

"Because it is a new process that started this round. The email mentioned something about networking and an environment with less distractions. Besides it's only a month, and who knows where I'll be placed when this orientation is done. It could be anywhere."

I really hoped it was Atlanta. I'd lived there for the last five years with Jo and Sable. But the government could and would place you anywhere in the world if they had a need. And given my power and access to multiple branches of magic, they might decide they needed me everywhere or anywhere.

Carelian, who'd grown to the size of a large Saint Bernard but less fuzzy, rumbled by my side, his tail swishing as we stopped in front of a door with my name tacked to it. I pushed it open and glanced inside fighting back a sigh. I'd become spoiled in my accommodations the last few years. This room looked like a reject from the seventies. Twin bed, desk, tiny closet with a built-in dresser that might hold my clothes. The air conditioner/heater combo was built into the wall under the window. When I added in the linoleum that hadn't been changed this century and the vaguely harvest gold faded paint, I almost expected bell bottoms and a disco ball to materialize.

"One month. We can handle it," I said trying to convince myself more than him.

~I prefer the accommodations at our apartment,~ he groused, walking into the room and inspecting every inch.

"You prefer the house in Albany with your own bed and a yard to go terrorize squirrels in," I retorted, but I didn't really disagree with him. Sable's job paid her over a hundred thousand a year. With the addition of our rent allowances for college we had gotten a nice apartment for the three of us, with double master bedrooms, and only a fifteen-minute walk to school for Jo and me. But that was in Atlanta. I'd inherited a house in Albany, New York, that all of us loved, but at this rate it would be another decade before I could live there.

Jo earned her bachelors, then her masters in Mechanical Engineering with a minor in Transform, and the draft had slapped her to work with the Army Corps of Engineers on some water rights stuff with Lake Lanier. She seemed happy and excited about what they were doing, even if half of what she and Sable talked about went over my head. It took me another two years to get my doctorate. I spent a lot of time in labs and my dissertation ruffled a lot of feathers.

But it meant Sable would be finished with her service next year. She loved her current job, and they had hinted at a promotion, but already headhunters were talking about some great jobs all over the country. I had no idea that an interest in water purification could be so lucrative. But for now she'd chosen Atlanta. Where they might decide to go depended a lot on where I ended up.

Jo and Sable had gotten married this summer, between my graduation and the start of my draft, though Jo had proposed at the Fourth of July. What I hadn't expected was that they had been talking to Esmere and Baneyarl about triads. When they married me in the same ceremony, I thought my heart would break with joy and fear. But I also knew those two were in my life forever. They had talked about having children when both of them were done with the draft and we were all settled. We were still working on what a triad meant to us.

I didn't know what we were besides family. Carelian and his mother, or malkin, Esmere, said we were a joining and that was all that mattered. The relationship between the three of us wasn't sexual, but it was real. I had finally realized it would never break, and adding Sable had just made it stronger. Though I still didn't know what making us into a coven would involve.

But now that I had finished my doctorate, it was my turn to serve. I loved what I'd learned, though I wasn't sure what job they would assign me. Being a double merlin, the only one they'd identified so far, meant I was overly powerful. Then if you added in Carelian, it meant I had even more power at my disposal. This power made a lot of people very nervous.

I'd earned my bachelors in Biology, Masters in Biology, and Doctorate in Quantitative BioSciences. It meant I was really excellent at researching things in labs and maybe even coming up with new medicines or procedures, at least that was my hope. I had a ton of minors too. Mostly I'd had time to kill and free tuition so why not learn everything I could? I'd earned minors in Spirit, Chaos, Organic Chemistry, and Criminal Justice. Steve Alixant, my mentor, sometime boss, almost friend, and fellow merlin, thought they might use me as a troubleshooter because I had worked with the FBI and had the CJ minor.

Personally, I counted the decade of my draft all as penance for my degrees and just wanted to get it over with. The last few years had been quiet with no one trying to kill me, pressure me, or even give me any hassle. Apparently, the last big drama, after I got my degree, with actual demigods from the other realms showing up convinced everyone to leave me alone.

It had been nice.

Either way, I had regular classes with Baneyarl, my griffon teacher, though we'd moved on to theoretical discussions and talk about how our scientific explanation of magic compared to how realm denizens thought about magic. Those discussions had dropped down to once a month and would go on hold until my draft settled down. The three of us usually made it a day out with friends, bringing food and other things from our realm. We'd started a spice trade that had made us a bit of extra cash and guaranteed I'd at least be able to pay my membership in the House of Emrys by that alone, though getting gems exchanged into cash was a pain sometimes.

A quick glance at my watch told me I had thirty minutes until the start of orientation.

I unpacked quickly, dumping my First Aid kit and bathing supplies on the shelf in the closet. It didn't take me long to locate the shared bathrooms or the laundry room. I pulled my phone out of my pocket and sent Jo and Sable a quick text.

Am here. Unpacked. Off to hear the lecture about my solemn duty.

Almost instantly there was a laughing emoji. We didn't go silent; you never knew when someone would kidnap you. Too bad we had to learn that the hard way when Hamiada, my house, had kidnapped both of them.

Enjoy. Ping us when bored. Still don't understand why they're keeping you there, but whatever. Don't eat anyone.

I pretended she meant that for Carelian, as I was much too nice of a dragon to ever eat anyone. Besides, for me being a dragon was a state of mind, not a form I could shift into. Shape shifting wasn't a magic any human had. I laughed to myself as I had a night shirt that read, "Don't poke dragons, for you are crunchy and taste good with ketchup."

With one last look around the room, I headed to the orientation location. Carelian trailed alongside me, too bored to even chase leaves. It looked like we were on the campus of a small college built ages ago.

There were small signs printed up saying orientation with an arrow and I followed, surprised I hadn't run into anyone yet. Sable said her orientation class, which had met daily for two weeks to make sure they knew the laws, how pay worked, and who to complain to if they had an issue, had over two hundred people and was more of a seminar class than anything else. Complete with homework.

I glanced at the cat by my side; he'd been too quiet and that usually meant he was up to something. "You don't have to stay. You can go sleep at the apartment, or even the house if you want." Carelian could step through reality to any place he wanted, though I didn't know if all Cath could do that or if it was a learned skill. I could sidestep to anywhere on Earth if I could visualize it clearly enough. I wasn't crazy enough to try to sidestep from here to another realm. Within realms I could sidestep if I knew where I was stepping to, but so far, I'd refused to do anything quite that insane outside of Baneyarl's space. Realms could be anything and could shift. Earth remained stable.

~No, my quean. I stay by your side.~ He almost muttered the words. If I hadn't been walking down the aisle to the front of the auditorium, I might have pushed him on it. As it was, I was too busy frowning. It was an auditorium, but in front of the stage were eleven chairs, obviously waiting for people to fill them. I had no idea if they were for the other mages here for orientation, or if it was for someone else. Except they all faced the stage, not the audience. I moved over to the side, scanning the auditorium with both my eyes and my magic. I could sense magic if someone else was casting a spell or tearing open a portal to another plane.

But I didn't sense any magic or portals opening. It felt like a building, nothing more or less. Carelian had disappeared into the shadows, of which there were more than I would have thought. Did no one believe in turning on lights?

I didn't see Carelian. Not that I was particularly worried about him, but he'd been known to give people heart attacks in sheer fright when they saw him. A light flashed into the auditorium as someone else opened the door. I looked up the aisle to see who was arriving. The lack of good light, not to mention the door opening again, prevented me from getting a clear look. I knew they were people and that was it.

I rolled my shoulders and brushed down my pants. Today I was dressed in my nice but powerful clothes, jean slacks, a soft green tank top, and a lightweight jacket in grey matching my slacks with interior pockets.

That paired with low heeled boots and my hair in a smooth braid, I knew I looked a bit remote and older than I was. Which was the intent of this outfit. Over the years I'd learned just how powerful clothing could be.

When the newcomers got closer, I frowned, more than a bit surprised. Mages—well most mages—didn't emerge until after puberty. At a minimum you had to get a bachelors, but most got masters or even doctorates like me. That meant most mages were in their mid to late twenties when they started their draft. I was a bit old at earning my doctorate at twenty-seven. Most people were out by twenty-five or so.

The group of people walking down struck me as odd. At least two had tattoos on their faces besides their mage tattoo, their clothes were beat up or screamed attitude, and a few were much younger than me, maybe only twenty-two, which I guessed was possible, but it seemed off. I'd been a college student. We had this self-possession, almost arrogance especially in the later years as we got used to magic and its limitations. These mages didn't look anything like that and it made me uncomfortable.

"Yo, looks like we get primo seats. What up?" said one of the men, his skin either a light tan or the lights were worse in here than I thought. He flashed a grin that I'm sure was supposed to be charming but it came across as wolfish and hungry.

"Waiting for orientation to begin," I replied, not sure about anything. I still didn't know where Carelian was or what he was up to.

"Same. Should be bad ass, get our draft done, and make some sweet moolah. Can't wait." He just smiled that same hungry smile and I nodded, scanning the others. A mix of men and women. One or two looked interested in the set-up, the others just looked as if here was the last place they wanted to be. I couldn't disagree with that sentiment.

Before I could move over and try to introduce myself, sharp footsteps rapped out on the stage. A figure moved out into the light that hit the center front. The man was dressed in a navy three-piece suit with wing tip shoes, his hair in a short neat office cut. He strode out and drew our attention with a level of presence I couldn't help but admire.

He stood and I felt his gaze ruffle over us, though I couldn't see any details about his eyes.

"I would say welcome, but you aren't. You're here because it is my job to make sure you can become productive members of society or to make sure society never has to deal with you again."

Chapter 2

Section 115.2.4

During any mage draft service security may prove paramount and electronic devices are at risk of being compromised. Any reasonable request to confiscate or limit access to electronic devices by either your draft contact or your draft supervisor will be supported. Refusal may be regarded as a national security matter.

ORDER

Wait, what?

All of my attention snapped to him and tweaks of discomfort in my stomach flared into full blown churning.

"Take a seat, now!" His voice rang through the room like a shot. Four years ago I would have been scrambling for a seat. Two years ago I might have ducked my head and slunk over there. But I'd practiced channeling my inner dragon. I watched the others scurry, eyes wide or a snarl on their faces. The one that worried me the most was a girl with strawberry blonde hair. She didn't even seem to register anything he said, just drifted over and sat. I couldn't see her clearly but something tugged at me.

The only chair left was one in the middle, front row—of course. I walked over at a slow measured pace and sank into the chair, trying to emulate the grace Lucille Blanding exuded.

Lucille managed James Wells' estate. While she kept everything ready for me to inherit, she also ran her own business and intimidated everyone who knew her. I'd talked her and Indira Humbert, my other mentor and merlin, into giving me attitude and poise lessons. Carelian approved. He felt his quean should be more regal. I still wasn't sure I could pull it off, but now seemed the perfect time to put everything to use.

Legs crossed, I tilted my head up, giving him my serene expression. I admired how he used height, light, and the auditorium to give him an illusion of power. But the question was: to impress or cow? From his statement I was thinking cow, but the other people here didn't make any sense. Sable said she was with all archmages. As was Jo. There wasn't another merlin here, and while I wasn't perfect at guessing, almost none of these mages felt that powerful.

"All of you are screw ups and represent a danger to our great country. I am authorized to make sure you understand your responsibilities as a mage or make sure you will never be a risk to anyone ever again."

The male mage who had spoken to me sneered and called out, "What ya gonna do to us? You ain't no mage, you're nothing." He grinned maliciously as his words rang in the auditorium. Flames blossomed over his fingers.

"Ricardo Juarez." The man on the stage didn't seem worried at all. He walked around to the steps on the side and proceeded down with slow ponderous steps. "Lieutenant in the California Kings. Never convicted of anything, but suspected in multiple crimes, any of which carry the death penalty." He kept speaking as he walked, stopping in front of Ricardo.

Up close I could see his hard face, with no laugh lines anywhere on it.

"You got that right. No crime, no punishment." Ricardo laughed as the flames created flickering light around his face.

"That is how the law works. But if I was to do this?" The man swung at Ricardo; a hard fast jab aimed at his chin. It never connected. Ricardo leaned back then spun out of the way, standing, his face suffused in a scowl of rage. Our speaker stood there, a silent smirk on his face.

"You stupid pendejo!" Ricardo spat and fire jetted out toward the man before I could even react.

But rather than being scared, the man sidestepped the flames and drew a gun. The movement so smooth and fast I didn't realize he had a gun in his hand until I heard him speaking. "Pursuant to Section 1.3.4, attacking an officer of the draft is a class A felony and the punishment is death." He pulled the trigger and a dart slammed out and hit Ricardo in the neck.

Ricardo gasped his hand flying to his neck, eyes wide, face pale, then in a slow crumple like an ash remnant he collapsed. Two men emerged from the shadows and headed toward us.

All of it happened before I could even think to react. I watched it all with my mind frozen in surprise. The man turned and looked at us, and I saw the smirk at the corner of his lips.

"Take this as a given; if you break the rules the consequences will be severe and immediate. It is my job to make sure all of you know exactly what your role is as a drafted mage. Any breaking of the rules will be noted and addressed." He glanced over to where the two men were carting Ricardo off. "He will be tried and executed. Everything here is videotaped and nothing is done without us being aware of it."

"You killed him," gasped out one of the women. Dressed in a long bohemian gown with lots of crystals, her face was whiter than the quartz around her neck.

"That would be inefficient and create extra

paperwork. I hit him with a tranquilizer dart."

"Lie," my mind shouted, though nothing else had been a lie.

"He will go through due process like all of you will, because all of you are dangerous and don't know your place." All of that was truth, though I knew I'd never see Ricardo breathing again.

He scanned the assembled people, who all had pale faces. "Now that you understand your place, my job is to make sure you know the rules and I will do everything legally in my power to make you cross the line. I delight in it. You know you are all losers and I just plan on making sure you all are removed from the game, legally." He smirked right at me as he said that and I felt everything snap into place.

Three years they'd been planning this and I was the reason. They didn't think they could control me, so they planned on killing me legally. And starting the draft activated the draft laws. It gave them power over me they didn't have before. I narrowed my eyes, but settled back into my chair, a smile pasted on my lips. I knew every law regarding mages, each section and the history of it. Jo, Sable, and I had studied every loophole and I knew this was a game of me keeping my cool.

~Carelian, want to join me?~ I asked, still smiling at the man.

~I thought you'd never ask,~ he purred and stalked out of the shadows. I heard a few muffled shrieks as he came up and sat next to me, and I couldn't blame them. I smiled at the man, keeping my calm, cool façade.

"Oh yes, Merlin Munroe. I was warned about your familiar," he said with a flat tone. "Be warned, any law you break the consequences apply to it too."

That made me laugh and I could see multiple people looking at me, eyes wide, sure I was insane. "You are welcome to try, but remember, he is his own person and the second I die, there are no more restraints on him." I blessed Baneyarl and Esmere for the hours upon hours of political coaching they had provided me, pointing out that people would threaten Carelian to get to me. But they also pointed out that nothing short of a blitz attack or an area attack would get him. And Tirsane only mentioned me being killed legally; Esmere was perfectly capable of taking any revenge she wanted no matter how I died.

The very fact that those beings had talked about retaliations on humans made me wonder what else the title Herald meant, but no one would say. Apparently it was like saying I was invited to dinner—what that involved could mean absolutely anything. Up to and including I was being served as dinner.

The man glared at me and I smiled, letting my hand rest on Carelian's back. Silence was power. He glared at me for a moment longer, then stalked back toward the stage. "For the next month, you had better watch your step because I will be watching yours. My name is Brian Kamp, Director for the Draft, and I will be overseeing your re-education to make sure you understand the importance of your role in our society."

I heard others shifting and muttering, the empty chair in our midst a reminder of what we were facing.

"Now, turn over all your phones. Now!" His voice cracked through auditorium and the others scrambled to pull out their phones. I went through the law in my head and sighed. I pulled out my phone slowly, and Kamp moved toward me, a small bag in his hand. "Drop it here."

"One minute," I said and saw him about to snarl something, but I cut it off with a sweet smile. "After all, we want to make sure we maintain security. Don't we?"

He opened and closed his mouth a few times trying to come up with a retort.

As he spluttered, I pulled up and wiped my phone. I had Jo and Sable's numbers memorized. As it finished wiping, I pulled my credit cards and ID out of the case. I powered it down and dropped it in the bag, forcing a smile. "There you go."

Carelian didn't move from my side as Kamp sneered at me and moved to collect the rest of the phones. I sat back and forced myself to think. If I thought through everything they could possibly pull, nothing would surprise me. I watched the others and saw two of them crying as they dropped their phones in the soft bag. Who knew what secrets the phones might reveal? Which was why I'd wiped mine. No one needed to know who I trusted or relied on.

~Is there a purpose behind this theater?~ Carelian asked, yawning, showing off his teeth if anyone thought about moving closer.

~Isolation I suspect and the enemies I made when Hamiada tested me on behalf of magic have probably come home to roost.~

Hamiada was the dryad that was part of my house. She'd kidnapped Jo and Sable, and I had to go rescue them. To save them I had to pass three trials. By the time I returned to Earth I had a yard full of Draft officers waiting for me. They were offended that I'd stepped out on a murder investigation. I'd managed to avoid being found in violation of the laws, but I'd also created an enemy that day—Director Harold Lefoin. I'd kept tabs on him and he had risen to Deputy Chairman for the Draft Board. The only position higher was Chairman and that was usually a senator. It meant he had a lot of power, but I'd been hoping he'd forgotten about me.

Carelian snorted in my mind. ~Like I would ever leave you. You will never be isolated while you have me.~

~They don't count you. But they think it removes Jo and Sable from me.~ I was worried as all of this seemed to be geared toward me or maybe just those who weren't seen as following the party line enough. That idea set off too many alarm bells in my mind.

The other mages had found their way back to their chairs and all of them were sitting there on the edges of their seats, most looking frantic, though a few looked bored, and the redhead hadn't moved.

I watched Kamp drop the bag of phones on the stage, wincing at bit at the crashing noise they made. At least mine was in a good case but still. Oh well, worst case I'd get a new phone.

"Now that you understand the seriousness of this, here is the agenda for the next month. You will learn the laws and your place in them and what your requirements are for the draft. Most of you owe the government four years, Munroe here owes us ten. I doubt any of you will finish your draft. You're all too stupid or too arrogant to live that long. But since we want to make sure that you remain healthy, we are trialing a mandatory physical education requirement. You will be showing up every morning outside for PT. This isn't optional. The first part of the afternoon will be spent reviewing the laws. Then you will go to training for how to use your skills as the government requires from you. You must prove you understand how the laws apply to you." He paused and looked at all of us, contempt clear on his face. "Do you understand?"

"Of course," I replied as I looked at him.

His gaze locked on my face and he smiled. I knew without a doubt that this had been arranged specifically for me.

"Then go get what you need, a notebook might be helpful. For the next month you won't be allowed off campus. Remember violations can be construed as intentional avoidance of draft mandates. Meals will be provided starting with breakfast tomorrow morning." With that he disappeared into the shadows with our phones, leaving us to stew.

Section 1.3.4

Assault or offensive use of magic on any draft officer during draft service is regarded as a Class A felony and if authorized by the Draft Board and the OMO, the officer may have the person executed immediately.

CHAOS

The echoes of his steps hadn't finished fading away before I was up and headed out of the auditorium, my mind spinning. Everything, even the PT, came across as a trap and a reason to sanction us for not following instructions. No one mentioned PT in the assignment email, so I had no workout clothes available, much less sneakers to run in.

My strides were brisk across the campus, but my mind still processed what had occurred in that auditorium. Why were these other mages being lumped in with me? While having a gang lieutenant who was a mage seemed like a terrible idea, things like that had to have happened before. Was this something that happened on a regular basis? I'd obviously gotten too complacent over the last two years. All I'd done was research and study. The biggest excitement was going to Baneyarl's.

I turned it over in my mind as I reached the dorms. Esmere once said everything was politics, and I had the bad feeling this was going to prove that. The first political decision I had to make? Make friends or keep everyone away from me. I needed information, and I needed it fast. Of course, I also needed clothes, shoes, and more hair scrunchies.

I scanned the room, but just because I didn't sense magic didn't mean there weren't electronic listening devices. I started inspecting the room—overhearing me I could defeat, but cameras I needed to remove. Fifteen minutes later I finished checking every bit of the room and no camera.

~Carelian, can you open a rip to Jo and Sable?~

He had sprawled out on the bed, taking up the entire thing. I added a note to pull in his bed too, otherwise I'd be sleeping on the floor.

~I figured you would need to talk to them.~ There was a small spike of pain as the rip formed and I quested out. It had taken me a while to get to the point that I could talk to Jo and Sable this way. In the beginning, I could just send thoughts to them but they couldn't respond. After much practice with Baneyarl, we advanced to full mindspeech as long as Carelian facilitated it. It had something to do with him as my focus, but he groomed his balls every time we asked about it and didn't reply. He could be a jerk when he wanted to be one.

~Jo? Sable? Got a minute?~

~Hey, Cori? What's going on ?~ Jo responded, and as always mindspeech had a bit more flavor to it than verbal words. Her worry and curiosity coated the words like sugared candy.

~Sable?~

~Yep, here too. We're getting dinner ready.~ Sable sounded more relaxed, but she had a go with the flow attitude I admired.

~So I need a few things. This whole setup reads as a trap and I'm going to need to deal with it, or they are going to use it as a reason to kill me.~

~WHAT!?~ The dual exclamations spiked into my brain and I groaned as I sat down on the uncomfortable desk chair. The students in the seventies must not have had any sensations in their butts.

~Easy please. Shouting like that makes me think Carelian decided to use my brain as a scratching post.~

~That would be useless. Scratching posts should pull against my nails, not give at their touch.~ He sniffed and I flicked a hand at him.

There was a moment of silence then Jo and Sable snickered. ~I think you just got dissed by your cat,~ Jo said, sounding much more relaxed.

~This is not a new thing,~ I muttered, glaring at Carelian who was busy making sure every hair on his tail exhibited perfection. ~So the Draft Board is playing games. I'm pretty sure they are trying to kill me in a way they don't think Tirsane and Salistra will have an issue with. Other than that, I'm not sure what is going on. Granted, I'm also not sure Tirsane and Salistra remember their threats,~ I stated as I rose and walked around the room.

~They do. They talk to Esmere about you sometimes,~ Carelian provided.

~That doesn't help me feel more secure. Either way someone is trying to kill us or use me or both. But I'm not sure yet.~ I paced in the tiny room, already missing the bigger space of my bedroom at Sable's.

~Okay? None of that explains why you're talking to us via mind speak,~ Sable pointed out and I sighed.

~The person heading this program collected our phones. I think they're trying to play the isolation card, or make sure people can't check out what they are being told while in class. But they've forgotten how much people in my generation communicate via computers. Sure no phone makes it annoying, but with a computer I can talk to anyone. Maybe both, but either way I need a list of things and not having a phone or being able to leave campus makes it difficult. In theory, we're allowed off campus tonight, but I suspect there is a curfew he didn't bother to tell us about.~

~Only you Cori,~ Jo laughed and it wrapped around the words in my mind. ~So what do you need?~

~A few things. I'm going to need exercise clothes and tennis shoes. If you can get those, I think my loving familiar would be willing to step over and get them for me.~

~Depends. Will they share dinner?~ he asked sitting up. ~Chicken?~

~Yes, oh bottomless pit. We'll throw another one in the air fryer for you,~ Sable said, and I could hear the mental rolling of eyes. Carelian ate more than both of them put together. Be interesting to see if the Draft Board was ready for his food needs.

Carelian purred in our shared mindlink. ~Yes, the crispy fat is delicious that way.~

~I'll get a bag put together for you,~ Jo responded. ~What else?~

~I think we should set up a check in. Carelian, if something happens to me, I need you to go to Jo and Sable and make sure they are safe. Please?~ That was my one big fear. That if I was targeted, Jo and Sable would be as well.

~Always. They are my queans too.~ He rose and pursued his head stropping across my leg.

I rubbed his ears just the way he liked as I thought. ~Right now I think that's it. They took my phone though, so let Steven and Indira know. Otherwise, can you order me some pizza to deliver here? I don't want to leave campus and open myself up to other issues.~

~Yep. Address match up to what was on the email?~

Jo asked.

~Yes, or at least the rideshare had no issue finding the place.~ I looked around and didn't see a fridge, but food was an excellent icebreaker. ~Jo, can you triple the order? I want to see if I can at least make nice with the other mages. Not that I trust any of them right now, but I don't get everything that is going on. It feels like I'm in some weird movie plot with layers and layers of conspiracy.~ I groaned and sank back down on the uncomfortable chair. ~Oh yeah, I need a notebook and stuff. Heck, I might need my laptop and a printer if he's going to have us do homework. This is just ridiculous. The email said just show up with enough clothes for two weeks and be ready to network.~

Sable snickered in my mind. ~I'd be much more worried if it was anyone else, but this sort of stuff seems to follow you. Remember your stalker last year?~

~Yes. Finally had to call Charles and ask him to come convince the guy that I was involved with him and our familiars were sex partners. I still can't believe the guy bought it.~ I shook my head, remembering the incident. Charles Wainscot and his familiar Arachena had become friends and occasionally came over. He was an odd personality, even by my standards. He thrived in the logic of order and loved his databases. I suspected he had the skill set and personality to be a black hat hacker if he wanted. Lucky for us he found working for big corporations managing their data and security much more interesting. As well as being a white hat hacker for me occasionally. He didn't come on our visits to Baneyarl, but he'd been up to the house in Albany twice, and he and Baneyarl had some epic conversations about the nature of morality.

~More Arachena informed him if he continued to discomfort her chosen's mate she would use him as food for her children,~ Carelian said in our minds and I turned to glare at him.

~She what?~

He just flicked an ear at me, not expanding on his comment. I sighed. ~No wonder Charles kept getting funny looks on his face. I bet she was telling him things. Oh yeah, let him know what's going on too. Ugh, never realized how dependent I was on my phone.~

~No worries. Everyone that knows you knows us too. *Mami* will be annoyed but I'm sure she'll expect a visit as soon as you get an assignment,~ Jo said, soothing my worries a bit. Isolation was an effective technique. If I couldn't talk to them I might already be freaking out.

~Okay. Get everything ready for Carelian and I'll be here waiting for pizza. Add some chicken wings? I'm suddenly starving.~

~One order for a dorm full of starving students placed. Should be there in about forty-five minutes. I'll have your stuff ready in about ten, but since I know Carelian will want at least two chicken breasts, I'd be surprised if he's back before the pizza gets there.~ Jo sounded sure and calm and that made me relax.

They are safe. I got this.

And I did. The last few years had been quiet, the stalker registering more as an annoyance than anything else. I only did minimal magic in classes, working with Baneyarl on the big things, and I'd gotten very good at giving offerings that were almost invisible. Blood, skin, hair on my legs, so anyone watching would think I almost never did any magic. Which had been part of the plan originally, but then it became second nature. The problem was going to be making sure I didn't give them any reason to enact the laws against me. I smirked, almost looking forward to it, but worry still churned in my stomach. They had already proved how ruthless they were willing to be.

~Watch yourselves. I don't know if they'll try to use you against me, but I wouldn't be surprised by anything.~

~We will. You make sure you return to us as you left.~ Sable sent me a mental hug, and I responded in kind, already missing them.

~See ya, Cor. Have fun storming the castle.~ Jo's teasing ended the connection.

I looked at Carelian, who had stepped off the bed and was stretching, taking up most of the available space. "I should have asked for another room, just for you," I said with a smile.

~This is distressingly small,~ his voice dismissive.

I opened my mouth, then slammed it shut as I remembered the possibility of someone listening in. ~What's wrong? You've been grouchy all day.~

He sat and stared at me, his green eyes the color of his mother's fur. ~I have been edgy. Something is wrong. This being a trap almost relieves me. But I feel like there is a target on my back.~ His fur rippled down his spine as if trying to dislodge something and worry shot straight through my heart.

~Be careful. Even you can't prevent a bullet slamming into your skull.~

If I lost him.

My mind stopped, and I took a deep breath. ~If they hurt you, I'll destroy them.~ It was said with calm, cold intensity and I meant it. They could push me all they wanted. But if they took him from me there were no words to describe what would happen.

His ears laid back against his skull, then he chuffed. ~Good. My malkin would assist, as would Baneyarl. Even my littermates might step in.~ He leaned into my hand and I scratched his chin. ~I would expect nothing less than vengeance should they take me from you in such a cowardly way.~

~There would be. Same if Jo or Sable were hurt. But do me a favor, don't get hurt. I need you too much.~

He licked my hand. Then a spike of pain as a rip formed and he stepped to another realm. It sealed back up, leaving me there. Alone.

I sat for a while letting my mind rummage through what little I knew. I don't think they realized what they had started. But I had become complacent, thinking I could be invisible and unnoticed. I stood and walked over to the mirror on the closet door and gazed at the image reflecting back. The tattoos on my temple, the mark of a mage, filled with more colors than anyone else proved I'd never been invisible.

Time to rattle some cages. Remind them that poking dragons is a stupid idea.

Chapter 4

Section 1.105.1

All mages are required to undergo a draft orientation where the weight of their debt on society is to be fully explained as well as the consequences of not bearing that weight. If any mage is regarded as lacking the ability to carry their burden, measures may be taken to ensure society is not at risk.

SPIRIT

By the time pizza arrived, I'd changed into jeans and a tank top. Summer in West Virginia, which is where this little "orientation" was located, tended to be hot and muggy. But I still looked nicer than I had before Indira Humbert educated me in using fashion as a weapon and armor.

Indira Humbert was my mentor and my teacher for my first year at GA MageTech. Over time she had become a friend. As a merlin, she understood all too well how easy it was to be used. She used her experiences as a cautionary tale, and I'd taken it to heart. But she also used her sexuality as a weapon, something I couldn't do. Using clothing to set up expectations and control reactions was something I'd grabbed and almost started to enjoy. Almost—I still lived in tanks and shorts when no one besides Jo and Sable would see me.

I met the delivery guy at the door and accepted three large pizzas and two boxes of wings, the smells filling the hall with mouthwatering scents. I turned and headed into the common room. It was basic to the point of stripped. It did contain a long counter and a sink against the far wall with a few tables and chairs that looked like they'd survived multiple generations of college students. To my delight, Jo had asked the pizza place to include paper plates and plastic utensils. The lemon pepper wings, my favorites, were calling to me and I worked on getting a meat lover's slice and a few wings.

I settled down in a chair facing the entrance to the room and satisfied my hunger as I waited and listened. Carelian hadn't returned yet, which didn't worry me. He was probably getting spoiled by Sable. Jo tended to be more sarcastic and not as much of a pushover. Sable, on the other hand, spoiled him rotten, which he firmly believed was his due.

The sound of a few doors opening, then closing, followed by footsteps on the stairs, reassured me my idea had merit. It took about three minutes, but one of the draftees walked into the room, followed by two others. The three of them were simultaneously together and apart as they drifted in. My pizza took the majority of my attention, but I still watched them as they tilted up their heads, letting the scents seduce them.

One was dressed in something that I swore I'd seen in Halloween shops. The long flowing black dress and the Chaos symbols everywhere. The only thing missing was a black pointed hat. She had long brown hair with ragged ends, telling me her offering wasn't smooth, which was another giveaway. Almost everyone took the Cosmetology course and learned how to use certain aspects for offering. Some of us learned a lot more, but then appearance was everything.

Huh, that's an idea. Purposefully give up offerings like that in chunks, make someone underestimate or think I'm awkward.

My offerings were almost invisible, but it might be a

good idea for misdirection. It was layer upon layer of subterfuge, but this was why my life had been about politics for the last few years. No matter how boring I thought they were.

The other two were men, one looking like he belonged in a goth band. Hair dyed black, the roots were a giveaway, with eyeliner that even rock stars didn't do, and white skin that made me wonder if he was allergic to the sun or layered in face paint. Even the tattoo of Spirit on his face was in drab colors.

The other one was about as opposite as you could get. Tall, muscular, a golden boy if I'd ever seen one. He had Order on his temple, and a smirk on his face. His clothes were of the same quality as what I wore out, so I pegged him as having either money or training. Most mages got paid well, but not usually until after the draft was over. Of course he was the one making a straight path to me.

I continued to watch, trying to figure out their roles here. The girl and emo maybe I could see. But why was this guy one of the failures?

"Hello gorgeous. I ended up not thinking about the fact that all my cards were in my phone. You know how it is, everything is cloud based, which makes it difficult to get dinner tonight. Mind sharing your pizza, and next time dinner is on me?" He had a brilliant smile and I could almost believe his words. None of them were a lie, which was well done, but they didn't ring sincere.

"I figured people might need some food. Sure, help yourself, there's plenty." I included the other two hovering at the edges of the common room.

"That include us?" the Halloween refugee asked eyeing the pizza.

"Sure does. But would you bring me another slice of the combo?" I asked, watching as golden boy already had three pieces piled on his plate. The spilt second indecision as he turned and had to decide where to sit was amusing. But I didn't react, just watched the others.

He strutted over, and the image of a rooster in the yard jumped into my mind. I wondered if he'd look as silly running from Carelian as that bird had. My smile threatened to escape my control. I prevented that by taking another bite of pizza.

"Since you were so gracious as to share your food, may I impose on your company also?" he asked. The other two were still perusing the food options.

"Sure." I waved at the table. I'd made sure I had one of the bigger ones. It would comfortably sit six.

He settled down to my right, smiling at me. It was a very practiced smile, and I wanted to ask where he'd taken lessons from. But that might have been my own cynicism. "Benjamin Trainor, but all my friends call me Ben."

Oh, he was smooth. So why was he here with the losers?

"Cori Munroe," I replied as the other two approached.

"Hi, can I, well may we sit here?" emo boy asked, his voice low and shoulders sagging as if he already had processed my rejection. The girl peeked over his shoulder like a cross between a scolded puppy and a hopeful toddler.

"Big table. Sit down. I'm sure you heard I'm Cori. What are your names?" I saw the flicker of disappointment cross Ben's face, but I pretended to ignore him. I needed to pry out their secrets.

They settled in and the girl's eyes flicked across all of us. She was so ridiculous I couldn't help but think of her as a girl. Even as a teen, Jo had more presence before emerging than she had now.

"I'm Neil," the emo muttered, focusing on the food

and not us.

"Hi, um, I'm Claudia. I'm a Wiccan," she offered. I fought back a sigh. Wiccans should have been exceptional with how the elementals worked, but they lost sight of it every time by relating it to females only. As far as I'd been able to figure, Magic had no gender, but most human languages didn't have neuter pronouns for sentient beings. And it just came across as rude. Even the denizens felt uncomfortable calling Magic it. But while Magic might be referred to as she, her domain didn't care what was between your legs.

"Benjamin Trainor," offered Ben again, though a lot less enthusiastically than he had to me.

Everyone fell silent as they ate, and I tried to figure out how to ask why they were there. I had a criminal justice degree; I should be better at extracting information. Esmere would have already had them spilling their stories. She also had five-inch claws.

"So did any of you know the guy, Ricardo?" I asked, watching them under my lashes. It wasn't hard to pretend the pizza and wings absorbed my attention. I was hungry.

"No," murmured Claudia.

"Attacking a draft officer was stupid. What did he expect?" Ben said, his voice arrogant and I did an internal wince. The lessons learned in the other realms had been seared into my brain.

Neil shrugged, still not looking any of us in the face. While that annoyed me, he also wasn't concentrating on anything other than food. "Figure we're all dead. Isn't that what he said? Knew I'd end up like this." Self-defeat colored every syllable out of his mouth and I had to fight the urge to slap him.

Instead, I pretended to be naïve. "What you mean? Did you piss off the Board? What could you have done?

I mean you've been in college. How much trouble can you get in? They don't go around killing people."

Neil didn't answer. He shoved the remains of the pizza slice into his mouth, eyes down. I let my gaze drift over the others, a curious expression on my face.

"No clue," Ben said, a smile on his face but my magic screamed lie. "I figured it's a clerical error. I'm not planning on getting into any trouble. Get through the draft and get back to work." That part was true. None of this made sense.

Claudia shifted in her seat, a blush rising up her face. "I might have been caught trading magic services for money," she said, her voice almost a whisper.

"So?" I said, drawing out the vowel as I twisted that in my head. "That's not illegal as long as you report the income."

She coughed. "I might have been doing it for insurance claims."

I flickered my gaze to the strong Fire on her temple and it clicked. "You were doing arson for hire? Are you insane?" At that point I couldn't figure out why she hadn't been charged and executed already. Law enforcement didn't deal with arson nicely.

She sighed. "I'm not very good and it only scorched the floor."

The desire to beat my head on the table was spiking hard. I shot another glance at Ben, who was munching through pizza like he didn't have a care, but his leg was tapping out a rapid staccato.

"Neil?"

"Don't wanna do college. Took early draft. Just going to teach me to keep me in control."

I tilted my head. He wasn't wrong, but it was more than that and he'd raised his head as a person to watch, so yeah they were going to hit him hard.

We all fell silent and worked on food. I thought about talking to the others, but so far I only had a slight idea of what was going on and why they'd thrown me here. Claudia had finished her one piece with all the meat picked off, when another guy walked in. He'd been one of the mages in the auditorium, but seated behind me. Very well built and carried himself like an athlete, his skin somewhere between Jo and Sable's in tone. He had long dreads knotted in sections that I recognized as offering marks. An easy way to make it fast to offer, I'd used it myself.

"Yo! Who ordered the pizza?" he asked even as he headed toward it.

"I did. And feel free to help yourself," I said, amused.

"I will," he retorted over his shoulder, flashing a smile that Claudia went all gooey at. A minute later he strutted over, flipped a chair around, straddling it. "Well, I see two sexy women, I'm sure we'll have lots of time for fun later. It's rad that they're including PT as part of the draft training. After all, a fit body is necessary for a healthy mind. I'm Dwayne Jordan."

Neil and Ben were looking at him with matching sneers. I had to avoid laughing at their reactions.

"I doubt we'll have much time for fun. But we were discussing the comments made by Kamp at the orientation," I probed, wanting to see what he'd say.

"Merlin cares." It was the popular dismissal lately. I thought it was stupid. "Dad'll get me out of this in a week or so. There's no reason for me to be here and I've got some sweet ladies to get back to."

The conversation died, and the others left after eating most of the pizza. I sat and thought, but couldn't come up with any more ideas, just lots of concerns.

Carelian lounged on the floor of the room when I returned, and the scent of chicken filled the air.

"Have a good dinner?" I asked as I grabbed the two bags on the floor. One bag contained my school backpack, which had my laptop and notebooks in it. I pulled that out and set it on the desk, checking to make sure I didn't lack anything important like power cords or mouse. But everything was there as I expected.

~It was excellent. Chicken is a wonderful meat. Not as good as salmon, but still delicious.~

"I had pizza. It was decent." I didn't even try to make him feel guilty. It did no good. I switched to mindspeech, just in case. ~So did you get any of your concerns dealt with?~

He yawned, widely. I just stared at him.

~It still feels like an ambush, and I cannot see the trap. Esmere agrees it is targeted at you, but it is being used to clean up other loose ends.~

~I agree. I've figured out one or two of the loose ends, but not all of them. Why are they here or what did they do to piss off everyone?~ I put everything away and got ready for bed. I suspected someone would be banging on my door at five am.

"Ugh. Coffee!" I turned, looking around the room— not even a cheap pod coffee maker. "Oh, this is cruel and unusual punishment. No coffee?"

Chapter 5

Section 20.21

Upon injury, excluding situations where providing aid would put others at risk, no person involved in the draft may be denied medical aid. All mages' injuries or illnesses should be tended immediately by qualified medical personnel to prevent risk to their own selves and others.

ORDER

I staggered up as my alarm went off at four-thirty A.M. The idea of sending Carelian to get me coffee presented an almost overwhelming temptation, but I resisted. He had elected to sleep at the house in Albany, which I couldn't blame him for. The small room would have required him to sleep on the floor, which was only acceptable when he decided to do that. It also prevented me from stepping on him when I rolled out of bed that morning. Fifteen minutes later I had sweats, a sports bra, T-shirt, and sneakers on. Sure enough, at four-fifty there was a pounding on the door down the hall.

"Time to get up! Daylight is wasting. Get your asses in gear!" The yelling voice didn't sound like Kamp, and I would have been surprised if he lowered himself to work out with us.

I opened the door before the wanna-be drill instructor could hammer on it.

The man standing right outside my door sneered at me. "Glad to see someone knows how to get up in the morning; you might make it after all." The man was a few inches taller than my five-six and weighed double what I did, and all of it was muscle. He had his skull shaved and hard, light blue eyes. Those same eyes raked me up and down, then spun, marching to the next door that presumably contained a mage. "Outside and lined up. You have five minutes!"

I made my way downstairs, still wishing desperately for coffee.

Dwayne Jordan was already outside, looking overly peppy and enthusiastic. I began to stretch a bit, wary about what was planned. As I warmed up, I positioned myself to see who made it down the stairs. Claudia showed up, dressed in a tank top and shorts and sandals. At least they looked rugged, but I still suspected they would be less comfortable than real sneakers. Ben dragged himself down yawning, in a pair of jeans and polo shirt and I cringed, but mostly I wanted to scope out the others.

The redhead came out wearing the same sundress she'd had yesterday and strappy sandals that didn't look like they'd survive any amount of hard use. Neil followed her, surprisingly dressed in black sweats, shirt, and tennis shoes. I tried to think of the four that were missing.

The instructor bellowed, and I saw three people scurrying down and one sauntering. The saunter belonged to a pretty woman with ebony skin and cheekbones that would make a model sigh with envy. Though she wore so much make up it looked caked on her face. The tights she wore left nothing to the imagination, especially when paired with the bra clearly visible under her loose tank top. At least she wore shoes that looked possible to run in.

The other three just looked out of place. A dark-haired woman wore clothes at least two sizes too big for her, and her hands just shook as she stood there.

Another male, Chinese I thought, had no expression on his face. While he wore exercise clothes, they reminded me of what you got issued in high school, they had no personality.

The last made me sigh. Skinny, with horrible acne, glasses, and braces, his eyes were locked on the ass of the spandex wearer, and given the light pants he wore, the effect she was having on him was obvious. He came across as a stereotypical over-sexed nerd.

That thought made me stop and I looked at them. Most mages were college graduates; we'd learned how to interact with people. Even Charles could be polite if he thought it was worth the effort. Out of this group, not counting myself, at least three if not four were obviously not versed in being social.

This is a rigged setup, and it's too obvious. So who here is a ringer? All of them?

The only person I could be sure of was me. This got more twisted with every piece of information I got. The desire to call for Carelian flashed through my mind, but I didn't need to have him antagonize everyone and he would for sheer amusement factor. There was still the redhead and someone else missing.

"Line up, single file. I am York Beauchamp. You may call me Sarg or Beauchamp. I've been hired to make sure you wimps can handle the field. We're going to start off with a nice run and see how many of you can't hack the life you'll be leading." He looked at the getups a few others were wearing and sneered. "And how many of you will be running back to mommy."

Oh, if only that was an option.

My internal sarcasm levels were high and all I wanted to do was find coffee and go back to bed. The order didn't matter.

"Let's go, mages," he barked and gestured for us to

36

head out. We started in a slow line with only Dwayne looking at all enthusiastic. York proved he kept himself in excellent shape by circling around us and yelling at anyone who lagged. I don't know what he said, but it motivated the person he chewed out as they picked up their pace. I saw a flash of red at the end of the line and figured it was the missing girl.

Jo had insisted I get in shape and after my first six months of college with multiple people trying to kill me, I'd realized it was a very good idea. I would never enjoy working out, in fact it sucked. That being said, I'd still spent a lot of time on treadmills, stair masters, ellipticals, and weight machines. Jo was much more fit than I, but I'd gotten to a nice maintenance level where I had muscles without looking buff.

The pace that York set equaled a slow jog compared to what I normally did. I wanted to pick up the pace just to get it done as soon as possible. At the rate we were going it would take an hour plus to cover the distance, which annoyed the daylights out of me. Not that I had anything in particular I needed to go do, but still I wanted to be done with this getting sweaty crap.

The path was headed back to our dorms, and I sighed in relief. A shower and hopefully food where there would be coffee would be excellent. He pulled us to a stop and didn't even look winded. Being near the beginning of his little line, Dwayne had been ahead of me, I hadn't been able see how the others were holding up. Now I could turn and look at them and I froze.

Most of them were fine, if exhausted and looking like they were about to drop. Claudia was limping badly from her shoes. They hadn't been made for running like I thought. The redhead, however, had blood trailing behind her at each step as she sniffled. My desire to support this farce snapped, and I was at her side, ignoring Beauchamp.

"Sit, now," I snapped out the command even as I helped her to the ground.

"What do you think you are doing?" yelled York, looking like he was about to get into my face.

"Helping her. Per Section 20.21 I'm providing medical assistance." I didn't bother to yell. He wasn't as important as her feet. At some point the strappy sandals had fallen off or been discarded, but she'd continued to run. Why? Her feet were shredded with bits of rocks and twigs in them. Why the hell wasn't she screaming or crying?

"Umm, per...umm section," he stumbled, and I heard flipping. I glanced away from her feet to figure out what he was doing. He had a small book in his hand and was flipping through it. I saw the word "laws" on the front.

I shifted my attention from her feet, which while oozing blood weren't life threatening, to her face and I wanted to be sick. In the dim auditorium I hadn't really seen her, the shifting lights and the little display from Kamp had ensured I focused on him, not the others. The epicanthic folds at the corner of her eyes, the sweet smile, face streaked with tears of pain, told me everything I needed to know.

"Section 20.21: injured mages are to be treated by qualified medical personnel." He stressed the word qualified and tried to sound menacing. It didn't even register as I looked at a mage with Down syndrome. I knew the stats; it was covered in one of the basic Mage Laws courses. Less than one in 10,000 mages had birth defects or disabilities that could not be overcome like dyslexia. The teacher never said what was done with those mages who couldn't use magic, and I had too much going on to follow up on a question of statistical curiosity.

Now that statistical anomaly looked at me and smiled.

"I am a qualified and registered paramedic."

"In Georgia," he growled, as if proud of his comeback.

"And Alabama, Tennessee, Florida, North Carolina, South Carolina, and West Virginia. I made sure to get licensed in all those states." I looked up at him. "Now explain to me why I have a patient with Down syndrome bleeding." There was no compromise in my voice and I didn't care. Here I was in the right and he knew it.

Something akin to shame flickered over his face before he stiffened. "I'll call for medical. Keep her contained until then." He pivoted and headed away from us. I didn't bother to watch him go. I instead moved my attention to my patient.

"Hey. I'm Cori. Do you know your name?"

Her smile widened, even if her lips trembled a bit, and she nodded her head.

"Can you tell me your name?"

"Bridget. I'm Bridget. You had a cat." Her voice was sweet and guileless. I wanted to cry and scream.

"I did. Would you like to pet him while I work on cleaning up your feet?"

Her eyes sparkled, and she sniffed up a trail of snot leaking down her face. "Yes."

~Carelian can you bring me my med kit and come outside please? I have someone that would like to pet you.~

He must have heard something in my voice. ~I enjoy pets.~

I needed saline to clean out her wounds, but most of my mind was locked in a vicious circle of trying to figure out what to do. The law didn't make allowances for mental capabilities, only hospitalization. And her feet would be easy enough to treat, though normal medical advice would be to stay off of them until healed.

The sound of multiple gasps had me lifting my head and looking at the other mages. They had gathered around me before I'd seen their mixed looks of pity and horror. Right now they weren't looking at Bridget or me. They were focused on the dorms. Sitting on the ground, I peered through their legs and smiled.

"Here he comes. He loves to be petted and his ears scratched." I felt more than heard the rustle of people getting out of Carelian's way as he parted the group.

~Med kit. What happened?~ he growled out as he looked at her torn up feet.

~This is one of those instances where your mother and I would have a difference of opinion,~ I sent him as I dug into the kit.

"Bridget, this is Carelian, my familiar. You want to pet him?"

Her eyes were wide as she looked at him, and I couldn't blame her. He probably weighed about what she did.

"He bite?"

"No. He won't bite you." That I could say with a hundred percent certainty. Carelian lay down next to her so she could easily pet him, and she did. Her slow awkward movements were all gross motor control and almost no fine.

How did I miss what she was?

The problem was I knew how I'd missed this. I was focused on the person orchestrating this and unsure if the others were allies or opponents. But that meant I'd missed the innocent they'd put in here. Offering to the wolves? I didn't know, and I could hear Carelian's purr as she carefully petted him.

I had her feet clean and bandaged by the time York came back. The man had lost what little respect I might have had for him with this stunt.

"The ambulance is coming and they'll take her to get fixed up," he barked out. I nodded.

"I'll catch up when they take custody of her." He started to protest, and I gave him a flat stare. "I am obligated to stay with my patient until someone else takes charge. You wouldn't want me to break the law, would you?"

He snapped his teeth shut and turned to the others. "The PT is cut short today. If you don't have the right clothing get it today. We have extended the open campus until lunch. You have," he paused and glanced at his watch "four hours. Breakfast is available at the cafeteria until eight-thirty. You have class at one in the ground floor of the Chaney building, room 103." He turned and stalked off a few feet, obviously waiting for the ambulance.

I ignored him.

"I'm going to get food. That was a nice warm up, but nothing you could really call a workout. See you later, losers." I didn't have to look up to know it was Dwayne. I didn't care.

The others dispersed, and I let them. I watched the girl caught up as a pawn in a game she didn't even know existed and wondered what to do.

Chapter 6

Section 1.1.1

Any mage that refuses or evades the Mage Registration and Service Act is declared an active danger to the integrity of the United States. A special task force shall be established to hunt down all rogue mages and ensure they are not a danger to the populace at large. At no time shall avoidance of the draft be regarded as acceptable.

CHAOS

The ambulance had picked up Bridget and the two EMTs were kind to her, so at least for the next few hours I had faith that she would be okay. By then it was eight and I knew I needed food to survive the day. Carelian and I ran to the cafeteria and flew through the sparse breakfast offerings. Yet another thing that made no sense. I might need Carelian to go get me some energy bars just so I had something to eat.

The cafeteria did have coffee. Not the best, but it was drinkable. And they had real cream. That made my day better. I sat in the back, having grabbed one plate for Carelian and one for me. He'd demanded bacon, and I gave him an evil eye. Despite what he thought, bacon for every meal wasn't healthy. The serving person had protested that they had familiar food available. We'd looked at it, and it was the cheapest brand possible. I just looked at her and said, "You convince him to eat that." Then walked away.

He got his bacon.

The food at least was edible, nothing compared to

how Jo or Sable cooked, but edible. I ate the eggs and bacon thinking about Bridget. I had no idea what to do about her. I also didn't know what happened to mages in the past that had disabilities of her level.

Okay that was a lie. I was very sure they had been killed. The mage reportedly hurt in an unfortunate training incident.

I wanted to be sick. The idea had disturbed me when I learned of it, but what could I do? It was a theory, a statistic, and I'd learned it and moved on. But now it was a person, a young woman with hair that was almost pink in the sunlight, and a smile that had no guile or plans behind it.

~The young woman is simple?~ His voice had a lilt to it, as if he wasn't sure what word to use.

~Simple or disabled. She had a genetic abnormality that causes confusion with the instructions her cells follow. There are many side effects.~ I could recite all the details about the chromosome and how it affected its victims, but it didn't matter. Bridget was here and I didn't know what to do about it.

~Ah. And you allow them to live?~ His voice was careful. The clashes over culture had been many over the years, especially regarding prisons. Almost all the beings from other realms I'd met had a horror of them.

I flinched at that, but I had expected it. A few years ago, while Carelian was off on a hunt somewhere, Esmere and I had a conversation about damaged children. She saw one with either cerebral palsy or something else in a wheel chair in a movie we were watching. I'd explained about disabilities and damage. She'd been deeply disturbed at the idea that we allowed damaged children to live.

I'd laughed. "What do you expect us to do? Kill them?"

~Yesss,~ she'd hissed in my mind. ~Just like I killed mine that were not right. You don't allow the damaged ones to live, to reproduce.~ She stepped into a rip and didn't speak to me for a month. We'd mutually agreed to not discuss the topic, but I understood where she was coming from. On Earth animals often killed those that were damaged or deformed or injured. And the realms had nothing like hospitals, though Esmere was a healer.

The idea struck me for the first time if that was why she had become a healer, because she'd had to kill her own children. That she was looking for a way to fix them. I pushed it to the side as I tried to figure out the issue of Bridget and the department looking for ways to kill their problem children. I had identified why four of the mages were here with me.

So far it seemed like we were all risks or dangerous. None of us fit into the nice little mold the Draft Board thought we should.

I finished eating and headed back to the dorm. He'd said we had until after lunch to be back on campus, though calling anyone without a phone was a pain. Walking back in the dorm building, I noticed a land line.

"Okay, I haven't seen one of those in a while." I looked at the phone and realized I had no idea what number to call for food or supplies.

Taking the phones had been a brilliant move and annoying.

"Screw it." I didn't have time or energy to deal with doing it the long hard way. Part of me wondered how the others were managing it. I jogged up the stairs to my room, Carelian behind me. I changed to mind speech, just in case they were bugging these rooms. ~Can you open a rip, please? I need to talk to,~ I paused and glanced at my watch, trying to figure out where they'd be right now. Sable should be at work in her office. She usually wasn't in the field until the afternoon, but Jo would have been in the field for an hour. ~Sable.~

Carelian was agitated and pacing back and forth. ~You will have to kill the sweet girl?~

I blanched and swallowed, my breakfast suddenly considering making a re-appearance. "I don't want to kill her at all. I wouldn't kill her. That is not my plan. I want to avoid her getting killed at all costs." My voice overly loud and I sighed, sinking down on the bed.

~Will you be able to?~ His words sank like lead rocks into my chest.

~The rip please.~ I had zero desire to talk about the death of someone. But his words conjured images of her throwing an angry fit, fire lashing out everywhere with no control, just emotions. Elementalists were more likely to have that happen, and Bridget had no idea how to control the powers she had.

I saw his glare and ignored it. How in the world did I argue something that I didn't know how I felt about? The spike of pain appeared, and I sent a knock to Sable.

~Sable, have a few?~ I sent the message, flopping back on the tiny bed. Carelian was right, my king bed was much nicer.

~For you? Always. What's up?~ Definitely the isolation was an excellent ploy. But it just served to make me wonder who they had isolated Bridget from.

~A few things. One, can you get me a coffee maker and coffee? Running before I even get a cup is completely unfair.~

~Wow, they do like taking your life in their hands. But sure, I can grab a simple drip coffeemaker.~ Sable knew my opinion of pod coffee makers. ~And some decent coffee.~

~Thanks. The food won't make me rave about it, but I won't die, so I'm fine there.~ I paused, trying to figure out what else I needed and how to broach the subject.

~Cori? What's wrong?~ Her gentle thoughts poked at me and I sighed.

~What do you know about mages that are disabled or damaged in some way? I mean, what happens to them?~

There was a long pause and I could imagine the crease of her brows as she looked at me. ~What do you mean, what happens to them?~

~If a mage with massive disabilities, and I'm not talking Jo's dyslexia, but like cerebral palsy or something else, emerges. What happens?~ I think I was hoping she knew of some magical place where they were made happy and taken care of. Maybe I just wanted to believe that.

~I don't know. Other than the case studies, where I think most of them had to be killed to stop them from hurting others, I'm not sure I've ever known one. Why?~

With a mental sigh that felt like it came from the dark recesses of my soul, I explained about Bridget.

~Oh Cori. Only you. I don't know. I can ask, but I think we both know what the response will be.~

~Oh yeah, discomfort and avoidance.~ I knew that reaction all too well.

~Anything else I can do besides the coffee?~

I looked at the computer and my clothes. ~Yeah, I'll need a printer; he's going to expect papers nightly. If I had a printer, I could be nice and let others use it.~

~Ouch, your orientation is much different from mine. I've got an extra one at home you can use. I'll send it over. If I can figure out how to send it with Carelian.~

~Thanks, Sable. I miss you guys and I've only been here a day.~ I laughed in amusement at myself.

~We miss you too. Feels weird not having you there.

You'll figure it out.~ Sable's reassurance didn't really help.

~Thanks. Remember, daily check-ins. I have no idea what else they are going to try to pull.~

~Got it. No burning down the campus.~

~Hey, I'm not the firebug. Have it swallowed by the earth, now, that's a totally different option.~ I stuck my tongue out at her in my imagination.

She just laughed and closed the connection. I looked at Carelian, speaking out loud. "I do seem to end up in regular disasters, don't I?"

~Part of why I am your focus. The last few years have been boring.~

I snorted. "Working my butt off wasn't boring."

~No one died, no trips to realms. Booooring.~

"Glad to know I exist to amuse you."

He lifted his head from the floor, ears flicking my way. ~What else did you think you were for?~

I groaned and levered myself off the floor. Nothing would be ready for me until this evening, and I smelled like I felt, hot and sweaty. With a grunt of effort, more emotional than physical, I heaved myself off the bed and grabbed my shower stuff. Time to brave shared showers.

They weren't bad, but it wasn't until I stepped out that it dawned on me I had no towel. I stood there dripping wet for a long time. I glared at my workout clothes. Using them to dry off would defeat the purpose of showering. With a sigh of exasperation I picked up my sweaty clothes and my shower stuff and walked back to the room, dripping water as I went.

"Huh, Miss Perfect feels the need to show off the perfect body too? What? You that desperate?"

I paused ten steps from the door to my room and rotated to face the speaker. I didn't bother to try covering up. One of the advantages of years of working in fire stations was I'd been yanked out of the shower more than once and seen more than enough bodies in various stages of undress to not really care about nudity. Besides, the hallway was muggy and being naked almost felt comfortable.

It was the female mage who'd worn too tight clothes last night and still wore the skimpiest shorts for running I'd ever seen. She'd managed to find sneakers, which relieved me because running in stilettos would have been a recipe for disaster. Or entertaining. She had her hair in a natural afro creating a puff of curls around her head like a halo, skin as dark as Sable's, and a figure like Jo's without the muscle. The sneer on her face detracted from her beauty.

"It's been a while since I've had to remember to take a towel with me," I said mildly. "Too used to hotels or my own bathroom."

"You sure you weren't just trying to use your body to distract others?" She canted her hips toward me with an aggressive glare at me.

I glanced down at my decidedly normal body, white skin—I never sun-bathed nude so I looked like a sheet of computer paper—tan lines, B size breasts, and hips that needed to lose a little weight. I spread out my arms, hair still a sodden lump down my back, and smiled. "Is it working? Are you distracted?"

"Huh? I mean, no. I'm not into girls," she sputtered, crossing her arms defensively.

"So, walking naked on the girls' floor, with what I assume are mostly hetero girls is supposed to distract you how?" I just stared at her, making sure I had a slightly puzzled expression.

"I mean, well, guys could come up here," she said.

"Have at them. Not that interested. But I am starting

to get cold, and I need to deal with my hair before class." I turned, heading for my door.

"You're weird," she said slowly.

"Nope. Name's Cori. Nice to meet you." I shot a thought at Carelian. ~Open the door please. And will you get towels when you see Sable?~

The door swung open and he snickered at me. ~I can lick you dry?~

I shut it behind me and gave him a look. "No. You'd take all my skin with it."

~Yum, fresh mage,~ he snarked back. I threw my clothes at him.

Chapter 7

Section 2.20.6
Infractions are treated the same as the general populace, however community service should be aimed at using the mage's skills in a way to benefit the local jurisdiction.

SPIRIT

They scheduled our law class to begin at one, and I wanted to eat again before that. The idea of law class again after taking it in college made little sense. Sable had sworn hers was much more interesting than what the college course had been and was much more practical. I grabbed a notebook and headed out, but paused by the door with the name Bridget O'Kief on the door.

~Anyone coming?~ I asked Carelian, trusting his ears much more than mine.

~Oooh, mischief? There is no one coming up the stairs, though there are people in other rooms.~ He turned and peered down the hall.

I turned the knob, expecting a locked door. It would give me a chance to practice my transform abilities. I knew I should be able to make a key from any object by keeping it malleable and sliding it into a lock and adapting to the lock as I went. In theory. It wasn't something I had played with that much.

But the knob turned in my hand and the door swung open. My conscience battered at me but I needed to know who she was. If I could figure that out I might be able to contact someone. I stepped in and looked around; I needed more than a name. I shut the door behind the two of us and looked. The room looked identical to mine, even down to the same linoleum pattern. A duffle bag sat in the closet and the bed was ruffled like someone had slept in it. There on the desk was a small purse, and I rifled through it, finding—to my joy—ID. I copied down the name and address in my notebook.

It was something, if nothing else maybe someone to call. If I could find the number.

Dejected at not finding any other contact information—phones were important—I put it back and went to the door. ~Anyone?~

~No,~ he said, a whisper even in my mind. I opened the door, and we slipped out. We headed down the stairs to the cafeteria again, and I made a mental promise to memorize all the important numbers in my life. Having a phone made you dependent on it. I needed to make sure I knew how to contact people without it. I couldn't mindspeak to everyone.

Noise echoed up from the lobby as I came down and glanced in. Standing in there talking was the spandex girl, Neil, and a Chinese man. I debated about stopping to say hi and finally turned into that side of the lobby. Either way, I needed to eat and I really hoped they had better food for lunch.

"Hey." I flashed them my paramedic smile. The one that said I'm here to help and I'm not scary. They froze and looked at me, as if I'd caught them doing something. That just made me more curious. "I'm Cori. I met Neil last night, but I don't think we were introduced."

The woman smiled at me, her earlier bravado back. "Oh, I'd say we've been very intimate, but my name's Yvette Jones. You look cuter with clothes on."

I just smiled. "It's nice to meet you. But I thought you

weren't into women?" Years of Jo and Sable flirting with each other and teasing me meant sexual things couldn't phase me, though I still didn't understand the interest in sex. Jo and Sable sure seemed to enjoy it.

She flushed a bit and shrugged, glaring at the other guy.

"Feng Long," he said, his voice flat. Neither of them offered to shake or anything, they just stood there looking at me.

I blinked for a moment, then channeled my dragon. "I don't know about you, but I suspect class will be long. I'm headed to get some lunch first." Carelian brushed against my leg. "Oh yes, this is my familiar, Carelian." I petted his head while I talked, it was even with my waist.

"Doesn't that thing have to be on a leash?" Yvette said, her eyes wide as she stepped back a bit. "I don't like cats."

"He can be, but he is his own person most of the time. And protected under the law." I smiled at them, all teeth and no eyes. "Being polite is the wisest course of action."

The three of them nodded, but Feng's eyes were narrowed and focused on me.

"Well, see you at class if I don't see you at lunch." I waved, feeling like a prize idiot, then spun on my heel.

~This place is nuts. You still suspecting an ambush?~ I sent the thoughts to Carelian. My entire back crawled with the feeling someone was watching me. The lessons I'd learned when I had assassins after me didn't let me dismiss the feeling. I brought up a shield of electromagnetic energy and coated my body with it. Dirt or air could be much better, but dirt was too obvious and air I was null in. I could listen occasionally, but for a long-term spell it got expensive.

I rarely used this one as it tended to fry my phone or drain it. That we had learned the hard way. I could use metal, but then I needed a source of the metal and it made me look like the Tin Man walking around.

I tried to see if anyone followed me out, but if they did, I never noticed. We walked to the cafeteria with Carelian acting like an excited dog, darting various directions to sniff or investigate objects.

~Find anything?~ I asked as I filled up plates for both of us.

~No. But this entire place reeks of deception and schemes. How did I end up in a place that reminds me of the Court of Lords?~

I shot him a glance at that, no idea what it meant, but here wasn't the place to get into other realm politics. I didn't want to get involved in Earth politics if I had a choice.

In the cafeteria, I sat at a table, watching the bored kitchen staff. How much money was it costing to have all these people here for ten mages plus, what, two maybe three teachers or draft officers? Others trickled in as I picked at my food. The meals still sucked, but at least the hamburger was edible. The fries weren't, much to my disappointment.

Neil, Claudia, Ben, and Dwayne came in and I saw two others whose names I hadn't figured out. One girl dressed in ragged clothes with her hair lumpy and uneven came in, not looking at anyone. She got jello and an apple. Nothing more. The other was a young man who looked like he needed an extra thousand calories a day, and someone to tell him plaid pants for men hadn't been fashionable this century.

The girl just slunk to a table and picked at the jello. That surprised me given the amount of what I assumed were offerings missing from her hair. Mages needed food to stay healthy. The body prioritized what was missing. Unlike blood or skin, hair wasn't treated as something the body needed to replace, but even to grow hair required calories.

"May I join you?"

The voice pulled me away from my musings over the girl. I looked up at plaid pants, striped polo, and a nervous smile on a face with Entropy on his temple.

"Sure." I kept my voice light and friendly. "I'm Cori," I offered, and he grinned a nervous grin. What annoyed me was I don't think his eyes got above the neckline on my shirt. A modest scoop neck that barely hinted at cleavage. I'd decided a long time ago to dress for competence, not sexuality. That was all Jo and Indira. They loved having people look at their bodies. It made me uncomfortable.

"Jake," he muttered as he collapsed into the seat across from me. I heard a soft growl from Carelian, but I waved my hand at him under the table. I might as well see where this went.

"Entropy, huh? So did you get your degree? In what?" I started with pleasant conversation. At some point making friends instead of scoping people out would occur.

"Yeah, wizard," he said, identifying the middle rank of mages. "You have great boobs."

"What?" I had to process that to even figure out what he said.

"Boobs, yours are great. I'd like to see them sometime."

~If he so much as lays a hand on you, I will use his bones as toothpicks.~ Carelian snarled in my head, but I knew it was to me only.

My mouth opened and closed and I didn't even know how to respond. I looked around almost expecting someone to yell out "Gotcha" but no one paid much attention to us.

"That isn't appropriate," I managed to say. I was so shocked I didn't even know how to react.

He just shrugged. "I like boobs, you have good boobs. Better if I could see them. Ooh, can I touch them?"

That burned off my shock and I leaned forward a tiny bit. The spark of excitement in his eyes made me nauseous. "If you so much as touch me, it is assault and I will disable the tendons in your arms and legs so you can't run, can't do anything but thrash, and I will sit back and watch my familiar eat you, one bite at a time. You can scream and beg and plead, and I will just watch."

His eyes jerked up to look me in the face and I smiled, showing all my teeth. "Don't offend people. It will get you killed and the second you touch someone, it vaporizes all their restraints. I'd learn that lesson very quickly."

He just blinked, looking at me. I stood up, taking my tray, and walked over to dispose of it, then walked out. I pulled the magnetic shield back up as I stepped out the door.

~Who does that thing think he is? He is not good enough for my queans, any of my queans. He should beg to be allowed the honor to groom your foot.~ Carelian was almost sputtering he was so mad. His fur fluffed out, creating a ridge of spikes down his spine.

I didn't respond. My brain was having issues with the blatant sexism and almost harassment, but then most people weren't that stupid. And that was the part I was sticking on. Why would anyone say that?

Carelian was still sputtering in my mind as I reached the classroom. It was obvious which one it was, and I sat down at the back so no one could sit behind me. Taking out my notebook, I waited to see the students. I wanted a chance to analyze and evaluate each person when I wasn't trying to do something else.

The first in was Claudia, arms wrapped around her waist so that even in the muggy heat of a North Carolina summer she looked cold. Ben and Dwayne walked in together, joking and smiling, but they moved as if every muscle was ready to react. Maybe people were realizing how serious this was?

The straggly girl who needed a few thousand calories slunk in, followed by Jake, his eyes latched on her ass. I sighed. If we were a reject collection, I could understand some of the issues. But while I could see why Claudia and Neil were here, and even Jake if he was that socially clueless, that left unknown girl, Feng, Yvette, Ben, and Dan. Were they here just because, or to leverage me into something worthy of punishment?

That idea chilled me to the bone, even as I acknowledged the possibility.

The others strolled in, Yvette and Feng pretending the other didn't exist. Lovers spat already? I groaned and rubbed my temples. This couldn't be this huge of a conspiracy just to eliminate me.

It felt like something I needed to talk to Esmere about, but before I could finish processing that line of thought, Kamp walked in. He slammed the door behind him and most of the students jumped or started turning to look at him. I saw a few pale and Claudia and the other girl I didn't know shrank back a bit. Jake was sitting behind and between Claudia and Yvette, but I couldn't see what he focused on. Somehow I didn't think it was Kamp.

"I see most of you made it this far. Better than I expected, though I understand one of your number has already ended up in the hospital. That is a valid reason to miss class, though I wouldn't recommend it as a way out." He smirked and my stomach clenched. Where was Bridget?

"Now that we are here, we will dive into the laws that enable you to serve. Never think of your draft as a punishment, it is a reward for being allowed to live in this great country. Other countries ask more of their mages than we do, so it is up to you to prove you are the best and give your all to the job of serving your country." His passion and intensity had at least Ben, Dwayne, and Feng sitting up and looking proud.

He's a true believer.

I didn't know if that was a good or a bad thing. It just told me he believed in what he was doing, and wouldn't regret having to put a bullet in any of us "for the good of the country". That made me nervous.

"Before we start going over the laws that rule your life from now on, we will talk about the ones you broke to get here. And you want to memorize these laws. Because breaking them from now on could have serious penalties." He slapped open a notebook on the podium and started with the first person on that row, the choppy worn-down girl.

It tore at my conscience. I wanted to know what was up with these people, but at the same time the idea of hearing their crimes kind of creeped me out. I cycled through the laws, trying to come up with a concrete objection. But this wasn't medical and I didn't think he was a doctor, so HIPAA didn't apply. Before anything occurred to me, he started to speak.

"Yes, I think you all deserve to know exactly what sort of reprobates and in some cases monsters you have here with you. And let's start with Lizabeth Duncan."

The girl in question hunched down even further, and I prepared to stop him if he hit her. This whole thing felt like a train wreck.

And I'm in the middle, per usual.

Section 2.20.19

Mages have the right to use their abilities to protect themselves, defend others, and assist in times of need. Their magic shall be treated the same as a weapon with the same level of due diligence applied. Any reasonable expectation of harm can be regarded as need to protect themselves.

ORDER

But he didn't attack her. His body language shouted that he wanted to drag her to her feet and hit her until she hit back, but he just sneered and started to talk.

"Lizabeth Duncan. Drug addict. Five counts of using before you emerged and two since. One more arrest for using will bump you up to a felony level. But if we catch you dealing, that will make it a level B or A felony. And I'm sure all of you know what that means."

I knew I did, but apparently some of them gave him blank looks. Kamp snorted and walked to the whiteboard behind him. "Felonies are broken down into classes. E through A. Class B and A felonies carry serious time for the rest of us, but for mages they carry a death sentence. For Class E through C, you just get extra time. Isn't that right, Benjamin Trainor?" He wrote the letters A,B,C,D,E on the board.

The man in question stiffened and looked down at his desk. I felt magic build, and waited for an explosion, but Ben just curled into himself.

"Ah, Trainor doesn't feel like talking about what he did. What a shame. It was rather ingenious and doubled his draft to make sure his country had recompense for his actions." Kamp had this attitude that was worse than nails on a chalkboard.

A flush of red swept up Ben's face, but he just curled in tighter, though I could see his hands were clenched into fists. I moved my attention back to Brian Kamp who was smirking.

"Now that we know what the penalties are, let's go over why you are here, and what you can do to ensure you make it out of the draft." He snorted; contempt etched into every inch. "Neil Lang, inability to do the course work required. Refusal of secondary education and all assessment tests." Kamp actually frowned as he spoke, eyes locked on Neil. But did that qualify as a redeeming emotion from him or not?

"The refusal requires you to enter the draft now, but makes you a liability as you don't know how to you use your magic. Your coursework and first year will be different than the rest as you will need to be educated on how to use magic, but for this month, you'll go through the basics with us. Your fate is one of the few I am not positive about. Who knows, maybe you'll surprise me. It has happened before." He smiled and half of the class pulled back.

Neil just looked constipated and resentful. I couldn't blame him. Kamp's smile, which I think was supposed to be reassuring, looked more like a shark about to eat you.

"Claudia Morgan, attempted arson. Three counts, but at least two of them were dismissed as you didn't even get the rags to burn. You claimed you were forced into it. Lucky the judge felt sorry for you, otherwise you wouldn't be my problem now. Also a bit ridiculous that a Fire mage can't set things on fire." He focused on me while he talked. I just smiled back and split my attention between him and Claudia.

The woman looked ready to burst into tears. She needed to get over it and quit being stupid. But then my temper and patience were fraying. I took a deep breath, trying to re-center myself and quit letting this jerk get to me.

It felt like he was almost disappointed I didn't react, instead he turned to Yvette, smiling. "Yvette Thomas. Bachelors in Biology and arrested twice for solicitation. Three other possible charges prior to emerging."

I was sitting so I could see her profile and watched carefully. She didn't cower, just shrugged and smiled a sexy smile. "Ain't solicitation if I'm not paid. It's just a good time. And gifts don't count. Isn't a girl worth pretty gifts?"

"If you can learn to channel that attitude in the correct way, I'm sure you'll be an excellent mage for the draft. Otherwise, you might be here a very long time."

Her back stiffened and I swear I saw a bit of vaporization from the midst of her afro, but nothing happened and he moved on. While embarrassing people like this wasn't anything I enjoyed, it did give me a lot of information and I was writing it down. I had an idea of who to contact to get more information. Besides, I hadn't talked to Charles in almost two weeks.

"Ah yes, our perv. Peeping Tom charges, up skirt picture taking, installing recording devices in changing rooms, and drilling holes into the girls' locker room. All the charges were misdemeanors so far. But you've been following a set pattern, which leads to assault and rape." Brian moved so he stood directly in front of Jake, and I could only see the back of Jake's low pony tail. "I fully expect you to be stupid and try something with a female mage and she's going to rip your heart out. I will enjoy seeing you go down."

"Hurting me breaks the rules," he muttered, and even from here it sounded like he was pouting.

Brain stepped back and wrote a number on the board: "Section 2.20.19". "Okay mages,"—he sneered that part—"does hurting him break the rules?"

Everyone just looked down, unwilling to meet his eyes. "No. Not if he touches me first." My voice rang clear in the tense classroom.

Brian Kamp turned to me, his smile a bit more forced. "Please elucidate, Miss Munroe, for the others in here."

I gave him my biggest smile and let a bit more southern seep into my accent. I was a Georgia girl after all. You used the weapons you had. "If someone touches you it is assault. You are allowed to protect yourself however you want, including using magic pursuant to Section 2.20.20." I flicked my eyes over to Jake, letting them narrow a little. "Or allowing their familiars to protect them. Section 2.20.21."

Kamp's eyes tightened, and the smile didn't touch them as he stared at me. With an aborted snarl, he moved his gaze back to Jake. "Exactly. So if you decide to cross the line, I expect I will be cleaning you up in a body bag."

Jake's shoulders hunched with his arms crossing his chest. I wanted to roll my eyes, but as long as he didn't make my familiar get in trouble, I didn't care.

Kamp lifted his head and smiled. "Now next in our little group, Dwayne Jordan. All-star in high school. Father is a famous sports personality."

"Yes, he is." Dwayne hadn't flinched; he just sneered back at Kamp. "And he'll get me out of this mess. I'm not supposed to be here. I haven't broken any of the laws applicable to mages."

Kamp crossed his arms and tapped his fingers in a

fast pattern. "That is true. You weren't convicted of anything prior to emerging, and no one has pressed any more charges against you—so far. However, your father managed to get three date rape charges against you swept under the rug. And all the girls had their college paid for."

Dwayne shrugged. "They were interested. They just changed their minds. Not my problem."

"Before or after you drugged them?" Kamp asked, almost sounding interested.

While Kamp was fixated on Dwayne, all I could see was his posture. Dwayne was slouched in the chair and relaxed, bouncing his head as if listening to music.

"Either way, I suspect you will remain true to form. If you rape a mage during your draft, rest assured not even your father will be able to get the charges lifted. Assuming you live. Most rapists don't." Kamp snarled out that last part, sounding angrier than he had with anyone else.

"Whatevs. You can't do anything to me." Dwayne dismissed him and looked over at Ben, smirking.

I expected Kamp to do something, but he stepped back and looked at Feng Long. That man had sat down and remained perfectly still. Until Kamp focused on him, I'd forgotten he was there. He hadn't moved at all. "Feng Long." He said the name with such distaste it surprised me. What had this man done? "Former hacker, took down and held hostage multiple municipalities before you were fifteen. Sentenced to ten years with no electronics at all. Then you emerged. They had to figure out how to get you educated without letting you into computers, but it turns out you lost your touch in a decade without being able to use them. So they think your teeth are pulled." Kamp leaned close, and I was very glad that I wasn't sitting in the front two rows. "I, on the other hand, believe once a criminal, always a criminal."

Kamp straightened and Long hadn't moved, still sitting like a statue.

~That guy is human, right?~ I asked Carelian, wondering if he was something else.

~Yesss,~ Carelian said, his tone matching his lashing tail. ~Though I think both he and Feng are offal not worth saving. They should both be buried.~

I fought not to laugh at that image and sat back. So far he'd gone through everyone; that left me and Bridget. He smiled up at me and I just looked back at him.

"And that leaves Cori Munroe," he said, his voice sugary sweet.

"Oh? While I am fascinated to learn what I've done, what about Bridget O'Keif. Or doesn't she rate?" I said, not reveling in the attention but controlling it as everyone turned to look at me.

Something flashed across his face. "Yes, we must not forget Bridget. She won't be back until tomorrow, but her kind never last. They can't."

"What sort of shit is that?" I burst out, my cool vanishing.

The superior look vanished, and he growled. "The only option we have. If she cannot meet the terms of the draft, she will suffer the consequences. And if she misuses her magic, she will pay the price."

I wanted to protest; there had to be something, but even I couldn't come up with an answer right then. She wouldn't be back until tomorrow, so I had time. I could figure out something.

And what? Change the world? I don't have that kind of power.

I wanted to stew on it, but Kamp shook off whatever

momentary emotion had affected him. "Shall we talk about you, Cori?"

I grabbed my frustration and worry about Bridget and shoved it to the back of my mind. I hated when theoretical ethical issues were shoved in my face, but right now there wasn't anything I could do and I had no ideas.

"Yes, please," I said, faking disinterest. "Did I kill someone? Or am I in trouble for jaywalking?" My snark might have been getting the better of me, but right now we had a rapist, drug addict, perv, prostitute, and a hacker. Who knew what Benjamin had actually done? But I was starting to see they figured why not take care of all their issues at the same time.

He smiled, but it didn't warm me or anyone else. "No, you just think you're above the law and have to call in reinforcements to blackmail everyone into treating you like you are special. Yes, I know all about you." The sneer in his voice should have sliced me.

At this point everyone was looking at me with varying levels of curiosity and concern. Well, everyone except Lizabeth and Feng. For her part, Lizabeth just picked at her arm, and even from here I could see the spot of blood. Feng remained stiff as a backboard, looking straight ahead.

"No. I wasn't above the law; it didn't apply to me at that time via your own laws. As for reinforcements?" I let my voice dangle with sarcasm. "Trust me, I didn't ask them to come, they chose to. And if you had been there, you would understand that they are not beings I control."

"Oh, I heard all about it," he said shrugging. "Smoke and mirrors and adrenaline changing their perspective as to what was really there."

I looked at him and started laughing. There was a

snort from Carelian and I figured he was laughing too.

My laughter did get everyone's attention, even Feng. I couldn't stop the giggles at what they had to do to convince themselves that Salistra and Tirsane and even Bob weren't what they were.

"Are you laughing at me?" he demanded, his face paling.

I just shook my head, trying to get my giggles under control. It took me a second, and the color started flushing back into his face before I could get my answer ready. "No, I was just laughing at the idea of people thinking it was fake. It wasn't. And I really hope no one ever realizes how real it was."

He looked like he wanted to wrap his hands around my throat and squeeze. Instead he glared at me, hands shoved in his pockets. "By the time you are done here, I will make sure you understand your place in our world."

The phrasing surprised me. I covered my mouth, trying to stop the giggles. "I'm sure you will." He stood there for a minute, trying to decide how to respond. With a huff of annoyance he spun and went back to the board.

"First section." He wrote on the board with hard jabs. "We will cover exactly what Miss Munroe did. Why it is illegal. And you will be required to write up a one-page paper explaining why what she did should have been breaking the law."

"Except it wasn't," I said sweetly. "So the only way to write a paper proving that I should have been punished is to either change the law or the situation."

He glared.

I smiled back at him. The arguments between Steven Alixant and Harold Leofin had proven that, and I knew that.

With a snarl Brian Kamp turned away. "Your

assignment is to write a paper on all the things the Agent in charge did wrong. That if the paperwork had been followed, Cori Munroe would have been punished for breaking the law."

He said this to the class as a whole and I responded. "Oh, I can definitely do that. But there is no way for anyone else to have any idea what the particulars were. So what would you like them to do?" I leaned forward and tried to ignore Carelian snickering in my head. I could be a real pain when I wanted.

Kamp growled a bit, and I knew I had him. The case had been filed, finding in my favor and he had to be aware of it. "Everyone else will write out the first three sections of the Mage Laws and provide an example situation where they would apply."

"Umm, do you have a copy of those?" Claudia said meekly.

"You implying you don't know them?" he sniped at her and I sighed. The poor girl was about to get his irritation with me played on out on her. Not fair.

She looked around the classroom and I could see the panicked looks on most of their faces. Feng didn't react at all. He was just weird.

"Well, look it up on your computers. You have limited internet just for that purpose," Kamp snapped as he put the pen back down on the tray under the board. He must have been overly frustrated because when the pen landed, the tray snapped off falling to the floor with a crash. "Okay, who did that?" he raged, whirling to look at all of us.

I checked for Murphy on me—nothing. Then I looked at him. Murphy, well multiple Murphy's, were wrapped around him, almost cloaking him from view in mage sight.

Ugh, great.

With a muffled sigh, I dispersed them, making sure I offered up leg hair. I didn't need anyone to realize I'd used magic.

"Let me remind you, using magic against me is a violation of Section 1.3.4. In fact let's go over that section." He started to drone about the laws, and I settled back to watch the class. There were only two mages in the class with relativity beside me. And there had been at least three or four spells on him. This would be more interesting than I thought.

Chapter 9

Section 2.20.1
If convicted for a Class C, B, or A felony, the penalty is immediate death given the impossibility of controlling a mage.

CHAOS

The introductory session on laws governing mages and the draft was long and boring, at least to me. The others seemed clueless as to the laws that they were required to follow. Carelian started to snore an hour into it, though no one else seemed to notice. I made notes on a few aspects Brian Kamp pointed out that I hadn't thought of, but often he twisted the specific law to make it appear as punitive as possible. There were a few cases where I completely disagreed with his interpretation, but most of them were things it would take a court case to solve. I had zero desire to be involved in a court case.

We left with the assignment of a one page paper about the first three sections of the mage laws, while I had an after-action report about that day. Good thing Steven and I had debated it nonstop, and I knew all the details.

No one walked near me as I headed back to the dorm. Which didn't hurt my feelings at all. I didn't want much to do with any of them, though maybe Yvette and Lizbeth had my sympathy. Maybe.

It felt like I had crossed a minefield by the time I got back to my dorm with Carelian by my side.

~I'm going to visit my malkin then stop to see my

other queans. I will be back tonight with your requested things.~ He said that slightly disparagingly.

"Thank you, Carelian. I do appreciate you doing this for me." I spoke idly, figuring letting any listeners wonder would only help me. "But I think you just want to avoid the food they are likely to serve."

I heard the humor as he replied. ~Wouldn't you prefer to eat Jo's cooking, or even Sable's to what you are likely to be served?~ With that parting remark he opened a hole in reality and vanished. I sighed. He wasn't wrong about that.

No phone meant no music, or at least subpar. There was Wi-Fi and I connected, then set up a VPN to make sure what I did online wasn't tracked. Because I needed some help.

I pulled up a chat program and my word processing program. I needed to get the paper out of my way and try to prep as best I could.

I stared at the chat program for a long moment before I clicked on the icon for Charles Wainscot. Over the last few years he'd grown a lot, and the acne had faded, turning him into a handsome young man, if a bit stern and overly orderly. Jo had asked once, and it was a true ask, if Charles and I would get together. It had been after the stalker issue.

Because it was Jo, I had given that question a lot of thought, but shook my head and replied that it was unlikely. I liked him, I enjoyed talking to him, and the occasional hug was nice. But neither of us felt anything more than that. He told me once he was a very firm demisexual. And most people couldn't get past Arachena and his own cold logic to make it to the next stage. Personally, I thought if Jo or Sable had been bisexual they probably would have ended up dating him. I just enjoyed talking to him and Arachena, who had finally given in and agreed to talk directly to me. In her own words ~I build my own patterns.~

His avatar was a picture of Arachena traced in neon colors. She glowed with beauty. It was how she dressed up on the first Halloween Carelian and I celebrated. The first year he was with me we were too busy with the FBI, the OMO, and dealing with everything to even be aware of it.

Ch-ch was his handle online and what Arachena called him.

[Hey. Have time and interest to do a bit of digging for me? Only legal stuff.] I knew I needed to preface it with that. He was dangerous on a computer. The years of serving in the draft and working with computers had slowly moved him up into hacker territory. It didn't hurt that even complex algorithms just made sense to him.

[Are you in trouble again?] His reply was immediate, and I glared at shining letters.

[I didn't do anything,] I typed out, feeling almost hurt. Why did people think I was the one that caused these issues? I double checked there wasn't a Murphy's cloak around me. Just in case.

[That doesn't change the question. What happened?] His responses were lightning fast, and I sighed.

[Draft orientation was a setup. They are trying to legally eliminate me. I'm just trying to figure out what else is going on. You up for helping?]

This time there was a long pause before letters appeared. [You using the VPN I gave you?]

[Yes. And no cameras. I checked.]

[One minute.] I spent the time waiting to work on my paper. It came out pretty easily and a lot of the mistakes that Alixant had made, mostly from trusting me to follow the unspoken rules, were obvious in hindsight. But if he hadn't made them, they would have had legal justification to kill me. So overall, I was rather glad he'd screwed up.

[I'm ready. Go.] The words blinked at me and I had to pull my mind back to what I was going to ask him to do.

[Bridget O'Keif. She has Down syndrome. Mage. Soul, not sure of her power level. Here is her address from her ID.] I provided all that. Took a deep breath and typed. [I need to know if she has family. I don't know where she was pulled from or if she has a support structure. They took our phones and I suspect hers is the only way she had to communicate.]

In my mind I could see the expression on his face, cold, remote, and that clenching of teeth he got when anyone helpless was being abused. He was such a crusader about people not being bullied.

[So what do you want to do with that information?]

I stared at my computer trying to figure out that answer. [I don't know. Maybe know who to call? I'd like to know if they...] I paused. What did I want to know? Would they be happy Bridget was gone? Worried? Apathetic? Did she even have a home? Or did she live in a group home? [I just want to know. Maybe it will present me with an option.]

I could feel his steady gaze and shifted as if he was really there. [Okay. Anything else?]

[Yeah. Benjamin Trainor. Can you tell me what he was convicted of before emerging? I know it was a class E or D felony, but not what.]

[Is everyone you are with a felon?] Knowing Charles, he was serious about the question.

[Or close enough. Drug addict, rapist, peeping tom, do I need to go on?]

[Huh. Interesting orientation. Glad mine was much

more boring.]

[That would have been nice.] My life never worked that well.

[I'll ping you later tonight. Bye.] As always, Charles was abrupt and to the point. I shook my head, missing Carelian and his comments. I ordered multiple copies of the mage laws to be delivered here overnight. It felt like I was spending money like crazy on nothing, but a few hundred dollars this month would be fine. I still didn't feel rich, but I was well past the point of being broke. Scrimping for years had long-term advantages.

An hour later the paper was done, and I was ready for dinner, whatever that was going to be. But that meant dealing with the strangers at best, enemies at worst, and I didn't know if I had that level of patience today.

My grumbling stomach told me I didn't have much choice. I grabbed my key and headed out into the hall. I made note of the other names on the doors and found it interesting that they had empty rooms between all of us. But then with only five women that was bound to happen. I walked to the common area and saw Jake coming out of the little kitchen area.

He gave me a smarmy smile. I nodded and kept on walking. Of all of them, he was the weirdest. I heard him following me, but he never got close enough to talk, and I kept up a heightened awareness the entire time as well as a shield. Good thing I had closed-toed shoes; it made offering up my toenails almost invisible.

The same two servers were waiting for us with food that was just as unappetizing as lunch. So far breakfast had been the best meal, but how badly could you screw up pancakes and eggs? I picked at the salad, wilted, and started to wonder if there was a way around the closed campus edict. This was going to be torture, for the food alone if nothing else.

A tray clanged down onto my table and I looked up to see Dwayne dropping down in the chair across from me. Yvette followed him a moment later.

"Yes, please join me," I said, sarcasm dripping off of every word.

"Excellent. See, I knew you'd be glad to have me here." His smile was so polished and perfect I wondered how long he practiced in the mirror.

"Us," interjected Yvette with a smile. She settled in at the table and I watched them.

Double team or clearing the way?

"I wouldn't say that, but I'm not sure the company can be worse than the food." I held up a forkful of salad lettuce topped with canned chicken.

They both looked down at their plates and sighed. I was pretty sure that reaction wasn't fake or false. I forced myself to eat even if the temptation to side step home was getting larger and larger. A month of subpar meals would not kill me.

"So, you're the famous double merlin, huh?" Dwayne asked after eating a few bites. He'd grabbed meat with some type of mashed vegetable.

"I am a double merlin. Don't know what you mean by famous." I poked at the salad and decided if Carelian came back raving about what Jo and Sable fed him, I might have to refuse to brush him for a week.

"Oh, they talk about you," Dwayne said with a leering wink.

"And they would be?"

"The news, the houses, the government."

I shot him a hard look. "And you know this how?"

"People like talking to my dad. He has parties. I listen." He kept eating and Yvette shifted in her seat, paying less attention to the food than I was.

"And who is your father?"

Dwayne jerked back as if I'd hit him, his jaw tightening as he glared at me. "You don't know who my dad is?" His already dark skin flushed and he shook his head, making his dreads shake and the beads on them rattle.

"Should I? Is he the president?" To be honest, outside the president and a few people involved with the Draft I didn't know many famous people. I hadn't cared, still didn't.

Dwayne blinked at me and seemed to deflate a bit. "No. I guess you don't watch sports?"

"Nope. Never had time or interest."

"He's Andrew Jordan." I just looked at him, the name vaguely familiar, but I couldn't pull it to the front and I shrugged. He looked at me, face blank, then huffed out a sigh. "You are totally out of touch. My dad is a three-time NBA MVP and has his own company. He's an influencer when it comes to sports and is moving into politics. Like I said, he has lots of friends."

"Oh. Okay." It had never occurred to me that people outside of maybe the Draft Board or Steven Alixant's bosses might talk about me.

"So what are you going to do with all that power? If it was me, I'd be living like a queen. Having people wait on me. No one would push me around." Yvette pushed her food around her plate, but her eyes never left me.

The use of the word queen made me smile. "There isn't much I can do. Not and be exactly what Kamp is talking about. With power comes a lot of rules."

"If I was you, I would make them follow my rules. You're powerful enough they couldn't stop you," she insisted.

I gave her a funny look, wondering where she was going with this. "Really? How?"

"Well, you could always just eliminate anyone in your way," she hinted with a sly smile.

"Ah. I see. So who would that be? Kamp? The Draft Board? How about the OMO? What about the House or Senate?" She'd started to frown halfway through my recitation. "How many people am I supposed to kill? Thanks, but I think I'll play by the rules and do my time. Everyone else has." I stood up and grabbed my tray. "See you at PT tomorrow."

I turned and walked away, now even more nervous about the game they were playing.

Chapter 10

Section 2.20

All mages will face expedited trials for felonies. If deemed necessary by the jurisdiction they are in, drugs may be used to keep them unable to access their abilities if they are deemed a threat by said jurisdiction.

SPIRIT

Carelian had pulled everything from home over for me, including some salmon with broccoli from Jo. That got him extra brushes that night. I woke in the morning, had a four-ounce espresso, and was ready to go before Beauchamp started pounding on the door. Caffeine solved so many problems.

The others struggled out into the early morning air, and I was both relieved and worried to see Bridget shuffling out with us. She had nice tennis shoes on, but I still rushed over to her.

"Are you okay? Can you run?"

She blinked at me, then smiled. "Nice lady. Kitty? Kitty?" She looked around for Carelian.

"He's still asleep. Are your feet healed?"

Bridget nodded at me rapidly, still smiling. "Doctor fixed them. All good."

Huh. They got a mage to heal it.

I thought about it, and it probably hadn't been that expensive, but usually you didn't get doctors to waste offerings on something that would heal itself. Draft pressure? Anything was possible.

"Get in line. We're doing stretches then a nice two-mile jog," barked out Beauchamp.

I watched everyone else. Most of them seemed to have come up with sneakers and were at least accepting this aspect of life. But Bridget. My heart threatened to break as I tried to figure out what I could do even as my mind went in circles.

Our drill instructor led us in basic calisthenics, then started off at a slow pace. Bridget copied us with the exercises and for the most part did okay. I noted Beauchamp didn't yell at her, just locked his jaw every time he saw her mess up. But she could run at the pace he set. We went through the campus slow enough it wasn't too much effort to keep up, but fast enough that talking wasn't wise.

We were dismissed for breakfast with the warning of class at nine.

"You know how to get to breakfast?" I asked her, still worried.

"I have a map," she said with a bright smile. "But shower. I know my routines." She said all of this as if reciting rote information. I wanted to scream this wasn't where she belonged.

"Okay. Eat breakfast with me?"

"Okay!" Her voice bright and smile wide as she headed to her room.

I fought back tears, I didn't know if they were from rage or sadness, and headed to my room. I started another rich espresso, grabbed a towel and headed for a quick shower. Ten minutes later I had more caffeine in my system and was dressed to deal with Kamp. I made sure my paper was in my notebook.

"You staying here or coming with?" I asked the cat who had finally deigned to wake.

~Eggs are good. Rather have bacon.~

"Don't look at me. I just want decent food."

He stopped mid groom to just stare at me.

"Okay fine, tolerable food."

Carelian snorted and rose, following me out of the room. We went down to the entry and I looked round for Bridget. She came out a minute later, her hair still damp. Her eyes lit up the moment she caught sight of Carelian. "Kitty!"

She headed straight for Carelian, who purred and stood up straighter. They probably weighed about the same, so her falling to her knees to hug him didn't worry me. "Pretty kitty." She hugged him tight, then carefully petted him in long strokes from his head to the base of his tail.

~Sweet girl,~ he purred in my head and I nodded.

"Ready for breakfast, Bridget?"

"Can the kitty come?" she asked, standing up, but her hand still lingering on Carelian.

"Trust me, he likes bacon as much as I do."

"I like bacon," she chirped and began walking out with us. I saw the others glance at her and then pull away. I wanted to yell at them or beat them, but I understood and couldn't blame them. There had to be a way to save Bridget, but how?

She stayed mostly quiet on the way to the cafeteria, occasionally pointing toward a bird or something. Her hair dried out into frizzes and I had to resist the urge to braid it. At the meal line she took eggs and pancakes and extra bacon that I knew Carelian would get. I let it be. He knew the risks of too much bacon.

Everyone avoided us at breakfast. I figured 50% of the avoidance was due to Carelian, the other 50% to the girl. Yvette managed to smile and wave, but scurried over to another table rather than joining us.

I watched Bridget, my heart breaking. She came across as a bright sunny ten-year-old. And there was no way in the world she could follow the amount of education needed to use magic. At least in this realm.

We walked to the class, and I saw everyone trailing us. Fine. They could think what they wanted. I had to follow my own moral code, but I wondered what the fallout would be.

Kamp walked in, talking before the door finished closing. "Put your papers in the basket and let's get going. Today we are going to talk about legal ways to use magic."

I pulled out my paper and dumped it in, along with most of the others. Bridget didn't, nor did Neil. I settled back in my seat and Bridget kept most of her attention on Carelian. He reveled in her petting.

Kamp wrote on the board, "Section 73.2 Magic as Income". "Now let's use real-world examples. Let's say someone needs to get a bonfire started for a properly permitted party." He turned and looked at us, his eyes burning into Claudia.

I fought not to roll my eyes, but sympathy only went so far. How stupid could you be trying to burn places down for money? Arson was illegal for everyone, not just mages.

"Could you accept money or barter in exchange for starting the fire?" he asked looking at them.

The rest of the students didn't look up, well, except for Dwayne, he just slouched back in his chair looking bored.

"Claudia, surely you know the answer to this," Kamp said, leaning over her. He had to outweigh her by at least seventy-five pounds.

"If the value of the work performed is less than six hundred dollars accumulative, it does not need to be reported. If it is over that amount it must reported as income." Her voice was a whisper.

"And how much did they pay you to set fire to the house?" He didn't move from in front of her.

"Five thousand," she said so low I had to strain to hear the words.

"Ah, so that would have been reported on your taxes. But it wasn't, was it? So there you have tax fraud. Then there is what you were asked to start the fire in." He smiled and my skin crawled in revulsion. The man was taking active enjoyment in her discomfort.

She muttered something.

"Speak up. I don't think we can all hear you."

"An abandoned apartment building, okay!" The words burst out of her and Kamp smiled.

"Ah, but it wasn't abandoned, was it? How many squatters? Poor homeless that don't get the luxuries of room and board and tuition because they aren't mages?" He kept twisting the knife.

"Five," she said, her hands clenched. "But nothing happened to them. The fire didn't start." I watched, sensing her anger, embarrassment, and fear. "The fire never took off, it just smoldered and smoked."

"Yes, smoke and a pitiful little fire. That's why you're here. Almost managed to earn a bachelors. Short one semester, weren't you?" He kept asking questions that he knew the answers to.

"So while the judge let you off, saying you obviously didn't want to burn the building down, I mean how else could a Fire mage fail so badly? You lost your free ride and now you're here. A failed arsonist. All for a measly five thousand? You threw away your life for that? Why? Did you need to prove how stupid you were?"

Claudia was crying now and refusing to look up, her arms defensively across her chest.

"Well? What was the money for? You wanted to go party your last year? Or was your current wardrobe not fancy enough for you?"

He kept jabbing and poking, and even Dwayne was starting to look uncomfortable.

Claudia erupted, launching herself out of her chair so she was close enough her hair would touch him. "I needed the money, okay? I didn't have enough money to buy pads and tampons. Merlin, I didn't have enough to buy condoms or coffee. Five K? That would have lasted me the rest of the year plus, until I got into the draft. It was enough to make sure I had more than ramen and tomato soup. I was just tired of being broke."

Her words cut me like a whip and I couldn't sit silent anymore.

"Enough. Point made. Don't be stupid, and she was lucky. Why don't we talk about how to report any money you make on a 1099 even if it wasn't declared by the person paying you?" I spoke loudly enough that my voice cut above her shaky panting and the magic that I suspected was about to lash out didn't appear.

Kamp sneered at her, but he let her sit down. "Or maybe you can learn to manage money better. The government is generous."

I bit my tongue, hard, to prevent myself from saying something I probably would have regretted. Maybe.

He turned and started lecturing on the rules. I knew most of them, so I spent my time watching as Claudia curled up and seethed with embarrassment. Dwayne had his smirk back, and Ben just acted confident.

This whole thing made no sense, but what worried me more was how easily that could have been me.

"Get started on the assignment this week. Which laws cover the behavior expected of a mage." He dropped a bunch of the small books with the mage laws in them on each of our desks.

I saw the others grab them, even Feng. The

temptation to use telepathy had never been so great. Instead, I kept my mouth shut and watched as he grabbed the papers, flipping through them. I knew mine was the only one he'd probably read, and it didn't matter. Alixant and I had worked through what saved my ass and how we could both protect ourselves next time.

Bridget hadn't even bothered to grab a book and I kept waiting for Kamp to attack her, but he didn't. Instead he frowned and went through the papers again.

"Neil," he barked out. "Where's your paper? Bridget has an excuse as she wasn't here last class. You don't."

I don't know what I expected from Neil, but it wasn't a shrug. "I didn't do it."

"Why not?" Kamp barked a triumphant grin on his face.

Neil flushed the first hint of color I'd seen on him. "I just didn't." I could see his hands gripping the top of the desk, going white at the knuckles.

Where is Kamp going with this? Is this a power trip? You can't get killed for not turning in a paper.

"So you are refusing to follow orders?"

Oh Merlin, that can get you killed.

My mind raced, trying to think how to derail this, but I couldn't protect the world. I gritted my teeth and kept my mouth shut.

"What, too good to write a paper? Even Miss Special over there wrote one. I have to admit she at least understands the ramifications of what she did. But you're too good to do that?" Kamp had moved over and stared at Neil.

The kid, and yes he was young, maybe 19, flushed and tilted his head down. "No."

"Then tell me, why didn't you write a paper, emo boy?" The amount of contempt in his voice had me leaning forward, ready to attack, but I didn't know what to say or do.

"BECAUSE I CAN'T READ!"

Chapter 11

Section 2.20.32

Any mage under the influence of drugs, a psychotic break, or otherwise out of control and using magic in an uncontrolled manner is considered a clear and immediate danger. If others are at direct risk from their undisciplined magic use, immediate termination is authorized to prevent loss of life. The officer on scene will make the decision as to how to deal with a dangerous mage.

ORDER

Neil snarled, and I felt his magic casting out the all too familiar prickle of Murphy's Luck. I stood up from my desk and snuffed it before it could hit Kamp. That would give him way too much justification, even if Murphy was just annoying. Only luck meant he hadn't realized he wore it before.

"Last time I checked, an education was guaranteed to all mages. How did illiteracy slip through?" I asked Kamp, while trying to make sure Neil didn't cast anything else. Luckily, his lack of education meant that Murphy was the easiest as it was pure intent, more so than any other spell beside Luck.

The random thought that casting Lady Luck might have been how people cast blessings on others flitted through my mind and disappeared.

Kamp actively spluttered. "He's lying. Everyone can read."

I didn't grace that with an answer. Though my blood boiled at the idea that so many kids slipped through the system.

"Neil, can you read at all? Do the letters move for you?" I tried to keep my voice kind, but I'm sure my frustration slipped out.

"Why do you care? I'm just a dumb idiot." He glared at Kamp. "Just get rid of me. That's all anyone ever wanted anyhow."

I locked my jaw and glared at Kamp. "If he is dyslexic or there is some issue with his eyes, the government has a responsibility to make sure he can learn. Section 1.135.62."

Kamp's eyes narrowed, and we locked stares. "He refused."

"He didn't know his rights. Do you want to throw away a mage because the education system failed him before he emerged?"

Kamp's jaw ground as he stared at me. "One chance," he snapped out. "Otherwise he isn't my problem."

I turned to Neil and for the first time in my life I was tempted by one of the lesser-known Psychic spells. Persuade. I wanted to make him get a clue, but all I could do was present him with the option. Being an adult sucked. "Neil. Do you want to learn to read and go to college? Get a real job." I willed him to understand what was being offered, to get the one slim chance he had.

He snorted and crossed his arms. "Why? To give more people a chance to pick on me and call me stupid. No one wants me. And I can't learn to read. I'm too dumb."

"Neil," I tried, but Kamp cut me off.

"He made his choice. This isn't your problem. Unless you're claiming mentorship status." The smirk on his face told me he knew what that would mean. And what I only learned long after was how much Indira and Steven had risked for me.

I stood back and shook my head. "No." I started to say something else but his look had me snapping my mouth shut. Anything I did would make it worse. I longed to shake the boy and make him realize here was his chance, but he was so angry he couldn't see and there was nothing I could legally do to make him realize it.

"Fine. You willing to give up being a mage?" Kamp positively glowed with delight.

"What do you mean?" Neil said, his voice wary.

"You're untrained and you're an idiot, but you aren't a criminal yet. Here is your one-time offer. Join the Army. You'll serve a decade. They'll teach you what you need to know. But you will be prevented from using magic ever again."

"How?" The words burst out of me and I cursed silently. I should have clamped a hand over my mouth, but I forced a smile and tried to pretend I hadn't just lost control.

He smirked. "If you aren't trained and you don't know how to make offerings consistently, it is relatively easy to neuter a mage." His attention snapped back to Neil. "Your head will be shaved and your nails cut to the quick every week. If you are caught doing magic for anything other than circumstances where your life or others' are at risk, you will be executed as a rogue mage. But if you make it out after a decade, you'll be free."

Carelian snorted in my mind. ~Like lack of hair or nails would stop you.~

I didn't say anything. Kamp wasn't wrong. Most mages only learned how to offer other genetic material via training and being taught how to isolate the cells. And after a decade of no magic and no easy offerings, he probably wouldn't even think about magic. It would be like most of the mages I'd met. After a while it was easier to do things the normal way than use magic.

Kamp picked up his phone and made a call. I went back and sat down, eyes still on Neil. He sat there, looking sullen and angry, and I let it go. I couldn't save everyone. I kept telling myself that. Maybe I'd start to believe it.

"Arrangement is made. Look on the bright side. They'll teach you what you need to know, and you're guaranteed a job for the next decade. It could easily be worse." If he had been sarcastic or even cruel about it, I might have lost my temper, but he wasn't. He sounded sincere, a true believer.

In some ways, that was even more stressful. He might enjoy destroying us, but he did it because he believed we were dangerous. When it came to me, I couldn't blame him. I was dangerous, just not in the way he thought.

Five minutes later, Neil was gone with two men dressed in suits. I found it odd that it was mostly men driving this, but for all I knew all the women were too damn intelligent to be caught up in this insanity.

The end of class was another assignment to list out ways to stay within the letter of the law for Wandering Mage Act and what the consequences would be if we didn't. This had been discussed to death in college and writing a one-page paper would only take me an hour at most. At least I had an e-reader so I could read while I had nothing to do.

It was a subdued class that headed toward lunch. We'd gone from eleven mages to nine. Maybe all of this was a draft version of Then There Were None. It sure felt that way. Bridget and I walked slowly; she was more interested in watching Carelian explore. I just didn't know what to do.

We entered and one of the servers was talking earnestly with Lizabeth. Everyone else had already gotten their trays and sat down. The food today seemed relatively safe, taco salad. I grabbed a salad with extra salsa and then grabbed a bowl of taco meat with sour cream for Carelian. The server started to say something and Carelian just raised himself up on his hind feet and the server's mouth clamped shut.

I fought giggles as I headed to the table. Bridget took good care of herself, getting her own food and following me, but there wasn't any way I could see her making it through the high-level STEM education. Or maybe I was making an assumption.

We settled down at a table, Carelian sitting in a chair to eat. I arched a brow at him and he just flicked his ears at me. He was showing off.

Bridget watched him eat, her eyes widening at his opposable thumbs. I wanted to ask Bridget a question, or lots of questions, but the bang of a plate hitting the floor jerked my attention to the side. Lizabeth was jerking backward in her chair, the plate laying discarded on the floor with utensils scattered like fallen offerings.

I jumped out of my chair and was headed toward her when she began to thrash, falling to the floor with her head thwacking it hard enough I winced reflexively. I had just made it to her side when hot water streaming into my face pushed me back.

"Merlin, she's tripping and her magic is lashing out," I muttered. Often you could calm a tripping mage by touch, but the table caught on fire, and the water from the steam trays came shooting out, creating whips of boiling water. I couldn't get close.

~Want me to attack her?~ Carelian asked at my side as everyone else had fled to the opposite side of the cafeteria except Bridget, who sat at the table. She watched all this with wide eyes but didn't seem scared.

"No. You might get hurt, and I'm not sure it would make any difference." I ducked as water lashed out at me. Lizabeth rose to her feet, laughing with a touch of hysteria.

"I can see it. I can see how to use magic. You're all idiots."

The air went hot enough I backed up another step or two. Then more water in the air, making it hot and almost like breathing steam. I coughed.

"Have to stop her before she kills someone." KO was still easier if I was touching, but I could get a directed wave here. I heard people behind me yelling, but I focused on her. The KO went out in the smallest cone I could manage, an area about three feet wide at about ten feet. The cop I'd seen cast one back in Rockway was still more skilled at it, but I could disable more people for longer now. I'd come a long way since the showdown outside my house in Albany.

The wave hit her and she looked at me for a split second as the magic collapsed, then I saw her start to crumple. Two cracks from a pistol shattered that weird calm. Her head exploded, brains shooting out the back of her skull and her body fell dead to the floor.

I pulled up my shield, magnetic energy swirling around me as I spun. Carelian had moved close to me so my shield would cover him too. Expecting a bullet to hit me any moment I turned slowly and saw two of the suited men I'd seen standing there, guns drawn. Looking at me, not Lizabeth's body on the floor.

"Are we going to have a problem with you, miss?" one of them asked. They really did look like goons from a movie set. I dubbed one Stocky, the other Hefty, just so I could differentiate them in my mind.

"Only if you keep pointing a gun at me or my

familiar. I am allowed to protect myself." I cast Lady Luck on myself, Carelian, and Bridget for good measure.

They exchanged glances and then one of them reached into a pocket with his left hand, pulling out a phone. A quick dial.

"Yes, sir. The target is down. There is another mage in between us and the target." A moment of listening, then, "Yes. That is her." Silence. "Yes, sir." The goon hung up and put down his gun at the same time as he put the phone away.

"You are free to go, ma'am," he said, his voice dismissive.

Lessons that I had taken to heart welled up as I fought to deal with what had just happened.

"That is Merlin Munroe. And I would like an explanation for what just happened," I replied, my shield still up.

Hefty and Stocky exchanged glances, then looked back at me. "We are just following orders, Merlin Munroe. Mr. Kamp will be here in a minute. Miss Lizabeth Duncan was determined to be a risk to others with uncontrolled magic due to drug use. This put her in violation of Section 2.20.32." They both looked nervous and contemptuous at the same time. I wanted to scream.

I turned around and looked at the splatter of brains, blood, and bone over the gray-yellow floor. Her face was all but unrecognizable. Even looking at the situation in hindsight, there wasn't much I could have done unless I hit her with a KO the second she started to convulse. Even then, it might not have worked.

I swallowed and turned to look at them. At least two mages, Benjamin and Jake, were throwing up. The cafeteria servers had fled.

There is nothing I can do. I failed.

Mel Todd

I made it three steps before Brian Kamp stormed in.

Chapter 12

Section 2.23.1

While in the course of their duties, a mage may find themselves needing to act in a manner that is against their moral or religious code. At all times their oath of service must be weighed against their own morals. While sex, murder, or even assassination may be the best way to resolve assignments, no employee of the government can be punished for choosing another resolution.

CHAOS

"Are you responsible for this, Munroe?" he shouted storming over toward me. I cranked up the power of the shielding to the point that the hairs on my arm were rising up.

He stopped a foot away from me, a frown on his face as his watch lifted up.

"Responsible for what?" I looked at him, trying to keep my emotions in check. That wasn't easy as I didn't know if I want to cry, rage, or worse of all just walk away.

"Her lashing out like that."

I stiffened as the pieces snapped into place. The server talking to her, the sudden reaction, and what the goons had said. Where the brains splashing hadn't affected me, the sudden realization of what he had done made nausea rise in my throat.

"You set it up. Your goons tipped your hand. You got her drugs. The server gave them to her and she OD'd. You knew she would. They knew she was out of control, even what law to use. And they were right here. When they haven't been present without you calling for them before this."

He stared at me, then shrugged. "She didn't have to take them. That was her choice not mine." A quick glance around the room. "Looks like there is some damage to clean up."

"But not as much as you had hoped?" I wanted to spit, to cleanse out the foul taste in my mouth.

He glanced at Bridget, then back at me and Carelian. "Collateral damage can't be helped."

Rage flashed through me and I forced myself to turn, appetite fled. "I believe I have class this afternoon." My voice stayed mild as I walked over to Bridget. "Are you ready to head to class, Bridget?"

Her eyes were locked on the figure on the floor. "Is she dead?"

"Yes."

Carelian rubbed up against her leg, purring loud enough I'm sure people against the wall could hear him.

"Okay." She stood up and took her plate over to the return station. Bridget headed out the door without looking back. I shot Kamp a hard look and he just smirked. Screaming wouldn't solve anything. Right now he had all the cards and all I could do was play the game. I hated playing games.

Bridget stopped in the middle of one of the grassy areas, lifting her head to the sun. "Pretty day." Her smile was the same sweet thing, and the image of her laying on the ground like Lizabeth flashed through my mind. There had to be something I could do. Anything.

There was no answer from above, so I pointed at another building. One we hadn't been in yet that looked like the old gym. "We go there next."

"Okay," she said with a smile and started off in her

rambling walk toward that building. I followed, my mind racing and my shield held high. I only saw Yvette walking behind us, still in stilettos. Why anyone would wear those, especially when walking across grassy areas, I'd never understand.

This was only the third day. At the rate mages were dropping, I'd be alone by the end of the week. What fresh danger did this class hold?

I took the lead when Bridget hesitated; she traipsed after me, perfectly happy to have someone to follow. The door with a sign on it reading "Mage Draft Training" opened into a large practice area that reminded me of a dance studio. There were ten chairs in the wide-open space and not much else. Bridget went in and drifted over to the mirrors, twirling in front of them. In the corner of the room was a small counter with cabinets above and below, and a basket of fruit sitting on the counter. The idea of going and grabbing an apple sounded appealing. Anything to get the smell of burned blood out of my nose. Maybe later, after I assessed the danger of this class.

I sat near the end, leaving one chair open for Bridget. It didn't take long before the rest of the students came in. They sat down, leaving the empty chair between me and the rest of them. I couldn't get the image of Lizabeth out of my head, and more than one of the others looked green.

Two minutes went by with all of us sitting there, not talking, and I missed my phone. At least then I could have been chatting with Jo or Sable, or if nothing else I could surf the net on it. Before my frustration could slip from my control, the door opened and a woman walked in. We all turned to look at her. She commanded our attention as she walked through the doorway and into the classroom. I could see most of the men reacting, but

I'd been exposed to Indira and Esmere enough to sit back and analyze.

She was only about five-four and not stunningly pretty. But as she moved through the room, she exuded power and confidence. The simple dark blue dress would have looked at home in the office or out for the night. What really caught my attention was the expression on her face, simple confidence.

"Welcome to my class. All of you have been chosen to work in the shadows of the country. Your assignments will be dangerous, but you will have the chance to make a difference, something many people never get. Here I will teach you the darker sides of your power. You will learn how to kill and investigate. If you have the temperament, you will learn how to tempt and kill. But most of all you will learn to see into the dark side of reality and make it bright."

I blinked. Looking around, I saw the others were hanging on every word. I fought back a groan. We were expendable. And since we were problematic, why not throw us at a problem that might kill us? It solved two birds with one stone.

"You mean I'll be working on my back again? Nothing new there," Yvette smirked as she talked. "Be just like my college days."

"Wait, you want me to be a prostitute?" Claudia looked like she might hyperventilate.

"No child," Yvette said in more of a drawl than I'd heard before. "She's talking Mata Hari's. Sounds fun to me. Always said sex was a weapon."

"You may call me Madame Verde. " She rolled the r, making it exotic to my Southern ears. "I will be your guide." Her eyes roamed over all of us, snagging on Bridget who was humming softly to herself as she sat on the floor petting Carelian. Nothing flickered over her face. Instead, with the same confident smile she turned back to us.

"As you can see, I am an Entropy archmage." She moved her hair and revealed an Entropy tattoo. "I have decades of experience with mages of all branches, and I can make sure you use your powers to the fullest." She gave a cool smile that made my teeth ache it was so cold. It was how Salistra would smile if she was a human. That idea made me want to run very far away.

"First lesson is getting in shape. It is part of the reason they are starting you with PT here. If you aren't healthy, staying alive is harder."

"But we're mages," protested Dwayne, who had a horrified and fascinated look on his face.

"So? That means you are just as easy to kill as a human. Most of the skills I will teach you are variations of what you can do, and we will go over all of them. We will start with elements, as most of you have either Fire, Water, or Air." Her eyes flicked to me, dismissed me, and touched on Bridget. That had me stiffening, but she didn't act like she was going to do anything, so I let myself relax, but kept the shield up. I'd lowered its power, but it was still there.

"How many of you did the boil water, freeze water, or blow paper around experiments?"

Everyone raised their hand, even Bridget, which told me she was paying more attention than I thought. Which meant what? This all sucked.

"You can eliminate targets with similar logic. If you can boil water, you can boil blood or the brain. If you can freeze water, you can freeze a joint, an eye, or a heart. This is more difficult without excellent knowledge of anatomy, but if you are just trying to kill, the brain is a large target that involves no specific knowledge."

"Are you really teaching us to be wet work spies?" Jake burst out, looking like it was Christmas and Halloween rolled into one.

"That would imply there is a wet work division, which there isn't. I will teach you how to use your skills to the best advantage for our country. Anything not cleared by your draft officer would of course never be tolerated."

I wanted to open my mouth and tell them about the various laws. But instead, I kept my mouth shut as I thought. They couldn't force me to do this, and I knew that. Did I tell the others? Trying to be subtle, I turned and looked at the other students. Claudia still looked vaguely horrified, and I suspected the Wicca leaning made it so the idea of killing someone, especially when she couldn't do it with fire from a distance, horrified her. Jake, Ben, Dwayne, and Yvette all looked almost excited. As if being someone that would die in their first year of service was somehow something to look forward to.

I leaned back, trying not to rage. She continued on, basically getting them to think outside the simple patterns that they would have learned in the classes they had taken. At least I thought they'd all had basic magic classes. I knew Yvette had her bachelors, and I assumed Dwayne and Ben did, but who knew.

A cart was wheeled in by the goon Hefty. It had a bunch of glass bottles on it all filled with different substances. "For Fire and Water, I want you to come up and practice boiling and freezing. For those of you with Air, I have these." As she spoke, she walked to the cupboards I'd seen earlier. Opening the top one, she pulled out a basket and walked back.

"These are excellent items to start with." She pulled out a handful of tiny origami paper cranes. "I want you to fly them to random points in the room. The more swiftly and accurately you can do it the better. Then we will get to smaller and smaller items." Her smile had that same level of chill as she pulled out cranes that were even tinier. "You'd be amazed at what people ignore."

The rest of the mages seemed excited and bubbled up to go look at what she had. Claudia even looked curious, the green fading from her face. Feng just moved like a tin man, all stiff and unemotional. Bridget didn't, she just made faces in the mirror at herself and Carelian.

"Miss Munroe, are you going to join us?" Madame Verde asked, her voice pleasant yet disinterested.

I smiled at her. "I am afraid I don't have any of those skill sets. And it is Merlin Munroe." My voice just as pleasant.

"Oh? I had heard you were rather skilled at Fire." Butter would not have melted in her mouth; her tone was so cool.

"I'm afraid you have me mixed up with someone else." I pointed at my tattoo, clearly visible as my hair was in a French braid. "No Fire. In fact, Earth is the only element I have."

"Ah, I must have been mistaken." She adopted a thoughtful look. I looked away as if I didn't care about her and watched the mages. Too many of them were paying attention to us, but they were at the same time busy boiling liquids, freezing them, and making the little cranes fly around. Yvette had a smile, the first real one I'd seen, as she zoomed the cranes to different parts of the room.

Jake came over to us, his eyes locked on Madame Verde's breast line. "I don't have any elements either. What should I do?"

Verde turned and smiled at Jake. "Merlin Munroe

and I were just discussing that." She made a show of peering at his tattoo. He was Psychic, with Non-organic, and Relativity. It vaguely disturbed me that he had so many of the same skills I did, and he qualified as a first-class creep. "Relativity is an interesting skill set. But as always, Psychic is the power with the best offensive skill. You are an archmage?" She directed that to Jake, who puffed up and managed to get his eyes off her chest for a moment.

"No, a magician," he admitted. I gave him points for not lying.

"Ah." She deflated slightly, and I wanted to roll my eyes. Indira had spent a lot of time with me on how honeypot crafting went and why it worked so well. It also turned out I was largely immune, as was Charles, because neither of us was attracted to bodies. It made sitting back and watching people be stupid rather amusing. "Then I shall have to teach you both how to use KO."

I swear Jake's eyes lit up. "Yes," he hissed out. "That would be wonderful."

My skin crawled as I watched him get aroused. Steven Alixant was becoming a nicer and nicer man the longer I was around some of these creeps.

"Remember touching someone sexually if they are unconscious is nonconsensual and can be regarded as rape." He looked at me and I smiled, showing all my teeth.

"I know," he muttered and took a step away from me.

"Do you know how to use KO?" Madame Verde looked at me, waiting.

"Yes." I didn't bother to hide it; I was sure that had been recorded.

"Excellent. Show me please?" Her face remained

absolutely smooth, but a glitter in her eyes set my alarms off.

~Cori,~ Carelian warned. He still was over with Bridget, but I could feel the weight of his regard.

~I know.~ I tilted my head toward Jake. "On him?"

"What?" he squawked, taking three rapids stutter-steps back. "Not me."

"No. I meant me." Her smile serene and I saw the trap.

"Ah. Then is this an official duel?"

"What?" That surprised her.

"A duel according to Section 2.45.1."

"Oh. Yes, I suppose that would be acceptable." Her excitement had died, and I wanted to laugh. If I had KO'd her, it would have been a witnessed attack and I would be at risk.

I raised my voice. "Duel accepted. Witnessed?"

A chorus of voices, ranging from excited to annoyed, rang out. "Witnessed."

Chapter 13

Section 2.45.1

In certain situations, differences between mages cannot be settled equitably. Or the measure of a mage may need to be taken in situations where simple tests are not as informative. In these cases, or when an instructor needs to assess a student, a duel may be an option. While killing blows should be avoided, they may occur. This is counted as an unfortunate accident, not a crime. Only experienced mages should duel, and duels between students or mages in the draft should be avoided if at all possible. Matching rankings is also recommended.

SPIRIT

~You have the memory?~ I sent to Carelian.

~Yes. May I eat her after you kill her?~

~First, I'm not going to kill her.~ I rose from my chair and moved to one end of the room. ~Second—ew. Really, I don't think humans taste as good as you think they do.~

~Meat is meat. Hot sauce solves everything.~

I glared at him but couldn't come up with a valid rebuttal. Taking the simpler path, I turned to Verde who stood at the other end of the room. The others had pushed the cart over to the side and stood watching, with a bloodlust I recognized from the other realm all too well.

Why do people want to see me in the middle of a fight?

Her smile mocked me and I sighed. Esmere and Baneyarl had made me practice and offer until I'd lost a full six inches of hair. But at the same time, I didn't want the Draft aware of what I was capable of. But again, I only had Earth as one of my elements. Though I could use my null branches, it was best if I never showed that off unless I was about to die. I stood there frozen as to what to do when I felt her call Fire.

I expected to see a fireball headed my way, or maybe a stream of fire. Instead, the area around me started to get very cold. I cast Disrupt at her and the air warmed up as she rocked back a bit. Her eyes narrowed, and I saw her dark brown eyes glimmer.

She responded in kind, hitting me with a much harder Disrupt than I used and I had to use my Bio-Kinetics skill to brush it off. That skill was one I'd been working on. In the Relativity branch, Bio-Kinetics gave me advantages if I paid attention to my body.

I could tell she was getting ready to hit me with more Fire. The elements were babbling with excitement. This needed to end before it got too involved and people started asking exactly what I was doing. Much of what I did was almost invisible. And I'd prefer to keep it that way. But big and splashy made more sense in duels. Which is why I found them kind of stupid.

The power in the classroom let me call electricity, and I let some of my hair go in offering. Not a lot, even my pales in Non-Organic were more than most people's strong branches. I shot a bolt of electricity toward her, but didn't have it follow her when she sidestepped. It ground out, hitting the floor.

"Impressive. I didn't know you could throw electricity." She didn't sound impressed, she sounded annoyed. Maybe something that wasn't in the file.

"A simple trick. Much like this." I cast Murphy on her and pulled Lady to me. I could see her trying to figure out what I did, but I wasn't about to enlighten her.

103

Instead, I hit her with the burst of terror I'd felt when Jo and Sable had disappeared. That got a reaction from her.

Verde sprang backwards, her eyes wide as she looked around, panting. While she was trying to recover, I followed up with a narrow beam KO. It slammed into her before she'd shaken off the emotions and she crumbled to the ground.

"Wow, that was too cool. Where did you learn that?" Claudia was babbling and Jake looked like he was about to have a meltdown standing there. The others just looked wary, except for Feng. His eyes were narrowed as he stared at me.

I walked over to Verde. "Madame Verde, are you okay?"

Her eyes popped open, and the first real expression I'd seen on her flicked across her face, a snarl of rage. Then I felt her grab Entropy and throw Age at me. A growl slipped out, and I hit her with another, more powerful Disrupt. While she wasn't powerful enough to age me, she could age some of my cells, and that would both cause damage and hurt.

The Disrupt hit her and the magic fizzled out. "Don't be stupid again. You know darn well using Age or Disease is frowned upon in duels." I managed to not snap out the words, but I stepped back, ready to react if she tried something else.

"I dislike losing," she said as she stood up and this time Fire flew at me.

Earth sprang to accept my offering and a wall of dirt, there was always dirt everywhere, appeared between the fire and me. The fire hit it and dispersed across the earthen shield. I pulled the dirt together into a ball in my hand and mentally asked Earth to send it to her as hard as it could. It hit her at chest level and exploded over her, knocking her to the floor.

Dirt covered her dress and face, caking into the lines on her face and aging her visually.

"What is going on here? Munroe, I'll have you executed for attacking an instructor."

I heard Kamp's voice and sighed, turning to look at him. He was standing behind the others, rage and calculation clear on his face.

"I wasn't attacking an instructor." I dusted off my slacks. "It was a duel to test my skills."

"Is she telling the truth? Was this a duel or did she just attack the instructor?" The way he weighted the words told me he wanted people to say no.

Carelian brushed up against me. Verde managed to pull herself up, looking like she'd been playing in the dust. It destroyed any level of elegance to her appearance.

Verde glared at me, but Bridget spoke first. "Duel witnessed and agreed. Per Section 2.45.1." Her voice guileless. The other mages glanced at each other.

"Yeah, we witnessed it. Was very outré. Not sure of everything that was cast," Benjamin provided, shrugging at the glares.

Kamp's jaw clenched hard enough I was about to offer up the names of dentists. He stared at Verde. "Is there an issue here?" He glanced around the classroom, a sneer on his face. "You don't seem to be teaching them much."

Verde blinked at him, her eyes narrowing. "Oh, I think they are learning more than you would think. Now, if you don't mind, Merlin Munroe here provided excellent examples of KO and Disrupt. There are other students who would benefit from learning how to use it so accurately."

Kamp glared at all of us one more time, then

stomped out, his annoyance palpable.

Great, I win and I just make more enemies.

The glare from Verde at showing her up not only in front of students but Kamp too promised retribution. I sat down hard into one of the chairs and watched the students. Claudia and Jake were gazing at me in a way that was almost sexual, and my skin crawled. Feng seemed to ignore me, but he was always angled toward me. Yvette just focused on her crane. Dwayne and Ben seemed to be ignoring everyone, though the green tinge had left their expressions.

"So now that you've made them realize how easy it is to kill people, are you also going to tell them the consequences if they attempt to do this to anyone?"

Verde sent me an arch look. She was trying to dust the dirt off herself. "The same consequences there are if you attack anyone. But if you're going to kill, do it right the first time."

"Because watching the blood boil in someone's body is so much more pleasant than seeing someone's brains blown out and splattered all over the wall?" My tone was hard and struck like a slap, and I heard Claudia start to gag as I pulled back into the forefront of their minds the image of Lizabeth laying there.

Verde shrugged. "If you're stupid, you'll die. Better you die now than when you could hurt other people."

I tilted my head in acknowledgment, even if I would have preferred to burn her hair off. Why was I always getting in these situations? I took morbid enjoyment in the Murphy's Cloak still settled on her. If she didn't notice it, oh well. Not my problem.

"She isn't wrong. While I might be opening your minds to what you can do with your powers while you work for the draft, don't think this is in any way permission to kill. The Draft Board and most other governments look down on mages killing for any reason." The words sounded like they were pulled out of her. "But you still need to learn this." She cast me a cold look. "There are some apples over there, why don't you work on Aging?"

It wasn't a suggestion. Effecting nonchalance, I walked over to the cabinets and picked up the apple. A whisper of thought. The apple decayed in my hand, withering so fast that the bacteria didn't have a chance to reproduce. Instead, I had a desiccated apple. How much offering would it take me to age a person twenty years? The answer whispered in my mind and I swallowed. Something like that should have cost me dearly, instead it would be half an inch along the bottom of my hair.

The knowledge of what I could do for so little made me want to throw up. Where the brains hadn't upset me, this did. No one should have that level of power. What was worse was knowing how easy it would be to just age the heart, not even the valves like I was going to target a few years ago.

~You are a powerful quean, you must never forget that,~ Carelian whispered in my mind and I turned to look around him.

The joy from the other mages at learning how to freeze a cup of liquid in the center of a container or boil a teaspoon of water at the bottom of the jar, chilled me. Those particular skills were deadly, if used correctly.

~Why does power have to mean the ability to kill?~ My frustration leaked out , but the laughter I received surprised me.

~Cori, power doesn't mean killing. It means power. What you do with it is what defines you. You are a dragon, be one.~ His laughter took too long to fade, and

107

I glared at him across the room. Bridget was playing with her hair, but it kept vaporizing.

~What is she doing?~ I felt the weight of everything on me.

~Playing with Seeing. She is trying to find her mom.~ His voice had a note of sorrow to it.

I fought a lump in my throat. Seeing let you look through buildings, through the very molecules of the world, but you had to know what you were looking for and how deep to see. Otherwise you might see the bones in your arm when you meant to see the veins or the dirt in the ground when you were trying to see the bone. I could do it in theory, but it took a lot of offering and you needed to know exactly how far to look. That sounded much easier than it was.

My attention shifted back to Verde as she spoke. "Everyone. Please remember this. We will be working on branch-specific attacks tomorrow. There are ways to take out people quickly and easily. Anatomy will be the focus of tomorrow's class."

I let it be. If finding her mom kept her happy who was I to challenge that.

Verde strode out of the classroom trailing dust before anyone said anything. They were a quiet group as they gathered up the material and left. Feng veered off to one side while everyone else headed to the dorm building.

~One minute,~ Carelian whispered in my mind before fading into the shadows. I frowned at his disappearance but smiled at Bridget.

"I'm heading back to the dorms. You good?"

"Nap. I want a nap." She smiled and humming slightly, headed directly to the dorms with her swaying walk.

I followed, watching her, but she didn't seem to be

talking to anyone and I let it go. She was functional enough to be alone and make it to her own room. Could she survive as a mage? Was I protecting someone that didn't need it?

Chapter 14

Section 2.32.10

If a mage is unable to serve due to sickness or other physical ailments that will not pass with time, an alternative may be agreed upon. Four years are owed, but they may be exchanged for help with experiments, testing, or even non-invasive medical experiments. All avenues should be explored prior to declaring a willful refusal to serve. All mages can do some sort of service.

ORDER

The questions didn't leave me as I headed into my room, having watched as Bridget disappeared into hers. I made another cup of coffee; I needed to cleanse my mouth and mind. Once the smell of decent beans and some cinnamon had worked their way into my psyche, I pulled up my computer and connected to the Wi-Fi. Messages were waiting from Jo, Sable, and Charles. I didn't bother to fight the smile that appeared and I relaxed a bit more.

Sable and Jo were both online. I sent them morning greetings, along with the information about Lizabeth's death. I couldn't call it murder. No matter how much it felt like a setup, no one had forced her to take the drugs, and trying to prove that Kamp had laced them with something would be almost impossible. The whole situation was looking worse and worse, but running away wouldn't solve anything. It needed to be changed or stopped, but right now I didn't know how to do it.

I hate politics.

I pulled up Charles' messages, interested in what he had found.

[Cori. Bridget O'Keif. Age 21. Emerged about eight months ago. Her mother has been fighting with the Draft Board about her serving in the draft since then and is on social media trying to get her daughter back. High functioning Down syndrome, has a regular job and graduated high school. Her mother, Margaret, has tried to get exceptions for her, but none of them were acknowledged.]

The information sat there waiting for me. I read it a couple times processing the ramifications. Bridget's mother had managed to delay her entering the draft for eight months when her daughter couldn't or wouldn't go to college. It implied a lot about Margaret's stubbornness or political power.

[Is her mom someone important?] I paused, then typed again. [And thanks for this. You aren't putting yourself at risk, are you?]

[Not an issue. And not really. Most of this is on social media. Important depends on how you look at it. She is the protocol officer for the Secretary of State's office. Something about Public Affairs? But she doesn't seem to have any real connections to anyone on the Draft Board. Mostly she is relentless and uses the laws to her advantage. Mostly section 2.32.10.]

[Ah] I sat back, thinking. This meant that Bridget had a home and a mother or family that loved her. But how did I get her out of this? How did I get myself out of this? The rest of them. Were they worth it? Dragons did what they thought was right. The problem is I didn't know what I thought was right.

[Any word on the others?] I finally typed. The coffee helped ward off the coldness I felt as I waited.

[Claudia is an idiot. Dwayne is a rapist and a spoiled

school boy. Yvette. She said she was an escort right?]
His responses were almost instant. The man could type like he had as many arms as Arachena did.

[Yes.]

[If so, she was a high paid one, and sailed through her degree with ease. She is a wizard, with a BS in Biology. Also, she started her draft a year ago. So there is no reason for her to be there.]

That actually explained a lot. She went too hot and cold. Undercover work was not going to be her forte.

Charles was still typing. [Neil is a drop out and failure across the board.]

There I had to interrupt. [Not exactly. I suspect he's hugely dyslexic, worse than Jo, and the system failed him. They've washed him out into the military. They'll remove his hair and nails and teach him to never use magic.]

[Huh. That wouldn't stop us, any of us.] There was a warm fuzzy feeling in him thinking of our small group as us.

[True, but he's never learned how, so it will. Lizabeth is dead. They killed her today.] I explained that in short, tight words. And that I thought it was a set up.

[How do you end up in these situations, Cori?]

[I don't know. Though I suspect there is a cosmic level Murphy's Cloak on me courtesy of Magic.]

A laughing face appeared. [That would be about the only thing that makes any sense. Feng and Ben are the interesting ones. The felonies Ben is charged with? All are FTC crimes. He figured out how to manipulate the stock market and made a few million. But they caught him. He forfeited the money and has the double draft service. But what is interesting is I think he is still doing it, and this time it's legal. The young man will make it out of the draft and walk back to billions. He's a pattern genius and I'm pretty sure he's written software to read market fluctuations.]

That surprised me. [So white collar crime? Not anything where anyone was hurt?]

[I'm sure a few hedge funds are cursing his name, but yeah. Nothing violent or even dangerous.]

[It was only illegal due to a technicality, wasn't it?] That just popped into my head. But it was the only thing that made sense.

[Exactly. One he probably didn't know about because eighteen months ago, it wasn't illegal.]

It all fit together nicely, a way to control people, and so far, most of their "criminals" were just misguided or desperate. So far, the only ones I really thought were true criminals were Ricardo and Dwayne. And maybe Jake. I still didn't know if he was a creep or a burgeoning serial killer.

[What about Feng?]

Rather than the rapid typing there was a pause. [This is one I wish we could talk about. VPN is up, right?]

I double checked just to be sure. [Yes.]

[Feng is an archmage and has a double master in psychology and biophysics. He's also three years into his draft. And he's damn near a ghost. No social media, no life, just working under the draft. I haven't figured out what department he works for. Do you need me to find out?]

[Nah. I figure Kamp put him here. I just don't get Feng's game. I'm not sure he has said more than four words to me.]

[Well watch him. Anything else you need?]

[Besides to not be dealing with all this? When I get my placement, dinner? The six of us?]

[That would be nice. Arachena says she misses the queans. What is it with that name?]

[If you figure out, let me know,] I typed, shaking my head. [Carelian refuses to answer me. He's just says I am. So who knows?] In my mind I could see him laughing.

[Cath.]

[Exactly. Okay, I've got a paper to write, and this is only day three. Thanks again.]

[Any time.] His icon winked out. I pulled up the writing program, and the door to the room opened. I spun, ready for an attack, Lady Luck around me and a shield ready to snap up. But it was Carelian. His ears laid back against his skull. He slipped in and shut the door, locking it. I relaxed. Locking the door needed to become something I did every time. Another thing to remember.

~We need to talk.~ He sent it with a sharp force that surprised me. I'd never heard him this insistent.

I started to respond out loud, but his lashing tail and twitching ears told me something had really upset him. ~Always. What's wrong?~ I made myself sit back and pay attention to him. He started to pace in the room, but gave up as it took three of his strides before he reached the wall and had to turn. He threw himself down on the floor and aggressively groomed his front paws, all claws fully extended.

Rather than prompting him, he had his own sense of timing, I waited until his tail calmed down.

~I followed the one you call Feng. He smells of deceit and corruption.~

I nodded, watching him, trying to figure out what had him so agitated.

~He called someone, speaking in Mandarin or maybe Cantonese.~ He managed to mutter in my mind, which felt odd.

~Wait, he had a phone?~ I said sitting up, surprised.

Carelian shot back both ears, opening and closing his

114

claws in annoyance.

~Okay, sorry. And you speak Cantonese?~ I just looked at him, confused.

~Realm creatures understand all languages. Does it matter right now?~ His tail lashing increased, and I raised my hands.

~Nope. Got it.~ He had been able to speak Japanese, so why was I surprised he could speak another language? Or maybe it was more he sensed the intent of the words. Either way, I wasn't going to push it right now.

~He spoke about you. Mentioned your skills were higher than expected and you were not the flighty woman they had been told to expect. They would need to step up the efforts to get you to misstep.~

I shrugged. ~That isn't a surprise. Charles told me he is already half way through his draft. So he's a plant here to try to make me mess up.~

Carelian paused. ~Charles would see true. It matters not. What is of dire importance is the next part. The person he spoke to, yes I could hear both sides of the conversation, I have ears on my head not useless bits of flesh like most humans, asked if the rates were declining. Feng responded that there were fewer mages regarded as threats in the last year and they had managed to increase the rates of accidents during the draft.~

I frowned, trying to process what this meant. ~Someone is trying to kill mages in the draft? I thought the draft did that well enough?~

~What is truly disturbing is the second part of that conversation.~ His tail was lashing again, and I tossed him the pillow to attack. He'd shred it, but they could add a pillow to my bill if they cared.

His claws sank in, and a few rakes with his hind

claws and the pillow shredded. I'd need another one, but I could live for tonight.

~Blood and soft flesh would make me feel better.~ I waited, wondering what he was going to say. ~They spoke about the rewards for eliminating any mage before they sired or birthed children. Bonuses for female mages.~

"THEY WHAT?" The words bust out of me at almost a yell as I looked at him. I felt the familiar prickles of Murphy and dismissed it with a frustrated thought. ~They are purposely killing mages and getting bonuses? But Feng is a mage.~

Carelian's tail flicked , sending bits of fluff floating through the room. ~Yes. But from something that was said, I don't think he is from your country. I think he is from China. They are actively trying to reduce the number of mages your people have available.~ He paused, eyes still slitted. ~He mentioned a woman, one he called Jade Laughing. That she would expect results soon. There was a meaning there, how he said it. But I don't know what it meant. Ruler, boss, manager? Some sort of meaning like that.~

My stomach churned. I set my coffee aside, wishing instead for some milk. ~Did they know you heard them? Carelian, did they see you?~

~Do you think I am a kit to be so easy to spot?~ he hissed inside my mind and I shuddered. It tickled in a horrible way. ~No. I stayed until he finished the conversation. It wasn't very long, but he did ask what the bonus was if he managed to get you to cross the line and be executed. Because he thought he had enough of you figured out to provoke.~

I sat there, my body shaking with either rage or fear, I didn't know which. ~And how much was that?~

~Two million.~

I whirled to the computer, pulling up the chat again. [Charles. You there?] I typed quickly after triple checking again my encrypted VPN was up.

[Hmm, should I start charging you?]

I couldn't even find it in me to be snarky back.

[Do you have access to the stats for mages and how many have died over the last few years. And then tell me how many of them had children before they died.]

[Cori, what is going on?]

I typed so fast I had to go back and correct my words to make them legible as I explained what Carelian had overheard. [Do you have stats on deaths while in service, broken down by age and gender?]

[Have? Not at my fingertips. One minute.]

I resisted the desire to fidget, though I was already ready to go to the gym just to burn off energy and stress.

[Here. This is stuff that is publicly available, though not obvious. What are you looking for?] His letters appeared rapid fire as he typed, and I garnered my thoughts.

[What is the percent of women entering the draft that finish it alive?]

[46%]

I blinked. [Are you telling me 54% of all women that enter die?]

[That is what the numbers say not me.]

[Men?] I typed out.

[67%]

[Causes?]

[As a whole: 21% Suicide, 46% Accident, 10% Illness, 23% Ronin.]

I stared at the numbers and felt sick. [They are killing mages. How much have these jumped in the last three years?]

This time he was gone for fifteen minutes. I

distracted myself and Carelian by brushing him. A ping from my computer pulled me away, but both of us were much more relaxed by that point.

[Remember there are no stats yet for this year or last year, but in a three-year span the death rate has increased by 321%.]

No matter how long I looked, the numbers didn't change. Someone or some countries were purposefully working to get mages killed during their draft.

Chapter 15

Section 1.135.62

All mages are entitled to an education. Disabilities such as speech, hearing, language, or learning shall not be used as an excuse to deny an education. All efforts shall be made to provide material and support in pursuit of this education foundation. Unless the mage chooses of their own free will to not learn they cannot be penalized.

CHAOS

Charles and I debated until dinner time, and he brought Jo and Sable into the discussion. They were both horrified and promised to double down on making sure they didn't have issues over the next year or so. Sable only had a year left, Jo had three. Either way they needed to be very careful. While Sable was in a stable job, Jo worked outside and accidents could happen.

We didn't come to any conclusions or answers. In fact, mostly the only thing I became was angry. Who the hell decided they got to kill people and push mages to cross the line so they had an excuse to kill them? It made perfect sense, though. The draft was the perfect time to get someone to break the rules because you were always watched. Always.

I came to no conclusions and collected Bridget for dinner. She was more agitated than usual and kept asking where her mother was. Stress and worry wrapped around me, but she just talked about banana pudding and vanilla wafers, and I smiled and tried not to cry. I created some bullshit paper and the four of us talked late into the night via chat as we tried to think of what to do about anything.

[I don't know, Cori. But all I can say is Arachena says the Herald will figure it out. I must admit I don't understand her faith in you, but if anyone can, it's you.] Charles and the others signed off after that and I crawled into bed, worried. Carelian slept with me and I wrapped around him, letting his purr and warmth soothe my soul.

I was waiting outside when York showed up. He nodded at me and went and banged on doors getting everyone up. Bridget came over to me, aiming more for Carelian than me. We went through the morning exercises, which at least warmed me up, then we started our jog. Carelian disappeared before the first turn. Running long distances was not anything he preferred to do. He commented often that he wasn't a unicorn.

Bridget actually ran pretty well, and I gave her mom silent props for the beautiful daughter she had raised. We were at the halfway point, the road and main gate to our right when she stopped.

"I'm going home now." She turned and started walking toward the gate.

"Bridget, come on. We have to finish the run." I jogged over to her. "Everyone else is going this way."

"No. Done. Going home." She kept up a steady pace toward the gate. "Want to see Mom."

"Um, Bridget. Your wallet and id stuff are in your room, right? You can't go without that," I offered, desperate to get her to stop.

She paused, then shook her head, red hair flying around in an ungainly mess. "No. Will get later. Going home now." She kept walking in a steady manner that seemed somehow unstoppable.

"Bridget, you can't leave," I said, trying to keep up

with her.

"Yes. Going home," she insisted.

York must have noticed we were gone, because his shout boomed from behind us. "Where do you think you are going? The route is this way. Just because you can do magic doesn't mean you get to wander off when you feel like it. Get your butts back with the others!" I could hear footsteps as Bridget kept walking, her mouth set in a firm line as I walked backwards in front of her.

"He sounds angry. We should get back with the others." Every word was a lie. Right at that moment, I really wanted to just burn down the world, but I couldn't let this young woman get killed. There had to be something.

"Bridget O'Keif, halt!" he yelled, having easily caught up to us.

"No. I'm going home. I want my mom." Her fists were clenched, and she didn't stop walking.

"Bridget O'Keif, if you don't stop now you will be in violation of the draft orders provided by Brian Kamp," York barked out.

Merlin's Jizz. That can get her executed.

My mind raced faster than ever, but I didn't make any traction. There wasn't anything I could do besides die with her.

"He's not my mom. I want to go home." She stopped and turned to him. "My mom tells me what to do. No one else. I'm going home." Her lips trembled.

York leaned close, his nose inches from hers. "You will start running along the route and you will go to class. Is this understood?"

Her eyes widened and tears slipped down her face. "No!" Bridget screamed, and I flinched back as a solid inch of hair vaporized from her ends. A wave of fear, anger, and confusion slammed into me like I'd been hit by a wall of water. I had to swallow a scream.

~Cori?~ Carelian sounded panicked, and I whirled looking for him. He cowered on one side of the road while I saw York bellowing in rage.

"That is an attack. Stop," boomed out York.

Magic spun out from her; her hair visibly shorter as I felt Murphy's Cloak surrounding us. Things started to form out of thin air, shapes and figures, and I stared at them.

She's calling ghosts.

The knowledge horrified me. All I wanted to do was cry, or scream, or run away. ~She's projecting her emotions,~ I told Carelian and myself. I swallowed hard, the sharp taste of bile-tainted coffee rising up my throat as I grappled to not react. "Bridget, stop it. You're scaring people."

"Home. Now!" She was sobbing, but absolutely unmoved.

I looked around for York and saw him over off the sidewalk on the phone. The other mages were all huddled together under a large oak, looking at us with a mixture of horror and anticipation. I had no doubt he was calling for backup, and I couldn't think of anything to stop her. I could KO her and try to convince Kamp.

"Bridget, I'm sorry." I moved toward her, my necklace thumping on my neck as I tried to get to her.

"No!" she screamed and starting stomping her feet and waving her arms. I felt something grab my very being and pull. I could hear others screaming and knew she was pulling at all their souls. I panicked and did a wide KO, hard. It bounced off of something, which I hadn't known was possible, but Bridget shuddered and the pull stopped.

My knees almost buckled, threatening to send me tumbling, but I staggered and stayed upright. Bridget swayed and looked around, her eyes wide and dilated.

"Freeze. Get on the ground now!"

The words came from behind me. I glanced over my shoulder to see that Hefty and Stocky had appeared, guns drawn and pointed at both of us. Kamp stood between them.

"Bridget O'Keif, get on the ground now. You are under arrest for violation of section 2.20.32. If you come with us quietly it doesn't need to get unpleasant," Kamp said, his voice carrying from where he stood, the other draftees behind him and Bridget behind me.

"No. I want to go home!" She was bawling in earnest now, taking big gulping breaths of air as tears ran down her face. "I want my mom!" The muggy morning seemed to cry with her as I felt water running down the nape of my neck.

"Kamp," I shouted. "She doesn't understand."

He looked at me, anger written large on his face. "It doesn't matter. She almost killed everyone here. Do you think I don't recognize a Sever?"

I flinched. Sever was what I'd used on that gun man a few years ago when Japan was still trying to kill me. Only Spirit mages were taught it, but it ripped your life from your body. Philosophers were still arguing what that implied, but for the rest of us, it meant you were dead.

"There has to be something," I was begging as I swiveled between the crying girl and the furious Kamp.

"There isn't." He looked at the two goons. "Take her. If she does anything, you know what to do."

The men, pale grim looks on their faces, nodded and moved forward, guns at the ready. York had moved over to where the mages stood. Both a guard and a witness to what was about to go down.

"No!" I shouted, feeling my own tears pressing

behind my eyes. The pale faces of the other mages remained in my vision like after images. Desperate, I ran my fingers over the Spirit symbol on my necklace, my birthday present from Jo after I emerged. That first year at GA MageTech, the birthday party in Baneyarl's realm. My fingers stroked the scale secured behind the symbol. Tirsane's scale. Her words rang in my head as if she was repeating them right now. "It is a token. If you ever need me, break it. I will know. Use wisely."

But what could she do? She wouldn't change the laws here, that much had been made clear. A random comment Hamiada had made that day in the glade when Jo and Sable had been freed from the trap she'd put them in, whispered through my mind.

Before I'd finished processing the thought, I ripped off the necklace and snapped it in half. "Tirsane, I need that favor." I yelled the words, fear making my voice high and sharp. I glanced at my right wrist, and the circle of magic symbols were in full color, radiant almost. They pulsed with the beat of my heart.

Carelian looked at me, his ears already laid back against his skull. ~Magic's breath,~ he cursed and raced to Bridget.

Kamp, who had been following his two goons at a slow pace as they approached Bridget, turned to look at me, face draining of blood and emotion. "What did you do?" His voice low with some emotion I couldn't define.

A slash of pain spiked through my head and I gazed at the pieces of scale in my hand. Doubts assailed me and I looked up at him, all my bravado gone. "I'm not sure."

The rip formed about ten feet between where I stood and Bridget. The two goons had pulled back and now flanked Kamp. Their faces were all ghost white. I don't know what I looked like, but I'd started this, I'd better see it through. Wishing I wore something besides shorts, a sports bra, and a now sweaty tank top.

~Are you sure, my quean?~ Carelian's voice was oddly hesitant.

~Doesn't matter. It's done.~ I didn't take my eyes off the rip even as I waited for a bullet to the skull by Kamp or his thugs.

The rip stopped growing, now taller than the oaks that dotted the campus. One second it was a distortion in the air, one you couldn't see through, the next Tirsane slithered out. I hadn't seen her since my private graduation party. The Guzman's had thrown me a small party and Baneyarl, Esmere, Tirsane, and Jeorgaz had shown up, which after their wedding appearance didn't really surprise me. At the party she'd barely been six feet tall and spent most of the time laughing with her snakes looking just as amused. Salistra had also been invited, much like you invited the scary fairy, but didn't attend, to my personal relief.

Right now Tirsane displayed what I called her regal mien, her face beautiful but impassive, her height at least twelve feet tall, and her snakes alive and hissing. Her scales glittered in the morning sun and water started to condense on her skin. Her impassively beautiful face turned to me and my mouth went empty creek bed parched.

"Merlin Munroe. You have called in your favor?" Her voice so pure and exact that my eardrums felt lacerated.

I bowed in a short, yet sincere motion. "Tirsane. Thank you for coming."

"You called. I had promised. I do not break my word." There was a world of warning in her words and the possibility I had made a huge mistake rattled my soul.

Chapter 16

Section 3 - Wandering Mage Act

In as so much that the lack of what would be offered by the mage does not affect either their health, appearance, or reputation, the request of any official from either the federal, state, county, or city government for assistance to prevent either the serious injury or death of any person or persons, whether known or unknown to the mage, must be granted. The mage must provide said assistance until the offering boundary is crossed. At such time the mage may demure with the words, 'The cost is detrimental.

SPIRIT

I took a deep breath and tried to control my shivers. Either I trusted Tirsane or I didn't. Either way, I'd started this domino chain of events.

"See this young woman?" I fought to call her a woman when I saw a child that I desperately wanted to protect. "She has a birth defect we call Down syndrome. It makes her... simple." How in the world did I explain the myriad of ramifications that went with Down syndrome? In the end, I fell back on the words Carelian had used.

"Ah," she murmured and slid over to Bridget, who stood there, eyes wide, tear tracks on her cheeks, as she looked up at the demigoddess. Carelian stood next to her purring, and I saw Tirsane linger on him before shifting her gaze to Bridget.

"What is your name, child?"

I found my ability to breathe locked in my chest as I watched. Maybe this is what seeing things in slow motion was like—terror and hope in one dreadful compilation.

Bridget looked up at her, sniffing snot back up. "Bridget O'Keif." She looked at Tirsane closely. "Are you a snake? I didn't think snakes were as pretty as you are."

Tirsane laughed, the clear tones shattering the hold on everything, and I swear even the leaves started to rustle again.

"I am a gorgon, child, and thank you. Why are you crying?" Tirsane didn't get smaller, but she did seem to crouch, lowering herself to not loom over Bridget as much.

"They won't let me go home," she said, a tremble appearing in her voice. "I want to go home."

Tirsane turned her gaze to me, and only the fact that I had met her multiple times before, some when she was being much more terrifying, prevented me from either fleeing or crumpling to the ground. "Is this true?"

"It is draft orientation. All mages are required to serve. She isn't allowed to leave per the terms of the law because she is a mage," I said, managing to keep my voice level.

Her gaze slid from me and I sagged a bit. I took evil pleasure in the whimpers from behind me.

"I'm outta here. I ain't getting paid enough to put up with monsters."

My rage spiked at anyone using that word on Tirsane. I turned and saw Hefty booking it across the campus, leaving Kamp and Stocky standing there. Kamp had a wet patch on the front of his pants.

"I'd watch my language. Tirsane is not a monster." I growled out the words. Scary as all get out, yes. But then I'd seen Indira in a full rage and she could be terrifying also.

Kamp shot a terrified look at me, but I didn't give him anything. I just pretended it was an afternoon with Tirsane at the house, serving tea and cookies. Her favorites were spice cookies.

"And you are the representative of the draft?" she asked in her silken tones that reminded me of a knife slipping through silk.

Kamp's head jerked up and down as his mouth worked, but no words came out.

"And is what the child says true? You will not let her leave?"

He swallowed three times in rapid succession before trying to speak. "Law says taking her is required. She can't control her magic. Attacked others. She broke the law." His confidence got a bit greater as he got those words out and stood up a bit straighter. "She has broken our laws by attacking us. Her life is forfeit."

"Ah." Tirsane settled down and looked at me, her face showing nothing but serene perfection. "Herald. You know I cannot interfere in your laws. At least, not without grave consequences. So what favor did you want? While I could whisk her away, I do not believe she would find life in the realms congenial."

I shuddered at that idea. Bridget there in the realms, by herself. No, that would not be a good idea.

"No, Tirsane. I would never ask you to break the laws of Earth." At least not blatantly ask, subtly hint oh yes. "And Bridget is not suited for living in the realms." I wasn't suited for it, most humans weren't.

"Then what are you requesting I do?" A hint of curiosity in that arched brow with her snakes waving around her head.

Bile bubbled in my throat and I steeled myself for my insane request. I took one last glance at Bridget and hoped she didn't hate me for all eternity for this, but the idea of them killing her, killing others like her couldn't be continued. The image of Kelly, the murderer who had been autistic—the court had confirmed her diagnosis after she was executed. The stats from class flickered through my mind, deaths that were real now, lives destroyed. If this could be stopped, these people saved, I had to try. Which meant I was going to play god.

"Hamiada mentioned once that you could drain magic from someone," I said, my voice clear in the oppressive humidity of the morning.

She went still, even her snake froze. Heart pounding, I stood there as she slowly turned to look at me.

"Yes, that is one of my abilities." Her voice laden with hidden weight.

I heard nothing from the mages around me. Even Carelian had gone quiet, as if they all held their breaths. "Then I formally ask, both as the favor you once granted me and the Herald of Magic—"I paused. I was taking a leap of faith here, and I might be the one who paid the price, but I couldn't not try"—that you drain all magic from Bridget and others like her, so none of them will be subject to laws they are not capable of obeying."

"Hey, wait, what-" Kamp started out protesting and made two steps toward us. I could see him out of the corner of my eye.

Tirsane glanced at him and snarled. That perfect face turned into something from the deepest recesses of our minds, and I saw Kamp turn white as a pale sheet of stone seemed to coat him. If I hadn't been so sure Tirsane didn't mean me harm, I would have screamed like the other mages. I could hear shrieking that I pegged Claudia for and rapid footsteps that I just knew were Jake and Dwayne. But I didn't take my eyes off

Tirsane.

"I wish to ensure I understand the Herald's request." Her face back to beauty as she leaned in close. The snakes all arrowed in on me, stopping about two feet from my face. "The Herald is not only granting permission, but making the request of Tirsane to remove magic from any human not capable of meeting human laws."

There was a wealth of minefields in that, but no matter what, I didn't want to see people dying because the laws didn't take into consideration their own shortcomings. "Anyone not mentally or developmentally capable of using magic according to our laws. Yes." Nerves had my digestive system in knots and I had to convince myself that throwing up would be very unhelpful.

A slow, almost malicious smile spread across her face and my doubts quadrupled. What had I done?

"So be it." She turned and went back to Bridget who had sat down, her head on Carelian, sniffing.

~Do not hurt her. She is a sweet girl.~ His voice echoed in my mind and I knew he spoke to Tirsane.

"I would not. There is no purpose served in hurting one such as she, though Esmere would not understand you protecting her," Tirsane countered as she crouched down, her snake body lowering her so her waist almost touched the ground.

~True. But I am not my malkin.~

"True." Tirsane looked at Bridget. "I am going to touch you, then I promise, they will let you go home."

"Home?" Bridget lifted her head, voice trembling. "I can go home?"

"Yes." Tirsane's voice was gentle. Her hand reached out and cupped Bridget's face. In this size, Tirsane's hand covered most of the back of Bridget's head and the entire right side of her face, the tattoo hidden behind her palm. "This might feel odd."

Then something happened. I couldn't explain it or even be sure of what I sensed. That feeling before lightning strikes, the intake of breath before you scream, that pull when a rollercoaster drops you. It was all of those and none at the same time. Magic moved, swirling through the campus, more tangible than I'd ever felt, though that seemed like a lie. It built and swarmed and throbbed and hung over her, a storm cloud waiting to pour.

I looked around, part of me expecting to see army troops rushing in or portals to all the realms appearing. But it was the quiet I'd seen on TV before a tornado struck. That analogy didn't make me feel any better. My attention was pulled back to Tirsane by her snakes hissing. Then all magic broke loose.

The heavy waiting sensation snapped, and I heard everyone behind me yelling and various calls to get out of there. I didn't bother to turn and see what was going on, all my attention was riveted on Tirsane, Bridget, and Carelian. The dam holding the magic in the air ruptured, and it streamed into Tirsane. I couldn't really see it, it was more like a heat mirage, or a crystal-clear river; you only saw by what it distorted. It flowed into Tirsane and she glowed. At first a subtle glow around her edges, then brighter and brighter, until she looked like a rainbow was about to burst from her skin. Her snakes waved in the air, thrashing either in pain or ecstasy, changing colors as magic poured into her, into them.

Then it stopped. Like a sudden summer shower, it stopped, and the day cleared, suspiciously cool and bright. I forced myself to take in a shaky breath and walked over to them.

"Carelian, are you okay?" He looked a bit wild, all his

fur puffed up, but his ears weren't laid back, though his tail jerked around.

~That was a rush I hope to never experience again,~ he said slowly in my mind. His entire body shook and his fur started to smooth back, though his eyes were so dilated as to be black.

"Bridget, are you okay?" I asked. Her eyes were about as wide as Carelian's and she was panting a bit. Not from fear, I hoped.

Tirsane pulled her hand away, and I blinked. The tattoo was gone. Bridget moved her head incrementally and looked at me.

"Yes. I okay. Kitty?" she asked patting Carelian.

"He's fine."

"Snake lady?" she asked, eyes still so wide she looked almost deranged.

At that question I turned to Tirsane, who was curled up on her tail, looking like she'd stuck her finger in a light socket.

"That is a good question. Tirsane, are you okay?"

I had been unaware she had nictitating membranes until multiple lids opened and closed over her slit pupil eyes. They were blown open too, and a shudder ran through her.

"I thank you for the inquiry. I am fine, if a bit... drunk? Yes, drunk. That was unexpected."

"What was?" I asked, worrying that I had caused her to get hurt in some way.

"Cori, how many people on your planet are mages?"

The question surprised me and I reached for my phone to figure out the answer, but of course it wasn't there. I tried to remember that stat. "I think about forty percent are magician or higher. They think maybe as much as another thirty percent are hedgemages, but they almost never use magic."

"And of those, how many would meet the restrictions you provided me? What would the number be?"

"Um..." I did the math in my head, not fast, but I did it.

Seven billion and forty percent, that would be about 2.80 billion. And if half of one percent of those were like Bridget, you'd be looking at quite a few.

I finished my thought out loud. "Maybe 14 million? I mean, that is just a guess."

"Oh." She sounded shocked and if I didn't know better, I'd almost think she was about to pass out. "That might explain it. Those unable to wield magic are very rare in our realms. I had figured a few hundred, maybe a few thousand at most. Millions?" She started to giggle, and I stared at her in shock. Tirsane giggling didn't seem like anything I'd have expected.

~Mayhaps I should call my malkin?~ Carelian asked, and he looked as freaked out as me, his tail puffing back up.

"I'm fine. Just a bit overwhelmed. Salistra will be chewing diamonds she will be so mad and jealous." Tirsane gave herself a shake and pulled herself back up to her full imposing height. "I thank you, Herald, for the boon you have granted Spirit today. I feel what I was given was in much greater value than what you asked." She stood there a minute, gazing at me and around the campus. "Ah yes, I think this is the best way." One of the snakes, it had red, yellow, and black bands around it, slithered off her skull and onto her hand.

Okay, that was both cool and creepy. They can separate from her head?

"Give me your arm." The imperious statement had me sighing. At this rate I was going to have a full sleeve of tattoos and none of them were things I had chosen.

Well, I did like the cat nose and whiskers, but still.

I held out my arm, the cat nose and whiskers on the inside of my left arm, then the simple green snake from Tirsane, and the unicorn horn, with four segments—an indicator as to my debt to Salistra. I took a deep breath, expecting another bite. The snake slithered down her arm and wrapped around mine. It was warm and smooth, the scales rasping as it slid over my skin. As it circled my arm, looking for a place to bite I assumed, it shrank, getting smaller until it was only about three inches long. With a sudden move it slid under my skin and started to slither toward the location of the snake tattoo. I shrieked as it moved inside my arm, positioning itself to the same location as the tattoo. I clawed at my arm, my entire body revolting at the wiggling crawling sensation under my skin. Then it floated up to the surface of my skin and melted down into the existing snake tattoo. The colors of the tat changed to black, red, and yellow.

"Merlin's Balls! What was that?" I was still frantically patting my arm, hyperventilating, but there was only skin. Nothing was there though my body still shuddered in remembered horror.

"Ah, a little token. Should you need me, touch the snake and call my name. I trust you will not abuse that gift?" Her attitude should have been serious, but she still looked like she was stoned.

I kept shuddering and rubbing my arm, managing to bite back the shrieks of "Get it out" by sheer self-preservation. It was a good thing I didn't have a knife; I might have cut it out.

"No. No abusing," I babbled, my hands shaking with the desire to claw the snake out.

"Then I believe it is time for me to leave." She turned and glanced at Kamp. "And I think you have learned your lesson from trying to bait our herald?"

I followed her gaze and Kamp was standing there, no longer stone, but just as white. "Yes, Ma'am. So noted."

She gave one searching glance at me, then turned and slithered back to the rip. It closed up behind her and a level of tension evaporated from the area. I knelt next to Bridget. "You sure you're okay?" Focusing on her and not my arm.

"Yes. Can I go home now?" she asked, her voice plaintive. The space on her temple where the tattoos used to be empty, revealing pale freckled skin.

"Yes, I think so." I turned to look at Kamp, who nodded in a jerky motion. "Let's call your mom."

The smile that spread over Bridget's face was blinding. It made me think maybe I hadn't screwed up.

Chapter 17

Section 1.3.1

All mages that retaliate to a draft officer with magic will face the equivalent of a court martial. If found guilty their draft service shall be doubled.

ORDER

"I would like to know exactly what happened." Harold Lefoin stared at me; his arms crossed as he sat behind the desk in the office. He'd aged since I last saw him about three years ago. There was more silver at his temples, more belly at his waist, and the stress lines added to his serious demeanor. But he still had the same attitude he had that day outside the house when I had to face down him and his agents. There Tirsane, Salistra, and Bob—the representative of Chaos—had made an indelible impression on everyone involved. I was still vaguely amused that I hadn't been arrested or shot on sight.

Kamp had provided Bridget's phone and we had called her very relieved mother. She would be here in another hour or so to pick up the girl. Carelian was acting as babysitter. I'd been sequestered shortly afterwards, in the politest manner possible, telling me the director wanted to speak to me.

The time to wait had probably been a mistake on their part. It gave me time to pull myself together and make sure that I met Lefoin as a dragon, even if I was still dressed in shorts and a tank top. And no matter how much I just wanted to dissolve into a babble fest, I needed to keep what advantages I had.

"Which part? Where you set up a group of mages to be killed? Where I found an option you hadn't considered? Or where I saved the life of an innocent?" I smiled at him. My hair was in a braid and I'd managed to wash my face, so while not looking elegant, I didn't look a wreck.

"Munroe," he growled and I kept the half smile on my face.

"I'm sorry, but am I under arrest? If not, I believe I am missing classes."

"They are canceled," he snapped. "And I need answers from you. What happened?"

"You should know. After all, you were about to sentence a girl to death." I kept my voice perfectly level even if my hands fisted tight enough to drive the nails into my palm.

"That wasn't me," he stated, glaring at me.

"And here I thought the boss was in charge of his minions' actions. Does that mean you'll now sacrifice Kamp on the altar of your mission?"

He settled back into his chair, my attempt to get a rise out of him failing. "What my employees do or don't do is not your affair. Explain what you ordered that thing to do."

I arched a brow at him and wished Tirsane was here to have him call her that. He wouldn't survive the experience. "I did not order Tirsane to do anything. I asked if she could drain magic from Bridget, and make her no longer a mage. If she couldn't do magic then the laws didn't apply to her and she could go home."

"And that is all you did?" His voice had a dangerous tone and I thought about how much information he might have gathered in the two hours I'd waited.

"The way I phrased it asked her to do it to all mages incapable of using their magic in accordance with the laws."

"And she just did your bidding?"

"Ha!" The laugh burst out of me and I clawed my reserve back into place. "Tirsane does not do anything I bid. Think of her more as a ..." I paused trying to think of the correct analogy. "Ugh there isn't anything I can compare her to. She's a demigod. And I suspect she thinks of me as a pet. So the best analogy I can make is I'm a blasted dog begging for treats and she gives them to me because I'm cute." I threw up my hands in exasperation. Holding on to being an arrogant merlin was hard. And since I didn't understand Tirsane how was I supposed to explain her to anyone?

"Hmmm." He stared at me until I was clenching my leg muscles to not fidget. "I can't decide if I should curse you for your arrogance, and find something to sentence you under, or say thank you."

I managed not to start. It helped that he still looked like he would prefer to bury me in an unmarked grave.

"And why is that?"

"Whatever trick your friend did, any mage that was mentally deficient, injured and unable to use their magic, and even a few with Alzheimer's, are no longer mages, down to not having any mage tattoos. We managed a few tests and all of them come up as norms. Not a shred of magic in them."

I nodded, trying not let my reactions appear on my face. Maybe people like Kelly wouldn't be able to kill. That would be preferable. And I still wondered if it had been the right thing to do.

"My question is exactly what do we now owe that creature? What did you promise?" He sat forward his eyes never leaving my face. "What did you give in exchange?"

My arm twitched as I imagined I could feel the snake

slithering under the skin again, and I gritted my teeth.

"Nothing. It was a gift to me that I could ask her a favor. I did." I didn't say anything else about the other marks or the Merlin-blessed snake. Even thinking about it made me want to gag.

"Hmmm."

We sat there in silence, me with my legs crossed under me so I wouldn't fidget, him just glaring at me. I don't know how much longer we would have stayed there if a spike of pain through my temple hadn't caused me to flinch. He jerked upright frowning at me, but before he could speak a rip opened up along the wall in the office where we sat.

"What in the world," he growled, turning and pulling a pistol from the small of his back. It was up and pointed at the rip in a fast smooth move. I had to give him points, the form was accurate and I had no doubt at all he could use it.

Salistra stuck her head in through the opening. Her current size meant her head took up the same amount of space as a very large human.

"What are you doing here?" demanded Lefoin.

I suppressed a sigh.

~Corisande Munroe. How could you? Tirsane is all but drunk she has so much power. You gave her all that power and now she is going to lord it over the rest of us for eons. And you didn't even ask me!~ Her voice was sharp like a dagger through my mind and I stifled a sob, and saw Harold groan and clutch his temple.

"I'd forgotten how very much that hurts," he muttered exhaling sharply through his nose.

~After all I've done for you, and I get dismissed like that?~ Salistra, her head in the rip, jabbing her sharp horn at me, ignored him completely. ~Now I can see why she likes you so much. You invited Esmere also didn't you? Did you invite,~ the pain that lashed inside my head at the real name of Bob slashed through me and gave me a bloody nose.

"Enough. I didn't ask you because I owe you, not you owe me. And I didn't know it would work that way. Though I probably should have. And I won't be doing anything like that ever again. No, I didn't invite Esmere. Frankly, I expected to die." I didn't quite shout the words, but I found myself standing and glaring at her, ignoring the horn that could kill me without any issue.

~Still! Tirsane keeps telling me how smart you are. Why didn't you think to invite me?~ It was an outraged huff and the tip of the horn got closer to me all the time.

~Because you are a drama queen and go and pull stunts like this.~

I jumped as Esmere spoke and I felt her walk behind me. I heard Harold cuss, but I was too busy paying attention to the new complication.

~I am not a drama queen. I am Salistra and she of all people should understand my due. What good are humans if they forget us when they have excess magic they wish to expend?~

The ideas laden in that sentence made my head spin.

"Salistra?" I said quietly and she whipped her head to look at me, the horn grazing my chest. "I promise, next time I have excess magic to get rid of, I'll summon all of you. Okay?"

She glared at me, first out of one eye, then turning her head stared at me with the other, then huffed. ~See that you do. If it is sufficient, I may erase the debt you owe me.~ Without another word she yanked her head back and the portal closed.

~I swear she's only happy when virgins are plaiting flowers in her hair prior to her corrupting them. Are you okay, Cori?~ Esmere sat in front of me, looking me in the eyes. ~Do I need to eat him for you?~ She cast a look at Lefoin, who really didn't look worried enough.

"No, thank you," I replied on automatic.

~Ah. Shame.~ She wandered over and rubbed the side of her face against mine. ~That was amusing though. I wonder how long her high will last. Ah, if nothing else, Cori, you are entertaining.~ With that she vanished, only the smallest pinprick of pain telling me it was a portal opening, not a side step.

"Why me?" I muttered under my breath.

"You know, Munroe, I think I'm starting to believe you that you are their pet. Though the cat seems to like you what with the rubbing." His voice was bland and I reached up, touching my face.

"Don't read too much into that. She was marking me as hers. Though how that works between her and Carelian I have no idea. Either way, I seem to be the property of multiple beings." I touched my tattoo then my arm with the markings from each of the realms.

"I see."

I winced and knew it showed on my face as I remembered where I was and who I was talking to. I never seemed to remember some people were the enemy unless they were absolute jerks.

"Is there anything else I can answer for you?"

"There are many questions I have. However, I am not going to say I am displeased at having fewer mages. Especially those that put my people in positions where they have to make decisions that are not easy to live with."

I nodded at that. I still had issues with what happened, but Bridget was alive. That thought sustained me at the moment. With a bit of effort I pulled my serene persona back to myself; it was getting easier to do, but was that a good thing or a bad thing?

141

"Is this going to be a habit of yours?"

"Do I look insane?" The words burst out of my mouth and I sighed and closed my eyes, clenching my fists. "Let me rephrase. If I could have thought of any option other than the one I took, given the time I had, I would have gone with it."

"Hmmm." He sat up, elbows on the desk and hands clasped. His attention on me was absolute and I just smiled, even as my stomach grumbled. "My problem, Munroe, is that you are dangerous. And while you could argue all mages are dangerous, you are worse. You don't see the limitations inherent to magic or, worse, you don't have those limitations. You are a destabilizing factor in a system that is rather precisely balanced."

"By killing people that don't allow themselves to be limited?" I asked, a bit of annoyance slipping into my voice.

"Yes." His answer was automatic and I blinked in surprise. I'd expected dissembling, or something. "I don't owe you any answers, but in the spirit of cooperation, as I believe you may be around for a long time, I will. Mages are deadly. You saw what happened when one with limited ability to control her skills had a temper tantrum. You were there in the cafeteria when the other girl overdosed."

I started to open my mouth to argue, but his hard look had me snapping it closed and I nodded for him to go on.

"You have had first-hand experience as to how dangerous someone who can't control themselves or their magic can be. I get no pleasure out of ordering people to be executed, but can you image the fear and riots that would occur should a mage lose control like that in public? There would be witch hunts and mages would retaliate and the whole damn world would fall into chaos." His hands slammed down on the desk, making me start, and he leaned forward, eyes intent. "If keeping our society in one piece means others have to die, so be it. It has always been like that no matter what lies we like to tell ourselves."

I gritted my teeth and kept still.

"But that leaves me with you. I have no doubt you will make it through whatever pressure we could put you under and while I still feel you are the most dangerous person around, executing you is not an option."

The temptation to smirk rode high, but I didn't move, even if my muscles were trembling with the desire to slap him.

"However, I believe you have more constraints on your actions than I originally thought, though it remains to be seen if they keep you on the straight and narrow or make you into a rogue. Either way, you will be watched and don't think I'll hesitate to take you out if there is any opportunity." Lefoin pulled a small manila envelope out of his jacket. "This class is going back to what has always worked in the past. You are free to stay anywhere you want. There are three classes held from 1-5 the rest of this week to teach you payroll, benefits, vacation, and all the other stuff that comes with the draft. Then you are expected to report to your assignment. There is time built in to find a place to live."

The envelope slid across the desk to me. I didn't touch it quite yet. "Your assignment is in there." He paused and shook his head. "I've loathed everything you and your friends have managed to do over the last few years. But now, I'm almost curious to see how you handle this. If nothing else, it won't be boring."

He nodded once, pushed away from the desk and left the room before I even had a chance to say anything.

I groaned. "Why me?" I stared at the envelope like it was a trap. Which it was. I didn't bother to look inside. I wanted to check on Bridget and Carelian and get my phone back. Getting to take a shower wouldn't hurt my feelings either. Ten minutes later, I was back at my dorm, and my phone hung in a bag on the door knob. It got tossed on the bed, and I went in search of Carelian.

He lay sprawled on the floor of Bridget's room, purring and enjoying Bridget petting him while she babbled to the woman sitting on her bed. She looked up at me and I saw the same red hair and green eyes. But what really set me at ease was the sheer relief I saw in her eyes.

"You must be Cori," she said as she rose off the bed.

I nodded, still a bit freaked out from the theatrics with Salistra and Esmere.

She engulfed me in a hug so tight I couldn't breathe, but I just let her hold me. The lack of oxygen had started to become an issue when she stepped away. Tears glistened in her eyes. "Thank you. Bridget and your familiar explained what happened. I was worried, but I didn't think they'd go this far. But you've saved her. I've been torn since she emerged and while she made it through high school there was no chance of college and they took her and... " She stopped and took a deep breath, blinking back tears. "Just thank you. She's my daughter. Maybe not what I expected, but I love her all the same."

I shifted, uncomfortable with the thanks. "I'm just glad it worked. It was... well..." I wasn't about to tell her how close her daughter came to being killed. "She'll be okay." I smiled at Carelian. "Though both of them might be going through withdrawal. He doesn't often get doted on this much."

~Which is a crime. I should be treated like this all the

time.~

Bridget's mother smiled at Carelian's comment, but focused on me. "Oh, I'm sorry. I'm Margaret O'Keif. And your friend has been very generous with his time." She sat back down smiling at her daughter.

"Did you get your stuff back? Have they told you anything?" I was hesitant to pry, but I still worried there were consequences beyond the obvious.

"Yes, they returned her phone." Her voice got tight on those words. "That did provide me a significant amount of stress. They want to test her before we leave, to make sure she really isn't a mage any more. But then she is free. We both are." The woman looked ecstatic and I smiled. At least I'd done something right.

"Then I'm glad you two are happy." I walked over to the desk and wrote my number down on a pad of paper with the pen laying there. "Here's my number. If anything happens, call me?"

Margaret looked doubtful but I squeezed her hand. "Really. Call."

"Thank you. Thank you so much for everything." She looked like she might start crying again and I kicked Carelian's tail.

"Take care. Bye Bridget." I managed to make my voice semi-chirpy. Carelian stood and wound around her before heading to the door.

"Kitty go?" She sagged a bit watching him wait at the door.

"Yes. But you get to go home."

"Home. Bye Kitty. Bye Cori." She waved at both of us, then stood looking at her mother. "Home?"

"Just about. Let's get your stuff."

I let them be and headed to my room. I needed a shower and I needed to deal with the assignment in my pocket. Either way it would get me out of this disaster and let me start working. I was really hoping for a lab position, something that would use my degree.

"You good?" I asked Carelian as we walked back to my room.

He didn't answer as I grabbed clothes to change into and plugged in my phone to charge.

~I am unsure. What you did for Bridget was good. She is too sweet to be a mage. But...~ The word hung in my mind like a question mark.

I headed to the showers. Wind had kicked up dust and dirt and it had mixed with my sweat, making me feel and look like I'd been through a tornado.

~What will the consequences be?~ He spoke as I washed my hair. Days like this I missed my short hair.

~I don't know. Tirsane seems happy with me, even if I'm trying not to scream every time I think about the snake under my skin.~ I couldn't resist rubbing it as I spoke, the sensation of it wiggling into my muscles and under my skin still haunting me.

~Malkin found it amusing. But it got the attention of a lot of beings, other lords of the realms and even Bob.~

I groaned, leaning back to rinse my hair. ~I don't need any more tattoos, thank you.~

~I do not want to lose my queans. Your triad is too strong. They will fear you.~

~Who is they?~ I rinsed off and grabbed the towel, wrapping it around me. I was going to be perfectly happy going home this afternoon. I missed my own bathroom.

~The other lords.~ He sounded wary and worried. That did not help my emotions.

~Well they can take it up with Tirsane. I'm still not sure about that entire thing, and a bit freaked out at the idea I could give her permission to do anything. But either way, it is over. I want to get dressed, finish a class on the paperwork, pack up and figure out where I need to go for my assignment.~ I walked back into the room, where he lay sprawled out on the bed. "And getting a decent bed to sleep in also would be nice. Wonder if I can just side step to work." That idea had serious merit and I would need to consider it.

~I will be glad to be home. Your bed is much more comfortable than this thing. Though I have decided I need more pets,~ he stated, not lifting his head from the bed.

"Uh huh. Bridget spoiled you." I pulled on clothes and finished toweling dry my hair. Definitely a bun day.

~That was simply treating me appropriately,~ he countered with a yawn.

"Spoiled," I shot back as I sat down at the desk and stared at the envelope.

~Worth it,~ he purred. ~So where are we going?~

I took a deep breath and picked up the envelope and slit it open. "Let's find out." I started reading slowly, saying key words out loud. "Assigned to the ambassador as a liaison. Starts in 2 weeks. Located in DC, ugh. And are they kidding? Merlin's balls they are IDIOTS!" I yelled that last word and Carelian jerked up, looking around.

~What? What happened? Where are you being placed?~

I turned to look at Carelian. "The Japanese embassy in DC," I snarled.

He blinked at me then started laughing. He didn't quit until I threw the pillow at him and threatened to make him eat the familiar food in the cafeteria.

~You would never do that. And if you attempted, I would either hunt or go see if my other, kinder queans would feed this poor starving Cath.~

I let it go. I had two weeks before I needed to be

there. I was going home.

Section 2.23.2

Every mage will be assessed at the end of their orientation for the best fit for them with the needs of the draft. They may be shuffled to different duties during their service to ensure the best use of varied skill sets.

CHAOS

I packed up and sidestepped home. I spent the rest of that week sidestepping to the classes on how you had to report time, policies, and all the other administrative things that seemed to go with any job. The odd thing was it didn't matter what agency I might work with; the Draft Office still paid my salary. I didn't care enough to figure out the accounting logistics, though I enjoyed my base rate. Having a doctorate helped, even if I owed them a decade. There were notes about hazard pay, extenuating circumstances, and even death benefits. That made me sigh, but I carefully put Jo and Sable on everything. If I died, they'd each get half.

"Carelian, what happens to you if I die?"

~I grieve.~

"That isn't what I meant. Do you go home? Do you die?" Terror gripped me at the idea he might die because I did. I was at my desk at the apartment, trying to finish filling out all the paperwork and setting up retirement accounts.

He lay on his bed that he'd dragged out from under mine. He swapped between sleeping under my bed or next to it. Though I suspected he slept on my bed when

I wasn't in it.

~Normally, yes. But I am bound to my queans by choice as surely as I am bound to you. It would hurt, but I would still be Carelian, and they would still be my queans.~

"Bound?" I didn't like that word. It smacked too much of slavery.

~Quit being human. I chose. I am satisfied with my choice. I have faith that whatever our ends, ours will be ones to be proud of.~ He draped his tail over his nose, his eyes closed.

I sighed and finished up the paperwork. Laundry and packing next. My laundry was all clean, but I needed to fold, put away, and then figure out what to wear for my first week of work.

"Cori, you home?" I heard Sable call out from the front room.

"In here. Packing." I had just finished putting a pile of undergarments I knew I wanted to take with me on the bed when Sable pushed open the door.

"Packing for?" she asked and flopped on the bed, her ring glowing a bit brighter since it was near me. Jo and Sable had matching bands on their right ring fingers, whereas their marriage bands were on their left.

"Figured I'd head up a few days early. Get a hotel and make sure I know where I'm going."

She frowned, sitting up. "I thought we decided you'd stay here and just sidestep."

I nodded. "I am. But I have no idea about where to sidestep to. So I need to go there, find a few places. Make sure I know where I'm supposed to be and how to get there."

"Ah. Makes sense. You flying?"

"It's in DC. I thought maybe I'd take the train? Enjoy the trip. That way Carelian could come?" We'd flown once, and he refused to do it ever again. He detested being up in the air, but we were both too worried about what causing a rip out of an airplane would do, much less where he might land. It was a very long trip to Vegas. He had sidestepped back.

"That makes sense. Okay." She laid back down.

I laughed and went over to the bed, sitting down against my headboard, and buried my toes under her back. "So what's up?"

"Jo's birthday is a month away. Our first one since we got married. I have no clue what to get her. Or you for that matter, but I have a lot more time until you."

"Ah. You're right. I was going to cheat and give her one of the books I found in James Wells' library. It's all the design schematics from the owner of Indian Motorcycles. Why Wells had it I have no idea, but it looked neat and might convince her to custom build you one. You know that's what she's been thinking about. Starting a custom bike shop. Not that she wants to start it until we can all move to New York."

"Oh, that is a great idea. But that doesn't help me."

"I suppose a date night is too plebeian for you two?" I teased, tickling her with my toes.

"Stop that. And yes. I want something awesome." Sable held my toes down so I couldn't wiggle them.

"What is the first anniversary gift type?"

"Paper or clocks. How lame is that?" Sable sulked, pushing her curls off her face. "Like she wants reams of paper."

I snickered. With her dyslexia, reading would never be her favorite thing to do and Jo really did prefer hands on. "Oh! I have an idea and it plays double duty. There is a paper making class I saw in one of the art magazines here in Atlanta. Why don't you take that, and make stationary for Marisol, and a bunch of thank you cards to use as we go through life. Custom made by mages." I snickered at that.

Sable sat up. "Make our own paper? Oh, that could be fun. I could send letters on that to Mom's relatives and my Aunt Lashonda would enjoy that as a gift too. She loves creating baby baskets for friends, having those as custom cards would be cute. That is a great idea. Thanks, Cori." She sat up and kissed my knee as I rolled my eyes at her.

"Hey, thank Carelian. I only saw it because I was picking up the magazines he scattered at the grocery store the other day."

~There was a bee. It needed to die.~

"Bees make honey," I retorted. It was an old argument.

~It was not that type of bee.~ His response was icy.

Sable laughed as she bent over to pet him. "You still pissed about getting stung?"

~Yes.~ The mental word was almost a hiss of annoyance.

"I think he's still more pissed about his face swelling up and us laughing at him. Don't go poking your nose in bees' business. They fight dirty." I slid off the bed, heading to my closet.

~I fight dirtier.~ He huffed then stretched out for Sable to worship him properly.

"Though if I get her this for her birthday, what am I going to do for our anniversary?" Sable faced me, but her gaze had turned inward.

"Well, save that for her anniversary and take her out for an evening of dancing. Or get her a new corset. The leather one she has is getting worn out."

"Ah ha! Corset! Perfect." Sable's entire face lit up. "I know exactly what to get her."

"Good. Because I need to make sure I have business

formal wear." I stared forlornly at my closet. "And I don't."

"What?" Sable moved over, putting her chin on my shoulder as she peered at my clothes. "How can you have so little? And yeah I see what you mean. They are mostly statement pieces."

"Ugh. I don't want to go clothes shopping." It was more of a grumble than a whine, but it didn't change the sentiment.

"Too bad. Though..." she trailed off. "I'm worried about your assignment."

Her words dashed the happy fuzzy feeling I'd let myself sink into.

"You too?"

"Cori, I don't think they have forgotten what you did. Or do you think they didn't tell their people here?" She pulled back and looked at me, worried.

"Oh probably, but that was what, almost four years ago? Surely they can't have held onto the grudge for that long."

Sable gave me a look. "This is the country that still reviles the name of a samurai who betrayed their emperor in the 1300s. Yes, I think they can. Honestly, after the bombs during World War II, I'm surprised they even have an embassy in the US."

I shrugged. "I looked it up. They've always had one. But from what I could figure out most of the time there isn't anyone there, not like an ambassador. It's just staff to take notes and send messages."

"They will know you. And him." She pointed at Carelian. "Unless you're leaving him behind."

~No she is not. She is first quean. I go where she goes. If you need me call and I will be there, but I go with her.~

We both turned to look at Carelian. He hadn't

moved from his bed, still curled up in a tight ball, but his voice had no give to it.

"There is that answer. Means the hotel I find needs to be one that caters to familiars, not that he can't open doors or even use keycards if he wants. I'm going to have to put you back in the harness, if nothing else so you can use cards and get in doors."

He grumbled slightly, but didn't argue. Sidestepping only worked if you knew where you were stepping to or were insane, like when I stepped to Japan. Here at home, we always had an area that was kept clear so I could sidestep to it. Magic tended to protect you, but that didn't mean you needed to be stupid.

"And what was the title you were assigned?" Sable asked, a thoughtful tone to her voice.

I thought for a minute, then shook my head. "I wasn't. Just assigned to the State Department as a liaison to the ambassador for the Japanese Embassy."

"Huh. Then business professional," Sable stated with way more assurance than I ever felt when it came to clothes. "You have good jackets, but you need more slacks."

"Those jeans slacks. They are comfortable and I know what size I am." I moved to the computer to order them. I'd bookmarked that manufacturer years ago.

"Oh, you're no fun." Sable gave me a pout. I was completely unmoved.

"You want shopping, grab Jo. You want someone who always has a med kit and can save your life, then you want me." I'd finally taken Jo's nagging to heart and learned to tolerate exercise. I'd become an avid hiker, as Carelian loved it, it kept me in shape, and there were lots of places to go. It also made me popular with the Search and Rescue teams as Carelian could beat most rescue dogs hands down. I'd gotten my certification after the debacle in New York. It let me mix my skills and gave me an excuse to stay in shape.

"Fine. Be that way. You probably need some shells, DC is muggy." She referred to light tops you wore under jackets when you didn't plan on taking off the jacket often.

"Point." I added a few shells into the cart. I did love this designer.

Sable just rolled her eyes. "You'll be fine. Where are you staying?"

"You are way ahead of me in the thoughts department. I'm still trying to figure out how to get there. Then figure out what in the world they are going to do with me. I have a doctorate in quantitative biology. What do I know about relationships between countries? Much less Japan who hates me."

"You know all the rules. What happens if you fail at an assignment?" Sable asked, sitting back on the bed.

"They're not rules, they're laws. And..." I paused, running through them again. "Nothing. They can reassign me, fire me, but I still work for the Draft Board so they just place me elsewhere." For the first time in years I thought about Paul Goines, the mage who had double emerged when three of his coworkers died. He hadn't been liked and had hated it there. I did not want to become him.

"Then go, do your best. Just remember, they are out to get you."

I snorted. "That has been made abundantly clear. What about you? Any reaction about marriage or the joining?" I pointed to our rings. "And we still need to play around with the changes." I was referring to the changes in our magic.

"No." Sable twisted her ring and smiled up at me. "But I'm still happy you said yes. I worried about ambushing you like that."

"I'll admit to sheer shock, but it prevented me from overthinking it, so probably a good thing."

"That was what Jo said. If we proposed, if that's the right term, and gave you time, you'd have torn it apart and rebuilt it in horrible ways for months."

"Probably. But yeah. Maybe Esmere, when she is done being amused by Tirsane, will come explain it to me."

Sable giggled. "I wish I could have seen that. "

"No you don't. Tirsane is imposing most days. When she showed up like that she was terrifying." I looked at the new snake on my arm and sighed. "Oh well. Washington. I need a decent hotel, and not top of the line. This is all coming out of my pocketbook, and I haven't received the first paycheck yet."

"And get you train tickets and get him a snazzy harness. Or maybe," she paused, looking at Carelian. For his part, he twitched and curled up tighter, likely sensing indignities in the future.

"He did look adorable in the vest. If you want him to go to parties and have people underestimate him, a tuxedo vest might be worth it." She sounded very serious, but I was laughing.

"I have a work vest for him. There is also the S&R Vest plus the wedding vest." I snickered. "If I dress him up too much people will assume he is just a big animal. Besides, if he doesn't want to wear them, I'm sure not making him."

"Exactly. It's camouflage. No one would realize that he is probably more intelligent than half the people there."

~Camouflage? A way to stalk prey without them realizing I am about to pounce?~

"Exactly. Plus it would let you carry simple things

and not interfere with your movement. And most people still don't realize you have opposable thumbs." Sable peered over the bed at him. "Sound good?"

~No, but disguising a hunter is always wise. I will submit to your camouflage.~

Sable managed to repress most of her squeal of delight and sprang over to where I was on the computer. "I know just the place to order them from."

I gave in to the inevitable and concentrated on not letting her get Carelian something embarrassing, laughing the entire time.

Chapter 19

Section 1.50.1

No mage shall be required to offer more than 75% of easily available offering (hair/nails) for any job or required task. Nor can they be required to utilize anything saved or personal possessions. If the mage so chooses to, they have that right, but their possessions are theirs.

SPIRIT

The train ride up to DC from Atlanta had been nice, and Carelian had watched out the window, though he muttered about the lack of hammocks.

~I still do not understand how it is always the same. You say if we take this ride a year from now, it would be the same outside.~

"Yes. Unless we have changed something like tearing down a building or cutting down a tree."

~That is both amazing and boring.~ He kept watching out the window though, and I didn't have an answer.

I'd arranged for a rideshare to pick us up and take us to a hotel a few blocks from where I was supposed to be Monday morning, giving us all day Sunday to explore. While there were a few looks at Carelian, most people just moved out of his way.

Sunday we explored the capital and while we didn't do any museums, it was fun to find good places to sidestep to that looked like they were almost never populated. Maybe I could come back some weekend. Carelian was especially interested in the Natural History museum and thought Esmere might find it entertaining as well.

I'd called Steven and Indira to see if they had any advice, and let them know all the drama that had occurred. They were both aghast at what had been going on and worried about what Tirsane had done. The consequences of that might be years down the road.

On Monday, I hung on to the mantra of starting off like you plan to continue. None of my work attire was drab or boring. I headed to work that morning in sensible low-heeled boots, my jeans slacks, a vivid burgundy top, and an asymmetric jacket in steel gray. Carelian walked beside me in a vest of gray with a pocket for the card key and a clip for his own badge. Steven had warned me they might require him to have one, so I was prepared.

I walked into the building a full hour before I was supposed to be there. While I knew who I was meeting and where the building was, office numbers and processes had not been included in my assignment. Which I figured was on purpose.

Steeling myself, I walked toward the security desk, scanning the metal detectors that employees were starting to go through. My start time was eight-thirty. I figured an hour was enough time to get everything done.

"Good Morning. I'm Merlin Munroe. I start here today and I am supposed to meet Daniel Lorison." Carelian rose up on his hind legs, putting his front paws on the desk. When he did that, he was barely shorter than me. "And this is my familiar, Carelian."

The security guard, an older Hispanic man, paled a bit, and I saw two guards paying very close attention to us. I had my phone in my purse. I pulled it out and set it on the counter. This way if I needed to pull up an electric shield because someone got too jumpy, I wouldn't fry my phone.

Before the security guard could speak, a man in a suit walked out of a door behind the desk and stepped over to us. "I have this, Officer Ruiz." The man shifted his attention to me. He was at least forty, skin the color of graphite, with short tightly napped hair, an unmarked temple, and no evidence of laugh lines. "I'm Lieutenant Strivent. Let me check if you are on the list."

I curved my lips, still watching the tense guards. I wasn't sure if it was me or Carelian causing their stress.

"Corisande Munroe? Identification, please?" He said the words with no warmth, but I pulled my state id out of my purse, handing it to him, my merlin status clearly marked on the id.

He tapped a few more buttons. "Very well, Miss Munroe. We need to get you a badge and," he paused, giving Carelian a hard look. "Will he go where you go?"

"It's Merlin Munroe or Doctor Munroe, depending on your mood. And he goes most places I go. Though he has little interest in human waste disposal methods outside needing to use the facilities." I kept my face perfectly straight as he blinked and glanced at Carelian.

"Then he'll need a badge too. Name."

~Carelian Tail-lash Xeonise,~ Carelian said, and I saw the man jerk. But he nodded and wrote it down.

"Is all other information correct?"

"I don't know. I haven't seen the information," I replied, and his jaw clenched. This was almost as much fun as tweaking Alixant back in the day.

He lifted up the computer screen and turned it toward me. It showed only my information. It had an old picture of me, addresses, family, etc.

"It all looks correct." I thought about mentioning the marital status, but to be honest the laws didn't count it as married, but they didn't not count it as married. I decided not to mention it.

"Excellent. Move over here please." He gestured to a station to the side that looked like a camera. I grabbed my bag and moved over. He tapped a red dot on the camera.

All too aware that he'd love for me to look awful, I made sure the smile was on my face before I focused on the dot. It flashed, and he nodded. "Now your familiar."

Carelian went up on hind legs and bared all his teeth. I saw multiple people flinch back. The lieutenant took his picture and nodded. "I will get your badges ready. It will give you access to all the areas you require. If it doesn't give you access to an area, you don't need to be there." I would have taken offense except it sounded so rote I suspected he said that to everyone.

"Thank you." I looked around. Was I just supposed to stand here and wait for my contact to show up?

"There is a waiting room over there. Mr. Lorison will meet you shortly. I will provide him with your badges." He directed me to a small area with chairs and three walls and no windows. It felt too much like a shooting gallery. Either way, I walked in and positioned myself against one of the walls so I could see anyone walking into the area. I had expected much more paperwork, but maybe all the time we spent in class doing it had paid off. All I could do was hope that Lorison showed up early.

He didn't.

At exactly eight-thirty on the dot, a man walked into the waiting area. He was about five-ten with white blonde hair, ice-blue eyes, a three-piece suit, and wing tips. I pushed away from the wall as I was the only person there. I didn't see he could be anyone else except my contact.

"Mr. Lorison?" I asked, walking over to him.

"Nice to see you are punctual." He scanned me up and down and sighed. "Not my style preference, but you will do. First, here is your badge. Where is your familiar?" Carelian had been laying behind some of the chairs, doing that specific Cath sort of invisibility where until he moved he was almost impossible to see. At the question Carelian stood up and I could feel his soft laugh at the start Lorison gave. He looked at the picture on the badge, then handed it to me. "He will need to wear it at all times, as will you." He cleared his throat and stood up a bit straighter. "My name is Daniel Lorison. You will refer to me as Mr. Lorison, Adjutant Lorison or Adjutant Daniel Lorison depending on the situation. How should I refer to you?"

Part of me wanted to laugh, but I kinda admired the way he stated his expectations so clearly. "Technically, I am Merlin Doctor Corisande Munroe, but that seems a bit ridiculous. At work I would prefer Merlin Munroe, but my friends just call me Cori." I somehow doubted he would become a friend but I could hope.

"Very well then, Merlin Munroe, this way if you please. Pay attention to where we go as I will expect you to find your own way in the future. Your badge will get you anywhere you need to go. If there is a keypad assume you do not need to go there." He walked and talked with exacting precision and we ended up in a room with three cubicles and two offices.

"This is the office for East Asia and Pacific Affairs." He walked into the smaller office and nodded at a chair before taking a seat behind the desk. "Japan, while they have had an embassy here since September 1949, has not been particularly active. Until the last decade, they have attended social functions and signed multi-nation accords, but little else. Our trade agreements with them

162

are rudimentary. However, since the death of James Wells, they have stepped up their interaction, pressuring the government and the estate of James Wells for access to his research notes and his valuables. I am sure you are well aware of this."

I had a sinking feeling I knew where this was going. "I am. I convinced them killing me was not in their best interest." Or more exactly Jeorgaz had.

"Well, we need to lean on your goodwill."

I arched an eyebrow, suddenly annoyed. "I am not required to give up personal possessions as part of the draft laws. In fact, it is explicitly called out that I am not required to sacrifice anything beyond seventy-five percent of easily available offerings during my duties. I cannot be required to spend blood or other offerings, much less give up personal possessions."

His smile was tight. "Of that we are aware. But the need to have a sustained relationship and trade agreement is great." Lorison took a deep breath, and I prepared for whatever bombshell he planned on dropping. "They have come up with a vaccine and pill series that could help prevent or even cure cancer. They are guarding it very jealously and for all we know it might not even be real, or what few laboratory reports they have let slip may be falsified. But if it isn't, we need this. Cancer rates for the last few years have doubled across the board and we are worried the inflation is not natural."

I sat back and looked at him. Thoughts raced through my mind. It was too perfect, too pat of a set up. But why worry about it. Surely if they wanted me dead this badly they could have killed me. I'd been sloppy the last few years. But the not natural comment set off thoughts, especially given what Carelian had overheard.

"When you say not natural, what does that mean?"

163

"The rates of people under thirty developing incurable cancers has increased by twenty percent and most disturbing, those from magical families or that have already emerged has jumped by fifteen percent in the last five years."

Those numbers sounded bad, but I had no idea what it translated into for real numbers, and some cancers like basal cell could be treated while others like myelofibrosis and other blood cancers could be maintained for decades without much else besides drugs. Longer if there was a mage willing to do marrow manipulation.

"What exactly are you asking?" I thought I knew, but assuming would make my life much more difficult than it already was, and I was curious how much they knew.

"We want to offer them access to the research you inherited in exchange for allowing us access to their cancer research and methodology." He sat very stiff in the chair, but I suspected that was his normal posture regardless of the situation.

"It feels like the government is being very free with my possession. What do I get out of it?"

"We are prepared to negotiate."

My eyes narrowed. What was going on? I'd never heard of the government negotiating anything. Carelian was very focused on all this. ~Do you believe this?~

~They want something. Something very special. Ask for the moon, they are in a bad place.~

~But I don't know what I have that they want. Which means I'm playing blind,~ I protested. I was pretty sure I'd seen a letter from Lucille, but I hadn't bothered to open it yet. Technically this was the first day of the draft.

"Okay. What exactly are you offering and asking? Access to research is too wide ranging. I need specifics."

Really, they could have stuck me in a lab. I would have been perfectly happy. Or sent me to medical school, or anything. Why this runaround? How much of it was because of my power levels, and how much was what James left? Why didn't they just steal it or something? Banks weren't that secure.

Daniel wet his lips; fingers still laced. "It is hard to know exactly what we would need access to. Would you have a list of what research and documents he had?"

"Not at this time." I didn't even know if a list existed. This was getting weirder and weirder by the minute.

He shifted and I swear he was going through a decision tree as to what to talk to me about next. "We are working hand in hand with China regarding these issues. The lead negotiator has asked for your assistance. While you are there, perhaps you can work with the Japanese liaisons and offer that you are willing to share the research with them."

I bristled a bit, but kept my cool. Sidestepping home would be way too showy and would tip my hand. But I had to fight my urge to start setting things on fire. Forming the triad with Jo and Sable gave me greater access to their branches, and fire was a greedy gift, loving to be used. It meant not letting my temper get the better of me.

"I'm not sure why the government, or more accurately its employees, think I would simply turn over that which is mine," I said, my voice getting cooler no matter how much I wanted to burn things.

His lips tightened, and I realized he didn't like this any more than I did. So why not have fun? That thought made me relax. "I am willing to consider it. I want five years of my draft waived."

He blinked, and I saw him bite down his reaction. "I

do not think the government would be willing to do that."

"Maybe not. But that is what I'm asking. Granted, until I can be told exactly what research they want copies of, I'm not sure what information I have available to share."

He seemed a bit gray around the edges, but nodded. "I will take that under advisement."

"So the next question is, has anyone asked if the Japanese are even willing to talk to me? And does the negotiator know I can't legally step foot on Japanese soil?"

At this, Daniel's perfect mask fell and an expression of horror and worry settled in. "What exactly are you talking about, Merlin Munroe?"

Section 2.22.2

At no point may a mage be ordered or even instructed to do any action that would place them in violation of existing laws. They may not be punished for refusing to follow an illegal order.

ORDER

I smiled. I'd never said much about what occurred, just that the royal magician had agreed to relinquish his claim on the inheritance and the emperor of Japan had backed him up.

"Here is what was said, you draw your own conclusions." I pulled up the memory in my mind, Carelian translating had burned it into my memory. Too bad that didn't work with my classes; it would have made some of them much easier.

"Japan will not interfere with Corisande Munroe after this point. She is considered anathema to this court and word will be spread that she is neither to be attacked nor helped." I said each word clearly and slowly, the strange echo of Japanese with Carelian speaking softly in my mind a bit confusing.

Daniel settled back again; his expression smooth once again. "That does not sound all that bad."

I gave him a look. "Anathema? I am detested or loathed or even cursed depending on how you look at it."

"Maybe they won't know it is you or will have forgotten," he offered, but even he didn't sound like he believed it.

"I suppose anything is possible." I looked at my watch and sighed. It was a bit after nine. "I can't address anything until after I've gone through the stuff I've inherited. You and your bosses need to decide what you are going to offer me to give up my own possessions. Remember, I could just sell them on the open market or give them to Japan as recompense for the damage I did there, though I still feel that was completely justified. So what do you want to do now?"

Daniel looked like he wanted to beat his head against the desk, an expression I recognized all too well from most officials that dealt with me.

"I'll take you to meet the liaison. It would be helpful if you knew what research Merlin Wells left." He rose from his desk and I matched something niggling the back of my mind.

"Mr. Lorison?" I said before he opened the door.

"Yes?" He turned to look at me, waiting.

"You were only surprised at the amount of time I asked for, not that I wanted the draft shortened." That was actually a guess, but he nodded, a sharp jerk of his chin. "How many people think I will die before my draft is over?"

I could never say why I asked that question, it just leaped out from all the puzzle pieces coming together.

He looked at me for a long time, then turned back to the door. "I'm afraid I have no idea what you are talking about, Merlin Munroe."

The way he answered told me everything, and I nodded. We didn't talk as we headed down to a hall with cubicles in the middle and much smaller offices on the other side. As we walked, Carelian garnered more attention than me, but everyone managed to resist the desire to rush out and pet him. I swear he gave off a pheromone that encouraged it. But today he walked and acted like he had somewhere important to be, and it seemed to work.

Daniel stopped at a small office and rapped on the open door. A woman, probably about ten years older than me, looked up from the desk that took up the majority of the room. She had short black hair, parted down the middle, and falling neatly to either side of her face and stopping at chin level in a sharp bob. It created a black frame for her pale face, narrow nose, and brown eyes. She lacked the normal fold I'd seen on most from Asia. I suspected she was half white, though her skin color and hair screamed Oriental. She rose and squeezed around her desk, her body more dumpling than noodle.

"Lorison?" Her voice was sharp and flat, with a softness on the vowels that reminded me of Sable when she spoke to her mom's family in Japan.

"Pearl Takishi, this is Merlin Doctor Corisande Munroe."

The woman looked me up and down, then transferred her gaze to Lorison. "How long do I have her for?"

"Until the problem is resolved or someone else screams louder. Good luck."

He spun on his heel and turned out the door. She pierced me with a hard look. "Don't think because you're a mage or the fabled Cori Munroe that I'll give you any slack. I aim to be director by the time I'm fifty and I'm not letting any prima donna ruin that for me. I will get this negotiation to work and you will help me. Do you understand?"

I quivered for a moment, trying to not say everything at once. "I understand that I am here to help you work on an agreement between China, Japan, and the United States. I also understand that I am under no obligation to offer up my personal possessions to my job."

She stared at me, then nodded. "Good. You understand how this works. Now what do you know about Japan?" She turned and moved over to her desk.

"That they quit trying to kill me a few years ago and that their royal magician and emperor are not happy with me in the least."

"Not helpful, but it's a start. I'm sure Danny boy made it seem all nice and easy. That Japan has a cancer cure and we want to give them the research Wells did to persuade them to share. And I'm sure he dangled a carrot or two."

I didn't say anything, I just sat down in the only chair. Carelian flopped at my feet, flipping on his 'I'm so cute' mode.

"We'll here's the stick. I want this agreement. I want China and Japan and the US to enter a long-term medical research open information trade. Mages on both sides have jumped their understanding of viruses and bacteria by at least a hundred years, but because of how our draft is structured, we don't have a lot of archmages or merlins that go into medicine."

I kept my mouth shut. I would have loved to have done that, but was discouraged. Either way, I would be free sooner. Nothing said I couldn't go back and become a doctor.

"China is willing do it for some trade agreements. There are some spices and foods that they would like greater access to. Japan, however, is balking. They don't feel we have anything to offer. Their xenophobic tendencies and continuing resentment for the incident during World War II have made them a difficult partner."

I stared at her. "By incident you mean us detonating nuclear bombs on two of their cities when mages tried to side.. um.. teleport the uranium out of the atomic bombs and ended up pulling the nuclear bombs across the world, activating them, and subsequently destroyed Hiroshima and Nagasaki?" That cautionary tale was why few mages teleported and why I'd never carry anything more powerful than a laptop.

"Like I said, incidents." She waved her hand in dismissal. "But they are still interested in the research you now have, no matter what they say." Pearl moved her mouth in a way that only resembled a smile if a shark lunging at you resembled a smile. "So what do I have to do to get you to give it up? You're the newbie here. I can make your life hell and you'll never be able to prove a thing. Worst assignments, late hours, sending you home at rush hour, only to want you back as soon as it is over. I will get this deal even if I have to drive you crazy to get it."

I blinked. It took a few seconds for everything to process. I looked at Carelian; while he didn't express anything, I could hear his amusement. Then I looked back at Pearl and started laughing.

She jerked her head back as if I had slapped her. I didn't fall into full blown laughter but more of a giggle. "What?" The demand made me grin.

"I've had people actively try to kill me. And I held up. You treating me like shit only guarantees I'll keep it all to myself and actively try to blow the deal, because I have no reason to support it. And you forget, I can play that game just as well. Tires always flat, nylons with a run, tea always cold, food just this side of going bad, batteries that die before important calls. I can do it just as easily and if not better because that level of magic costs me almost nothing." I gave her the same smile she'd given me. "So would you like to start again and convince me that working with you will be more rewarding than watching you destroy yourself?"

Pearl stared at me for a long time. Her eyes narrowed, then she nodded. "Good. We understand each other. Work with me and I'll help you get out of here sooner. If not, I'll get you transferred someplace else. Maybe Alaska."

I shrugged. "I always wanted to see the glaciers."

Pearl narrowed her eyes. "I almost admire you. I might actually like you. After we get this agreement."

My nails bit into my palms as I smiled and tried not to seethe. So much for research and working with anything that interested me.

"First, you need to get up-to-date on the two countries and exactly why Japan wants that research. I hope you read fast because you are going to have a lot to read."

Pearl typed like her keyboard was granite and needed to be pulverized. A minute later a young man with dark hair, an Order tattoo, and an earnest smile, stuck his head in. "Yes, Mrs. Takishi?"

"Take Merlin Munroe here, help her get her computer set up, log into the various websites, and I sent you the links she needs to download and read." She shifted her attention to me. "I expect by Wednesday you will be able to see exactly why it is in all of our best interests to make nice with Japan. Be here at ten and we'll talk."

I nodded at her and rose from the chair, following the young man. After a double take at Carelian, the rest of the day was spent doing the normal things I'd expected. Logins, computer issues, bookmarks, and figuring out where the cafeteria was. By the time I walked out at six, I was exhausted and felt like my brain might explode. I carried the computer in my hands, stressed about dropping it. I needed to get something to carry it in. I resisted the desire to just get a backpack. Indira would have had a fit if I ruined my look with a backpack.

Luckily, there were a number of shops that catered to the office workers of the DC area. It didn't take long before I had a matching set of office luggage. A smart briefcase in burgundy that would hold the laptop, my phone, a notebook, and other basic supplies, but still look slim and elegant. It matched with a much larger wheeled case that held the briefcase, lunch, my coffee cup, and even extra clothes if I needed to go somewhere after work. I'd seen people, both men and women, toting similar office bags behind them.

Once that was accomplished, we walked back to the hotel. Enroute, I placed an order for dinner so I could eat while I read. Carelian couldn't make up his mind, so for now he'd live with the dry Cath food I'd packed.

I spent the walk staring at the people and scenery, Carelian guarded my back, and we were never crowded, no matter how many people were on the street. It had a different vibe from Atlanta, though it was about as humid to my annoyance. We made it to the hotel, and I was rethinking my suit for DC wear, or at least for walking to and from work. I'd have to see about sidestepping more, or changing clothes. Staying in shape had too many benefits to let it go. Dinner arrived about the same time I did, so I grabbed that and headed up.

~Are all human work places so laced with poison?~ Carelian asked after we got back to the room. He'd been rather quiet, and I wondered what was going on in his head.

"All? No. A certain portion of them, yes." I stripped, getting into comfortable clothes. Then I curled up in the club chair. I had Indian food and reading in as my plan for the night.

~Humans are crazy, though I suppose my malkin would enjoy the games. Why did you not kill that woman?~

"Carelian! You know I can't just go around killing people. Humans aren't prey." We had discussed this before, but something about a Cath worldview didn't understand anyone permanently in the not prey category.

~She threatened you. I thought about biting her.~

"I'm glad you didn't. It would have caused issues. Though I may need to talk to Jeorgaz and see what is so important about Wells' research. And to think all I wanted was a nice job in a lab or something." The words had just left my mouth when I felt a subtle stab in my brain. I looked over toward the door and sighed as a rip formed.

"Yes?"

~I would like to talk to you. Please come over.~ Jeorgaz's voice filled my mind. I glared at Carelian.

"If I find out you guys are spying on me or worse, you can read my mind at all times, there will be consequences." I stood, bringing my food with me. My lunch had consisted of an apple. I was hungry.

~Reading human minds is confusing and way too much effort.~ Carelian dismissed that idea. ~Besides, they are boring and full of things that make no sense. Thoughts and words are all that matter, maybe pictures. It is more likely it is a coincidence, nothing more.~ He stepped through the portal, tale flicking. ~Besides, I'd rather hunt for dinner.~

I rolled my eyes and stepped through into flames.

Chapter 21

Section 2.20.21

Any action done by a familiar in protection of their mage is regarded as an extension of the mage's abilities and will be treated as such by the rule of law.

CHAOS

Even almost expecting it, I couldn't completely muffle the shriek that slipped past my lips. I reached out on instinct asking the fire to move away. It did, though sluggishly.

I stood there telling myself that I wasn't burning alive and continued walking into the space. I'd wondered what a phoenix would consider comfortable for a home realm, but this hadn't been what I thought. The glade, the setup seemed very similar to Baneyarl's, was ringed in flames of every shade. From white blue to fierce red to pale orange, but I only felt the warmth of a mild summer day. Trees were randomly scattered through the area, but some were in full summer leaves, other spring blooms and yet others barren winter. They all were either fruit or nut trees and I watched birds and insects flit from one to the other. An arbor of grape vines was where Jeorgaz sat, eating some of the juicy grapes that glimmered from under leaves. He was the size of a large hawk, but the colors made me think more of an exotic parrot.

"That entrance is a bit startling for a human."

Jeorgaz tilted his head then ruffled out his feathers. ~I do apologize. I had forgotten. It has been very long, and James was the last person to visit. He found it amusing, though the first few times he was discomfited. Please come in. You are free to help yourself to any fruit you might like.~

~I wish to hunt, Jeorgaz, do I have your permission?~ Carelian glanced at the birds, but I didn't think that was what had his nose sniffing the air.

~Feel free outside the ring, it is Chaos. Do not bring anything through you can't eat. I prefer a quieter life.~

Carelian brushed by me, rubbing his cheek on my leg, then dashed through the fire. I held up my dinner, still in its biodegradable cardboard. "I'm going to eat, if you don't mind. You caught me about to start my dinner."

Jeorgaz flipped a wing at me as he settled down on his perch, tail feathers of blue and red drifting in the faint breeze. I dropped into a cross legged position and opened up my container. I had chicken tiki masala and naan bread, and I was hungry. Scooping a forkful onto my naan, I took a bite. It wasn't too bad, nothing wonderful but good enough that I could enjoy it.

I needed to eat more than prod Jeorgaz. He could speak at any time, so I admired the beautiful birds, the odd scenery, and ate.

~So there are more people asking about the research James and I did?~ he asked when I was about halfway through my food.

"People?" I said with a snort. "Try the government trying to bribe the Japanese. Though I don't know if the royal magician is still involved. I'm not even sure the Japanese suggested it." I took another bite as he eyed me.

~Interesting. To be honest, I was surprised Hishatio didn't try to acquire the information over the last few years. He never took well to having his desires thwarted. James found it an admirable trait, I found it a much darker aspect than he. He wants what James discovered badly. Enough to risk my ire. Even manipulate countries to get to it. The infighting between nations has not improved with the OMO meddling.~

I took another bite, thinking. I needed to focus on what I could control, and the idea of the Office of Magical Oversight meddling was a can of worms I didn't want to deal with at this moment. "What is the big deal about the research?"

Jeorgaz flapped his wings, looking at me, and I got the feeling I'd surprised him. ~You haven't looked at what we found?~

"Nope. I think there is a letter from Lucille about it, but I haven't bothered to read it yet. Really, it's a few boxes of notes, or a bank deposit box. Until today I didn't think much about it."

~I will never understand humans. Technically, it is a large number of notes. But not in a box or bank box. Lucille,~ he paused, shifting his wings. ~I actively miss her. She was James' friend, lover, and manager for as long as I knew him.~

"I do not understand you familiars. Yes, James died. That doesn't mean you can't go talk to Lucille. I wouldn't expect Carelian, Esmere, or Baneyarl to quit visiting Jo or Sable if I died. They are your friends too, not just me."

He gave me a funny look, then ruffled his feathers.

~Lucille should have the key to the storage units. What we gathered, researched, and the gifts not kept at the house. James and I traveled the realms often, and he had many friends.~ Again he paused and looked at me. ~That is not accurate. He had many beings he knew. You have those from realms attending your parties and celebrations. James had meetings and came here. I do not remember him ever having fun with those from the realms.~ A sadness had entered the bird's voice and I put down my dinner. I'd eaten enough as it was.

"He treated you like specimens?" I asked softly. I'd spent enough time in the Albany house to realize that James was fascinated by familiars and the other creatures, the same way I was fascinated by various techniques with medical experiments. But I'd never gotten the idea he thought of them as friends or even equals. Me? I'd never had any doubt Carelian was a person.

~Maybe that is it. He asked my opinion but...~ Jeorgaz railed off and began to viciously preen one of his feathers. ~You have caused me to doubt my relationship with him. I had thought he was a friend, but maybe I was wrong.~

The old joke Carelian and I had came back to me and I smiled at the phoenix. "Maybe you are thinking about it wrong. It isn't that he thought of you as a pet, but more he was your pet, and who pays much attention to what their pet really thinks." I kept my voice gentle and light. "As I am very sure Carelian thinks of me and my partners as his queans, more than we ever think of him as anything other than our friend."

Jeorgaz pulled his head up and looked at me then began to trill. The sound mixed with the fire to create a chorus of bright cheerful notes that forced me to smile. ~Perhaps you are right. He was my pet and at times a bit dense. That brings us back to the research. It has much that is fluff or is about Bob and will be of little use to anyone. But there are items locked away that would be of great danger should people get their hands on them.~

"Now I'm curious. Why was James able to get this information?"

~Me.~ His voice was flat, with little pride or

satisfaction in it. I made an enquiring noise and he turned around on his perch letting me see his back. ~Usually only lords can travel to different realms, but phoenixes are unusual in that we have access to all realms, with or without a tear. James realized that and convinced me that humans learning about the other realms was in all of our best interest. I am no longer sure.~

"Ah." I nodded. "I'm sorry. Humans are complicated and arrogant. Though I still think Cath have us beat," I teased.

Jeorgaz laughed that trill again. ~Cath are superior, at least they think so. Did you know that Salistra attended your joining?~

That brought me up short, and I stared at him. I specifically looked for her and had not seen her. "Tirsane said she decided not to come." I didn't think Tirsane had lied to me. It was possible, but why?

~She wasn't going to, then changed her mind. She watched as a humming bird. I'm not sure anyone knew she was there, but I could see her. Birds of all types cannot hide from me.~

I shuddered at the idea of that much power in a tiny body. Not to mention how she did it, but there were some things that were better left unknown. "So what about the research? I wasn't going to but there is a lot of pressure on this. While no one can order me, it would make my life much easier. What is in there that they can't know about?"

Jeorgaz turned around to face me, shifting from one clawed foot to another. ~Being a familiar means you are bonded to that person. It clouds your judgement. You want what your mage wants, to the point of ignoring wisdom. Cath are more resistant to that urge, not that you have an overweening ego. I made errors in judgement that now after my Ashing I see I should have never agreed to.~ He picked a berry off a branch near him, and I tried to not get my stomach twisted in knots. ~One of the things in the notes is the secret to calling-" he broke off as an unearthly yowl filled the air causing me to leap to my feet.

"Carelian?" I said, turning to look for him. I hadn't paid that much attention when he left.

~Oh what has that Cath done?~ Jeorgaz muttered. His wings spread wide, and he looked much more like a falcon than a peacock.

Another howl as Carelian burst through the fire, panting with a set of slices along his ribs. ~We might have incoming,~ he muttered, turning to look at the flames still flickering away. His ears were laid almost flat along his skull, whiskers sleeked back, and his mouth hung open in a snarl.

"Carelian! Are you okay?" I rushed over, dropping to my knees to inspect his side. Four parallel gashes raked from his right shoulder to his back flank. They bled sluggishly, exposing muscle, but no bone or tendons.

~It will heal. I think it is coming.~

~Cath, I told you to not bring back anything you couldn't eat.~ The bird sounded annoyed as he flapped and launched himself into the air hovering above me.

~I didn't bring it back. It thought I was dinner. I am no one's prey,~ Carelian hissed, tail cracking like a whip.

"You hit me with that and you're getting kibble for a month," I warned. He left welts.

He hissed at me, and I pulled back, surprised. I couldn't remember him ever hissing at me and meaning it. ~Get ready, it's coming.~

"What in the world did you piss off?" I asked, as I stood. The desire to tape up his side warred with getting ready to fight whatever was coming.

~Yes, Cath. What did you annoy?~ Jeorgaz sounded just as annoyed as me, but Carelian didn't bother to look at the bird. Instead he hunkered down, gaze still locked on the ring of fire. I shot a worried look at Jeorgaz, who flapped lazily in the glade, which I swore had warmed up by a degree or two.

~I annoyed no one. Something thought I was a good lunch. I disagreed, vehemently ,~Carelian spat, anger in his voice, and if I hadn't been borderline terrified, I might have laughed. His ego was very persnickety.

A roar sounded through the clearing scaring the birds, and I snapped to attention. Earth shield ready, and I'd learned a few new tricks to keep people in place. Quicksand could be formed quickly or mud. It amounted to the same thing.

The flames flickered and a form charged into the glade, skidding to a halt about ten yards from us. It had the body and head of a lion, but there were two huge leathery wings beating a draft of fire and dust from the torn-up ground. Instead of a tail with a tuft on the end, there was a scorpion's stinger raised up in the sky with a point that looked like it could go through my body. It also had a set of lines going down one side of its face and rents in one wing that matched. The facial ones were bleeding, while the skin on the wings just hung there, useless.

On reflex I snapped up an earth shield between us and it, pulled electricity to me, and turned to glare at Carelian. "You dragged a manticore here? A Merlin blasted manticore?"

I really didn't know if I wanted to strangle my familiar or just jump back to the nice sane Earth realm, where all I had to worry about was a conniving government and random serial killers.

Chapter 22

Section 95.1

The Office of Magical Oversight will manage and maintain the mage database and keep secure all information therein. The US government will accept their jurisdiction and tests as binding when it comes to mage ranking and management.

SPIRIT

I braced myself, ready to fight for my life as it roared again. This time I could hear the pain in the sound.

~Mi'Kal, what have I told you about playing with others and not telling them.~ Jeorgaz's voice cut through the clearing and I jerked my head up to look at him. ~Not everyone is so understanding of surprise play.~

The manticore's wings drooped, and it hung its head. ~Sorry. He was pouncing a rabbit. So I pounced him.~ There was excitement and sheepishness in that voice. ~Pouncing is game. But he hurts me.~ I swear it sounded like he was about to start crying.

Now Carelian turned his head to look at Jeorgaz.

~I did say not to bring back trouble,~ Jeorgaz sighed, a level of exasperation in his voice. ~Cori, Carelian, this is Mi'Kal, a manticore. He is the equivalent of your three- or four-year-old.~ The manticore sank down on his haunches and looked mournfully at his torn wing and then rubbed his paw gingerly across his face. His mane was a darker brown than his coat, which looked tan. The scorpion tail throbbed a dangerous red at the end, and I couldn't help but swallow at the idea of it slamming into anyone.

~It hurts,~ he said, pain and sadness in his voice.

~Yes, I suppose it does. Carelian, you caused the damage; you fix it.~

~This is not my fault. I had a three-hundred-pound creature pounce me; I retaliated.~ Carelian's tone was flat, eyes narrowed as he stared at Jeorgaz.

~And I did not say that his wounds were not earned. I am telling you to repair the damage you caused.~ Jeorgaz flew over to Mi'Kal. ~And you will remember this as a reason to not pounce because you are bored and want someone to play with.~

Until that minute I had not known that lion faces could pout, but the pout on Mi'Kal's face was enough to make a harder heart than mine melt.

"Please, Carelian? I believe he has learned his lesson," I asked, unable to hold any anger at what was obviously a cub. "I believe you caused more than a bit of damage when you were younger." I referred to the tuna can incident that we still teased him about.

Carelian hissed, his tail still lashing, but he relaxed his body and stretched. ~That was to inanimate objects. Fine. But even you would have fled if that had attacked you.~

"Absolutely," I agreed. "And I probably would have been screaming in terror the entire time." I reached down to pet him. "Your actions were smart."

His ears flicked up, and he sighed, walking over to the pouting creature. ~You attacked well. I did not hear you. It was a good attack, though making sure your prey can't fight back is wise. Let me see your wing.~

I watched, fascinated. I'd never seen Carelian actively use magic besides opening rips between the planes. Carelian sat next to Mi'Kal looking small in comparison to the manticore. His tail went up and drew a line backward from the edge of the tear to where it would have started. I knew he was Chaos aligned, but we'd never talked about branches to know what magic he had or how he used it. Mostly because every time I brought up the subject he fell asleep or pretended to.

Where his tail rested glowed and I could see tissue rebonding, reforming there as he pulled his tail up. He did it again and again until the wing was whole, though pink and shiny.

~Don't use it or stress it for a few days, the skin is still tender and will tear easy.~ Carelian's voice was firm and a bit annoyed.

~Close your wing, Mi'Kal, and keep it closed until I tell you.~

~Yes Jeorgaz,~ the manticore muttered, folding both wings tightly against his back. Carelian repeated the process with the wounds on his face. I could see Carelian was exhausted, but he didn't stop until all wounds were healed.

~No roaring for three sleeps,~ he growled, stalking back to me. ~We done? I would like salmon. I'm starving, as someone interrupted my dinner plans.~

"How did you do that? Why don't you talk about your magic? And now that I think about it, why didn't you heal me after you bit me?" I couldn't figure out if I just wanted answers, or I was offended that he hadn't healed me.

He threw himself at my feet, eyes closed. ~Because. And I did heal you. Did you not notice it disappeared by the time you went to the noisy city and there are no scars?~

My mouth opened, then I stopped and looked at my arm. He was right. I couldn't even find the marks. It had stopped bleeding later that night and I'd taken off the bandage, not thinking much about it.

"Oh," I said, feeling my face burn. Some days I really

was an idiot. Swallowing, I turned to Jeorgaz who had escorted Mi'Kal out and was soaring back to his perch. "I should probably get going. But you were saying what was in the research?"

Jeorgaz landed and shook his body a few times, making sure all the feathers were laying correctly. ~Yes. There are many things in there, though we never stumbled upon the death of mages causing rips and encouraging emergences. But there are things in there that would be best kept out of Hishatio's hands. I do not believe he would use it responsibly, but perhaps I'm wrong."

"And that would be?" I had no idea what they could have found.

Jeorgaz sighed. ~There is a way to make a permanent stable passage to a pocket realm.~

I blinked at him, and processed what he said. I even saw Carelian lift his head, ears flickering. ~Does my malkin or Tirsane know?~ Carelian asked, his voice tight.

~No one does, I believe, besides you two. We realized what it meant and buried the information, but I think James mentioned our discovery or the possibility of the stable portal to Hishatio. A stable connection that you could harvest resources from would be of incalculable value. Whichever country had it would reap riches, but it would also allow any realm denizen, both sentient and not, into your world.~ Jeorgaz looked oddly embarrassed, if a bird could manage to be embarrassed. ~Right now only mages can create rips, and only Lords or those like Tirsane or Salistra can step back and forth. Foci can always go home and to their mage, but the door closes soon after they step through. This would create a permanent passage to a pocket realm that stays there until undone by the mage.

I stood there as that revelation filtered into my brain.

"This is bad. Very bad," I said finally as my mind took all our worst ecological disasters and multiplied them with magic involved.

~Hence my worry.~ Jeorgaz preened vigorously, not looking at me.

I wanted to groan. "I need to go through that data. Though at this point I'm almost tempted to just destroy all of it, and say it was lost. It might be safer than that information ever getting out."

~It is your property; you have to decide.~ Jeorgaz's voice was not sympathetic. I glared at him.

"That is not helpful. I'm getting pressure from my bosses, the government, and probably other people I haven't even met yet to hand over the data and you tell me if I do it could create the biggest land grab in history? Thank you so very much," I said, my voice dripping sarcasm. But internally I was trying to stop the freak out as every bad thing I could think of cycled through my brain.

~And that is why you are an excellent inheritor for James. You understand the consequences to what his research means. But that is just the one I am the most worried about. We discovered many things, there may be others that are just as incendiary. Things that mages, countries could twist to harm many.~ If a phoenix could smirk, he was, as he imparted that last bit of wisdom.

~I am still hungry. Shall we go or do I need to leave and find my own sustenance without someone pouncing me?~ I had never realized pounce could be used as a swear word.

"Yes." I turned to Jeorgaz. "I may have questions later, but I will try to look at the information this weekend. And I won't make any promises until after I have seen the research."

Jeorgaz ruffled his feathers. ~And that is why I knew you would be a better choice than Hishatio. Be well Corisande Munroe.~

I nodded goodbye, and we stepped back to the hotel room. I tossed my food container and placed an order of salmon for Carelian. There were a few places that would deliver raw fish specifically for the familiars; capitalism had major advantages. I nibbled on one of the pieces of naan I hadn't taken with me as I thought.

My desires went from one extreme to another as I contemplated the situation. Information, I needed more information. "I'm going to try to read the material I was provided. See if I can figure out what is behind this, besides just imperialistic tendencies."

Carelian lay in the middle of the hotel room floor, looking exhausted. ~Smart. I just want food and then to sleep. That level of healing is not my normal energy output.~

I frowned, worried. "Are you okay?" I stared at him worried about the scratches on his shoulder. "Do you need me to look at your wounds?"

~Am fine. I healed them too. Exhausted. That is draining.~ He closed his eyes, even his tail laying still. I let him be and read until there was a knock on the door. Carelian woke up enough to inhale his salmon, then he jumped up on the small couch and was asleep minutes later sprawled across the length of it.

Japan was interesting. One of the more standoffish countries—the other being the American Indians—and the nuclear bombs and magic had strengthened their xenophobic tendencies. Was the medical research they had that important? And no matter how I looked, I couldn't figure out why China was so interested as well. The treaty that was being proposed would give both the

US and China access to this research, though there were other trade agreements and a host of other clauses in them as well. It read like a wish list from politicians, but I knew something else was going on. Countries didn't try this hard for the boring stuff.

I closed the laptop, rubbing my temples. A headache was forming with all the manipulation going on. Being a paramedic would have been so much easier. My eyes fell on Carelian, who was still snoring away, and my joining ring. But if I wasn't who I was, I wouldn't have all this. It was worth a headache or two.

Bed called, and I gave in. Tomorrow would be interesting with more going on. Or maybe if I was lucky I'd be horribly bored.

Chapter 23

Section 1.140.3

All mages from other countries must be declared and their tattoos must be clearly visible. All delegates to the United States, excepting the American Indian Nation, must have standard tattoos and present themselves as such.

ORDER

I walked in the next morning at seven-thirty. I'd figured if I got in early maybe I'd have time to get my cube set up and get a better handle on the lay of the land. And figure out where Carelian could sleep and not get stepped on nonstop. He was still tired, but still followed me in, watching everything.

Pearl stuck her head out of her office as I walked by with my laptop. "Huh, you might have a chance yet. How far did you get on your reading material?"

Protesting that she said she would ask tomorrow would do me no good. "I skimmed most of it. While the history of Japan was interesting, the players involved don't make sense. And China pushing for this so strongly and making sure we are involved makes even less sense, but I was going to look at other treaties today and see if there was a common factor." I took a drink of my coffee and hoped I could figure out where to get more.

She tilted her head at me. "Not bad. Keep at it, maybe you might have some value." Then she yanked her head back inside her office and shut the door.

I gave the door a wary eye and continued to my

assigned cubicle. The question of should I be annoyed or relieved that I was being treated like any intern niggled at me. Either way, it didn't matter. I logged in and then went back to my research. If nothing else, I was learning things and was always interested. I found more coffee, decent but not good, and then went back to reading. Every link I clicked took me to more rabbit warrens, and I felt like I'd never be able to figure it all out.

A door opened, and I heard Pearl snap out my name. "Munroe."

I pulled my head out of cultural aspects of Japan and stood, glancing at the clock on the computer. It was already after ten. Pearl was in her doorway and nodded when I got my head high enough for her to see. "Yes?"

"Get your stuff. Be prepared to listen. We have a meeting with Japan and China's representatives in ten minutes." She stepped back into her office as soon as the words escaped her lips.

"Okay," I muttered as I sat down and tried to get my stuff. Not that I knew for sure what I would need. I spent a few moments debating what I should take. Finally I decided I needed to look assured and confident, because that was almost never a bad option. I grabbed my new briefcase and slipped the computer in with the notebook I'd started with questions to myself. Double-checking that my badge was clipped to my jacket, I walked over to Pearl's office.

All of my clothes were pantsuits. I really didn't like dresses. This meant I was dressed in black jeans slacks, a silk shell top in dark green, and a simple Chanel style jacket in black and silver plaid. It had interior pockets and didn't bind. I looked nice and not too extravagant.

"You coming?" I asked Carelian, who had spent the morning under my desk working over his fur. He'd slept solidly all night as far as I could tell.

~Yes. I am curious about how the prey will react to you.~ He rose and yawned, displaying all his teeth.

~They aren't prey, they are liaisons and my coworkers.~ I said that mentally not wanting anyone to overhear. The office had filled up while I worked.

~Prey. They shall bow before my quean and you will prove your worth.~

I snorted. His perception of the world around us sometimes made me laugh. The rest of the time I was glad he didn't truly decide humans would be acceptable dinners, though I wondered if that was just because he liked salmon better.

"I'm ready," I said from the door of her office.

Pearl looked up and nodded. "Good." She stood up and pulled on a suit jacket of stark white that matched her slacks over her blue blouse and I frowned a bit. "What?"

"Um, not to be rude, ma'am, but I'm pretty sure both Japan and China regard white as the color of death and purity." Blue meant different things in both cultures, but the fact that in America we rarely wore white outside of weddings or blouses made it a statement.

"You have been doing the reading, excellent. And good. I want them to know it is death to cross me and I will gladly wear it to their funeral."

I fought back a snicker. "Very well."

She paused at the doorway gazing at Carelian. "I take it he is coming?" I just nodded. "Tell him not to shed on my suit. Red means something very different."

~Why does everyone think I can control shedding? Besides, you should be honored I would grace you with my DNA.~

I could tell he was talking only to me, so I just rolled my eyes and hurried after her. For all her dumpling like attributes, the woman walked fast. I followed her down

191

the hallway to another bank of elevators, down, out of the building, into another building up to another floor, then down a hallway with nothing but closed doors.

"We are here. It is just the two of us. China decided to demand a last second meeting and the other person, Scott Yang, assigned to this negotiation had to take today off. You don't speak Mandarin or Japanese, do you?"

I shook my head. "No, I don't, but-" before I could say more she waved a hand at me.

"It doesn't matter. We conduct everything in English to make sure the language is the same, but being able to hear their comments makes life easier. I can speak Mandarin and Cantonese, Scott speaks Japanese, but the diplomat from China normally speaks to his aides in Min Nan and while I can get words, I lose much of it." She shrugged. "Take notes, and see if you can dangle the carrot of your research to get this treaty."

"That is still mine, and I'm not playing any games with it at this point. Besides, I think you will be surprised at how they react to me."

Though I'm really hoping they don't try to kill me.

"I am sure you are overreacting, and why would two flunkies in the Japanese political machine recognize you? They are like us and employ thousands." Pearl dismissed my concerns as she walked into the conference room.

I followed, keeping my face impassive as I pulled out the laptop. A quick search on Japanese and Chinese customs helped a little. At least I now knew not to shake hands, just bow and smile with closed lips.

Before I could figure out much more than that, the door opened and a staffer escorted in a man and a woman. I stood up as Pearl did, and they halted a few steps in. Their eyes scanned both of us, then they bowed slightly.

"Mrs. Takishi. Mr. Yang is not here today?"

"No, Mr. Yamigoshi. He had a prior commitment today. Merlin Munroe, this is Special Dignitary Shiro Yamigoshi and his assistant Hana Tamagio. This is Merlin Corisande Munroe, she will be working with us and helping to seal the deal."

Both of them stiffened and stared at me for a long moment. They turned their bodies so they weren't even looking at me. "Mrs. Takishi. We look forward to Mr. Yang returning. Where shall we start today?"

Pearl frowned, glancing at me. I stood there, hands clasped in front of me, not doing anything.

"The liaisons from China should be here shortly. Merlin Munroe would-"

Mr. Yamigoshi cut her off. "Thank you. We will take our seats and await their arrival. We should start with the trade incentives and then go to what China will offer." They nodded to her and took a seat as far from me as they could. I had sat at one end with my back against the wall, while Pearl had taken the head of the table to my left, as a matter of course.

They sat and started talking between themselves.

Carelian whispered in my head. ~They are talking about the dishonor of having the forbidden one here. They almost walked out.~

I fought with the idea of telling Pearl, but decided at this point letting her know Carelian could speak their language and how bad a miscalculation this was would better serve me by keeping it under my hat. Before Pearl could say anything, the door opened again and two more people walked in. Where the two from Japan were lean and fit, this man was rotund, if not obese. He made Pearl seem curvy in comparison. He was followed by a young man whose face was covered by his hair as he constantly looked down.

"Mrs. Takishi, I have arrived. Let us begin the negotiations as China needs this to further our country's climb out of feudalism." His voice was hard and flat, and a bit high. Nothing like the jolly voice I had expected from a rotund man.

"Chun Wen, this is Merlin Munroe. She will be working with us to ensure an agreement is reached."

He looked at me and sniffed, then took a seat at the table in the middle. The young man, who had not yet been introduced, scurried over and set up a computer and lay documents and a pen in front of Chun, like a waiter setting the table.

Chun murmured to his assistant, who nodded.

~He asked if the leverage was in place and if there was any change in existing plans. Freedom should pay their debts as they have accepted the money all these years.~

I made a note of that while I pretended to pay attention to stuff on my computer.

Pearl cleared her throat. "The meeting tomorrow with the ambassadors is set up. But we need to finish laying out what the terms of the agreement are. Currently, while the biological research called Naosu is still the primary goal, there are also trade and the open research agreement we are pursuing. The US is willing to offer open information trade with government medical research as well as copies of the research James Wells did."

"The government doesn't own that, and it is not up for trade at this time." I snapped out the words as I matched the glare Pearl sent to me.

Dragons don't let anyone browbeat them.

She ground her teeth and looked at both sets of people. "Is there anything else that can be offered in addition? The spices and technology bans toward China will be altered and lifted," she paused to slide a piece of paper toward Chun, "and we agree to increase our purchases of tea and rice from China by three percent."

I tried not to fume, but I wanted to strangle her.

"That sounds good, but five percent would sound better. The open sharing of medical research between the three of us would be good for the health of all involved." He smiled and my truth sense pinged hard.

I blinked. My truth sense stayed at low levels and I usually tuned it all out, not caring about the lies people told each other all day long. The people in my life rarely lied to me, and if they did—like about my cooking—it was because they loved me. This was a red alert, and I jerked my head up, looking at him. I was the only mage in the room, and maybe he didn't realize. With a quick jerk, I tucked my head down and started to pay much more attention to the conversation.

"I would need to check with the White House, but I don't believe a five percent increase is out of consideration. But only if China drops the tariff on ..." Pearl kept on arguing details and I focused on Chun. Most of his words weren't lies, but they weren't everything.

I'd never focused much on truth sensing, I could use it as I'd proved in New York, but in the last few years I rarely bothered. It got so annoying you just tuned it out. Now I didn't. He only lied about how he was sure it would help all three countries. That didn't surprise me; this was politics after all. But why had the specific phrase "the health of all involved" been so strong of a lie?

"Merlin Munroe?" I jerked my head up at Pearl's words, annoyed she'd called attention to me. Right now my fading into the background was much better. "Please help our Japanese liaisons with the wording of-"

Pearl was cut off, and from the way her eyes widened, I assumed it was either so rude it shocked her, doubtful, or so unexpected she didn't know how to react.

"We have no need of assistance. We will need to communicate with our emperor as to which way he would like to proceed. We are asking for the removal of all remaining sanctions, the agreed upon medical research sharing, and tariff removal for all exports." Mr. Yamigoshi stated this in a flat voice, never once looking my direction. For all the attention they paid to me you would have thought I was a piece of furniture.

I let everyone go back and forth for about two hours. Not once did any of them address me and Pearl gave up, just shooting me notes on the internal messaging system.

At four pm, and my stomach was growling, both envoys stood. "That is enough for today. We will return on Thursday. I expect Mr. Yang to be here." It wasn't a question from the Japanese. Chun nodded and smiled. The young man with him, who still had his face covered, rose and followed him out.

We both stood there, then Pearl turned to me, her voice cool. "What was that all about?"

I sat back down and gathered up my stuff. "I warned you that Japan would not interact with me. And I will NOT," I growled out that word, staring at her, "give up my personal possessions. There is nothing here that is worth it to me. Unless you want to knock five years off my draft?"

Pearl stared at me and sat back down, her eyes not moving from me. I ignored her and packed everything up. I was starving and needed to go to the bathroom.

"Why couldn't you be a pushover and scared of

offending authority?"

I smirked as I looked up at her. "Because you aren't that scary, trust me. So I'm not going to fold. What is the next move? Oh, and if you care, Chun is lying about wanting this to benefit everyone."

She waved her hand, dismissing that as she started to pack up. "I expect every word out of their mouths to be a lie. It is the nature of diplomacy." Silence fell between us, and I felt Carelian move under the table. "I need this. We need this. Both for my career and for the country. If the research on this new virus plays out the way we hope, it could revolutionize the way we deal with any type of cancer. It will let us target specific cells in the body without the need for radiation or chemotherapy. We need this." There was something dark and personal in her tone, but she straightened and kept talking. "I can't order you to turn over the information that Wells left you, but I can entreat you. For your fellow Americans — we need this."

I didn't say anything else. She hadn't lied, but there was something else in her tone. Neither of us spoke another word. She left, and I looked down at Carelian. "Well?"

~This should be fun, though it is a boring way to chase prey.~ He didn't say anything else on the subject, instead prodding me to leave and get food. He wanted beef. That sounded good to me.

Chapter 24

Section 1.141.5

All government employees must follow their department rules in dealing with foreign mages. Culture clashes are not allowed. Mages must be clearly identified and may not actively use magic on mages from other countries under most conditions.

CHAOS

The next day was spent with my mind in the world of treaties. I focused on the details of treaties with Japan and China. There were so many, all with multiple layers that made no sense and sometimes actively contradicted each other. I had no idea how people did this day after day. It was boring, confusing, and frustrating all at the same time. Carelian spent most of his time sleeping, but I'd already promised him a long hike this weekend. There was a place we could step to and head out over the Appalachian trail. He enjoyed catching the occasional snack, but mostly just chasing things for entertainment. After I settled down we'd have to talk, because he'd go crazy coming to work with me all the time, but for now he said he needed to be here.

Thursday morning I walked into the office, already feeling the boredom and drudgery weighing at me. If they made the offer good enough, I might turn over James's research just to end this hell faster. If we hiked on Saturday, I could go over it on Sunday. I was pretty sure Lucille could get the information and the keys to the house for me.

A man I didn't know waited at my cubicle. When I

got close enough he snapped out at me, "There is a meeting at six pm." His voice had the odd flatness of someone who had learned English via listening to computers. "Be ready to stay late. Negotiators in China are getting up early to meet with us. They will have the authority to talk through some of the issues with the current line items. Japan will not be there."

I looked up at him, he was at least three inches taller than me, and half smiled. "Hi? You are?"

He huffed at me, and I narrowed my eyes waiting for his response. "Scott Yang. I'm the lead with Pearl on this treaty. I heard you have already pissed off the Japanese. The two of us are going to focus on China and see if we can nail down their aspect. Then if we get into meetings with Japan, we will see what happens. If nothing else we can use you to rattle them and piss them off. Might be worth a try." He stared at me the entire time and I fought not to hunch my shoulders.

"That might work. You may need to have someone check into how mad the emperor still is at me. But I'll be ready."

Scott nodded at me and turned, leaving without another word.

I sighed and glanced down at my foot rest. "Feel like going to get some dinner later before the meeting? You don't need to come to the meeting you know, it will be all boring and lots of talk."

~My quean, I stay. Though food and a walk would be good.~

I worked through lunch, occupied with research and trying to prepare for Chinese rage. At four we wandered out, ignoring the double takes that Carelian got, and the occasional shriek of surprise. I didn't care about taking a longer lunch. I needed food and so did he, as I figured we'd be there rather late.

At five-thirty, I walked through the cubicles until I found where Scott was. He had gathered his equipment together in a slightly heftier briefcase than I had.

"What?" he asked, not looking up at me as he finished.

"I don't know where we are meeting."

"The room number was in the invite." He stood and pivoted, staring at me, the look not unfriendly but definitely not welcoming.

"And this is day four, which means I have no idea what that means. My orientation has consisted of threats, browbeating, innuendos, and showing me where the coffee and bathrooms are." I stared back at him. The coffee part had been non-negotiable.

"Valid. Follow me." He turned and headed out, going the same direction Pearl had gone on Tuesday.

~Do none of these people have lives or a personality?~

I shrugged helplessly at Carelian and followed Scott. He walked like a man on a mission and I felt myself getting out of breath trying to keep up with him.

I needed to get back to working out and more weekend hiking. Never enough time, I swear.

He stopped after an elevator ride and weaving through multiple mazes, insuring I was truly lost. "The meeting is in that room with the double doors. Video conferencing is set up. I am going to use the facilities prior to the meeting. I advise you to do the same." Without waiting for a response he spun on his heel and headed toward the door marked Men.

"I'm starting to think they don't have personalities," I muttered to Carelian. I headed toward the double doors, Carelian pacing by my side.

~Stop,~ he whispered in my mind and I came to an immediate halt. I glanced at him and waited. ~The

Chinese are discussing something called project Devastate. That they suspect it will take three more generations of concerted effort to see a significant change. A comment about still seeking data on what causes emergence.~ He looked up at me, ears back. ~I am unsure what they mean, but I do not believe it is for our benefit.~

I shrugged and headed toward the door. There wasn't any way to answer that. I pushed it open and Chun and his assistant were seated at one of the tables. Another table sat parallel to them with a large TV screen on the wall between us. The layout of the room reminded me of an equal sign with a square at the end. They nodded to me, their bodies hesitating a brief moment as Carelian followed me in.

I returned their nods and took a seat at the end of the other table. At the earlier meeting, Carelian had been under the table before they arrived and didn't move until after they left, so he must have surprised them.

~Any chance they know about your ability to translate?~

~Doubtful. The number of mages with familiars is small, and many would never need that ability. You, however, are a powerful quean and will need all of my skills.~

"Hi," I said brightly, smiling at them.

They nodded and whispered in rapid Chinese, or Cantonese, or whatever language it was Pearl said he normally spoke in.

~I'm not translating that; it would defeat the purpose of you not knowing the language.~

I kept the soft smile on my face, nodded at them and set up my belongings. ~At some point I'm going to ask you what they said.~

~You really don't want to know. It was extremely

rude and if I suspected they meant what they said I might have practiced my skinning skills on them.~ His voice had a hard edge to it in my mind.

Maybe I didn't want to know what they had said.

Scott Yang came bustling in and spoke to Chun in a rapid fire of syllables, though it sounded vaguely different than what Chun had been using.

~What language is he speaking?~ I asked Carelian, keeping my head down and trying to look unimportant.

~No idea.~

I resisted the desire to stare at him. Instead I acted like my computer was the most interesting thing in the world. ~How in the world can you translate if you don't know what language they are speaking?~

~It doesn't work like that. I can hear what they mean by the intent.~ He paused for a second and I tried to be patient. ~There are meanings behind words being spoken. I cannot translate a TV show because the people are not here. Phones are very difficult because I can't sense the speaker. Are we done?~ I fought not to giggle. Carelian hated trying to explain how his magic worked. Esmere, on the other hand, loved it, but to a certain level for most denizens it came down to instinct. Baneyarl was one of the few that could explain it logically in a manner my Earth oriented self could make sense of.

Before I could ask him anything else, Scott stopped speaking in whatever language he hand been and nodded.

"Mr. Wen," he said, his voice formal. Chun nodded back at him, sitting up as straight as his impressive belly would allow.

Scott went to a tablet attached to the wall beneath the screen and typed for a minute. The screen flickered and lit up.

"Your colleagues will be on shortly," he said to Chun. Scott came over and took a seat at the same table as me, but much closer to screen. He set up as the video started to connect. The screen flickered and revealed a room that didn't look all that different from the one we were in. One big table with doors behind it, and the walls were trimmed in red, but otherwise it could have been anywhere. Two men were sitting at the table and nodded when the screen resolved.

"Nǐ hǎo!" the older one said. He was dressed in a severe black suit with a rather upscale parted haircut, while the man next to him had the more typical straight cut.

"Nǐ hǎo!" Scott replied. "Xu Lun, I am ready to hear your requests. Ms. Takishi gave me some details that Mr. Wen requested earlier. I believe we should verify if they are correct."

The man on the other end, who I assumed was Xu Lun, nodded. "Yes. While I have ultimate faith in Wen, the Emperor and the Minister of Trade have clarified some of his requests." He spoke excellent unaccented English, and I wondered if he'd been educated here.

"Then I am ready to review your details. Are we ready to work on the items at hand? Item one is the request to increase exports by three percent." Scott's voice was the same monotone, and I glanced at him, pretty sure Pearl would have recorded the request to increase to five percent.

"I'm afraid your notes aren't accurate," Chun said, his voice almost bubbly. "We are looking for a five percent increase."

"Ah, I apologize, but after much discussion with the Son of Heaven, we believe a ten percent increase is more sustainable." Xu's voice was smooth, but I couldn't sense this was as much a game as haggling. Something I had never been good at. I sat back and took notes, sensing when they got to the real number; six percent increase in soya bean, and three percent in gold from the United States. They had moved on to the next area, the ability to share data with the government medical research centers, primarily Johns Hopkins and Walter Reed.

This part at least interested me as I had no idea what research was being performed in either center. I would have loved to have been placed there to work. Playing with bacteria, or working with other diseases, even using my magic to manipulate growth in new ways would have been fascinating.

I looked up at the screen to the other side of the world as the double doors opened and an old man strode in, followed by three guards. He had long white hair caught back in a tail and I could see the multiple tattoos on his face indicating he was a merlin, though I had no way of making them out. He wore robes of gold in a style I hadn't expected to see outside the movies. But I didn't need the immediate bowing or clothes to realize this was the emperor. The dragon following behind him proved that.

Pictures of the Dragon of China were omnipresent when you searched the internet for information about China. It had been the same familiar since 1861. The emperor Tongzhi of the Qing dynasty emerged as a merlin and the dragon appeared, stating he was the familiar of Zaichun, the emperor's birth name. The succession ceremony had taken place in the Imperial Ancestral Temple courtyard. There was no hiding either the emergence or the dragon, as it was one of the few times the dragon had spoken to others. Thousands had come to watch the coronation, and it spread through the city like wildfire.

I had made a quick attempt to research the dragon—an online search or two—it never was referred to as anything except the Dragon of China. It was the poster child of every eastern dragon I'd ever seen. A ruffle around its neck in yellow, scales of red that darkened to black by his tail, with four legs and no wings, and a lion-like face but with a muzzle that was too long. He was gorgeous and intimidating at the same time.

"Emperor Qixiang, how may we assist you?" Scott had risen and bowed. I mimicked him, but I was focused more on the dragon. He was supposed to be Spirit. Part of me wondered if he'd like to come over to the parties we had in Albany.

"I wanted to check in and lay eyes on the merlin that has caused so much distress for Japan." He didn't sound at all upset about that. There was the slightest smirk on his face as he focused on me and I got the feeling he was just as deadly as the emperor of Japan, just in a different way. Even over the video conference I knew this man wouldn't hesitate to order someone killed if it furthered his purpose.

I flailed for something to say that wasn't snark or rude. "It is nice to meet you. Would you introduce your familiar?" I hated trying to figure out names.

The room went silent on both sides of the planet. What was the issue?

Chun Wen hissed at me. "The Dragon of China never speaks with lower mortals. He is a sign that the gods are pleased with us. The only way to address him is not at all. Only the emperor and his family may address him."

I blinked, pulling back a little. "That sounds awfully boring and even cruel." My words deepened the silence as everyone stared at me and the emperor wasn't even smiling a little.

~Humans are idiots.~ Carelian's voice wafted

through my mind, but I didn't dare turn to look at him, trying to figure out what he meant. A spike of pain, so fast it only registered because the image on the screen showed Carelian walking toward the dragon.

"Oh shit," I muttered as people in both time zones gasped in horror.

Chapter 25

Section 1.125.3

All declarations of need must be filed both with the Draft Board and the OMO for auditing purposes.

SPIRIT

"Call your cat back!" Scott didn't yell at me, but the words were shot out of his mouth with enough force to bring spittle.

"I don't own him." I barely looked at Scott, instead watching the guards who had grabbed their ruler and had him in a corner of the room, two of them in front of him with guns drawn, while the aides were flat on the ground, with their hands laced behind their heads. I assumed this was to show they weren't threats, and I couldn't blame them as the third guard was brandishing the gun and yelling in Japanese at Carelian.

Carelian for his part was sitting upright in front of the dragon, and I figured they were talking. It was a similar pose to how Arachena and Carelian often conversed.

The guard was still yelling in Chinese and getting closer to Carelian and the dragon, gun waving, and I could see other people approaching through the open double doors.

"You had better not shoot my familiar," I warned as I scanned the room looking for specific details. If things went wrong, I'd side step there and get two countries declaring me anathema, but there was no way I'd let Carelian get hurt.

"Merlin Munroe," Scott snarled. Everyone on our

side was standing and switching between glaring at me and at the screen as the guard waved the gun. The men on the floor looked like they were trying to become one while the emperor peered over the shoulder of his guards.

The only sounds were the guard and his rapid-fire commands, though I had no idea what they were saying.

The dragon turned and roared at the guard, and everything went silent. A low voice spoke, and everyone in the room pivoted to look at the emperor. I shot Scott a quick look, having no idea what had been said. He looked even more pale than he had a minute ago.

"He said to stand down. This is a friend of the Dragon of China." He swallowed and stared at the screen. The emperor kept talking and eyes were getting wider. Then the dragon and Carelian disappeared. Scott cleared his throat. "He said the Dragon of China was going to visit a friend and would be back when everyone quit acting like..." Scott cleared his throat and I looked at the emperor who had rage written on his face. "Like idiots."

"Oh." Before I could say anything more, Carelian's voice whispered in my head.

~Tiantang and I are in Albany. He needed a break. I might raid the cans and Malkin is coming to say hi. I'll explain later.~

~Be careful and try not to terrify anyone?~ I wasn't too worried; the clearing at my house in Albany was well shielded from any passing eyes. And while we weren't there often enough to have fresh food, there was a large amount of canned goods. ~If you need to throw a party, let me know and I can have groceries delivered.~

~I may. And the rulers of China might be in for a very big surprise.~ He all but snarled the words.

~Carelian?~ I asked, suddenly worried.

~Later. Don't kill anyone. I want to watch when you do.~

I huffed out an exasperated sigh and returned my focus to the room and screen, only to find everyone staring at me.

"What?" I asked, looking around.

"Where did your cat take the Dragon of China?" Scott demanded. For all his flatness earlier, I wondered if he was about to have a stroke.

"Carelian did not take Tiantang anywhere." Oddly some words were easier to say when Carelian said them in my mind and I didn't even stumble over the pronunciation.

Everyone looked at me blankly. The emperor surged to the front of his flunkies and glared through the screen at me. "Where is my familiar?"

"Apparently having lunch with mine. Talk to him. He'll respond, if he feels like it." I crossed my arms and glared back. "Or haven't you learned that a familiar is not a pet or a possession? They are a person just like you and me and have the ability to do what they want." I could feel the eyes of everyone on me, and I didn't care. I was sick and tired of people being treated as less because they were different. And while Carelian might like to play the animal occasionally, I would not let people who knew better disrespect him like that.

The emperor, I really needed to know his name, grimaced and gave a sharp jerk of his head. "Very well. Though I begin to see why Tomohito declared you anathema. Doing the same is tempting."

I bristled, about to chew him out, when he flinched the tiniest bit and held up his hand. "Peace, it was a poor joke and I will not be doing anything of the kind."

He may have been more believable if he wasn't grinding out the words and looking like he'd rather be chopping heads off with a sword than talk to us.

One of the guards yammered at him, and he snarled. It was both amusing and intimidating at the same time. It was also by far the most honest expression I'd seen on anyone since this whole thing started. He snapped out a few sharp words, and the guard fell silent.

"Carry on," he growled and turned and stalked out, the guards scrambling behind him. They looked freaked out, twisting and checking every space as they moved.

"I think they just realized there are beings for which distance and location is not an issue." The words came out louder than I intended and everyone looked at me, a bit wild eyed. I forced a smile to my face. "Welcome to my life. Shall we get back to discussing the terms to present to Japan?"

They stared at me, then nodded and slowly people sat back down. I sat at my computer pretending to be unaffected, but for the next two hours Scott kept giving me worried glances. When we finished at ten P.M., I was exhausted. I wanted a piece of fruit and bed.

"We need to talk in the morning," Scott said, but he was much politer than prior.

"Sounds great. See you then." I kept my voice chirpy as I packed up everything. He just nodded and raced away. I'd finish out the week at the hotel, then commute from Atlanta. I waited until everyone was gone, then I sidestepped to the hotel.

Carelian was waiting for me. I glanced around the room. The dragon would have been extremely noticeable in here, if not too big for it. "Tiantang go home?"

~No. He would like to talk to you.~

I gave Carelian a long look. "Not tonight. It is well after ten. I have to be back at work tomorrow by seven, and there will be a meeting involving me. Who knows what will happen. I might be happy to still have a job." I started stripping off my clothes. Work clothes were much less comfortable than a t-shirt.

~It is important. More important than sleep.~

That made me pause, and I gave him a hard look. He didn't blink or back down, just sat there waiting for my decision. "Did you at least put a cider in the fridge for me?" I didn't think I could handle more earthshaking news today. I was very glad I'd eaten, but I still was a bit hungry. There were nuts and snack bars there.

~Yes. I figured you might like something. Plan on extra coffee in the morning.~ With that parting comment, he slipped into a rip and away.

I groaned and pulled on a comfortable shirt and jeans, then my sandals. Dressed in clothes I liked, I stepped to the designated spot in the house. We'd set aside an area, taped off even. It was always kept clear of everything. It meant I didn't need to think, I just stepped.

Stress I hadn't realized I was carrying dropped off me. Taking a deep breath I walked into the kitchen, grabbed a cider. The fridge was mostly empty outside of that. I took a moment to pop the lid off and took a drink before heading out the back. Exhaustion settled on me like a weight, but it was still easier to deal with than the stress I had been carrying. I was glad I'd swallowed before I stepped out back, as it looked like they were having a mythical creatures meeting. Tiantang took up a chunk of the yard, with Esmere in kitty loaf position, Baneyarl sprawled out across from her, and Carelian across from the dragon.

They all looked up at me as I walked out. I smiled,

walking toward them. "Hey. Tiantang, it's good to meet you."

Up close, the dragon's eyes were swirls of gold with vertical pupils. While they were the same color I'd seen cats with, they seemed richer, more exotic. He blinked at me. ~Merlin,~ he said in my head. His mental voice had the roar of thunder as an undertone that made you expect lightning at any moment.

"Please, just Cori. The merlin crap is stupid. Besides, any of you could eat me before I could react."

~Humans are better marinated in fear. You would be too bland as you don't fear.~ Esmere licked her shoulder as she responded.

"I believe I don't want to know how you know that." I dropped next to Carelian, one hand petting down his back, the other holding my cider, legs out in front of me. "So what's up? Carelian said you needed to talk to me?"

The dragon looked at me, his scales blood red in the light from the back porch. ~You meant it when you said she would just talk to me. Your human is very odd.~

~My queans are unique and powerful. Cori is the best. She sees only the being, not the form. Tell her. She will have ideas.~ Carelian purred as he talked, and I rolled my eyes.

"He's biased. I'm not that great. I still don't use my magic as well as I should, and Merlin knows I'm making a mess of this job." I took a sip of cider, trying to let my frustration go. I knew it wasn't all my fault, but surely I could make it better. Though I'd prefer to help without giving up my inheritance. I didn't even know what it was yet.

Tiantang curled up tighter, his white frills almost luminescent in the dark. ~I was very young when magic returned, a rip opened underneath me as I cracked my egg and I fell at the feet of the man who would become emperor. I have never seen another dragon and what few familiars that came to court were never allowed in my presence. They told me they didn't want to risk me eating them. I lived my days in the palace, but only spoke to Qixiang, he of the most recent Child of Heaven, no one else. I was regarded with awe and fear and until Carelian spoke to me, I existed in loneliness. Each merlin in the royal family called to me and when my current mage died, I moved my link to the one closest, not knowing any other option. It never even occurred to me to talk to anyone besides my focus, but they rarely had time for me. So I have spent my time listening, learning, and not understanding just how huge this world was.~ He sounded like rain in a storm, sad and powerful.

"Wait, you've basically been in isolation with nothing but humans for over a hundred and fifty years?" I asked. When the great figure nodded his head, I wanted to run over and hug him. "Okay, that bites. I'm sure Jo and Sable would love to meet you, and if I'm not at work, you can come talk to me."

~Oh we have addressed that. I am working on finding his family. Dragons are relatively rare and most dragons are really only located in one area of the realms. We should find them in a few days if not sooner.~ Esmere sounded sure of herself.

"I'm very glad then that Carnelian tried to give me a heart attack and did that, but I'm not sure that necessitated me staying up and coming here," I prodded gently, while fighting a yawn.

I could sense the thoughts rippling between them as Baneyarl focused on his wings. It amused me how many of the realm beings used grooming the same way humans used playing games on their phones.

Carelian spoke, though he sounded reluctant.

~Tiantang has been listening and learning for a long time and to both his benefit and detriment, many in the palace think of him as nothing but a pretty animal. Even his current focus rarely speaks to him for advice or even friendship. But he has been listening for years and after we talked, much of what he had overheard fit into a puzzle he was unaware of.~ I knew how fast they could communicate huge amounts of information when they didn't need to slow it down for humans and words.

"Okay. And?" All I wanted to do was go to sleep. The cider hadn't helped, and the desire to go upstairs to my bedroom and crash was getting stronger.

This time Tiantang spoke in my head. ~And I believe Qixiang's sister is behind a plan to kill mages in your country.~

Section 2.20.22

Familiars are both pets and children. While their mage can be held responsible for their actions, it is understood that a familiar will not be expected to obey cultural or societal expectations. Nor will the mage be punished because of these.

ORDER

The sleepiness vanished as I jerked upright and stared at the dragon. "Did you really just tell me China is behind the mages that are dying?"

His long whiskers quivered. ~I am unsure how far the plan goes, though I do not believe Qixiang is aware of it as anything other than a dismissed idea. His sister Huilang is the Minister of Magic. He trusts her implicitly.~

I sat there trying to figure out what to do, ask, anything. Why did I get bombshells like this dropped on my lap? "You don't trust her?"

There was a long pause then finally Tiantang said, ~I believe she desires to see China supreme, no matter the cost.~

"And you?"

Tiantang rippled through his long, sinewy body. ~I am not in favor of killing mages, or killing in general. Any policy set on controlling by killing those you can not control carries with it the seeds of destruction.~

I sighed and set down my bottle. "I need more information. And I am very sure you don't really want America as a whole to react to this. It would mean war."

That much I was sure of. A foreign country actively killing mages that the government leaned on to create the basis of their scientific and military power? Trade would shudder to a standstill. I stopped, tilting my head as other things occurred to me. Or did we already know?

"Tiantang, did you ever overhear them talking about or with Americans? I don't believe this could be easily done without inside cooperation."

The dragon curled tighter, and I waited, worried even more. I really wanted to talk to Charles and take a look at his data. At this point, I'd need to start paying him.

~I am unsure. While I have learned most language spoken in the court, telling the nationality of a human is confusing. There are very few people that are not Chinese that are trusted by the royal family. They are like a wounded deer, startling at everything. And Huilang does not like me. She has lust in her heart at my existence and hates that I went with her brother.~

I groaned and dropped my head into my hands. There wasn't going to be enough coffee in the world for me to be able to handle tomorrow morning. After rubbing my temples, I raised my head. "Tiantang, I am very honored that you chose to share this information with me. But I have to ask why? What do you want me to do and where do your loyalties lie?"

It was a question I'd never asked Carelian. I didn't want to know. Part of me expected him to choose his mother or his people over me any day of the week. Humans were horrible. But then I didn't know all the machinations that went on over in the realms. Every being there focused on grooming. Carelian extended his back leg chewing on a spot, while Esmere cleaned her claws, Baneyarl focused on his wings, and the Merlin blasted dragon licked tail.

"That is not helpful nor reassuring." I stared at all of them, waiting for the answer.

Esmere glanced at the dragon, then at her son, and hissed. It was an annoyed sound that I completely agreed with and would have duplicated if I could have made that noise. ~You are all cowards. Cori, we don't think or follow the way you do and those who were selected to be focuses are even more strange. Tirsane, Salistra, Bob, and the others are not gods we worship, they are heroes that ascended to power most of us do not even dream of.~

~Nor do we want it,~ Baneyarl snorted then fell silent at a glare from Esmere.

~If you want to explain this, please do,~ she managed to hiss in my mind and he buried his head in his wing to avoid her gaze.

Tiantang was listening as avidly as I was. His upbringing must have been nonexistent, if all of this was new to him.

~You have an organized society, rules, and groups. We have a few rituals, some understood truths, but everything else is open. You saw the dedication to Magic. She/he/it is the only power we worship, but strength rules everywhere else. Those who are focuses, both per their inclination and Magic's choice are strong, stronger than most.~

I glanced at Carelian who didn't look at me, working hard on his hind haunch that was already perfect.

~We don't do loyalties to countries, gods, realms, or even branches of magic the way you do. We choose who our friends are, and they tend to be the only things we are loyal to. Our version of your families. Friends are more than lovers as very few of us have mates the way humans do. We have clans of those who think and believe in line with us. My son pulled you into our little clan.~ She huffed a bit and looked at Tiantang. ~You are not obligated to be loyal to anyone or anything, that is your choice.~

~Even my mage?~ His mental voice was somehow tremulous, uncertain. Not the strong, impressive thing I thought I'd hear from a dragon.

~Even your mage. There have been many that have lost their mages over the years for various reasons. This is always your choice.~

Tiantang curled up tight, appearing half the size I knew he was. ~I must think if that is allowable.~

Esmere shrugged. ~Think, ponder, take a century or two if you need it. But do remember humans are normally fragile and you can often ignore them until they decay unto death.~

I made a face at her and she ignored me.

~Your kindness has been extreme.~ He wriggled up, holding his upper body in the air like a cobra, and I waited to see what he was going to say, but a pain stabbed my eye hard and deep and I knew whomever was coming through was opening a much bigger rip than usual.

~Ah, Tirsane is here, and I believe she has brought a guest.~ There was a bit of disapproval in Esmere's voice. ~Cori, we have abused your hospitality sorely.~

I turned to look at the rip that was forming near the orchard. It was almost as tall as the nearest tree, which was eighteen feet tall. Tirsane slithered out, but she appeared in her normal guise, only about six feet tall. Before I could spend much more time worrying about that, something huge moved into the opening of the tear. It bent around the edges and a dragon stuck its head out.

I swallowed the yelp of terror that burst out from my

lungs and fell back into Carelian. The only reason I didn't start reaching for magic and figuring out how to kill a dragon—something that never had occurred to me before this second—was his purring.

"Ah, Cori." Tirsane nodded at me. "I forgot you were here. Zmaug, this is Cori Munroe."

The dragon was huge, like half as big as my house huge. The quarter acre yard in the back suddenly felt like a tiny sandbox with an adult in it. While Tiantang looked like the typical Chinese dragon that had been in that culture centuries before the magic spread, Zmaug looked like the dragon you saw when you looked for European dragons. Two wings, four legs, green scaly skin, and teeth as long as my forearm.

It glanced at me, a quick dismissive glance, then nodded before focusing on Tiantang. A hissing slippery sound came out of the dragon's long muzzle and Tiantang froze. A feeling of waiting, like a storm about to break, filled the air, then Tiantang said something. The liquid sounds halted and jerked slowly as they fell out of his mouth. It sounded the way I did when I tried to speak Spanish, slow and hesitating as I translated in my mind from English to Spanish.

Even with scales, horns, and wings, I could see the joy in her face.

~You have returned my child to me. I assumed he had been eaten. He was barely hatched when he disappeared. I never thought that Magic might have chosen him. And your world is so big, looking for him would be impossible.~ She turned her huge head back to him. ~It is time to go home.~

Tiantang turned to look at Carelian. ~You reached out to me. Let me know I am not alone.~ He turned to follow Zmaug through the rip and paused. ~Please tell Qixiang I have thinking to do.~

219

I choked and tried to breathe. Before I could protest, scream or get any words past my sphincter tight throat, they stepped through the rip and it rippled into something much smaller. My mouth opened and closed as I tried to protest.

"What just happened?" I croaked out.

Tirsane slid over to me and crouched down. "Is there an issue? And I did need to express my pleasure again at the little treat you provided me."

I wanted to follow up on the idea that they expected me to tell the ruler of another country that his familiar was doing a walkabout with his family, but I forced myself to look at her and made the sides of my mouth quiver. That was all I could pull off as I really wanted to run screaming after them yelling "Don't go!" Instead I pretended I was an adult and focused on the scary demigod. Which in retrospect, maybe I could piss her off and get her to kill me. That might be the safer way to go.

"What does death by a gorgon feel like?"

She arched an eyebrow at me and I realized I had said that out loud. "I am not sure. My racial magic causes all the cells in your body to fossilize. I imagine it would be relatively painless, though the few humans I have killed that way screamed the entire time so I could I be wrong."

Technically, I could make the earth open up and swallow me, but I couldn't see any way to do it and not damage the house or grounds.

"I'm glad you enjoyed the magic absorption. I think. I never asked, did anyone die because of that?" Lefoin had implied mostly it had been good but I didn't figure then had been a good time to press for details.

"Not from me draining their magic. The exactitude of your laws allowed Magic to guide me and make sure I took it only from those not capable of following your rules, not those who did not wish to follow the rules."

I heaved a sigh of relief. "I'm glad."

"Your discovery of the lost one has earned you many favors. So do not be surprised by the occasional visitor. Zmaug is a Spirit lord and her clan have long memories."

Putting my head in my hands and bawling about the things everyone expected of me, things I had no idea how to fix, wouldn't change anything. Instead, I stood up and nodded at Tirsane.

"You really need to thank Carelian. He started all of this. I'm just the schmuck trying to clean up the messes."

"Ah, but you are he. All four of you actually are regarded as the same. You share the rewards and the blame." I blinked at her, completely surprised. "So you did good. I must go. Baneyarl." They nodded at each other as Tirsane turned to leave. "You still coming over in the evening tomorrow, Esmere? Salistra is still not speaking to me."

~She is still in a snit? That filly needs a good stallion.~ Esmere rose. ~Yes. I will see you then.~

"Then good night all." She turned and slithered out the rip, Esmere and Baneyarl following with waves of goodbye.

I turned to Carelian and stared at him.

~Yes?~ He yawned wide as he responded, then blinked at me, slow and languid.

"Just how am I supposed to explain that the Emperor of China's familiar went to visit family?"

~By saying just that. What are they going to do? Your people almost never execute anyone and you have done nothing to deserve that. Besides, I would never allow my quean to be executed. I think I will sleep at home tonight.~ Before I could sputter out a response, he leapt and was gone.

I stood in the back yard of a house I rarely got to live in and contemplated going stark raving mad. Somehow I didn't think it would be that long of a journey.

Chapter 27

Section 2.20.23
Familiars that hunt are to be restrained from hunting other pets or endangered animals. Fines will be assessed if they are found to hunt these.

CHAOS

I slept in the Albany house. Hamiada made it so it oozed comfort, and I needed every bit. We'd created a good relationship, the dryad and I. Plus, adding fertilizer to her roots in the basement made her very happy.

I got my coffee there, then sidestepped back to the hotel. I didn't tend to keep clothes that would be appropriate for the State Department in Albany. Most of the time we were there, it was for a vacation. Which meant jeans, shorts, tank tops, nothing that wouldn't get me written up for walking in wearing. But having good coffee helped my mood, if not my trepidation. I checked out of the hotel and took three minutes to dump my suitcase back at the apartment in Atlanta. Just being in my room made me homesick. I hated this job.

With a sigh, I left the hotel and walked, hoping a solution would coalesce in my brain. It didn't. The walk, however, gave me time to work out worst-case scenarios and my responses to any questions that might be thrown at me.

By the time I walked through security, I felt almost serene in what would come next. Though the idea of the emperor's sister being a player in all this didn't make me feel any better. I was glad it was Friday. After I sat down at my cube, I shot a message to Jo, Sable, and Charles.

Dinner tonight? I need to talk to you guys. Super hush hush stuff. Charles, bring your computer?

I didn't expect them to respond immediately, as I was pretty sure all of them were in their commute at the moment. I logged in and started digging through my email. There were notes about the requests from the Chinese, and I pulled that one open first. I'd just been scanning over the treaty terms before and while the trade items were the biggest aspect, there was a list of little things from all sides. It was the Chinese side I wanted to review.

"Munroe, get in here!" Pearl's voice echoed through the office before the document finished loading. Carelian hadn't shown up yet this morning, and I figured he was out with his mother or still sleeping somewhere. He was at heart a cat and he had three different places to sleep right now. Who knew which one he would be at? I grabbed my coffee and pulled all the responses I'd come up with during my walk to work and headed into Pearl's office. Part of me was surprised she'd waited this long. I must have been here for at least fifteen minutes.

I entered the office and Scott stood on one side. I quirked a smile as the wait was explained. The two chairs seemed like challenges, and I accepted it and sat down, coffee cup in hand.

"Explain to me just what were you thinking?" Pearl did a good impression of a hissing Cath, but she didn't have the teeth to pull it off.

"Which moment exactly?" My hand wrapped around the coffee, heat leaching through the tumbler. Tomorrow I might need to get an iced coffee to help offset the surrounding tempers.

"When you told your familiar to kidnap the Dragon of China," she said, eyes trying to burn holes into me.

"Ah, I didn't tell him that." My voice stayed mild as I

sipped the coffee, watching her. Scott paced behind me.

"Then what did you tell him?" he said, his voice hard.

"Regarding that? I didn't tell him anything. He told me they were going to talk. Then they left."

"Where did they go?" Each word dropped like a chunk of lead from her mouth, and I almost felt sorry for her. None of them were going to like this.

"Immediately after that? I have no idea. But I met with them last night and Tiantang went to visit his clan. He passed on a message for Qixiang though."

Scott had moved around and stood in the space between Pearl's desk and the wall. "What would that be?"

"That he, Tiantang, had thinking to do."

I watched them sputter. "That's it. He left to go think? And how do you know what his name is?"

"He told me, of course. Tiantang de Xue. It means Blood of Heaven. It's a complicated story that is not mine to tell," I finished as I saw both of them get ready to pounce on me. "He will return or not when he is ready."

"Tell him to return now," Scott all but yelled at me. His emotionless way of speaking almost completely gone.

The walk to work had done me good and removed all the worry I had about their reactions. "You want me to tell a fifteen-foot dragon that is over a hundred and fifty years old, who has gone to visit family, that he needs to go home now?"

"Yes," he snapped.

"Have fun with that. I'll be willing to watch. The realm denizens regard sentient beings as acceptable prey and they are very much on the fence if humans are sentient."

They both fell silent, and I sipped my coffee. Finally,

after many glances back and forth, Pearl spoke.

"You do realize you've created an international incident here, right?

"No. I don't think this is my fault. I might have been the catalyst, but given how isolated Tiantang has been, I suspect it was a powder keg ready to blow."

"Well, what about the bird?" Pearl asked, her hand wrapped around a pen so tight I was scared it might snap.

This confused me completely. "Bird? What bird?" I didn't think they'd seen the backyard. Hamiada didn't tolerate cameras from others on her soil. And few people would be stupid enough to regard Baneyarl as a bird. But then this entire situation made no sense to me.

Pearl leaned back, staring at me. "I don't know if you are innocent or if I'm going to strangle you with my bare hands. I almost want you to give us the stuff and we waive your draft because you create drama wherever you go. Yesterday almost immediately after you left I got an irate message from the Ambassador to Japan. He was in country and had been meeting with the Foreign Minister over there and the Royal Magician. A flaming bird popped in and proceeded to chew out all of them at once. Letting the Royal Magician know he'd never get his hands on Well's research and if they dared to do anything to the rightful heir, there would be Chaos to pay. And that he should stop being an ass and work with you."

I groaned and thought about strangling the bird myself. That ploy had destroyed any chance I had of trying to give them things that didn't matter and hide the research. Which I still couldn't understand why someone hadn't broken in and stolen. But I'd figure that out this weekend.

"That would be Jeorgaz, James Wells' familiar. I do

not control him. He is an independent agent. And that is not something I would have requested him to do."

They both just stared at me. Then Pearl sighed. "Go. Finish up the notes that were requested. We'll work on the next day of negotiations. If nothing else, the Chinese might be a bit more conciliatory or they might be worse. Maybe the Japanese will remove the stick that's up their asses." She shifted her attention to Scott. "We need to get sign-off on the changes they requested. There should be some senators up now..." She kept talking as I rose to my feet and left the room. It seemed the wisest course of action.

The document was waiting for me and I dug right in. This wasn't as much fun as a lab or helping people, but it was still about solving puzzles, and that got my interest. It was buried in the lists of concessions and asks. While the big ones were what Pearl had told me, the actual documents had dozens of minor things that I would have dismissed without noticing, except for what I'd been learning. There, along with a comment about exporting five tons of salt a year to Alaska and an agreement to drop the tariff on video games by a half percent, was the cessation of the moratorium on allowing US companies to hire mages to work in factories they built in China.

That necessitated research. I knew how the US ran mage laws and what you had to do to hire one, it wasn't much different from hiring anyone else other than we had to show proof of completed draft service and our contracts always specified the amount of offerings that could be expected per pay period during our employment. Most mages could do it easily, though there were days when Jo and Sable came home with their hair looking a bit ragged from a rough day.

China had a different view on mages than we did. All

mages were enrolled in the civil service and tattooed, even hedgemages. Which meant they had a huge workforce of mages that they could use for twenty-five years. I shuddered at that idea. My decade was bad enough. A quarter of my life? No thanks.

But what did that mean? I had pieces but no answers and no one I could go to. I catalogued my resources: Sable, Jo, Sable's Dad John Lancet, Carelian, House of Emrys, Indira, Steven, and Charles. That wasn't much and outside of the House, none of us had any power anywhere. Could the House help? I didn't really have evidence, just overheard comments and pieces that didn't fit together.

Bringing in Hamiada, Baneyarl, or Esmere didn't sound smart. They had little patience for human relationships as it was. The impact of this would get thoughts along the lines of "kill them all" and not much more. And the world would have to be ending before I called Tirsane. I shuddered again thinking about the snake.

Before I could involve Indira and Steven though, I needed to go through the research James did. They would need to understand exactly what people were fighting over. Maybe I could use Jeorgaz's little fit and make it look like I was on the outs with him. It might work. I decided I needed to stretch and headed out for a little walk. There were strange looks cast my way as I walked out, but I pretended not to notice them. Either way, this assignment would be exhausting.

Once outside, I called Lucille.

"Yes, Cori?"

"I need to look at the research James left me? It's becoming an issue."

There was a moment of silence. "I see." And I suspected she did. She'd dealt with the demands of people wanting that research for years. Lucille Blanding was the manager for his estate and she would be until I completed my draft. Which meant another decade for her, unless I did get out earlier. "I'll leave the key to the storage unit on the front hall table. As well as the list of bank boxes and keys for them. I assume the house will let me in?"

Lucille didn't know about Hamiada, but she knew the house was more than it seemed. "If not, call me and I'll ask Carelian to come get it."

"Will do. And good luck." She hung up with her normal brusqueness. But that reminded me. I hadn't seen my familiar since last night. He hadn't been in the bed with me at the house or shown up at the hotel room.

~Carelian?~ I sent out. As long as he wasn't trapped in a private realm pocket, he should hear me.

~Yes?~ He sounded sleepy, but okay.

~Hadn't seen you today. Everything good?~ I frowned as I walked. I couldn't remember the last time I had gone this long without seeing him.

~Yes. Went hunting with Tiantang's clan. Ate too much. Sleeping. Home with queans tonight?~ he asked hopefully.

~Yes. I invited Charles and Arachena as well.~ I'd checked and everyone had responded with an affirmative. ~I need to get a key from the house for the research. I'm hoping I can grab it before we go home.~

~Good. Sleep now.~ He sounded like he was falling asleep as he spoke to me, and I kept my laughter to myself. An overstuffed cat made a couch potato look energetic. He'd see me in a bit, and I suspected the hunt was good for him—though I had no desire to know what they had hunted.

I walked back in, head high, ignoring the whispers

that followed me, and dove back into my research. I
needed to look at all the details from new angles.
Halfway through trying to figure out what Japan really
wanted, especially after the little stunt Jeorgaz pulled,
my computer screen flashed.

My head jerked back, surprised, and I looked at the
message. Call Incoming. They'd shown me how calls
would be via my computer. I put on the headset and
clicked Accept Call.

Whoever I had expected, maybe Scott or Daniel
Lorison, the person glaring at me from the screen was
not it. Emperor Qixiang glowered at me, close enough I
could see the wrinkles at the corners of his eyes and the
hair thinning on top, though it was carefully styled.

I stammered a bit. "Emperor Qixiang, how may I help
you?"

"Where is the Dragon of China? Return him, now!"
Even through the computer screen I could feel his rage
and I narrowed my eyes.

"I did not do anything with your familiar. He told me
to let you know he needed to think. I believe he will
return when he feels he knows what he wants to do."

"That is unacceptable," he growled.

My own annoyance bubbled up. "And treating the
creature that should be your best friend, the reason you
can do so much magic, and your link to your ancestors
like a dumb animal is? You should be ashamed of the
way you have treated Tiantang. He is over a hundred
years old. He should be valued and cherished, not
treated like something you can ignore. He is a very
intelligent being, not a toy." I didn't bother to moderate
my tone or volume, and I heard chairs squeaking and an
office door opening.

"You dare," he hissed. The number of people out of
sight of the camera who were having conniption fits

right now probably numbered in the dozens. I didn't care.

"Dare to tell the truth? Yes, and you know it. Tiantang is visiting family and will be back when he is ready." ~Carelian?~ I sent as I balled up this memory.

~Yes?~ He still sounded sleepy.

~Catch.~ I tossed him everything in the few seconds while Qixiang spluttered.

~Ah. Very well.~

"I will see you fired for this. No one can talk to me this way."

"Feel free. I'd love to be in a lab, or hell, on a lava field. The people I deal with would be nicer," I shot back. There was a glimmer of red scales behind him and muffled shrieks.

~I believe it is time for me to talk to my mage. Thank you, Cori.~ Tiantang's voice rumbled in my head, and I saw the emperor's face pale.

"Have fun with that conversation, Qixiang." I made my voice especially chipper and hung up. "Jerk."

"Corisande Munroe!" I heard Pearl bellow from right behind me. I turned and smiled at her.

"Yes?"

Chapter 28

Section 1.201.1

All mages that are enlisted are exempt from the hair regulations, except where it would cause risk to life or limb.

SPIRIT

Pearl spent twenty minutes yelling at me, trying to convince me to record a groveling message. I refused, and I didn't care, no matter what dire threats she came up with. That entire conversation had been between me and another mage and had nothing to do with my job here at the State Department. Pearl disagreed.

When I walked out of her office, I packed up my stuff and headed out. It was Friday, I was tired, and this was a job, not my career. The second I was out of sight of anyone I stepped with my laptop and everything to Albany. It only took me a minute to find the key laying right where Lucille said she'd leave it. Along with the instructions to the storage unit. I picked up another envelope and pulled out the list of banks, along with the box number for each bank. There were five. It didn't surprise me Lucille had all the keys on another ring and each was labeled with the bank they belonged to. But from everything Jeorgaz had said, the storage unit was what I needed to look at. I'd have to try to get to the bank before noon on Saturday.

To my surprise, the storage facility was very close. Not close enough to walk, but close enough to stop there now before I headed home. "I'll be back, Hamiada, see you," I called out to the house as I walked out.

Fifteen minutes, and one rideshare later, I stood in front of an unprepossessing storage unit.

How in the world had no one ever broken into this place and just stolen everything? The only alarm I could see was at the gate. Here, there was nothing.

Shaking my head and wondering what either I was missing or all the people who wanted this were, I twisted the key in the padlock, removed it, and pulled up the rolling door. It was dark, and I reached to find a light switch on the wall near the door. A flick and light flooded the area, revealing a few boxes on the side, and a door in its frame leaning against the back wall.

"This is it?" I'd been expecting boxes of notes, maybe a lab, or maybe more mementos like in the magic room in the house in Albany. But this? The boxes had a few file folders in them, they were either tax documents, contracts, or some pay stubs from decades ago. When was the last time I'd seen a pay stub?

From what I could see, there wasn't much else except the door. I walked over to it. Painted off white, it leaned against the wall, looking like it had been pulled from a house and stored here. I moved over and lifted it up. There was nothing behind it besides some very sad cobwebs.

I turned around one more time. Had all the research already been taken? It would remove both trouble and stress of being pressured for it, but would create a major headache for me. I turned and was about to walk out when I stopped and looked at the door. The memory of the door in the attic ate at me and I sighed and went back and turned the knob, pulling it open.

If I had been anyone else in the world, the door would have opened to reveal the same sad cobwebs that I had seen behind it. But it was me. And that meant, of course, when I pulled open that door, there was a gray and misty space beckoning me to step in.

~Carelian?~

~Am I never going to get any sleep?~ he muttered in my mind.

~You've been sleeping for at least ten hours, so I have little sympathy. I have a magical door waiting for me to step through. Want to come with?~

There was a minute of silence and I could see him yawning and stretching as he made his decision.

~Yes,~ he said and before I could ask when there was a pinch and he was rubbing against my leg. ~You should have hunted with us. It was glorious. Zmaug has a wonderful hunting ground.~

I laughed and petted him. "I do not think me, with my slow feet and lack of desire to toy with prey, would have been of much use."

~Humans. They do not understand how much fun the chase is.~

I gave him an arch look. "When it comes to realm denizens, humans are just as likely to be prey."

He yawned again. ~Humans are boring. They run too slow.~

I didn't want to know how he knew that, so I changed the subject. "Shall we?" I sent a text to Jo and Sable letting them know I was headed into a probable realm and that Carelian was with me. That made me feel safe as I knew he could get me out of almost any situation.

Carelian licked his chest for a minute, stretched again, and sauntered toward the gray enclosure, tail in the air. ~Well, since you won't let me sleep.~

I gave in to temptation and hip bumped him through the door as I followed.

He cast me an affronted look over his shoulder as the door swung shut behind us. The familiar grayness surrounded us. It felt like a realm space. Maybe this was an example of what everyone wanted to find. But really, a bunch of gray nothingness? They could have it.

"Hey, Cori. What are you doing here?"

I spun as Hamiada materialized behind me. Or at least it sounded and looked like the form she normally took. At a certain point I had to assume creatures were who they pretended to be, but I did crank up my truth sense.

"I'm looking for research. What are you doing here?" Though I had ideas bubbling up in my brain faster than I could sort them out.

"Oh, this is where James asked me to store everything. Come on, I'll show you." She spun, and a path appeared, leading out of the gray mist to a sunny meadow. In a perfect world I would have recognized it as the same place Jo and Sable had been held. But it looked like any glade or clearing I'd seen in the realms; green grass, breeze, trees, a stream, and a bright blue sky. Never a sun, always a breeze. Jeorgaz had called them permanent pockets. Permanent for what or whom? What could you take from here?

"There they are. You want me to drop them back into the study?" Hamiada said, and I had to wrench my mind back to paying attention to her.

"Wait, no." I followed her finger and stopped at the wall of boxes. There weren't five or six boxes like I expected, or maybe a bunch of binders. No, there were twenty-one crates, each at least four feet tall, stacked in a pyramid, because why not. "Could I, um, see like the top one?"

"They are yours; you can do what you want with them." She floated there on the tips of her toes, making me look for wires. Vines reached up from the ground and deposited the top box there at my feet. I stared at it, trying to figure out how I would pry the lid off, when vines came up, wiggled tiny tendrils under the cracks—making me think of the snake under my skin—and heaved it up. The lid was set down behind the crate.

"Thanks," I murmured as I inched closer and looked in. It was full of binders. And when I said full, I meant neatly packed and wedged in so tight I thought I might have problems pulling them out. Written on the spines were topics and dates. Some were thin, others three inches thick or more. I reminded myself that crying would solve nothing.

I stared for too long at the overwhelming amount of information in a single crate, before I lifted my head, looking into the blue sunless sky. "Jeorgaz, you busy?" There was no guarantee he would hear me, but somehow I expected he'd be very aware of anyone being here. I wasn't going to pry into Hamiada's personal life, but most of the higher ranked beings seemed to know each other. Or I was just being introduced to the people they knew.

~Yes?~ The words in my mind corresponded with a wash of heat and the smell of sandalwood, which I couldn't help but smile at.

"There are a lot of boxes and binders here and I had some questions."

I felt the flash of heat and turned to see him. He perched on a branch that had extended out from a nearby tree, his blue and purple tail feathers drifting in the breeze.

"This is a lot of stuff," I said, staring at him.

~I did tell you we looked into many things.~ He seemed serene, and it made me want to startle him. I might have been a bit cranky at this point.

"This is a bit beyond what I was expecting. Is there a binder, or master list with all the important shit in it? Or at least an index? Otherwise I'm going to spend a year just organizing it." A nasty thought popped into my mind. "Or I could give it to the government and ask them to organize it for me, detailing out everything it contains."

This time, he glared at me. ~I do not understand why Carelian likes you so much. That would be very unwise.~

"He likes me because I can be just as sadistic as a Cath with the correct motivation. So, master file?" I crossed my arms over my chest, giving him my best glare. And I was hungry. It added to my lack of desire to compete with him.

The phoenix shuffled his wings in obvious annoyance, then jumped up, disappearing in a flash of flame. Before I could start listing all the things I was going to do to him, starting with using his feathers in a pillow, he reappeared above me with a large binder in his claws, which he promptly dropped on me.

I stepped back and caught it. Though seeing him reminded me of earlier that morning. I had almost forgotten after everything else. "And do you know how much trouble your little stunt caused today?"

~Which stunt?~ He settled back down on the branch.

"Going and threatening the royal magician."

He fanned out his tail feathers. ~So? He will never be allowed to use what we discovered. And there were rumors from others that he was trying to figure out a way to steal it from you.~

I groaned. "Esmere would have understood. I needed it as bait, as leverage. Dangling the opportunity for them to get it. It was a way to manipulate them. Everything is so twisted up right now I don't know what I will or won't do. But either I contradict what you threatened them with, putting me at risk because that means you might not punish them if they kill me. Or I have to abide by what you said and never even tell them details of what they could gain access to." I glared at him.

The phoenix blinked at me, and I swear his colors dimmed. ~That did not occur to me. By my very nature I am fire. I act. James was also very blunt, if deluded as to who his childhood friend had become.~

The bird sounded and looked sad. All the bright colors had dimmed and the blue almost seemed to be spreading.

~It is his nature. Cath enjoy the game. Phoenixes are all about the flame.~

That didn't make total sense to me, but I nodded. "It's okay, but please don't? I don't know what to do with everything I've learned and as it is I need to figure out if I should just let you flame it all."

The bird brightened. ~I could do that, turn it all to ash and gone.~

For a heart stuttering second I thought he was going to flame in and burn everything to ash. But to my intense relief, he seemed to be seeking permission.

"That would create a lot of issues. Not to mention, I'm not sure what might be in there. Please don't." Begging might be over the top, but I could ask nicely.

He sagged a bit. ~As you wish. That binder contains what he called a precis of all the experiments and if he regarded them as failures or successes. Again, do not let others get a hold of this research.~ He sounded worried and part of me almost offered it up to him to destroy. But I wanted to look at it and I didn't want to throw away any bit of leverage I had.

"I'm not promising anything. Let me look, okay?"

He drooped again, even his tail feathers seeming to drag. ~As you wish. Call on me if you have questions. Hamiada, Carelian." He bowed as he said their names, then disappeared in a wisp of flame.

I kept my comments of "over dramatic much?" to myself. "Thanks, Hamiada. Can you keep this safe? I probably won't need it for a while."

"Of course. That is what this glade is for. Storage." I must have looked confused because she laughed, exposing her green round teeth before spinning. "James had me create it. Temperature always at what you call 75 degrees Fahrenheit. No insects, no rodents. Isolated and perfect." She whirled again.

"So he didn't create this? You did?"

"Of course I did. If he had created it, it would have vanished with his death, or maybe Jeorgaz's ashing. Either way, they don't last past the mage." Hamiada had a way of making her answers sound like I had asked the dumbest question in creation. I brushed it away.

"Huh. Okay, thanks. I'm going to stop at the house, then head back to Atlanta."

"Oh," she slumped down. "When will you stay?"

I resisted hugging her. "I don't know. Someday. I promise. Maybe Jo and Sable will have kids that you can play with?"

She nodded, a glum aura around her. "As you wish." Her form faded away as the last words were spoken.

I sighed and readied myself to step to the house. Normally I didn't step out of realms, but in this case I felt safe as the realm and the house were owned by the same creature. I stepped into Albany, grabbed the bank list, the binder still in my hand, and stepped home.

Standing in my bedroom, I groaned. Even as easy as stepping was for me, I'd used up almost half an inch of hair with all the jumping around. Oh well. I glanced at my watch surprised it was almost seven. All this had taken longer than I thought. The smell of spices greeted me as I opened my bedroom door. My feet carried me into the living area that faced the kitchen. Charles was already there and Arachena sat on a shelf we had put up for her. They turned as I walked in, still carrying the binder and the list.

"Hey," I said, smiling and feeling a weight drop off of me. "You won't believe the week I've had."

Chapter 29

Section 1.125.2
Medical advice should only be ignored upon clear
need or the draft officer's declared and avowed
proof of need.

ORDER

We all gathered for Jo's enchiladas, with Mexican
rice and margaritas. It was Friday after all. Carelian
showed up, but he only took a token bite of the beef
then sprawled out on the floor with Arachena perched
on top of him. We all served ourselves and related the
stories of our day.

I had figured my day would win, but no, Jo won. It
turned out there had been a denizen hiding in Lake
Lanier. It looked like a mermaid, but had tentacles for
hair. It had been breaking the filters in the dam, which is
why stuff kept getting into the system and breaking
things. At least that was the impression I got from her.
But the part that made her win was when she had to
swim down there and argue with it.

"I kid you not. I'm down there in the water with a
tank on my back, glaring at this thing that looked like a
Tirsane wanna be. She was pissed that we weren't
letting the water flow freely. I was trying to figure out if
I should fight her, talk to her, or call you." She laughed,
pointing her fork at me.

"Why me?" I protested. "What would I do? Sable's
the one with Water, not me."

"Ah, but you're scary. I thought maybe you could get
her to listen. But then, believe it or not, Carelian saved

me."

~Of course I did. But I don't remember getting wet. And I assure you, I would remember getting wet.~ Carelian didn't even lift up his head.

Jo snorted, then grinned fondly at him. "You let us practice mindspeech with you. So I tried it. I didn't think it would work, but I didn't know what else to do. And she freaked out. Completely stunned I could talk. We were down there a while and I promised her that I'd see if there was a water place in the realms she could get to, which I'll have to ask Esmere about, and she agreed to stop breaking stuff once I explained what the dams actually did. I tell you, I didn't know if I was going to make it up here again." She took a swallow of her margarita.

"Why? She was attacking you?" My mind whirled as I tried to think how I could have rescued her.

"Nah. I was running out of oxygen. Man, that chica acted like it had been years since anyone talked to her. I promised an answer next week, so Carelian, can you ask you *mami* for some help?"

~As I was the impetus for you to gain this ability, of course.~ The smugness in his tone had all of us giggling. Even Charles seemed to be fighting chuckles.

~Cori, I am on fire!~ The words pierced my brain, and I convulsed in pain as they seared into me.

"Hamiada? What?" I asked, swallowing through the pain. I recognized her voice, but I had to fight to concentrate as her panic lashed at me.

~Help,~ she begged, her voice fainter and panic stricken.

I shook off the pain and stood. Carelian already was standing, the sleepiness gone from his posture. "Carelian, can you take them the long way and I'll sidestep?" I asked, imaging the space at the top of the driveway, off the grass where nothing was kept.

~Yes. We will be there in a minute.~ I knew he would open a rip to the Chaos realm, then another one to Albany. It didn't take long, but still longer than I would take. I nodded at all of them and stepped.

The cool night air was tainted with smoke, and a wash of heat drifted across my face. The porch was engulfed, and it was crawling up the outside of the house. I could hear the faint sound of sirens in the distance.

"Hamiada, are you on fire in the back?"

~No, but I burn,~ she wailed, and I winced. Mindspeech cut through your mind like a headache on steroids when the speaker was this upset.

I grabbed hunks of the lawn and flowed them over the biggest flame spots on the ground as I ran for the only hose I remembered seeing. Sable had water, but she needed it available to use it. I cranked it on full bore as I felt a tell-tale flash of pain that meant a rip had formed.

"Keep the water flowing, Cori, I got it." I heard her and sighed in relief. A wave of water rose up and dashed over the flames. And they spread.

I stared, confused at the incongruity. Flames didn't spread from water, they went out. I turned, looking, then I saw a bottle laying on the ground, broken and smoldering. It clicked.

"Merlin's balls, they tossed napalm." I'd spent enough time in the chem lab to know the properties of napalm. Water would just spread it. "Jo move air away from it. I'll keep smothering."

We worked in tandem, Jo depriving the flames of oxygen while I grabbed lumps of earth, moving it over anything near the ground to keep it starved. The firetrucks, the source of the sirens, turned down the street we lived on as we fought to get the flames under control. I struggled to pull enough dirt up to smother flames, yet not damage anything. It wasn't like I could lift up a lump of soil and float it. I had to raise the earth up in a wave and have it crest over the flames. But that meant pulling at earth that structures rested on, like the porch. Moving it around helped, but the damn jelly-like napalm seemed to want to burn.

"Sable, can you convince Fire to go away?"

She made a face. "I've been trying, but it doesn't want to. It finds this all so yummy. Something about both the chemicals and Hamiada has it almost drunk. I've even offered blood, and it takes it, leaves one area and pops back up."

I'd managed to smother most of the fire on the porch, but there were still flames flickering up the walls and to the roof. "Jo, can you create a bubble over the entire house and move the oxygen out?"

She frowned, then nodded. "I think so. Air doesn't like to stay away for very long."

The serial killer air mage must have practiced extensively to keep air away from her victims so tightly. Though removing the oxygen would have been... My brain caught up to my random thoughts as I fought to smother.

"Jo, just keep the oxygen away, or have it bind with..." I raced through easy combinations. "Try turning it to ozone. That's three oxygen molecules, that doesn't feed flame, right?" I asked, desperate to stop the flames.

"You don't ask for easy things, do you," Jo muttered, her eyes narrowed and focused on the fires. I saw a whisper of offering flare from her hair as she stood there. My heart in my mouth, I thought about other things I could do if this didn't work.

The firetrucks came to a loud screaming halt next to

us and started grabbing hoses and connecting to the fire hydrant. We had contained most of it, but the roof still had spots aflame and I didn't want to think about the damage inert napalm was doing to the house.

~Hamiada, are you in pain?~

~Yes, no. Both.~ She responded so fast my head jerked back as if I'd been slapped.

~What can I do to stop the pain?~ I could hear Sable arguing with the firemen, who didn't seem to believe her. A spray of water, so much easier to pull from the air than anything else, slammed into some flames and they just rode it, spreading to another part of the roof.

Argh. Why doesn't anyone ever believe us when we say things?

I honestly didn't know if it was that we were mages, women, or both. But it annoyed the shit out of me more often than not. The chattering behind me increased, but I focused on Jo and Hamiada.

~Stop the fire. I will need sustenance... much later.~

~Got it.~ I looked at Jo. "How's it going?"

"Ozone sucks, it likes to break apart," she gritted out, stress clear on her face. "I can get it to create but it really doesn't want to stay and I'm also trying to prevent it from grabbing onto hydrogen and forming water. That would spread the flames further. I can transform stuff, but right now my options are the elements available. I can't use fire like Sable." Her words were short and sharp and her rings reflected light from the fire.

Rings, joining, wait, I can use both.

Esmere had mentioned it to me, but I hadn't spent much time playing with that aspect of our joining. If ever I was going to, now was the time. I arranged what I wanted to do in my mind. Carelian pressed into my side and I gave him a pet as I tried to pull off something that might not be possible. I created a molecule-thick coating of argon across the house and under the fire. Pulling on Jo's strong in Transform, I pulled in the element to create a shield that wouldn't burn. Then I pulled all the summer leaves toward me with Air, offering recklessly.

Please.

And it worked. Air accepted my plea, but only took a portion of what I had offered up, to my surprise. It seemed I could pull on Jo's abilities at the same level as she could. The possibilities stunned me as I watched my plan tumble into place. The leaves swirled around into a pile across the lawn, even being pulled from around back.

I looked at the fire and dangled food and more hair, not asking them to quit burning, but to change their focus to this easy food and not the house I had protected. At this point the only thing still burning was the jellylike fuel, but there Jo was, preventing an easy burn by removing the oxygen from the air.

There was a moment of pouting from the fire, then the flames leaped from the house to the leaves, which went up in a burst of flames as the hungry fire devoured it. I sagged with relief, as there wasn't a bit of fire on the house that I could see.

~Hamiada, are you still on fire anywhere?~ I waited for a response and tried to gather myself as a firefighter headed toward me. The leaves were almost gone, but Fire seemed to have tired of the game, or knew we wouldn't let it keep burning. A hose was getting ready to be aimed at the embers that were fading fast.

"Ma'am? You the owner of the house?"

"Yes." I faced him and saw the word captain on his jacket.

~I am good. There is much to repair, but you saved me. All of you.~ Hamiada's relieved voice floated through my head at the same time the captain spoke.

"Can you tell me what happened here?"

Hamiada must have heard the question because she answered in my mind and I repeated what she said.

"A car drove by. I didn't see who was in it, just heard it." I substituted heard for felt. Hamiada had felt the vibrations from the engine and their music. "Then there was the sound of a bottle breaking and fire started to spread."

"Do you know how many bottles were thrown?" he asked, staring at the house, not me, his brows drawn together.

"At least three, maybe five." Hamiada wasn't sure, as after the first two, she'd panicked and come screaming for me.

"This isn't something I've seen out here before," he stated, turning to look at me. "How'd you stop the fire?" His eyes flicked to the tattoos on my temple as he asked.

I explained what Jo did and then what I did, but I credited Sable rather than me. I didn't want anyone realizing how strong I was in fire now that we had joined. Getting tested again might be a very bad thing.

He nodded as he stared at the house. "Not bad. Usually we have different methods for the few mages that become firefighters. You can find it listed on various websites if you're interested, but make sure your chemistry comprehension is strong. Most firefighters tend to understand a lot about chemistry." He said all this abstractly, his attention still on the house and the smoldering bits. "We are going to scrape up the remnants of the napalm, and chemically treat everything. The truck with the chem should be here shortly. We'll double check nothing else is still smoldering. You good?"

I nodded my head, suddenly exhausted. Running

away tomorrow for a hike in the mountains sounded like a very good idea. He left, and Jo, Sable, and Charles moved over.

"So what exactly happened?" Jo asked, her voice low, even though we stood far off to the side away from any firefighters or the sheriffs that were making their appearance.

It took a few minutes to explain what Hamiada told me. Jo wrapped her arm around Sable and gave me a worried, pensive look.

"Cori, do you know who did this?"

"No," I replied, shaking my head. Carelian pressed against me, but he wasn't purring, his attention focused on the house. "But to be honest, at this point it could be anyone. The US wants me to hand over the research, China blames me for their dragon going away, and Japan still hates me."

There was silence. Then Charles chuckled. "You know, Cori, I'm starting to understand the nickname you had as a teen. Cori Catastrophe fits. Only you could have three countries pissed at you. Not people—entire countries."

I laughed, a bitter, unhappy laugh. "Great. Not exactly the start I wanted."

Jo gave me a wry smile. "Did you really expect anything else?"

"No, I really liked the daydream. Stupid reality."

Sable pulled me into a hug. "We love you anyhow, even if you are a walking trouble magnet."

"Yeah, but what am I going to do about this?" The question hung in the air long after the police and firefighters had left.

Chapter 30

Section 1.141.4

All passports from other countries and from the US must clearly display the class and branches of any mage above hedgemage. Anyone found counterfeiting this will be held as a rogue mage.

CHAOS

Sunday, Carelian and I sidestepped to a location in the Appalachians, well away from everyone. We'd found the spot on one of our hikes and it was far enough along that there really weren't any people around. Carelian went first to make sure the area was clear, then I followed.

We hiked for about three hours. Well, I hiked, and he chased and cavorted and acted like a kitten again. It felt good to be out in nature and by the time we were done, I'd worked out most of my stress and needed a shower from our effort. After getting home to Atlanta, I pulled open the binder and started to read.

James had wide reaching interests, and the binder was meticulously detailed. Too detailed from what I'd seen of his other writing, and the handwriting looked very familiar. I set that tidbit aside and focused on what he had discovered.

The high point was definitely the ability to create a stable realm, but I needed to find out the details. Something about how it was phrased made me think we had little to worry about. But right now, I needed to get a good idea of everything. He'd discovered the gem that was in the ring on my finger, asterine. It had more than the properties that Esmere noted. It could store memories, act as an amplifier, and was immune to heat. Only a mage could mine or facet it. I grabbed a notepad and started writing the things to not share with anyone I didn't personally trust. This was the first item on it.

I kept reading. The list seemed huge. He had notes on creating memory stones, how to get a familiar, uses for realm plants—some of the medicines might perform miracles. I put that one on a list for me to research. There was a list of creatures and their descriptions, the nature of the elements, at least five rituals that worked every time—though the ingredients needed would only be available to a few (phoenix ash, dragon scales, etc.). He had travel journals about what he found in each of the realms, the history behind familiars from the denizens' point of view, even information about how the realms connected to us, and theories about the Area 51 rips. Things I noted to never let out to common information were re-emergence, pocket realm creation, and stable passages between realms or pocket realms. An interesting discovery was a shield that could only be done in conjunction with water. It basically created a static water wall that no ship could pass through, though it required multiple mages working in concert to keep it up. It would only work if you had a small island, maybe in the middle of a river.

All in all, it was so much information my mind spun. The re-emergence, asterine information, and the medicines went on the list. I sat there staring at it. I knew I needed to talk to Lucille and Jeorgaz, but I needed to head to bed, as I really suspected tomorrow would be drama filled. I stepped back to the glade, Hamiada made sure I could easily access it, and left the binder there. I didn't want to risk anyone breaking in and finding it. If they were willing to burn my house, I didn't think they'd have an issue with breaking into the apartment.

Morning came too early but taking a shower in my bathroom with my products, after sleeping in my bed, and getting to make my coffee helped a lot.

"You coming with me?" I asked Carelian as he lay sprawled on his bed.

~Your work is dreadfully dull, but I do not trust the people you work with.~

"You can sleep under the desk and I'll spring for sushi for lunch?" I just had a bad feeling about today. I didn't have a phone yet that was work issued, and I'd purposefully not even opened my laptop this weekend. I didn't want to know or see what drama was going on.

~Mmm, shrimp,~ he murmured as he yawned, stretching out like he had no bones.

"Show off," I said. "I'm stepping to that corner." We'd scoped a corner out in the break room that never had anything in it. It worked for me to step to, then head out to my cubicle from there.

~Will meet you there in a few. No getting into trouble before then.~

Protesting would have been useless, as we both knew trouble seemed to find me. I grabbed my little shelled briefcase, straightened my jacket and sidestepped. The corner was empty, as was the break room, to my relief. I'd noted most government workers didn't show up at seven, making the odds in my favor, but I probably needed to see if I could find another place. I strode out to my desk, the case rattling faintly behind me. This also had the advantage of not having me walk past Pearl's office.

I sat down, pulled out the laptop, logged in, and groaned as I saw my email. It had been two days over the weekend. How in the world did I have eighty-three emails?

A fortifying sip of my coffee and I dove into my email inbox. At least half were from Human Resources with things I needed to do for paychecks and insurance, all the paperwork that kept the world moving. The others were Pearl issuing edicts, while Scott chimed in. Some of it was normal, discussing strategies, asking who to approach for approval, copying her as a matter of course. But the ones that showed up on Sunday were different.

An email popped in as I read about China's demand, and even in email it was a demand, to meet with us first thing Monday morning. The email was from Pearl, saying she needed to talk to me as soon as I got in. I considered not seeing it, but decided getting the fight over now was better.

~Carelian, you want in on my meeting with Pearl?~

As an answer I felt a flash of pain, then him dropping his chin on my hand. My nose twitched. "You talked Sable out of eggs, didn't you?"

~She had extra, they would have gone to waste.~

I gave him an arch look, then scratched his head. "Yes, they would have." I pushed myself to my feet. "Come on, the dragon awaits."

~Tiantang is much scarier than her,~ he said pacing next to me.

~Yes, but Tiantang can only kill me. She can get me reassigned to Alaska.~

~I've never hunted a moose. That could be interesting. You should order me moose; I must know how it tastes.~

I refrained from commenting and stuck my head in Pearl's office. "You wanted to see me?"

She jerked her head up and glared at me, her mouth opening. Then she snapped it closed. "Sit. Scott won't be here for a bit."

I walked in and sat. She didn't bother prevaricating at all. "The Chinese refuse to negotiate if you are involved. I'm pulling you off."

A variety of things fought for supremacy in my mind, and I tried not to blurt them out at once. "I saw an email regarding that this morning. I'm not sure that is the right way to go." I said the words slowly, fighting through my desire to throw my hands up and let them do whatever they wanted.

Pearl tapped perfectly manicured nails on her desk. "And why do you think that?"

"They are lying about something and if you keep me there, I suspect it will keep them off balance. And right now the dragon is on my side, if I have a side." That much I wasn't sure about, but whatever it was I thought that my credit with the denizen was higher than the emperor's.

"And what does that buy me?" Pearl sounded curious and scheming. The second was what told me I had a chance.

"I will draw their ire, and the fact that they want me gone means they are probably hiding something. Keep me there as a way to keep them off balance. I suspect Tiantang is chewing on the emperor right now and there might be a change in policy soon." I left it at that. I had no proof of anything else.

Pearl lifted her eyes to the door. "Well? What do you think?"

Scott heaved a sigh and moved all the way into the room. "She still isn't that much use as she doesn't speak any of the languages and Japan refuses to acknowledge her, but it might be worth it to have her in the meeting China wants today. It might prove useful to figure out what they really want, not just what Chun Wen is presenting." His former excitement had faded, leaving him back with his flat monotone. Listening to him talk was like listening to someone droning on.

With effort I brushed that away. "See what comes out of the meeting today." I didn't mention Carelian. There was no reason to give up that secret.

Scott looked at his watch. "They wanted it first thing this morning, as someone from China will be on the call. We should go now."

I nodded and rose, making a quick stop at my cube to grab a notebook before following Scott. Carelian yawned again, and I hissed at him. He was making me tired. He whipped his tail at me, smacking my thigh, clearly unrepentant.

We were at the conference room first, the teleconference linked up but blank. I hid to the side like a good peon and this time I just waited, wanting to see. Carelian had slunk under the table so he could see the people coming in. Scott fussed with his computer, trying to look busy, but tension radiated off of him. So I didn't buy his act.

Carelian's tail tapped back and forth on my legs as we waited. They had wanted to meet at eight am. No one showed up until eight-thirty. This was a standard ploy and didn't surprise me. Chun Wen walked in and stopped, his assistant still hiding his face.

"She isn't supposed to be here," he stated, glaring at me.

Scott shrugged. "We wanted to see if we could change your mind. Merlin Munroe has much to offer to any discussion."

~Cori, the human next to the fat one is doing magic. Chaos based; I can taste it.~

I sighed and slid my phone away from me as I pulled up an electro shield. "Please ask your mage to quit casting magic." I tilted my head as I felt it hit. "Disrupt Thought I believe. I thought all mages were to be disclosed and clearly visible." I tapped my temple, easily seen as my hair was back, whereas the assistant never looked up and his hair hit at shoulder length, hiding everything like a curtain.

Scott stiffened. "That is not allowed. I will bring this up to the ambassadors of both countries." His body stiff with outrage.

Chun shrugged and sat down in the chair, looking at us. "They will not care. I have more power than they do."

Scott let go of his anger and sat down as well. "So you are one of the assistant ministers. Trade?" Chun didn't say anything, just watched us. "So what do you want?" The assistant sat up and stared at us for the first time, a tattoo peeking out at his temple.

"We have been talking to Japan and we believe we have reached an agreement with them."

Scott leaned forward. "I was unaware that Japan had reached out to you. This was supposed to be a three-way negotiation."

Chun lifted one shoulder. "We had a common concern."

My stomach twisted as his eyes never strayed from Scott. This would not be good, no matter what.

"Which is? We addressed most of the issues earlier."

The corners of Chun's lips lifted, but there was no amusement in his gaze. "We have concerns with your pet merlin being at the table. Given the rightful enmity Japan feels for her, it seems counter-productive to have her here."

I resisted, bristling and getting pissed. Because he had a point. I had told them Japan would have issues with me, but I needed to try and do my job. In theory,

China had no predisposed issues with me. The thought I was only making it worse made me shrink with guilt.

"Ah." Scott leaned back; his hands calm on the table. "What do you feel we should do?"

"Personally, I think anyone that has offended a foreign government so badly should be turned over to them. They must extract their satisfaction. It is poor manners to throw such things in their faces. It is, how you say - a bad look?"

His voice was smooth as ice as he spoke, shifting his attention to me.

"All of us have our orders. She has value if Japan would only see it. She has much they want," Scott replied smoothly, as if they weren't talking about me like I was a toy someone wanted.

"Much that is mine and not my government's to give," I snapped, glaring at both of them.

Chun smiled that non-smile again and started to answer. I flinched at a stab of pain as Carelian bumped up against my leg. Then the conference room was full of dragon. The red of Tiantang's scales almost glowed as he writhed around in the limited space.

The assistant's eyes widened, while Chun paled, sweat dotting his forehead as he tried to scoot back, but there wasn't anywhere to go.

~Cori, you need to come with me.~ Tiantang's voice rang in my head and the gasps from everyone else told me it was a broadcast.

"Tiantang, I can't just go with you. What is going on?" I tried to sound pleasant, but I nudged Carelian with my foot.

~What is going on?~

~No. You must come now. You must witness.~ His tail went over the desk and wrapped around my waist.

"Wait, witness what?" The words had just finished

when he pulled and we disappeared from the
conference room.

Chapter 31

Section 1.142.5

Familiars of foreign mages are granted the same rights as local ones, no matter how exotic they may be. Any threat to a familiar can be expected to be met with lethal force.

SPIRIT

Being pulled along via a sidestep let me know I really, really, preferred to move myself. I fought dizziness and kept my eyes closed until I thought I might not fall over. I could feel Tiantang's tail still around me, while Carelian had followed a moment later, and he pressed against the front of my legs while his tail tapped on my thigh. It was rapid enough I knew he was agitated, but that meant not ready to kill.

I forced open my eyes and almost shut them again. I stood in a huge room, with black marble floors laid out in huge squares. Pillars the color of blood rose up to support a ceiling that looked like a thousand tiles, green and brown, while the walls were beige with red detailing everything, except the throne at one end with daffodil yellow cushions. The opposite end had two huge doors in a brighter shade of blood. But that was what I grabbed at a quick glance. My attention was on the people.

The room was not crowded exactly but contained more people than I could count. A face I recognized. The emperor stood on the top of the dais his throne resided on, while around him everyone stared at us. If he could have thrown laser beams from his eyes, I knew I'd be dead.

"You dare?" he snarled. I figured it was Mandarin, but with Carelian seamlessly translating I didn't worry about it. For a minute I thought he was talking to me, but Tiantang rose up, his tail dropping away from my waist. I stumbled a bit, leaning into Carelian's heat and strength.

~I dare. I am the Dragon of China.~

"And I am the emperor!" Everyone was backing away from him, and I felt water being pulled from me. I took a good look at his temple, something I hadn't really bothered with before. Water, Time, and Pattern strong, pale in Fire, and Air. A blasted elemental mage. People were chattering, their language wrapping around me like a dirge.

"I don't think so." I hit him hard with Disrupt Thought and felt my body reabsorb the water he had been pulling out as I broke his concentration. I started to reach for Earth. It was the best way to protect myself and give me the precious seconds I needed to concentrate and step home.

~ENOUGH!~ The mental roar went through my mind, my bones, my soul, and I whimpered, leaning on Carelian. He growled softly and wrapped his tail around me, grounding me.

I really just want to go home.

The people in the room cowered, some kneeling on the floor in various positions of fear and obeisance. The emperor looked shocked, and the three people around him all looked torn between yelling and smiling. It was a weird expression. The same guard types huddled near one of the columns, guns drawn, but they didn't know who to aim at besides me. Personally, I felt like I was the one that should be pointing guns at them.

I gently pulled Earth toward me, the stuff in the air, on the ground, and mixed it with my bioelectric field. It wasn't the best shield, but hopefully it would slow down anything coming at me. So many mages, and most of them looking at me with expressions I could not identify.

China had a type of draft, and all their mages were marked. But what really identified them was they, like the mages in Japan, all had a uniform to wear. The Japanese mages tended to wear traditional kimonos for women and men. In China, they all, except for the royal family, wore a Lanshan in gray with the color stating their primary class: Red for Chaos, Blue for Order, and Yellow for Spirit. The hall was full of mages, and if they were told to attack me, I'd retaliate.

~I have watched the Qing Dynasty for more than a century. My sacred right as a focus is to guide my charge, to help them grow into a mage worthy of Magic. I have failed in my duty. My choice was flawed.~ Tiantang's words flowed into my head and all eyes were locked on him. Well, everyone else's. Mine were firmly on the dais and the dangerous people there. From the looks on the emperor's face and the woman next to him, I might need to start worrying about contracts out on my life again.

"What do you mean your choice was flawed?" The emperor had his arms crossed on his chest and glared at the three of us. The temptation to hide behind Tiantang flashed through me. It still exposed my back to others, but I wasn't sure this wasn't going to break down into a magical firefight.

~I choose the emperor,~ Tiantang stated as he flowed in his glide-walk up to the throne, his face tentacle-whiskers seeming longer and floating out in front. ~And I no longer choose you.~ The tentacles whisked out and wrapped around Qixiang, holding him immobile. ~Corisande Munroe, Magic's Herald, I charge you to witness my disavowment.~

Ah crap.

I stood up straighter and looked at the dragon and the throne. "As Magic's Herald, I so witness." Really there wasn't anything else I could have said. And then Qixiang screamed. It was a sharp short scream, not of pain but horror.

Something pulsed in the air, and color bled from the man's face. Not his face paled, but the color from his tattoos was pulled out and fell to the floor like dust. The whiskers unwound and Qixiang stumbled back, his eyes wide and mouth open, like he was silently screaming.

"What did you do?" The whisper came from one of the people on the dais, but I couldn't even tell the gender of the person who spoke.

~I disavowed him. Magic deemed him not worthy. Now I must choose the ruler of China.~ His voice rumbled through my head like the voice of a god, and I saw more than a few people fall to their knees as he spoke.

A woman pushed her way to the front, the merlin tattoo clear on her face, Chaos ascendant. She had her hair in twists and knots that must have taken hours to style. Her nose was sharp, and she looked too much like the picture of the Mongols that had once ruled the majority of the world. "I am next in line for the throne, as I am the second oldest." Even with Carelian's translating, I heard the arrogance, pride, and avarice in her voice. She reminded me of one of the statues that Hamiada watched over. The look of needing power was the same.

~I think not. You would bring this country to great heights and destroy it in the process. Your grasping need for power is not balanced by mercy or compassion.~ The disdain in his voice would have made me crumble. The woman gritted her teeth and stood up taller.

"It matters not. The Qing Dynasty must continue and I am best to lead it. You can temper me with mercy or compassion." She said the words as if they had a bitter and disgusting flavor."

~True. The Qing must stay. Your father was fertile and your mother fecund. But your father had many concubines.~ The dragon turned, his head panning the crowd. But I kept my eyes on her. What little seen when I'd glanced at the set up for China told me she had to be Huilang, the oldest daughter and the Minister of Magic. Surely she wouldn't start something with Tiantang, would she? Her eyes caught mine, and that glare cut me to the bone. No, she blamed me.

Why is it always me?

~China needs a strong ruler who understands that together we are stronger, who can work with others and yet retain the pride in what makes China great. One that will lead the world to a better state.~ He had stopped before a group of mages. The woman Tiantang focused on wore the double strip of a merlin, Order and Spirit. ~Cixi, step forward.~

There was a gasp through the area and I saw a few heads peek up. This was worse than watching a tele-novella. Who was she, and why was she dressed as one of the mages that served China? I had no idea what was going on, and I couldn't make Jo pause it to explain everything.

A young woman, I figured maybe early twenties as she was a mage, came forward and bowed, her eyes darting to the collapsed emperor, or was it former emperor, on the floor and the incandescent Huilang.

"Yes, honored Dragon of China?" Her voice didn't quaver, and I gave her points for that.

~I choose you to be the Child of Heaven, to lead China to greatness.~

There was a soft murmur of words that didn't sound polite. The woman, Cixi, dropped to her knees, her head touching the marble floor in front of the dragon.

"Great Dragon of China, I am but a daughter of a concubine. I am not of the royal family." Her protest sounded terrified and if she could see the looks being cast her way, she had a right to be.

~Your father was Zhenhui. That makes you of the Qing dynasty. You and your children will lead China to the next great adventure.~

"She is not worthy!" Qixiang had managed to get to his feet and the age difference between them surprised me. Qixiang must have been in his late fifties. I revised my estimate of the woman. She might be in her thirties. Their father must have been active late.

Tiantang turned his head to stare at the man, mage no longer. ~I say she is worthy. I am the Dragon of China and I choose.~

"Guards, kill them!" Carelian tensed as he translated this, and I snapped up my dust and bioelectric shield, expecting a hail of bullets.

"No!" Cixi had sprung to her feet, protecting the dragon with her body. "No one may harm him." Her face glowed with conviction. The guards had guns up and were wavering, their ruler, the challenger, and the others, all pulling at their loyalties.

"Cowards. I am the emperor." Qixiang grabbed one of the guard's guns and pointed it at the dragon and even I knew he was about to pull the trigger.

"The Dragon of China is China!" Cixi almost screamed that and I sensed, or felt, or maybe it was tasted, the magic snap out of her. The bottom half inch of her hair vaporized and Qixiang gasped, eyes wide, then he just crumbled like a puppet with his strings cut.

Cixi stood straight and proud. "No one will threaten him while I breathe." The room had fallen completely silent and everyone stared at the girl.

~And this is why I choose you.~ He leaned down, his whiskers wrapping around her, and he breathed on her upturned face.

My tattoos had been put on by the office of the OMO, and I thought they did that here too. But as I watched hers changed. Before, she had been strong in Pattern and Soul as a merlin, now Transform went from pale to strong. I frowned, then remembered that a familiar not only lowered your costs, but gave you another strong. I reached up to touch my vivid tattoo. I had more than anyone else and frankly it would have been nice some days to not be so odd, but I wouldn't give up Jo, Sable, or Carelian for anything.

~It is done. Long live Empress Cixi of the Qing Dynasty.~ Tiantang's voice rang through the great hall.

All around them people were kneeling and bowing. I kept my eyes on the dais. The body of Qixiang lay there, a crumpled heap of flesh. The ministers shifted and kept glancing at Huilang. Her face was an impassive mask. Then she bowed deeply to Cixi, who stood looking more than a bit bewildered.

"Long live the empress."

That was the trigger and everyone else bowed, and the ramifications hit me. A dragon, a realm denizen, had just changed the leader of a country—had he changed it to a maternal lineage as well?

~Tiantang?~ I whispered, having no desire to speak out loud, not as the only foreigner witness to this. I'd be happy if they forgot I was ever here, though from the smoldering hate in various eyes I doubted that would ever happen.

~Yes, Herald?~

I resisted growling. This smacked of Tirsane and Esmere corrupting him, but I let it be. ~If you are done with me, I really think I would like to return.~

~Ah, yes. Thank you for your time. This was important and I promise to explain later.~

~Please?~ I let it go and poked Carelian. ~Ready?~

~Very. Meet you in the break room.~ I started to say yes, then thought about it.

~Can you check out the conference room? See if there is a safe place for me to step. I'd like to make it look like Tiantang returned me, and keep me doing this easily confidential.~

~Yes.~ He disappeared and a minute later an image popped into my head.

With a deep breath, I sidestepped away from the drama into chaos.

Chapter 32

Section 1.142.3b

All staff to diplomats must declare their status; however, those that never leave the boundaries of their embassy are not required to make declarations. Emergences that occur while on embassy grounds are exempt from testing.

ORDER

People were yelling, security was there, and the doors were thrown open. I stumbled a bit and hit the wall. Stepping that distance without an emotional spike was harder than I thought. Half the room spun to look at me, guards with guns drawn; the rest jumped away from me.

Silence fell as we all stared at each other. It wasn't broken until Carelian jumped up on the conference table and started grooming his balls. That had everyone relaxing a bit, and Pearl and a vaguely familiar man headed my way as everyone else stared at me then started to exit the room, half of them on their phones. By the time they grabbed me and sat me in a chair, most of the room was empty except for the security man, Pearl, Carelian, and Scott. He was at the far side of the room staring at his computer, but if he actually saw anything I'd be surprised.

"Lorison is on his way here. Explain what happened," Stiver ordered, and I stared at him until I recognized him from when I got my badge.

Merlin, was that only a week ago?

I licked my lips, exhaustion slamming into me.

"What did you see?"

Pearl and Strivent looked at each other, then over at Scott. "Yang, get over here," the lieutenant ordered.

Scott closed his laptop and moved over, his gaze even more stiff and jerky than usual. His eyes were glazed over, and he sat down staring at nothing.

"Repeat what you saw." The crisp order came from Pearl this time, but my eyes were on Scott, alarm bells going off in my mind.

"She was there, then the dragon. It filled the room. Then it grabbed her and was gone. As was she and her cat. They were just gone, poof." His words were mechanical even for him.

"Now explain-" Strivent started. I held up my hand, still watching Scott.

"Have neither of you two noticed he is in shock?" Scott sat there, his breathing shallow, and I could see his skin was getting gray.

They turned to look at him. "Oh, for Merlin's sake," Strivent muttered and was on his phone. "I need a med team up here, stat. Shock reaction to magic."

Pearl groaned and rubbed her temple. I think she might have glared at me if she wasn't dealing with this emergency. I watched Scott until med personnel showed up, and took the time granted to gather my thoughts and make sure I understood the ramifications of what I'd seen.

~Can all focuses make someone a mage?~ I sent to Carelian. ~If I piss you off, can you take my magic away?~

~You are a herald. I can't do that.~

I kept my head down, resisting glaring at him. Having anyone guess I was having an argument with him would be counterproductive. ~If I wasn't a herald, could you? Could Jeorgaz have made James a non-mage?~

Carelian focused very hard on hind paw, the noise of his grooming a counterpoint to the EMTs' chattering.

~Carelian!~ Mentally shouting was hard, but this changed everything if it was true.

He glanced up at me and curled into himself a bit. ~Tiantang was rash. It should not have been public like that.~

I pounced on that bit of information, feeling rather like a Cath myself. ~So familiars or focuses can grant and remove magic?~

~No. Yes. In a way.~

~Carelian!~ I managed to hiss his name, but then Pearl and Strivent were headed back in my direction. ~We will finish talking about this at home.~

He slunk off the table and disappeared under it. I suspected he was talking to Esmere or others, but this time I would not let it drop.

"So the dragon grabbed you, and...?" Strivent said as he dropped down in the chair next to me.

I took a deep breath and stuck to the barest facts. "I think he pulled me to China, the royal palace, as the Emperor and the people I think make up his court were there."

"China?" they asked almost as one.

I shrugged. "I didn't check my GPS or go outside and look, but it looked like China, as did the people." They grunted and waved me to go on. "He said he would choose a new emperor and drained the magic from Qixiang."

"He what?" Pearl blurted, her face paling.

"Oh, it gets better. He, being the dragon, drained the magic, refused to choose Huilang, and instead he chose the child of one of the concubines to be the next emperor— empress? A female. Qixiang then tried to kill us or them, not really sure who he was going to kill, and the new empress, Cixi I think, killed him. Tiantang then chose her and filled in one of her branches. She is now strong in Soul, Pattern, and Transform." I swallowed and held up a hand before they could say anything. "The really surprising part is the Dragon of China," I said it like that purposefully so they could get the impact, "announced her children would be the rulers of China."

Pearl looked poleaxed, while Strivent looked a bit confused. "What is the big deal about that? I thought China had always followed the royal family."

It took a minute for Pearl to respond. "They have, but always through the male line. If the Dragon supports this, China might become a matriarchal society or government."

Strivent shrugged. "Okay. So why did he want you?"

There weren't any mages in the room so I went with the simple truth. "He wanted me to witness it because of my status. He knew me." I hoped they'd assume I meant my double merlin status or State Department employment.

They both seemed to accept it, though I thought Pearl was more wrapped up in what this change actually meant than hearing what I said.

"And you aren't harmed?" Strivent asked.

I thought about that answer carefully. "Harmed, no. Stressed, exhausted, a bit off balance, but there was no harm done to me." At least as long as I didn't count my shattered patience and understanding of my place in the world.

Lieutenant Strivent sighed and snapped his notebook closed. "Ms. Takishi, as she wasn't actually abducted by the government and she was returned within an hour unharmed, I do not know what you want me to do. Even if you decide to lodge a formal complaint to China that is more in your arena of power than mine."

Pearl looked up from the table, glanced at me, then at the lieutenant. "I agree. For now it's best if we let this go. There will be enough fallout once the ramifications of this leak out. And right now I suspect we are the only non-Chinese nationals who know. So I'm not spreading the news." Her voice was flat, and she stared at me.

"Not like I know anyone important who would understand the consequences," I said, as opposed to promising anything. I would be talking this over tonight with my friends and family but who would we tell?

She grunted and went to stand.

"Pearl?" She paused and looked at me. "Where is Chun Wen?"

"He was here when you were taken?" she asked, an odd note in her voice.

"Yes. We were talking about how I should not be involved. Something about a bad look."

Pearl stared at me and shrugged. "I'm not going to worry about it now. There is no telling what his new master will want." She heaved herself to her feet and lumbered to the door. "Take the rest of the day off. Keep your mouth shut. See me when you get in tomorrow." The conference room doors shut behind her as she said the last words.

I stared at the wall and thought about his lie and Huilang's anger. I wasn't sure the emperor was his master. And I doubted Huilang was going to take this setback lying down. I needed to talk to Carelian and everyone else to figure out what to do. If anything. I couldn't really save the world, and most days I didn't think the world wanted to be saved.

"Let's grab my stuff and get home. We have a lot to talk about," I said to Carelian, my voice laden with meaning.

He chuffed as he slunk out from under the table. ~You will not like it.~

"This does not surprise me. Come on." Fifteen minutes later we were back at the apartment. I had changed into something much more comfortable. It was only eleven thirty; it seemed much later. I got some sweet tea and settled down in my chair in my bedroom and stared at him. Carelian was sprawled out, pretending not to care, but his tail gave him away; it rat-a-tatted on the floor at a frantic pace.

"Can you cause a person to emerge?"

~Me personally? No.~

"Carelian," I warned, my stress bubbling at the back of my mind.

~I can't. I was never given to Magic. I just didn't want to be like the litters before. Either dead or hunters that never bothered to use their brains or magic because it was too much work. I forced...~ His tone changed and his entire body went limp. ~I saw the opening near you and I chose. It is possible. I just didn't know when you choose after an initial emergence and come from the realms at the same time it can trigger one. The problem is, you should have never been merely a merlin.~

"What?" That made no sense to me. Merely? Merlin was more power than I knew what to do with.

~You were chosen early to be a herald. Heralds have all the branches in all classes. You should have been that. But I sensed you when I searched for a mage. I wanted your fire, compassion, your empathy. I wanted to be better than my siblings.~ He didn't look at me. In fact, he'd rolled over so he couldn't see me at all.

I parsed what he said. "And the other familiars?"

~Those that are gifted to magic watch and find a soul they resonate with. They then can force an emergence with their appearance.~

It felt like I was dragging the information out of him.

"Gifted. You mean like those babies during the trial?" The colossal mistake I had made thinking "sacrificed to magic" meant "killed". Especially my mind caught on the gorgon looking up at me. "Someone can have a gorgon as a familiar?"

~Eh...,~ he murmured. ~Generally, those that are magic and humanoid simply become lords like Esmere given enough time. The gorgon would probably work with Tirsane in a century or two, while the Cath and Chitterian would become familiars, though I suppose it is possible for a human to get a gorgon familiar, though unlikely. The human mage would die of old age before that child became old enough to speak.~ He sounded thoughtful, but that didn't answer my question.

"Carelian?" I prodded, and he flinched, his tail lashing harder.

~Yes. If we try hard enough, we can choose someone and the act of us entering this realm can nudge them to emerge if they already had the ability to become a mage.~

"Are you ever wrong?"

~I suppose it is possible, but I am unaware of that ever happening,~ he demurred.

"So Tiantang can really pull magic from someone? Even though he wasn't Magic Gifted?" I tried to balance it all in my head and Carelian growled. I thought I heard a whisper of words in my mind that sounded like "stupid dragon," but wasn't sure.

~There are focuses, and then there are focuses,~ he finally said. As he spoke, he curled up tight in a ball and I suspected he was getting ready to pretend he was too tired to talk.

"And what does that mean?" I demanded, exasperated. There were days where I didn't know if I was treading on religious taboos or state secrets. It was about to drive me crazy.

He lifted his head and gave me an incredulous look. ~I know I am impressive and magnificent, but I don't compare either in magic or prestige to a dragon, a phoenix, or a unicorn. All of them are cross-realm beings. Cath, all felines really, are Chaos. All canids are Spirit, all insects are Order as are most avians. But those three, and few others, are all realms. They are, for lack of a better word, merlins by nature. At best I am a wizard by your ranking. My link with you, being your focus, lifts me up as I lift you. But those~—he paused and buried his head under his tail—~those are ... our superstars.~

I fell silent and let him be. I had much to think about and no clue what it meant for me or mine.

Chapter 33

Section 1.2

Serving in the draft is regarded as similar to military service and all mages, magician and above, are held to it. They shall be notified upon testing as to their status and a draft officer will be assigned to monitor them.

CHAOS

Being home so early, I decided I could cook, but I sent a message to ask Charles to come over. Something he had mentioned in passing made me want to ask more questions. I told him to bring his laptop. Since even now my ability to cook was basic—I might not cast a Murphy's Cloak anymore, but I still managed to make every mistake and mess possible—I went for something simple. I had steaks marinating and ready to cook and salad and potatoes done by the time everyone showed up.

"Hey," Jo said as she walked in, looking less worn out than last week. "You're home early." I made a face, and she paused. "Uh oh. That look means nothing good."

"It means a story when everyone is here," I responded.

She gave me a sideways look, then scanned me up and down as if looking for wounds. "Well, you seem unharmed, and since you aren't in hysterics, I assume our favorite Cath is fine."

I rolled my eyes. "Just for that, you can cook the steaks. Go. And yes, I have one ready for him so you can sear it and he'll be happy."

Jo winked at me and headed back to shower and change. While she wasn't covered in mud this time—really, how did she end up in a job where she got to wear jeans and boots all the time?—she was still dusty and hot.

Sable showed up a few minutes later, also wearing jeans, though a nicer shirt. "Cori! Ooh, potatoes. Yes." Then she paused and looked at me. "Ah, story time tonight." She glanced at the table. "And Charles is coming. Okay, I'll put on real clothes."

"Oops, tell Jo that, I forgot." Both of them had a tendency to wear as little as possible at home, meaning short-shorts and a tank-top. There was no reason to flaunt skin in front of Charles. He was a friend, not someone to tease.

By the time they emerged Charles had arrived. The small indoor grill was heated up, the table set with everything else, and we laughed and talked as Jo seared everything to perfection. Carelian's was raw, of course. We'd taken to keeping mealworms in the fridge and Arachena was more than happy to have four of them for her meal.

"Okay spill, Cori. What's going on?" Jo finally prodded as we finished up the last of the steak. Charles settled back to listen while Arachena nestled in the ever-present hood of the hoodie he wore.

I groaned. "You remember that comment about it being between China and Japan as to who wanted to kill me more? I think China is in the lead." I spent the next fifteen minutes explaining everything. When I was done, they all stared at me, then at the two familiars, who I swear were practicing invisibility. Then they looked back at me.

"I really don't know if I should be impressed or horrified," Jo admitted. "Not everyone can add dethroning an emperor to their resume."

"Hey, that was all Tiantang, not me," I protested.

"Yet you were the one he dragged there. Seems to me you're going to get all the glory and the infamy." Jo smirked at me, and I threw my napkin at her. She caught it, of course, and used it to wipe her lips. "So what now? I mean, while it's cool and kinda freaky, I'm not sure how much of a role you're going to play."

That twigged the train of thought about how all of this had to have a puppet master behind it, even if I couldn't figure out why, the only one I could think of was Freedom from Magic.

I turned to Charles. "Remember when we were discussing the various politicians and how they all seemed to be backed by Freedom Foundation?"

He nodded, his light eyes watching me. I could never tell what he was thinking, but where Alixant was all snap judgements and annoyance, Charles was methodical, careful in his thoughts, even more so in his actions.

"I'm wondering if they are more than we think." I spoke slowly, still trying to work my way through everything. "Is there a chance they are behind Freedom from Magic too? And have they been getting unexpected funding lately?"

Charles gave me a funny look. "I have info on that. Let me grab it." He got up and grabbed his laptop from his bag. Sable and I cleared the dishes while he connected and logged in. We cleaned the kitchen while he typed away.

"So get this. Freedom Foundation is a non-profit, so they have to report their donations and income from any fundraisers. In the last fifteen years, they have had multiple donations from anonymous donors all for between five and nine thousand dollars each time, multiple times a month."

"And what does that mean?" I didn't have a clue, but from the look on his face, I thought it must mean something.

"There's lots of laws about this. But if I understand it correctly, if it is under ten thousand, they don't need to report who it is. And since they are all anonymous and probably come from different accounts..." He shrugged. "I'm a data person, not a tax law person, but that's what I've heard. So I find it odd they have so many donations that are under that amount."

I sat back thinking about it, but it didn't really tell me anything. "I don't suppose you can tell me where the money is from."

"Not without a warrant and a lot more access," he said looking at me. "And I'd much rather not end up in jail," he said dryly.

I raised my hands in surrender. "Agreed. I just don't understand any of this."

"Well, lay out the parts," Sable suggested. "What do we know? Maybe then we can figure out who to take it to. Because as much I love being a crime fighting team," she made air quotes as she talked, "I don't really think there is some guy running around in a mask we can pull off."

I snickered. "No, probably not. Okay, I can go over what I know. But I'm leaving out the stuff about familiars and Magic as a force. I don't think it's part of this conspiracy. Or more accurately, if it is, we're all in big trouble and should prepare to die."

They snorted at that, and I got up to grab a notebook. I wanted to write it down to see if that made it clearer in my head. I talked and wrote at the same time.

"We know there is a concerted effort both by our government and by someone else to kill mages, preferably before they have kids." Just saying the words out loud gave me chills. "We know Japan wants something in Wells' research, but not what. China has a minister of magic that may or may not be involved. We know Freedom Foundation supports the majority of senators in office."

"And representatives. I checked, they all have significant donations from FF," Charles interjected and I added that to my list.

"What else do we know?" Jo was leaning forward and staring at the list. "I don't know if them trying to twist the draft is separate or part of the killing mages aspect. And why is Japan involved in the treaty? Is the medicine they came up with that good? Why have a treaty for it? Why not just sell or patent it?"

I sat back, thinking. "That is a very good question. Medicine gets patented all the time. Why not just patent it? If you didn't want to share, you have years to sit on it or charge a fortune."

"Japan controls all their mages?" Sable asked.

"I think so. The Empress's Handmaidens for the women, and the Emperor's Servants for the men. Why?"

"Well, if mages developed this working for the emperor maybe they don't follow the normal rules?"

I shrugged. It could be. I looked at the list. "It really doesn't seem like much. I mean, we have the numbers and know they are real. But everything else is a conversation Carelian overheard and what Tiantang told us. Which could be things that were misinterpreted or even code for something else. If someone brought this to me I'd shrug and say life sucks, people die." I paused. "Okay, I wouldn't say that, but other than my fear, there isn't anything to act on. And the numbers are just that— numbers, not proofs of murder or anything else." I sank back with a sigh and stared at it. "Am I making things up?"

The three of them all stared at my paltry list. "No, I don't think so," Charles said when the silence had almost become uncomfortable. "While the Draft Board manipulating you is one thing, it isn't illegal, and I'd be very surprised if it didn't happen on a regular basis. Remember I said I needed my notes? You asked me about who backed the Freedom from Magic group. Well, I did some research and found out that they are actually under FF. And that took a lot of digging. But what is really interesting is that FF has been around since about 1875 and the president of that organization was a senator, one Claude Beaumont, and he sponsored the No Mage Official law."

We all looked at him, then back at the information I'd listed. "Really? We doing conspiracy theories?" Jo asked, frowning at the paper. "I get people not liking us because we can use magic, but really, for most of us we don't use it that often." Jo looked around, frowning and thinking about it. "I mean, I use it at work, quite a bit, but it is structured and specific, things that to do any other way would be really expensive or hard." She must have seen our questioning frowns, because she clarified. "If something breaks in the dam in crawlspaces or even where there is a tiny amount of clearance, to do it manually we'd have to pull it all apart, then patch it up. We are talking many feet of concrete, making a space big enough for a human to get into, possible flooding. It could be really bad. But instead, I go down there with backup," she said that strongly, glaring at Sable who smirked at her.

There was a story there, one I didn't know. I added it to my figure-out-at-a-later-point list.

"I run a small camera in there and I can transform it back to whatever was needed before it broke. So for half

279

an inch of hair I save millions. It's one of the reasons so many public works budgets are so low."

Sable nodded. "She's right. I do similar things, and the filtration system I designed needs a mage to run it, but still, for tiny offerings it cleans water up at pennies on the gallon instead of dollars."

Jo nodded at Sable. "But here? At home?" She looked around. "I think I've seen Sable use her magic to light a candle or heat up the massage oil. I occasionally will pull heat out of a drink to cool it, but otherwise I rarely use magic at home. Most mages are like that. We use it at work because we are taught to, but cooking?" She shrugged. "If I think it needs to cool down faster I might have Air rush across it, but it's just as easy to put it in the fridge for ten minutes. Why fear us when outside of work we almost never use it?"

We all fell silent, looking at my notebook and then each other.

~I know not if it matters,~ Carelian said and from the way everyone stiffened I knew he'd spoken to all of us. I turned to look at him. He lay on the floor, close enough to see us easily, but not so much we would bump him getting up from the table.

~Tiantang and I talk. He says Huilang lies. Not to Cixi, but her words, while true, are not honest. Her anger is palpable, but he has not called her on it. Cixi is worried, but she can't change anything yet. It will take time to have her power base solidify and Huilang has sat in this position like a Chitterian on a web for decades.~

The images of the angry woman I'd seen plucking strings and manipulating things struck me as wholly accurate, if not creepy.

"Any idea what she is manipulating?" Charles asked.

Carelian flicked his tail. ~Everything, nothing. Humans care about things that make little sense but she still doesn't realize that all familiars speak all the languages. She has mentioned something about changing the world for the new year. She is also very close to the trade minister. Tiantang says he thinks they are having sexual relations.~

The way he delivered the information made me smile, but what it implied worried me.

"I swear, Cori," Charles said, leaning back and giving me a long level look, "you managed to either stumble across a conspiracy involving high-ranking politicians and multiple countries or a bunch of players that have nothing to do with each other. And not a darn thing we can do about any of it. You're right. No one would look at what we have and do anything."

I sighed and tapped my fingers on my water glass. "I get what China wants; I think. I see what FF wants. But what does Japan want?"

"To be left alone," Sable murmured.

"What?" My head jerked up at that. "What do you mean?"

"Japan was always a bit xenophobic. Anything not of their culture and people was to be regarded with fear. I remember being in Okinawa with Dad and the way they just pulled away from him and me. I don't look much like my mom, and they always treated all of us like we were wild animals that might attack at any moment. I think Japan would be happier if they were isolated from the rest of the world."

That thought stayed with me for the rest of the evening, though we didn't come to any decisions. That thought wouldn't go away.

Section 1.3.2

While serving under the draft, all mages are expected to hold themselves to the highest level of morality. Misdemeanors and infractions may carry heavier penalties.

SPIRIT

I spent the evening flipping through the binder, trying to get my head wrapped around the sheer breadth of what James had researched. Some of them were a few notes and something along the lines of "Well, that was a dead end." And there wasn't anything else. Others seemed like he had spent years on it. How old had he been?

The one with the most research was something he called a water wall, that he had used mostly as an amusement when he hiked, but he had put a lot of work into it. Most of his notes had reams of comments. This particular invention had reams of math. I glanced at them, curious. This was a created spell or effect I guess, but only a merlin with Water, Air, and Entropy could do it. That limited it to a few merlins, though I didn't see why multiple archmages working together couldn't do it. But the math and the offering would be complicated. Keeping it up for an hour or even a day wouldn't be an issue. But if the math was correct, most mages would be out of available offerings in a few months.

Morning came too early, and I slipped an extra thermos of coffee in my bag. I wasn't up to their pod coffee today. Carelian said he'd be there later unless I called, and he curled back up. Though I suspected he planned on visiting his mother and others today.

Either way, I sidestepped in at my normal time, but the office was empty. I liked it empty. I settled down and pulled up the information on China, along with training videos I was getting nagged about watching. I watched the videos, but I thought more about the problems and if there really was one. I had to believe there was. Percentages didn't increase that much without a cause.

I glanced at the clock and frowned. It showed 8:03. The office was still quiet. While I normally was here a bit after seven, usually Pearl beat me in or was here a minute or two later. While two weeks wasn't much time to establish everyone's patterns, I found this unusual. A moment of doubt hit me and I double checked the calendar. Nope, it was Tuesday.

I shook my head and started up one of the harassment videos again when the loudspeaker went off over my head.

"Cori Munroe, if you are in the building please call ext. 311. Repeat; Cori Munroe, please call extension 311." It was a woman's voice, but I could hear the tension in her voice.

What in the world? Why didn't they just call my desk?

I hit pause on the video and picked up the phone, dialing the extension. "Yes?" a tense voice answered, not the same one that had spoken over the loudspeakers.

"This is Cori Munroe?" I had no idea what was going on.

"Oh, good. Please come down to the lobby immediately." Her voice changed to relieved, then stressed again.

"Is there an issue?" I asked, confused and looking for

my phone.

"Just come to the lobby immediately, Merlin Munroe," she snapped, and I could now hear fear in her voice.

"Leaving now." I hung up, made sure my phone was in my pocket and my badge was clearly clipped. Just in case, I grabbed my coffee and topped it up. This sounded like caffeine might be needed.

The emptiness of the building registered as I headed to the elevators and they opened for me and I stepped in, enjoying the smooth downward flow. The doors slid open and two guards were standing there, guns drawn, pointing at me.

Freaked out, I reached, pulling Luck over me as I added moisture to their primers, something I'd been practicing, and slammed my back against the wall so I wasn't immediately visible. I started to grab for electricity to throw at them as I tried to figure out where to go. Stepping seemed the best option. Retreat was always the best option.

"Merlin Munroe, it's okay. This is Lieutenant Strivent. Please come out." The voice was familiar, and fleeing at the moment seemed counterproductive. Still holding Lady Luck tight around me, I stuck my head out. The guards had put their guns away and seemed a bit sheepish. The lieutenant stood there, glaring at me.

"Yes?"

"Exactly how did you get in the building? I checked the records. The last time you swiped in was days ago. But people reported seeing you at your desk, and the log-ins confirm it, but I have no record of you going through security."

Ooops. Merlin, I didn't think about that.

I responded with the super intelligent, "Ummm." Trying to think of a truthful answer. I would have to make very sure from here on out I stepped to a place down the road and walked in, going through security. Now that it occurred to me, I could have caused major problems. That bit of guilt had me hunching a little more in shame.

He shook his head, eyes hard. "I'll address that later. For right now, come with me." He pivoted on one heel with the expected military precision and headed to the front.

The entire situation made no sense, so after double checking no one was pointing a gun at me, I followed. I kept my pace at a steady walk—I refused to scurry—and followed him through into the lobby. Oddly, there still wasn't anyone there besides a few guards, all of whom looked freaked out. In the middle of the lobby, relatively dark due to the tinted windows, he stopped and stared at me.

"What?" At this point I had no idea what was going on and I was about to sidestep out of there, even if it gave away too much.

"Someone wants to speak with you and is refusing to let anyone in until they have."

I looked at him, confused. He glared at me and jerked his arm toward the lobby windows. I followed it and had to focus to see through the tinting, then stopped. On the other side of the glass, in the large area where people would walk up from parking, the metro, or being dropped off, was a large western-style dragon. The dragon's wings were half mantled and I could see people milling about on the other side. A large crowd in fact. And I had a bad feeling I knew who it was.

"Are you kidding me?" I muttered, but a bit too loud.

"I do not joke about stuff like this, and I am absolutely not kidding that I want that blasted dragon off of my entryway!" His face had flushed red, and a vein throbbed in his temple.

~Carelian?~ I sent as I stared at the dragon.

~Mmmm?~ he murmured in a sleepy purr in my mind.

The glare Strivent gave me convinced me I should start moving in that direction. A fortifying swig of coffee didn't help. At this rate I was going to need to go to the higher octane stuff, maybe make my coffee out of caffeinated water?

~Is there a reason that Zmaug is crouched outside my work building?~

~Nope... wait, did you just say Zmaug is there?~

~Yes,~ I whispered as I pushed through the door. The odd tension-filled silence caught me as I went through, but the rush of cars and noise of DC surrounded it. I felt like I was in the eye of a hurricane.

The door clanged shut behind me, and a flash of pain and then pressing heat let me relax a bit as Carelian pushed against my leg. I didn't look down at him, all my attention focused on the dragon whose head was turning to look at me, but I brushed my hand along Carelian's skull, feeling ears laid back and a low rumble that wasn't a purr.

In the dark in Albany, she'd seemed big, maybe the size of an elephant. Sitting here in broad daylight, I could already see news vans on the street. She looked like the size of a Learjet. Her scales of bright green and pink-blue shimmered in the morning heat. Then there were her wings. Tiantang didn't have wings, and Baneyarl's were birdlike, and I'd never gotten a close look at Elsba's. If anything, I'd say they resembled the wings of the manticore, except where his had been the color of peach skin, hers were the color of rubies on a thick skin that at a glance brought to mind neoprene. Though I'd never seen a dive suit that was ruby red.

Either way, you couldn't look away from her. It wasn't just the color or the size or even the teeth that were longer than my forearm. It was everything, majesty, awe, power, beauty, magic. They were all rolled up in this creature and I had no doubt she'd landed here to make a statement. The problem was, I had no idea what statement that might be.

"Zmaug, you wanted to talk to me?"

~Ah, finally you have shown yourself. This place is much changed from the days of kings and knights.~ She looked around. ~It smells much worse and has noise that makes no sense.~

"You could have just-ow!" I glared down at Carelian who sunk his claws into my calf. "What was that for?" I demanded. His claws hurt.

He whispered fiercely in my mind; words meant just for me. ~Cori, do NOT snark off to the dragon that can fry you with a breath!~

I blinked at him as he stared up at me, emerald eyes almost invisible his pupils were so dilated. My attention shifted to Zmaug, who waited, looking at me. Dragon faces don't lend well to human expressions. Cats are much easier to read if you look at their body language, but I swear by Merlin she was smirking at me and taunting me at the same time.

"So, Lord Zmaug, what did you need to talk to me about?" Regardless of anything else I had no doubt she was a Lord, though of Chaos, Spirit, or Order I had no clue.

~My youngest. Though magic may have taken Tiantang before I would have approved, do not think I do not love that dragon.~ Her word had warnings and from the way everyone was looking at us, breath held, I figured they could all hear her responses. But why broadcast?

"I would never think that. The joy you showed when he was found belied that thought ever forming." I wanted to snort at my own speech pattern, but something about Zmaug made you want to be more formal or flowery. News videos rolled and I could see the flash, hear the click of cellphones documenting this. Oh well, people wanted proof there were dragons. This was definitely proof. They were going to blame me. I just knew it.

~That is wise, but I would talk to you in private. I, however, have more manners than my child. Would you be willing to speak to me in private? Your focus of course may attend.~

I looked at all the people around us, watching with avid, hungry eyes. "That would be my pleasure, lord." I switched to mind speech. ~If you do not mind, could you take me with you as opposed to me following?~ I kept the comment private.

She, however, did not keep her response private, and I cringed at the idea of all the people hearing this. ~And how in the realms would you find where I wish to talk to you if I did not open the way?~ Her front arm reached out and claws longer than my forearm wrapped around me. ~I have faith your focus can find you.~ Her hand, paw, something squeezed around me and reality disappeared before I had time to scream.

Chapter 35

Section 95.20

All updates to the OMO must come through approved channels. The relationship between the government and the OMO shall be upheld through the highest level. The penalty for destabilization of this relationship will be extreme.

ORDER

It felt like a sidestep mixed with a planar rip, but I was the one tearing. The need to scream bubbled up inside me, but before I could inhale to scream, it stopped. I stood swaying on my feet; eyes closed as I concentrated on not throwing up.

~That was not nice, Zmaug,~ Carelian all but snarled, and his growl of annoyance was audible as I swayed in place.

~I am not nice. I am tempted to eat her. But then she could not answer our questions.~ I recognized Zmaug's voice and forced my eyes open. My desire to be eaten was nonexistent.

The sky overhead was a reddish gray and I swear there was a volcano smoking in the distance. My feet shifted on the grainy gray-brown dirt where I stood. The lack of moisture in the air sucked away my breath as I fought to believe what I saw. It was the first non-lush space I'd seen in the realms. I figured various creatures would prefer different landscapes. What I hadn't expected was the conclave of dragons perched on rocks, laying on the sands, and sitting up all staring at me.

"Umm," I looked around at the variety of dragons. There had been one assignment in the history of magic about magical creatures, and it had covered the major ones, those suspected but not proven, and dragons. It had talked about wyverns, wyrms, and the differences between Western and Eastern style dragons. There was no proof of any dragon besides the Dragon of China. None of their theories prepared me for the variety of dragons eyeing me like I looked at coffee, deciding if it was edible.

Some were the colors of metals— bronze, gold, copper, steel—but others were the colors of fire or water. I don't think there was a single color in existence I couldn't find in their forms. I had expected them all to have scales like Tiantang or Zmaug, but some had leathery hide, and a few, those higher on the rocks, seemed to have feathers. In any other situation, I would be bursting with excitement and asking questions. As it was, I still expected to be killed any moment.

Zmaug may not have had her claws still around me, but I knew she was right behind me. Her snorts of hot breath on the nape of my neck told me that.

~Carelian?~ I swear my mental voice squeaked, but I was trying to figure out where to sidestep to, either Hamiada or home. But if they followed me and could breathe fire, those points sounded like horrible ideas. I need to get more safe spots. Hawaii on the volcano sounded good, or maybe the middle of the ocean.

I took a shaky breath and tried to decide if I needed to run for my life or bring up Earth shields. At least with all the dirt here I could make myself an igloo. The image of me hiding in a dirt igloo while they tried to cook me made me smile until I realized it would be like a kiln and would just cook me.

~Is this the one?~ An unknown voice spoke, and I

stood frozen in indecision. How much trouble would I get in for killing dragons? Could you kill dragons?

~Yes. She is the one Magic called. Tirsane and Salistra think she is the Herald.~ There was a level of derision there that had my back stiffening. Anger and annoyance cleared up my fear, as usual.

Ah, screw it. They would try to kill me or they wouldn't, but I'm a dragon too!

I turned to glare at Zmaug. "I would like to point out you brought me here. And if you have issues with what Tirsane or Salistra said, I have no issue asking them to join us here and you can take it up with them." I glared at her as I prepared to flee.

There was a collective intake of breath and I reached for water and air. Water didn't like it here, but it existed and if I needed to, I'd suck the moisture out of their bodies and soak the place with it. We had avoided getting tested again after our joining. No one wanted to take the chance the differences could be detected. But I knew I could pull on Water and Air much easier than before.

One dragon perched on a rock rose to his full height and jumped toward me.

~Don't flinch,~ Carelian hissed in my mind.

Locking my knees, I watched the dragon soar toward me. It had scales the color of lava, rippling from red-black to flame yellow from his head and spine down to his tail and claws. The yellow ended where talons black as obsidian jutted out. It landed about five yards from me, kicking up so much dust I called on Air to blow it away from me. There were too many medical studies on what particulates did to your lungs to make me want to breathe in any of that.

It stuck its head toward me. The head alone was more than half my height. The red-black scales around eyes of blue flame would have been stunning if I didn't need to worry about it biting me in half.

~Arrogant thing, isn't it?~ The voice rumbled as if coming from the depths of the earth, and I stared back at him.

"No, not really. But if you're going to accuse me of things that I did not choose, I'd rather have you talk to the people you're really annoyed at."

Zmaug laughed from behind me and a few of the other dragons chuckled. At least two had trickles of flame flickering out of their noses. I wasn't sure if that was cool, terrifying, or both.

~We should just eat her; she would be a small snack prior to hunting.~ I wasn't sure who said that, but it didn't matter.

"What is it with you denizens and eating humans? There will be no eating of me and if you want to bitch at Salistra and Tirsane, Merlin, if you want to include Bob, feel free. I am not in any way, shape, or form responsible for their actions." At this point, I could feel my heart pounding as well as my head.

~What do you want me to do?~ Carelian whispered. ~I can go get Esmere.~

I shook my head a little, my own annoyance had gotten the better of my desire to flee. They could go jump in a volcano if they thought they could push me around just because I was human. I got that enough from humans.

~They know my opinion. Besides, once you are dead, what would they do?~ Zmaug said, and I could hear the challenge in her voice. ~Besides, you are just a mage, a human and fragile.~ The heat behind me shifted, and I moved.

One of the awesome things about this situation was I didn't need to worry about collateral damage, hurting innocents, or property damage. They also, probably, didn't realize I could use Fire and Water too. But it didn't matter.

I flicked my hand at Carelian and I grabbed Time. I set myself out of the flow by about thirty seconds and sprinted away from Zmaug. Carelian had already bounded away in two huge leaps. I raced to him, dropped Time, absorbing the cost with barely a shudder and I did a blast of Disrupt Thought.

As I saw multiple dragons shake their heads, aborting actions, I called Earth. Massive clefts appeared in the ground under the various dragons, and those on rocks had their entire perch drop into the ground. At the same time, I used Call Mineral, latching onto iron, and offered a full inch of hair to have it go straight down. We had discovered years ago that most of the denizens had blood with iron in it. But pulling these minuscule amounts took a lot of offering. And I spent it without blinking.

All of this happened in about thirty seconds, making me glad I'd been practicing things to do, and it made it so much easier that I didn't care about all the side effects. Guilt lived with me because it was so much easier to kill than to do almost anything else with magic. There might be offensive magic skills taught to the Rogue hunters, but other than the Soul yank I didn't know a quick way to disable people and I was never sure I wouldn't kill them.

My life would be easier if I was a psychopath.

The thought made me smirk, but I kept my eyes on the landscape and the damage I had just done. They all lay in holes, dirt pulled over them in some cases as the walls of the holes caved in. Low moans and a screech or two broke the silence.

~You dare?~ Zmaug hissed in my mind and I crossed

my arms to stare at her where she struggled in the hole created by my magic, Call Mineral making it almost impossible for her to move.

"You grabbed me and threatened to eat me. Yes, I dare." I was ready to sidestep if I needed to but backing down would do me no good. "And if you keep up this rudeness, I will rip every bit of moisture out of your eyeballs and leave you blind forever." I kept my voice laden with a threat that I meant from the bottom of my soul.

If flame should shoot from her eyes, Zmaug would have roasted me. She started to struggle to get out of the hole.

"I wouldn't struggle too much. I have the iron in your blood pulling down. I haven't told it to rupture cell walls, but I can," I warned her, still a bit peeved.

We were having a glaring contest, and I wondered if my next move was going to be killing dragons or spending my entire life running from them. Either way, the idea sounded sucky.

Laughter, rich, gravelly laughter that sounded like the Earth herself was chortling, rolled through my skull making me flinch. ~Give it up, Zmaug. She won't run or back down. Plus this hole is uncomfortable and I'd like to climb out.~ It was the voice that I was pretty sure belonged to the dragon that was all the colors of lava. I pivoted to see him trying to shake dirt off his head.

"Excuse me?"

~Dragons,~ spat Carelian, the verbal part a long hiss. ~They love to play games.~

~Amusing, coming from a Cath who plays with everything. Pax Corisande Munroe. There will be no more threats. Nor need you fear your existence here.~ Zmaug sounded gentler and more like the dragon I had met the other night, not the one that had been busy terrifying me for the last few minutes.

I glanced at Carelian, who had dropped his butt and sat staring at claws covered in black dust. ~I'm going to need a bath,~ he whined. That told me more than anything to let them go. I stopped calling the iron, something that had been a slow but steady drain on me. I had to keep providing tiny offerings to keep Call Mineral active. Then I had to concentrate to encourage the iron to go toward the center of the Earth, instead of coming to me.

A long sigh of relief and multiple dragons rose out of holes, shaking themselves to clear off the dirt that now covered them. They had been deep in some cases.

I stayed way back, fully prepared to step to Atlanta if I needed to, but Zmaug shook herself free and climbed out.

"Want to start explaining?"

She snapped her wings out once, twice, creating a gust of air that threatened to knock me over, before settling back down. ~Tiantang raved about you and your Cath. I wanted to see if something as weak as a human could truly be the Herald. Tirsane tends to be too accepting of humans. I think it is a repressed desire.~

I arched an eyebrow, but I wasn't about to discuss Tirsane's issues. "And all this was to what? Test me?"

~I expected you to run or cower. The last person was on the ground with his head covered pleading for us not to hurt him.~ She said it the same way I would say the trash hadn't been picked up.

~There was that one a few centuries ago. He at least attacked.~ This was lava dragon again. He'd collapsed the side of his hole into a shallow divot and was laying in it, enjoying it, I presumed.

~True, but the idiot used fire. Outside of the Quetzals, fire is annoying, not much more. Then he screamed and ran into a lava flow.~ Zmaug paused. ~That was greatly entertaining. I had not realized humans could scream so loud.~

I shuddered at the imagery. "That still doesn't tell me what you wanted."

She sat up straight. ~You did me a great boon by finding my son. He is enraptured by the idea of a working partnership with a mage, as opposed to the subservient one he allowed himself be trapped in. Though I understand that was in part due to your Cath talking you up.~ I narrowed my eyes, noting she never said Carelian's name. ~ I will tell you I was both concerned and impressed that you had so captivated his ideals though he talked to you but a short while. That made me want to test what sort of person you were.~ This time she paused and looked around. A shake of her head as she looked back to me. ~Perhaps I went too far?~

"Ya think?" I said dryly, annoyed beyond all belief.

Zmaug snorted and dipped her head once. ~You would have made an excellent dragon. You bow to no one. Are you sure you would not rather have a dragon as a focus? They are much more impressive than a Cath.~

Chapter 36

Section 95.26
The OMO, while a necessary functionary for the draft and managing mages, is not part of the United States government and as such shall have no input on policy or enforcement of policy that is not directly related to mages. Even there they shall be required to work through the designated Draft Board chair.

CHAOS

The sputtering that came from Carelian made me laugh and it broke the tension in the area, though I still wished she could have gone about this another way.

"All of that is fine. But why the huge snag from my work? Merlin, why didn't you just ping me? I could have met you somewhere."

The dragon blinked at me, then glanced at Carelian, then at me. ~It... it didn't occur to me. I was unaware you were pingable.~

That excuse sounded extremely weak. Carelian snorted. ~You mean you wanted to make a big showy scene and remind people that Tiantang wasn't the only dragon. Plus, if word got back to him, he would realize you could command the attention of Cori too.~

~Maybe,~ Zmaug admitted, and I threw my hands up in the air.

"Really? I'm how you're keeping score in competitions among each another?"

From behind me came a familiar voice. "Well, you have to admit, it is working beyond any expectation I had. Why would we stop?"

I stiffened. Slowly I turned to see Tirsane slithering up from a behind a small hillock. She wore nothing but a smile, but her snakes bounced around hissing in a manner that seemed excited. I heard answering hisses from the Quetzals and decided I wasn't going to ask.

"Because I'm not your play toy?" I asked, though I really suspected I was. Shouldn't I be getting paid if I was going to be some reality show contestant?

Tirsane grinned, not maliciously, but in true amusement. "Mine? No. Magic's? Very probably." She shifted her gaze to the black flame dragon. "New look, Onyx?"

He flicked a wing, and more dirt cascaded off. ~It is more comfortable than one might think.~

Tirsane shrugged, her breasts rising impressively. I snickered internally. Here, there weren't any human males or Jo to enjoy the show.

"Have you finished trying to intimidate the Herald?" she asked, coiling up in the sand.

~Trying is correct. Your herald has a sting,~ Zmaug replied.

"If y'all are going to sit around and talk about me like I'm not here, I'll leave," I stated. There were so many other things I needed to do.

~Wait. I did also bring you here for a reason,~ Zmaug said, settling into a very cat-like pose with her feet in front and tail wrapped around while she sat on her hind haunches.

I glared at her. "And that would be? And it was something you couldn't just tell me any other way?" The dragons were now on my snark list. This entire day was going to be nothing but me dealing with the fallout from this. And I already was dreading what I would be dealing with when I got back.

~This was much more entertaining,~ Zmaug

admitted, and she had the same level of concern Carelian would in the same situation—none.

I tossed an offering to Air—being able to use the branches of Jo and Sable's magic was so nice—and blew dirt in her face. "You're right. That is much more fun."

Zmaug growled and blinked her eyes, ignoring the chuckles of Onyx behind her. ~Point taken.~ She shook her head again then sat up straighter. Her size made me swallow. Nerves and annoyance only got you so far when you had a being in front of you that looked like it was the size of a two-bedroom house.

~Since my son was rediscovered, I made it a point to start paying attention to the mages in his sphere. I do not approve of most of them.~

I took that comment with a huge grain of salt as I had no idea what a dragon may or may not approve of. The denizens were not human, and even contemplating their constantly changing morality gave me a headache.

~They want to control the availability of mages across the globe, with their country being the only one with an excess of mages. They believe it will give them a monopoly in various industries.~

This meshed with what I had been figuring out, but I still didn't have anything actionable. There wasn't much I could do, as most countries tried to do that on a regular basis.

~To that end, they have pogroms running to eliminate mages in most countries. Yours, Russia, Australia. And they talk of a new event that will gut the United States and make them the premier country for mages in your world.~

A shiver ran down my spine at that. "I don't suppose you have proof?" Not that I knew what to do with that information if she did have proof.

~No. Only overheard whisperings.~

"And why would Zmaug, Clan Leader of Dragons, care about the machinations of the human world?" Tirsane asked. I had to admit I was curious about the answer to that question as well.

~My son lives in that world. I would see him be happy and healthy there.~ I looked at her in silence, and so did Tirsane. I don't think either of us bought that answer. She huffed, and a trail of smoke trickled up out of her nostrils. ~And I dislike the idea of magic being so under one nation's control. Magic does not do well when her vessels are constrained so much. Atlantis is a warning to us all.~

Tirsane flinched and her arms dropped down to her sides. "True. If that is what is coming, it is right you have warned the Herald. I should not have suspected you."

Onyx snorted this time. ~Yes, you should have. Zmaug is a devious egg-layer. Which is why I chose her all those seasons ago. Who wants a boring predictable mate?~

I smiled as Zmaug preened and flicked her tail at Onyx, whacking him on the nose at the same time.

"Cori, can you prevent this?" Tirsane asked. I bit back the urge to scream.

"Unless I have proof, no. And even then, this is another country we are talking about. I have no ability to do anything." Tirsane glared at me and I suppressed a flinch. Her face had approached the beauty that turned people to stone and I couldn't help the fear. But I channeled it and glared back at her.

"I can't. Me rushing in and trying to kill the people behind this would just get me and then a lot of other people killed. And I don't know who is leading this. The Chinese plan for decades, centuries even. So does Japan. I can warn people but they are going to ignore me without evidence."

~They are talking about an event,~ Zmaug interjected into our staring contest. ~That they want to set it up so that they will prove their supremacy, make their rivals look at fault, and guarantee their hold on mages.~

I chewed that over, but event could mean anything. "Is there anything else you can tell me?"

Zmaug tilted her head one way, then the other, as if listening to multiple voices. ~They said they have virus samples.~

I froze. "They said what?"

She gave me a look and continued. ~But they want to hold them until the treaty has been completed. That Japan will look guilty, not them.~ She shook her head. ~I do not know if this is important. All rulers plot and scheme. I do. What are virus?~

My mind raced as I tried to figure out the ramifications of that. Why push for the treaty if they already had the virus? "Virus is the tiny lifeforms that cause sickness on Earth." That was as simple as I could put it; I wasn't about to get into exactly what a virus was.

Onyx's voice filled my mind. ~Much of what they said means little to us. But the way they said it, the hushed tones, the tiny meetings, even those they kill when spotted. We have watched humans for eons, and know to ignore their squabbles about mating, but it sounded important with how furtive they were, how much they hide their conversations.~

"How do you listen in?" I wasn't a hundred percent sure I wanted to know, but at this point I was grasping at anything that might help make sense of this mess.

~We have started creating micro rips and we take turns. Now that we know where he is we will not lose him. We mostly listen around Tiantang. I will make sure he is safe there. While we are hard to kill, it is not impossible. Mages, if they are ruthless enough, can kill us easily.~ She nodded at me with an odd level of respect.

I sighed. "I don't know if that makes it better or worse. It means that anything you overheard could have nothing to do with this situation or everything. For all you know, they could have been talking about a video game or a movie."

Zmaug shrugged her wings. ~Truth.~

I scrubbed my face with my hands, glad I pretty much never wore make up. It would have been running down my face by this point with the heat and my own stress. "Thank you," I said finally. "But next time, could you just ping me and say you want to talk?" I almost begged, but I shot Tirsane the same pleading look.

If I had thought dragons could blush, I might have thought Zmaug was. But she rose up, stretching her wings wide. ~We will protect our own. And as always, we are Magic's servants.~ It was said with an aura of ritual. She stood and pushed off, clearing my height with one leap before her wings beat and she gained height, stirring up dust. I pulled on Air to keep it away from me.

~Don't mind her. We will let you know.~ Onyx stood, stretching. ~It is time to go hunt.~

I looked around the area. "This is not your home?"

Onyx laughed. ~No, simply a sunning area. The heat feels wonderful. Be well, Cori Munroe.~

As if his words were a signal, all the dragons in the area launched themselves into the air and started beating their way through the sky, following Zmaug.

I watched them go and then turned to Tirsane. "So you are here why?" I doubted it had been to rescue me.

"I can't just check in on my favorite herald?" she

asked, not looking at me as she stretched, her snakes and arms reaching high into the sky.

"Aren't I the only herald?"

"Which makes you my favorite," she replied with a backwards glance at me.

"Then no. I don't believe you just happened by." My frustration bubbled close to the surface, but there was still only so much I'd snark the gorgon.

"Ah. Shame. Let's just say a little birdy told me some creatures had gotten grabby handed. The most interesting things happen when you get annoyed. I had nothing else to do, so why not show up?"

I sighed. "Then, since my activity has ended, I think I shall return and deal with the fallout from my very public abduction."

"Oh, that should be interesting. Should I watch? Are you planning on doing anything fascinating to someone? Could you skin them alive?"

"What? No, please don't." I paused. "How would I even-," I paused as at least one method to strip the skin off of someone jumped into my mind. Acids were so easy to create. "Never mind. I don't want to know. And no. I am positive it will be boring lecturing, bureaucratic nonsense."

"Ah, shame. Well please do remember to notify me. And I might pass it on to Salistra," she commented on a teasing note, still not looking at me.

I groaned. "If that is all?" I visualized where I needed to sidestep to, an area outside the lobby so I could walk back in.

"There is one thing I thought I would mention," Tirsane said idly, turning to slither away.

"Oh?" I paused. Her voice too blithe. This gorgon never said anything that didn't have layers of meanings.

"Remember that Magic does not like to be

manipulated, and the deaths of her children could have grave consequences." Between one slither and the next, she was gone.

I stared after her, worried and perplexed. "Carelian, do you know what she meant?"

He was silent for a long time, standing next to me, staring off where she had been. ~Specifically no. But if the event that has been mentioned culminates in the death of many mages, there may be a ripple effect.~

"That would do what?" I felt my temper fraying.

~That is the problem. With Magic, you never can tell.~

"Just great. You know, if you guys are trying to drive me insane, I think it's working."

Carelian flicked his tail at me. ~Whatever made you think we were sane to begin with?~

Chapter 37

Section 2.20.3

Misdemeanors will always have the penalty of shorn hair and nails cut to the quick. Jail time is deemed useless and the penalty will always include community service and draft extension up to five years. If the mage has completed their draft, they may have their community service doubled.

SPIRIT

I stepped back into the hot muggy air of DC and almost whimpered as the dust that had settled on me despite my best efforts instantly became mud sticking to my skin and my clothes. Alaska was sounding better and better.

I looked around, and other than a few gouges on the terrace out front, there was no evidence a dragon had been there not too long ago. Checking my watch told me it had been two hours, which oddly seemed about right. Some of the interaction had taken longer than it seemed, and fighting always made time fly.

"No attacking the humans," I reminded Carelian as we headed to the lobby doors. "But I won't argue if you growl and hiss and scare the socks off of them."

~You ruin so much of my fun.~ He flicked his tail at me as I pulled open the doors.

"Yes, I know." I walked in and sure enough, Lieutenant Strivent was standing there with Pearl and Adjunct Lorison. I suppressed a groan.

"Munroe, get over here," Strivent snapped, and I set my jaw. I continued walking at my normal pace.

~Are you sure I can't bite him?~

I ignored Carelian. "Hey," I said as I walked up to them, feeling disheveled, annoyed, and wondering if I would end up in Alaska before this was all over.

"What happened?" Strivent glared at me as he raked his eyes up and down my form.

I opened my mouth then stopped.

Center, calm, being snarky will get me nothing.

"I will be more than happy to tell you, but first I need a bottle or two of water, and are you really sure you want to have this conversation out here?" I gestured to the lobby, where people were already falling quiet to listen or stare at us.

Strivent glared, but Daniel nodded. "That would be wise. Mrs. Takashi, please get Merlin Munroe some water while the Lieutenant and I escort her to the conference room on the second floor."

I could see a mutinous expression in her eyes, but she nodded and spun around, heading away.

"Merlin Munroe?" Lorison gestured, and I knew it wasn't a request so I smiled and headed through security with him while Strivent followed. I frowned, looking at my empty hand.

Merlin blast it. I dropped my coffee cup there. I liked that cup.

It soured my mood a bit more. Not that it needed any help. Right now, I wanted water and a shower.

One brief elevator ride later I was in a conference room with two men and Pearl glaring at me. I ignored them until I had one bottle of the icy cold water gone. It helped wash the dust out of my throat though I would need to change clothes to be presentable.

They all just stared at me, and I sighed. "What would you like to know?" There were many, many days when I felt like running away. This was rising higher on my list of days.

"Who took you and why?" Strivent blurted.

"I would like to know if it was really a dragon," Lorison commented before I could respond.

"Yes, it was a dragon. Technically, it was the Dragon of China's mother and she—" I fumbled for the right words "—wanted to talk to me and didn't think about a much more civilized way to do it. Besides, she enjoyed showing off."

"But it looked nothing like the Dragon of China," Pearl protested.

I shrugged. "I wasn't going to get into an argument about dragon biology. If you want to know, I'll ask her to come talk to you about it."

All three of them shook their heads and I repressed a snort of amusement.

"What did she want to talk to you about? I'd like to point out the security clauses you signed said anyone, not just humans. You are not allowed to talk about many of the things you see here." Strivent had his stern face on, and I had an image of him before Zmaug begging for his life.

I kept my face calm and did not laugh at that thought. I hadn't remembered most of the security clauses because ninety percent of what I had been involved in so far seemed to be common sense or stupid. Nothing anyone would want to know.

"I have no reason to believe I divulged anything that would be regarded as secure information," I replied slowly as I thought about the conversation.

"Then if it was not to get State Department secrets, why would she kidnap you in such a public manner?" Strivent demanded.

I took another sip of my water from the bottle I hadn't drained. "She wanted to see the mage her son was so impressed with. The royal family treats him like a dumb animal and Carelian talked up our relationship a lot." All three of them shot glances at Carelian who sat in the chair next to me, licking his paw and then cleaning his face. He didn't even flick an ear their way.

"All of that because she's a helicopter mom?" Pearl's voice squeaked a bit and her face flushed. I somehow suspected she'd had a much more up-close encounter with Zmaug than the others.

"More a mom whose child disappeared over a hundred years ago and she just wanted to know who he was all excited about." I shrugged.

"If that was it, what took so long?" Strivent glared at me as if I was going to break and babble that I had given away state secrets, if I knew any.

"First, there was a dominance game, which I won. Then they talked about the things they overheard."

"WHAT?" That burst came out of three mouths and I sighed. This wouldn't go down well.

"They're worried about the uproar Tiantang caused and have been eavesdropping on the royal family in China to make sure they are not planning on hurting Tiantang. They heard things that concerned them and wanted me to know. Mainly that China wants to be the primary source of all mages and that they are planning something big." I weighed information about the virus, then shrugged. "They also overheard stuff that makes it sound like China already has the virus and just want the treaty for publicity reasons."

I expected some reactions, but not what I got.

Pearl waved her hand. "China has wanted to be the primary source for all mages for the last hundred years. They've done raids, seduction attempts, even pregnancy manipulation. We know something is working because we've seen drops in the birth rates of our mages, but everything is so random we haven't figured out a way to stop it. There is a commission on it already."

Lorison nodded. "They are always planning something. It is their culture to try to take advantage where they can, but only if they can plausibly deny it or shift the blame to someone else. And as for them having the virus." He gave a little half laugh. "I would be more surprised if they didn't. The treaty just gives everyone the legal right to use it and go public with what they have discovered."

I could read between the lines and understood what he wasn't saying. The US already had the virus too, though not all the research notes which in some ways were more important.

"You aren't worried?" I asked, all too unsurprised by their reactions once I thought about it. Everything was games here in Washington. Games I had no desire to play.

Lorison and Pearl looked at each other and shrugged. "Unless they can tell us what an event or a plan is, it isn't anything we haven't known for years. They are usually subtle and long term, so I wouldn't worry about it too much."

I blinked again.

"I'm worried," Strivent ground out, and I looked at him, my eyes widening at how clenched his jaws were. "What do you mean they've been eavesdropping on the royal family? How, when, why? Are they doing it here too?"

Oh. It hadn't really occurred to me, but from the throbbing on the side of his head, I worried he might have an aneurysm.

"Why, I already told you. When?" I shrugged. "Whenever they think about it or are interested. Maybe when Tiantang tells them something is going on. Other than that, I couldn't say."

"What are they planning on doing with the information? And you haven't said how they are doing this." Strivent didn't move his eyes away from me and I was starting to wish Salistra would stick her head in again. That reminded me of what Tirsane said, but I didn't think they would take that any more to heart.

"I think you need to understand the denizens. Or at least their societies."

"They have societies?" Lorison demanded, his attention back on me.

"Yeah," I said nodding my head, wondering if everyone was this manic all the time, or if I was just lucky. "There are select beings that are part of the Lords. I mean, I know of the Chaos Lords, so I assume there are Spirit and Order Lords also. Then they have their leaders. Tirsane the Gorgon, Salistra the Unicorn, and ... Bob."

They didn't say anything, just kept staring at me. "They don't live like us, more like animals but with magic and understanding that sometimes their prey is sentient." I groaned. "I don't know it, not really, but mostly it seems like a loose bunch of family groups that organize by species and realms. They don't have a government or cities the way we think of them, but they do have homes and places they consider theirs."

"So they are spies?"

I rolled my eyes at Strivent. "Spies, no. I mean yes, but no. They care about their families. As to how? Well they open tiny rips between there and here and listen. I've never done it, so I only heard them mention it." I shrugged.

"This is not good. I've never heard of someone being able to do this, but you know what this means?"

"Dragons can listen in on sex talk?" I hazarded a

guess, wondering if he would have an attack.

"Argh." He pushed away from the table in a violent motion that had Carelian hissing, exposing all his teeth. Strivent didn't even seem to notice. Instead, he paced back and forth in the room. "Civilians never get it, and you blasted mages don't think. If someone has a familiar, they can listen in anywhere. There would be no place in the world safe from eavesdropping. We would have zero operational security." His voice got more strident as he moved back and forth, arms waving. Even Pearl and Lorison were scooting out of his way.

~What makes you think we care that much?~ I could tell from the vibration that Carelian had spoken to more than just me, and the sudden stumble as Strivent came to a halt let me know at least one person had been included.

He stared at Carelian, so did Pearl and Lorison. I just shook my head and drained the remaining water bottle. I needed a shower.

"You're her familiar," Strivent protested, still looking around the room as if he thought someone else was there.

~Yes. And I care about her, all of my queans. Old men sitting in a meeting talking about things that will crumble to dust? No. If someone threatens my queans, I will kill them. Listening to words that are empty is not worthy of a hunter. Even the dragons only listen because they worry. If they thought their child or their clan was in danger, there would be no royal family. You are like a swarm of Chitterians, making webs and plans that no prey would ever fall into.~

Carelian jumped off the chair and put his head on my arm. ~They are not worth your time. This draft wastes what you could be.~ He spoke only for me, and I scratched his forehead.

~I agree. But duty is what I am shackled by.~ He knew the consequences of me walking away and I would never do that to Jo and Sable. So I'd suck it up. A decade was doable, right? The desire to give up the research bubbled hard, and I knew I needed to look it over again. Maybe there was a way out.

"Are we done? I need to go home and take a shower," I said, rising.

They looked at me and nodded, but as I walked out the door, Strivent called out, "We will be talking about how you are getting in without swiping your badge."

I nodded and left, not side stepping until I was outside of the building.

Chapter 38

Section 2.32.3

When needed, mages will be contracted to assist with police investigations. They are to remain available to the jurisdiction until the case is resolved, either via an innocent verdict, justifiable, or execution. Only under extenuating circumstances may they leave the jurisdiction and even then they should remain available if needed for the court hearing. Any mage not obeying that rule may be brought up on charges and executed for civil disobedience if found guilty of avoiding their duties.

ORDER

I grabbed my stuff, walked out of the building, making sure I badged out, and sidestepped home as I turned a corner. An hour later, showered and dressed in comfortable clothes, I collapsed on the couch and reviewed everything that had happened.

Jo and Sable got home after jealousy-inducing normal days at the office. While they listened to what happened to me, they didn't have any suggestions what to do with the information. I went to bed early and tossed and turned all night trying to figure out what I was missing. When I woke up, I was reminded I'd left one of my favorite mugs in that dry realm and had to go with another one. This one only held twenty ounces of coffee instead of thirty. I packed extra coffee supplies.

I sidestepped to the side of the building, Carelian scoping it out first, then walked in. I nodded at the glaring Lieutenant Strivent, swiped myself in, and headed up to my cubicle. Pearl called out as I walked by.

"Come see me after you log in." She didn't sound mad, but who knew at this point. I set everything up and had my coffee gripped firmly in my hand as I walked into her office.

"Morning," I said, trying to put some enthusiasm in my voice. I failed, but I did try.

Pearl gave me a considering look. I took comfort that it wasn't loathing, more considering, and I sat down without waiting for her to offer.

"It is at that." She leaned back in her chair, looking at me. "I read your file and to be honest, I assumed you were a troublemaker, a prima donna, or even just spoiled. To my pleasure, you were none of those things. What few things I've had you work on, you've done well and efficiently, even if you didn't bow to my pressure to give up information to the Japanese."

I arched an eyebrow and took a sip of my coffee. At this rate, maybe I needed to add something stronger to my morning drink. Could I get over-caffeinated enough to not be frustrated with this job?

"But after having you here for two weeks..." She paused and checked the calendar. "It's only been two weeks." A sigh escaped her lips, and Pearl shook her head. "After having you here," she continued, "I have realized much to my chagrin that the moniker of Cori Catastrophe is accurate."

I started to protest, and she just held up her hand, giving me a quelling look.

"I fully understand that with everything that has happened, you have caused none of it. In fact, you tried to warn people it wouldn't work. You, unfortunately, were correct. I cannot blame the dragon on you or even your familiar." Here she gave me a narrow-eyed look, but it seemed more resigned than exasperated or even angry. "Nor the incident yesterday, though knowing you were in the building would have saved us at least twenty minutes of stress wondering where you were.

I felt my face heat, and I nodded. "That won't happen again."

She didn't respond to that, still just looking at me. "Which leaves me with a problem," she said, looking at me.

I tried to keep my face a mask and focused on my coffee. Drinking it, letting the sharp bitter taste and the sweet following occupy my mind. It helped, a little.

One corner of Pearl's mouth quirked up. "What, exactly, am I supposed to do with you? The last few days I've spent more time talking about you with others than I have all the people under me for the last year."

I lifted one shoulder. What was I supposed to say?

"Here's the issue. You are mostly useless to me, and I'm annoyed at all the capital I spent getting you here when I can't use you." Her lips hardened for a minute, then relaxed. "My fault. I'm too used to bulldozing people, and I figured it was just paper you'd hand over without protest."

I kept my mouth shut since I still didn't know what Japan might want so bad. Jeorgaz's comments about the pocket reality made little sense, but I needed to review the research in depth to figure it out. And so far I'd only skimmed over the information, not processed it.

"Until we can move you to a different area, I'm stuck with you. Can you suck it up and not make our lives any more difficult than they already are?"

"Do I have a choice?" I asked, my voice serious.

"Sure. You can make everyone here hate you by whining and throwing a fit. But if you can handle being here until the New Year, we will work on getting you someplace where your skills are more suited."

I tried to keep the relief off my face. This was not where my personality or my skill set belonged. Though it wasn't like the Draft had a job search engine I could flip through and see what was available.

"I don't think acting like a spoiled brat would be wise of me. I can sit down and shut up until then." Getting somewhere that I could use my skills would make three months of drudgery worth it.

"Good. Now out. Since you can't help me, I need to figure out how to deal with all of this."

I rose and headed toward the door.

"Merlin Munroe?"

I looked back at her, waiting.

"If you hear anything actionable from your... friends, please let us know. The situation in China has a lot of us upset and right now everyone is scrambling to see if they can find an Ambassador to China with a familiar. The error in our ways has been made crystal clear to — familiars are not fancy animals to be admired. They are your..." She trailed off, frowning.

"Partner or friend. They call themselves our focus. And maybe they are. But they all have human-level intelligence." I stopped and gave her a long look. "Just remember they are not human and their interpretations don't always mesh well with human culture."

Pearl tilted her head. "Such as?"

I nodded at Carelian, who had stuck his head in the door as I was about to leave Pearl's office. He saw no reason to get up as early as I did, but he wanted to know what Pearl talked to me about. "He still thinks if I beat someone in a fight, he should get to eat them."

Her eyes widened a bit, then narrowed. "Ah, I see. Thank you. Please have a quiet rest of the year, Merlin Munroe. I have enough work to do."

I laughed as I left and went back to my cube. Pearl

lived up to her promise, and I had no more meetings with diplomats about treaties or anything else. Instead I had research projects, collating information, and being bored out of my skull.

After the second week, Carelian didn't even bother to come in, preferring to go roam. Though when he decided it was nap time, he sprawled out under my desk, where I'd put a large dog bed, and snored. Even if he said he didn't, he snored. It was cute.

Most of the make work they gave me didn't take me long and wasn't all that interesting, though the occasional research rabbit hole was. But what I needed to do was review the research James had done. The idea of being caught with it in the office ate at me and working from home just wasn't done at the State Department.

~I can carry and guard.~ Carelian made the offer after the third week of me needing to go somewhere in the Appalachians and hike to burn off energy. I'd already made a note to travel to the Rockies and the Cascade Range, so we had some more challenging places to go. That it would still be light there when I got off was also a bonus.

"What do you mean?" I threw myself into my computer chair, already wondering if screaming would alleviate my boredom.

~It is easy enough for me to carry. I can step there and here and bring it. If anyone tries to take it, I will take it back to where it is safe. There is great information in that data that I fear you must know.~

I stared at him, hope blossoming in my mind. Something to do!

"You would? That gives me something constructive to do, instead of this stuff." I waved my hand at the cubicle that even now remained barren except for my briefcase and coffee cup. Personal items were annoying in a place where anyone could walk by and take them.

~You are my quean,~ he responded, avoiding the answer. ~I can also go to the storage grove and obtain items from there.~ He opened his paw, revealing the thumb that most never suspected.

I pulled him into a hug and rubbed his ears just the way he liked. The next month flew by as I studied and learned and was almost happy if not for the feeling that I needed to do something, not just read about it. I could see so much in what James had discovered and the need to ask more questions, to probe, burned, but I also remembered what Jeorgaz said. I had no desire to treat any of my friends like specimens. They were too important for that.

Something had started to gel in the back of my mind as I looked again at the research. Jeorgaz was there at every step and assisted or lent his abilities to much of what James did. James had only been a regular merlin, not a double.

I paused at his ranking, frowning. Something Jeorgaz had said to me filtered back.

~Carelian? Do you know if James was a double merlin?~ I asked mentally as I was in the cubical. While most people were treating me like a pariah, that didn't mean they weren't paying attention. Though not enough to see exactly what I was taking notes on or reading. I never left the binder or notepad visible. If I had to go to the bathroom or get more coffee, I slipped them under Carelian's sleeping body. He made an excellent guard.

He yawned as I looked at him. ~I have no reason to believe he was. Though he died way before my time so I have no way to know. Ask Jeorgaz.~

I looked at my notes again, still processing what I'd almost put together. ~Jeorgaz mentioned once that phoenixes were all realm creatures. What exactly did that mean?~

Out of the corner of my vision, I saw him curl and tuck his muzzle under his paws. He could be so darn cute I wanted to take another pic and post it to Sable and Jo. The problem with cute familiars, they begged to be immortalized in images.

~Cath are Chaos. Always have been. We resonate better with that realm. Both our personalities and our magic. This does not mean other realms are barred to us, just that we prefer our own realms.~ He nibbled his shoulder hard for a minute, then settled back down. ~But there are some that resonate with all the realms. Most of the apex beings I guess.~ He hummed in my mind for a minute. ~That isn't right, but I don't know how to categorize it. There are those who resonate with all the realms, what you might call a triple merlin. We don't tend to designate that way. Maybe a full mage instead of the crippled versions of humans?~ He sounded thoughtful, and I recognized a conversation derailment and interceded.

~So how many of these all realm beings are there?~ I kept my head down, looking at the notebook. Anyone walking by had no reason to believe I was doing anything except reading and writing.

~That I know of?~ He sounded thoughtful again. ~Dragons, phoenix, sphinx, valkyries, and chimeras.~

I blinked at the list. ~How many are ever familiars?~

~Only the dragons and phoenix, the other three find Earth boring and humans tasty. Well Valkyrie don't eat humans, they just only care when they are dying. It is complicated.~ I recognized his I'm done talking tone, but I had one more question.

~Do all focus's help their mages?~

He flicked an ear at me. ~Of course, that is what we

are, a focus of magic.~

~But——~

My computer beeped with an incoming call. I paused my talking to answer it, fumbling as always for my headset. "Cori Munroe," I said, wondering who was calling. I didn't talk to anyone in the State Department, and everyone else had my personal number.

"Merlin, this is security. We have someone here saying they have a meeting with you. Shall we escort him to the level one conference room?"

I looked at my calendar; it was empty, as I had thought. "I don't have anything scheduled."

"Yes, ma'am. He said it was imperative he speak with you?" The guard sounded hesitant, and my alarm bells went off.

"Who is it?"

"Hishatio Yamato."

Chapter 39

Section 2.20.20

At no point should a mage be held liable for protecting themselves from harm. It is acknowledged they are living weapons and will be granted the right to protect themselves even if death is the result for the attacker.

CHAOS

I managed to not run down the stairs or give in to the desire to pull the fire alarm as I went down to meet him. Why in the world would he be here? And did he travel via mundane means, or could he sidestep? As far as I knew, I was the only mage who could do it with little effort, but that meant nothing. The more I learned, the more I realized how much we didn't talk about because we didn't want the OMO or the Draft to learn.

Pearl had been on the phone, so I sent her a quick email letting her know before I headed out. Carelian strolled alongside me. The elevator took forever, but I got it to myself as it slid down, delivering me to what was certain to be a stressful meeting.

Maybe I need to take up meditation? At this rate my blood pressure is going to be permanently high.

"He is waiting in here, Merlin Munroe," a guard said as I stepped out on the second floor.

I'd learned the second floor held smaller conference rooms for ad hoc meetings, while the fourth held ones with teleconference abilities as well as more seating. The guard led me to a room, and opened the door, ushering me in.

Lady Luck snapped up around me while I prepped to pull up an electrical shield, even if it screwed up my phone. Carelian darted in first. I stepped through, all my attention on scanning the room for danger. It was a normal, boring conference room. A square table with four chairs, a white board, and one man standing in the corner looking out the window to the lobby. He turned to look at me as I stepped through, and I recognized Hishatio.

He wore a severe suit in dark gray, with his hair bound in braids pulled away from his face. There was no color in anything he wore, he was all shades of gray and black. But his eyes held something that I didn't expect.

All the various ways to say hello flitted through my mind, and none of them seemed appropriate. I wasn't actually happy to see him and I had no idea if this was a meeting of allies, enemies, or business related.

"Hishatio. This is unexpected." I let the door close as I stepped all the way in.

"I suppose it would be," he replied, his eyes flicking once to Carelian then staying on me. "I swear I am not here to harm you."

The words surprised me, though they did not reassure me.

"That's good; people yell at me when I damage buildings."

An emotion flickered across his face and he nodded his head, hiding his face for a moment. "Yes, that tends to annoy those tasked with maintaining it." He lifted his head. "Please. Sit. I would like to talk to you."

I ran my hand over Carelian's head as I walked over to a chair. After making sure I had a clear shot at the door and had the apartment location clear in my mind, I sat. Sidestepping there would take me less than a second if I was desperate enough.

Hishatio sat down at the opposite end of the table. He folded his hands and looked at me. "You have created much consternation among the diplomats for Japan."

I almost protested it wasn't my idea, but managed to keep my mouth shut. Never take blame that isn't assigned.

"And how would that be?"

Carelian had jumped up in one of the other chairs, pinning Hishatio between us. The man didn't look happy, but he didn't move.

"The consternation of our representatives was extreme. They are not supposed to be in the same room as you. Yet to leave would have created unacceptable loss of face. It was an unfair position to put those who have little agency for their actions."

I fought to keep my face smooth, though I wanted to wince. My current life was enough like theirs that my sympathy was high.

"I tried to warn my superiors that Japan would have issues with me. Unfortunately, I have little agency in this situation either."

He frowned, his eyes tracing the symbols on my temple. "But you are a merlin, a double. More powerful than any we know." The words seemed dragged out of him. "Why do they waste you with this?"

I gave him a cold smile. "They wanted my inheritance to influence you, as badly as you wanted my inheritance."

He tilted his head to one side. "A valid if misguided effort on their part. If you didn't crumble with people trying to kill you, why did they think you would fold because they put job pressure on you?"

Laughter burst out of me, and I couldn't stop it. Hishatio quirked an eyebrow at me as I tried to get a hold of my laughter. I lifted a hand in mute apology.

"I was not laughing at you. More at the accuracy of your statement. But then, when have politicians ever been logical?"

He nodded his head in acknowledgement of my comment. "I do forget how much easier it is sometimes with one ruler, not a gaggle of people that all want to go in different directions. I am not sure I would be able to handle it." He glanced out the window. The lobby and all its activity displayed like a miniature world outside of ours. "You all seem so chaotic in your actions."

I shrugged, watching him. Why was he here acting all nice? It made no sense.

"The emperor does not know I am here," he said into the silence that had fallen between us.

I jerked a bit at that. "He doesn't? Then why would you come? Why did you come?" I might have been a bit exasperated at that point. This was Esmere's game, not mine.

"I knew James. We were old friends. He grew up in Okinawa. Military brat." Okinawa was the only base in Japan, placed there as part of the war. Sable's dad had been stationed there too. The parallel was interesting, but it didn't actually mean anything. Hishatio didn't look at me as he spoke, and I tried to figure out why he was here and even more why he was telling me this stuff. "We talked and dreamed as kids. Even more as teenagers. Then we emerged and our discussions became more focused and directed. But still we remained friends though his familiar disliked me from the day he found it." There was bitterness to his words, and I felt a flicker of sympathy.

The room fell silent, and I waited to see what else he would say, and I played with the idea of calling for Jeorgaz.

"A lot of the research we both did. But his familiar meant he had more power and access than I ever could. And he was done with his service in a scant decade. My oath as the Maiyutsu-Shi is in place until I can no longer fulfill the duties of my office."

At no point had he looked at me, and I wondered what he was looking at. Memories? Dreams? Why was he here?

"I am not a good man," he said, his voice hard. He jerked his head up to stare at me. His eyes resembled blank screens, reflecting my own expression back at me. "If I thought you did not already have a will set up and that killing you would get me what I want, what my country needs, I would try to kill you."

"That is not in the book about making friends and influencing people," I muttered. My shield waited for me to call on it, the offering easy, and I could always step anywhere, though I obviously needed to practice rolling to another place as opposed to standing up to step.

A huff of amusement slipped past his lips. "I suppose not. But I would rather have you as an honest enemy than a false friend." He shook his head, his long hair moving like a snake's body in the reflection from the windows.

"I'd rather be no one's enemy if I had a choice. Maiyutsu-shi, why are you here? And while I am curious about yours and Jeorgaz's issue, I don't know how it affects me."

His eyes had not left mine, though I kept glancing away, uncomfortable with his flat stare.

"I need that research. It is everything we need. I am authorized to offer you the research on Nauso and revoke your abomination status." He didn't blurt the words, he said them calmly and logically and alarm bells went off.

"Why do you need the research? And if the emperor doesn't know you are here, who authorizes you?" I asked, then shot a question to Carelian. ~Can you ask Jeorgaz to come here? I don't understand what is going on.~

~Done,~ he replied back

I watched as Hishatio studied his clasped hands. The relief to have his eyes off of me was palpable, but I still wanted to know the answer to my question. "Mr. Yamato?"

"The empress." I sucked in a sharp breath at that. From everything I read, she almost never interfered in matters of state, preferring to stay in the background and manage her Handmaids, the female mages in Japan.

"Why?" He looked up at me, his face blank, so I clarified. "Why is she sending you here and not letting the emperor keep control?"

"Ah. Tomohito has his pride, Akiko bends like a willow. She sees the need and can let herself bend. But she sends me as the sacrifice." He didn't sound upset, just stating the way his world was.

Before I could figure out how to respond to that, though I did register how close he was to both of them to call them by name, there was a flash of light to my left. I turned to see the form of Jeorgaz flapping in the air, then settling on the back of the only empty chair.

"You," hissed Hishatio and I marveled again at his skill in English that he could make the word sound like something filthy.

~Mite in the feathers you are,~ Jeorgaz snapped back, and I groaned.

"Both of you are two damn old to be acting like kids. What's your problem? Your best friend died and you're his familiar. Why aren't you supporting each other rather than fighting?" I paused and turned to Carelian. "Just so you know, if I drop dead, get killed, or whatever, I expect you to stay by Jo and Sable's side, supporting them and letting them support you. None of this spitefulness back and forth." I was dead serious. The idea of Jo and Sable developing a relationship like this with Carelian almost physically hurt.

The bird and the royal magician just looked at me with shocked expressions. A bird looking shocked was rather amusing.

"What? If you're going to act like spoiled kids, I'm going to treat you like spoiled kids." I crossed my arms and glared at them.

"He started it," Hishatio protested, then sat back and bowed his head. "It is unseemly to fight with an animal, and immaterial to this conversation. We need the research. We will offer much."

Jeorgaz had all his feathers fluffed out. ~He is a mite in human clothing and exists only to drain the blood from those who are foolish enough to host him. Trust him not and give him nothing. You can't afford the price. ~ Until that moment, I hadn't realized birds could hiss and do it mentally.

I looked at both of them, blinking, then pushed my chair back and got up. Without another word I walked out, Carelian a step behind me.

Chapter 40

Section 2.20.16

Familiars that remain after a mage has died are to be treated as an endangered animal and only disposed of in extreme cases. At no point should the familiar be approached and apprehended. If they pose a danger, they will be eliminated immediately and then given full rites if possible.

SPIRIT

The door hadn't even closed behind me as I headed to the elevators before I heard mingled cries of "Wait," and ~Stop,~ burst out. I didn't. I went and pushed the down button. A walk in the fresh air, muggy and polluted it might be, sounded better than sitting in there.

The click of the door being pulled open sounded behind me. "Merlin Munroe, please. We do need to talk."

"And I need people to quit being mysterious or childish. Am I going to get my needs filled?" I turned around as I spoke and waited.

~Yes. Please come back. ~ Jeorgaz sounded resigned and maybe a bit sheepish. I could see a splash of color beyond the door that Hishatio held open.

"Are both of you willing to act like adults and explain what I, a lowly flunky in this place, can do to get you to go away?" My tone was dark because I was just annoyed.

"I can," Hishatio replied.

I searched his face, but found only resignation and

acceptance. With a sigh I nodded and walked back into the room. We all resumed our seats and I stared at Jeorgaz.

"I've read through almost everything. And unless I'm missing something, the aspects you were worried about the most are not an issue. Even if I gave Japan the information to create another pocket realm, it would be very difficult for them to create one, and I believe you could easily derail that."

~How?~ Jeorgaz demanded, even as Hishatio spoke.

"A pocket realm? Why would we want a pocket realm?" He had a confused look, and I stared at Jeorgaz, who avoided my gaze by preening.

"A pocket realm could be established by a merlin, and then it could be mined or exploited, then closed and done again and again until in that area all magic had been drained." I watched Jeorgaz as I spoke, snickering as his feathers puffed.

~That should not happen. It would damage much.~ He sounded aggravated and worried, so I quit being a jerk.

"Okay. I'm not sure how, but here's the catch—it only works if the mage has a familiar and that familiar is an all realms familiar. Which, unless there are some I don't know about, means the Dragon of China or the Phoenix of Paris here on Earth. Or if a realm denizen creates it for them, like Hamiada."

The bird froze mid preen, then lifted his head to look at me. ~Oh.~

"Yes, oh. Again, unless I'm missing something, if you tell the focuses not to, and they don't assist, there is no way for any mage to form a pocket like that. Or the permanent portal."

Jeorgaz brightened, and I mean literally. His feathers became brighter and barely visible licks of flame flickered around him. ~I had not considered that. Yes. I must talk to Tiantang and Flora. There are no others, but I can watch and see.~ With that last comment, he vanished in a wash of flame.

I groaned, shaking my head. "I will never understand how most of these denizens think," I muttered, mostly to myself.

"I do not blame you. I never understood why he disliked me so. I met him for the first time as a chick. James had opened a small portal testing something, and an egg tumbled into his hand quivering and rocking." Hishatio had a soft look on his face. "I met Jeorgaz about two months later. I admit I might have been rude, fledging birds are not exactly elegant."

I wanted to say what Jeorgaz had said about Hishatio. Social conventions urged me to explain, soothe feelings. Instead, I changed the subject. "As you can see, what you want is not available to you or any of your mages. Can the hostilities cease?"

He blinked at me. A frown creased his smooth brow. For the first time I realized he had to be in his eighties, yet there was only a hint of gray at the temples to provide any clues as to his age.

"Neither I nor Japan have ever cared about creating a portal realm. At least not until now."

"If that isn't what you wanted, why in the world were you trying to kill me?" I didn't even bother to hide my frustration. Those six months of fear—watching where I was, worrying about Jo, Jo's blood on my hands—and my desire to be polite snapped. "I had to kill a man who tried to kill me. He put a bullet through my best friend. I almost lost her. Then those two idiots attacked me in a building? What, by Merlin's blood, was your problem?"

Hishatio stiffened, his posture becoming more rigid.

"You were a threat. You had information my country needed. Information James had promised would be mine. And the solution inherent in that research justified the cost."

"How do you justify trying to kill someone?" I didn't shriek the words, but my anger was pulling on my magic and I could see how easy it would be to reach out with Fire and do something. Something horrible.

That made me tamp down my emotions. If trying to kill someone was beyond the pale, I was pretty sure setting them on fire was just as bad. Especially when they weren't trying to kill me.

"Because my country will die if I don't find what he promised me," he hissed, eyes glaring into mine. "I don't care about the majority of what he discovered. He had so much free time it didn't matter. You Americans aren't still trying to recover from the destruction of two cities and over half our mages!"

I pulled back as if slapped, my anger deflated. "What?"

"No, they don't tell you about that, do they? They just say two rogue mages detonated bombs on my country and people were unfortunately lost. No, your history washes everything clean, and this is simply a horrible accident." He leaned forward, rage making his eyes sparkle. "Those were our two major training centers for our mages. Being at war or not, you took out over seventy percent of our mages in those two accidents. Most of them were young and barely starting families." The sneer on that word made me want to weep. "We lost a full generation of mages and at least two more since then because of those actions. Japan is barely competing in this world where the power of your mages determines your political capital on the world stage. I would kill more than one girl to keep my country safe."

If he had started breathing fire, it would not have surprised me.

I sat and marshalled my thoughts. The war had happened right about the time he would have been born. So he hadn't been affected, but obviously it was burned deeper into the psyche than I knew. Not that I knew much about it besides what the history books said. Both mages had died in that teleport incident. But his passion made me think maybe it hadn't been an accident.

~Mind your manners, mage. My quean was not even born, nor were her parents, when this occurred. She bears no responsibility for the actions done prior to her birth.~ Carelian hissed the words, and they helped anchor me.

"I do not deny things were done between our countries," I said, "but Japan was not blameless. POW camps that used the prisoners as subjects to test mage abilities, to twist and find new ways to fight, to kill? Many of those who came out of those camps lived short lives. And we won't speak of what your ally Germany did." I kept my voice flat. The war had cost so many lives. Hitler's pogrom had killed mages, Jews, homosexuals, anyone that didn't meet his ideals. He felt all Germans should be archmages or higher and feared hedgemages polluting the blood. They were rounded up and treated the same as the other undesirable groups.

"I'd like to think we've progressed past that."

He bowed his head, his breathing evening out. "It changes nothing. I only regret that I did not succeed in my attempt. But not out of any animosity toward you personally. Only what you represent. You block that which could save us." He ground out that last part, then closed his eyes, hands flattened on the table.

"If it isn't what Jeorgaz was worried about, what do you want?" I asked, exasperated and confused. The amount of passion surprised me. No greed, just desperation, and that made me very uncomfortable.

"I don't know!" His English slipped, and the words came out heavily accented. His hands went white as they pressed against the table. In jerky motions, he stood up and went to the corner of the room so there was no table between us. He knelt on the floor in that same jerky movement. It almost felt like someone was controlling him like a puppet. The promise he made to the empress? What had she made him promise?

Kneeling, he then bowed all the way down until his head touched the floor.

I watched. This was wrong. I shouldn't be here. I was the wrong person for him to be talking to. This man, enemy though he was, should not be bowing to me. I started to speak, but Carelian stopped me.

~No. Let him continue.~

I clamped my lips shut and waited.

Hishatio lifted his head and looked at me. "I beg you. With the offering of my life. Grant unto me that which James left for me. The salvation of my country."

He remained kneeling and waited for my answer.

What the fuck?

It took me a second to get control of my reaction, and I glared at Carelian, hoping he had an answer.

~I do not know, but this is deadly serious. He is willing to die to get what he is speaking about.~ Carelian seemed oddly pleased and I didn't have time to deal with his smugness.

"Hishatio," I managed, then sighed. "I am royally tired of being a string pulled between various entities, but I promise you—I do not know what James left that would help you. It's not that I won't trade it, it's that I

333

don't know what it is."

He seemed to shrink. "Truly, there were no notes left to send anything to me?"

"I haven't gone through everything. But I will continue to look. I will not promise to give it to you, but I will tell you if I find it. It's the best I can do." I regretted the words the second they were out of my mouth, but I couldn't change them.

"That is more than I expected, but I will pay with my life for the research." He had regained his normal fluidity as he stood back up, but he now looked old where not minutes before I had regarded him as ageless. He set a card down on the table. "Here is how you may contact me." He flicked a glance toward Carelian. "Via mundane means, that is."

I watched him, then nodded slowly. "I will look, I promise. Though I still think if you had just told me this in the first place I probably would have just given it to you."

He turned his head to the side, as if in pain. "I judged you by my own reactions. I would never have allowed such treasures out of my life. You are well within your rights to kill me right now and none would blame you."

"Umm, yeah, I'm pretty sure I'd be charged for murder and I'd blame me. Revenge doesn't justify murder." The idea made me gag slightly. Killing someone with adrenaline rushing, expecting to die at any moment, I could understand. The desire to save myself, save Jo, let me do a lot of things. But standing here now, to just kill him—no, I wasn't that person.

"I forget. In Japan you would not be held accountable. I must leave. I have other assignments while I am here." He turned and headed toward the door.

He had shrunk somehow. Walking past me, he

seemed smaller and older than when I first saw him. By all rights I should hate him, want him to die, but mostly I just wanted to cry for him and for the country he would sacrifice everything for.

The door shut behind him and Carelian looked as upset as I felt.

"Well?"

~He is scared. And feels deeply. I do not know the answer, my quean, but he serves and would die for his belief.~

I nodded slowly and headed back to my cube, not sure of anything.

Chapter 41

Section 95.4

All mages are required to be registered with the OMO. Any mage found that has not been registered past the age of 27 is deemed rogue. All rogues will be offered a one time opportunity to serve in a double draft; refusals will be treated as a terroristic act and acted on appropriately.

ORDER

Early November arrived, Halloween had been a blast, and about lunchtime the atmosphere in the office became electric with excitement. I'd spent the time looking through everything James had left me, all the notes, and there wasn't anything. I had no idea what Hishatio wanted, or thought would save his country.

I had gone through all the paperwork left for me in the bank boxes, and none of them had anything about stuff to give to Japan. I still didn't know how I felt, but his emotions had been real and while neither I nor anyone I knew had anything to do with the bombing of Hiroshima and Nagasaki, I couldn't help but feel a touch of guilt and wondered if I cared about my country as much as he did his.

The only places left to look were all the boxes that James had left in Hamiada's grove. I planned on going through those over Christmas.

I was still a non-person in the department, and to be honest, I worked harder on making sure I knew everything James had researched than I did on any actual work. My boredom levels were epic, and I was about to just quit showing up. Why bother?

The muffled whoops, something I'd never heard in the office before, had me standing up and peering over my cubical walls. Striding toward me with a grin on his face was Scott Yang. I had to look multiple times as I'd never seen him smile before, and it changed his entire face.

"Did something happen?" I really hoped it was something minor, not like aliens showing up or Atlantis reappearing. Maybe Pearl had won the lottery?

"The treaty was signed and ratified. It's already filed with records and we can let other departments know to start working toward implementing the changes. This will look excellent on my resume." The smile still looked odd on his face, but I didn't tell him that.

"Excellent." And it was excellent. It meant maybe they could get me out of here, as my primary reason for being here was now gone. Now I could be assigned somewhere that I could actually do something.

"Yes. There will be a party hosted by China to bring in the American New Year. It is a great treaty."

I just nodded, still weirded out at his expression. Relief washed through me as he headed to Pearl's office and I sank back down into my chair. Another two hours and I could go home.

"Merlin Munroe, I have an assignment for you." I heard Pearl speak from the entrance to my cubicle.

I saved the document I was working on, a simple breakdown of treaties by country and number, turning to face her. "And that would be?"

Pearl glared at me in exasperation. "Check your email. There's a list of all the criteria of who China wants to invite to celebrate the signing of the treaty. I need you to get the initial list and verify with the OMO their locations and status. The State Department will provide stipends for travel up to a certain amount. There is a plus one built into the funds for spouses and what not. Work with the Public Relations office for the location and invitations. Your job is to verify the mage status of each invitee. You can access the Office of Magical Oversite website and obtain more information since your FBI clearance was never revoked. This will make it much faster for us rather than requesting it from the OMO and waiting for them to provide the information."

I didn't have a reason to refuse the assignment. To be honest I was bored to tears. The email glared at me and I tried to convince myself this would be fun. I pulled out the requests, frowning a bit at the list of names, then logged into the OMO website. After cleaning up the data, which took me a good hour, I uploaded the list and waited for the OMO to kick it back.

Twenty minutes later I had another list from the OMO and I bounced that against my cleaned-up spreadsheet. Most people didn't realize it but half of being a scientist was being able to look at data and manipulate it. I was very good with spreadsheets.

It was a list of people, about half of whom were registered in the OMO. The others I started to look up. The State Department had some very nice search databases and many of the people were ambassadors and other high up people in embassies or otherwise.

I got the list from the OMO, sorted in alphabetical order and started to list out the addresses that people would need to send to. I froze as I realized this wasn't just drafted mages. And I knew some of them. Jo's name was there, as was Sable's.

Chills rippled down my back and I started to pay attention to the data and what it said. Every mage on the list was an archmage or a merlin. And by my count it included most well-known merlins in the United States. I kept looking and frowned when I saw Shay, Indira, and Steven included on the list. I got a bad feeling when I saw Hishatio was to be invited, as well as some of the representatives in the UN.

Trying not to freak out, I went and pulled out the information on previous parties. And I didn't know if I felt better or not. There seemed to always be a high percentage of mages. I kept digging, but it looked like merlins got invites to most parties. That I wanted to check on, as I knew I'd never gotten one.

I grabbed my phone and texted Indira. She and Steven were still dating and didn't seem in a hurry to make it formal, though they had moved in together. They lived near Quantico as Steven still worked for the FBI, and Indira did her own research and took temporary jobs that interested her.

We still got together every month or so, and I'd just seen them at our joining. If anyone would know, they would.

Do you two ever get invites from the state department or government for parties and stuff? I typed, then paused. *And hi, my job sucks.*

A laughing emoji appeared, then words. *That exciting is it? And in answer to your question, yes. About 3-4 times a year. Most of the time we decline, but most merlins get asked occasionally, it is a mixture of showing off prize thoroughbreds and pandering.*

I looked at this for a long moment. *Then I shouldn't worry about a party where well over half the guests are merlins?*

Why worry about a party at all? And no. Some of those still under the draft may be required to come, but the rest of us usually decline. A long pause, then a curious emoji. *What is going on to make you worry at all?*

Dinner this weekend? I responded instead and went back to the list. The idea of trying to text all the conflicting emotions and thoughts in my mind sounded impossible.

She agreed, and we made plans to go to dinner and talk about the stuff going on, something I really hadn't told them about so far.

I paused, frowning when Bridget O'Keif's name popped up on the list. She wasn't a mage, Tirsane had seen to that, so why was she on this list? I logged back into the OMO website and pulled up Bridget. Oddly, it had the phrase "Under Review - Possible Deceased" on the top of the record, something I'd never seen before.

Deceased? Surely she wasn't dead? A flicker of panic raced through me.

What had Charles said her mother did? I racked my brain and then gave up and shot Charles a text. He responded back a minute later with her job. Being on your own computer with a chat history helped immensely. She worked for the State Department. It only took me two minutes to find her internal phone number.

The list and the pending invite gave me a reason to call her, and I did want to know how Bridget was doing.

I stared at her number, then back at the lists. Did that Under Review show up in the report? Checking to see if any other mages had Under Review flags ate up another ten minutes, then I gave in. I needed to know things; it was my weak spot. Besides, if Bridget had died I was going to fall apart. I'd done everything I could to make sure she didn't die.

Headset on, I dialed the number.

"Margaret O'Keif, may I help you?" The vaguely familiar voice filled my ears and I couldn't help a furtive glance around, as if I was doing something illicit.

I really need to quit feeling like a kid with their hand in the cookie jar.

"Ms. O'Keif, this is Cori Munroe. I, um, met you at the draft thing. Bridget having her magic pulled away?" I was pretty sure she'd remember me, but that didn't mean a strange voice would click for her immediately.

"Miss Munroe!" I could hear the powerful emotions in that voice, and I wanted to blush. "I am so glad to hear from you. Is your draft here? The number is local."

"Yes. I'm in the State Department." I took a breath. "Is Bridget okay? I mean nothing happened to her afterwards, did it?" I didn't know if I wanted to know the answer, except that I needed to know the answer.

"Bridget? She's fine. Actually better than fine. No more magic. They tested her multiple times and have one scheduled every six months, but it was like she never had any magic. Even the tattoos seem like they were never there when you look at her skin. I don't know that I'll ever be able to thank you enough."

I sagged in relief. "I'm glad. I was worried as the OMO has her as deceased."

Margaret snorted. "Yes. They talked to me about it. They don't have any other status they can use and they refuse to remove the record. So they marked her as dead. I don't care as she isn't someone truly in the work force even if she does have a job. But I heard a rumor," she hesitated as if unsure she should say it.

"That this happened to lots of people everywhere?" I asked, my own amusement leaking through.

"Yes. Did it?"

"From what I've been told, yes. The OMO has mentioned they want to talk to me, but they haven't followed up yet." And I sure wasn't going to remind them.

"Then you helped many more people than just me. I've been dreading the draft since she emerged. Stupid laws," she spat, but I could hear the grief and sorrow behind her words at the same time.

"Yeah," I murmured, but didn't comment, as I'd also seen the damage Bridget could have done with her anger. "I did have another question for you though if you have a minute."

"Merlin Munroe, you can ask just about anything of me and I'd try to give it to you." She laughed, the sound making me smile. "It's a good thing I don't really have access to anything super-secret. You'd be able to get it out of me."

I snickered. "I don't really think I'm spy material. I lose my temper too easily." Clearing my throat, I refocused on the list and my confusion. "I'm working on a list for a party to celebrate the signing of a treaty."

"Oh. They saddled you with getting the guest list and addresses for the Biological Treaty between the US, Japan, and China?"

I blinked, surprised. "Yes. How did you know?"

She laughed again. "I deal with a lot of the parties if they are multinational. And this party has a lot of people excited. There hasn't been a big party this year. It has all the people that want to see and be seen hoping for an invitation. Anything this big will get a lot of attention." Margaret paused for a minute. "Ah, Bridget was on the list because she is a single female archmage. That makes sense. I think you can safely remove her from the list." She sounded sad and amused at the same time. "While I do not doubt she would love the chance to dress up and go to a fancy party, I suspect others would not be as happy."

I sighed. "No probably not. You mind if I call if I have any other questions?"

"Anything you need, Merlin Munroe."

"Ugh, Cori, please?" There were some people I had no desire or need to intimidate.

Section 95.18
The OMO will provide addresses and other information for mages under the draft. The government will update the OMO should any information be found to be inaccurate.

CHAOS

"What do you mean, you don't want us to go?" Jo's voice managed to be calm and curious, but from the set of her jaw I knew she was pissed.

"Because something is going to go wrong. Not just my crazy luck, but something else." I hated that I sounded like I was pleading.

"Cori. Explain," Jo said, her voice icy cold.

I laid it out. Most of it she already knew, but I added the last bit about how the party would be the perfect opportunity.

"So you don't know for sure that something will happen?" Sable had stayed silent, watching us argue since I'd asked them to not go when they received the invitations in the mail. I'd not had any control once I validated the list, and removing their names, or Indira and Steven's, would have been too obvious.

"So you only think, not have any proof?"

Sable's calm, reasonable voice was the death knell for any chance I had of getting them to not go.

My shoulders sagged, and I shook my head. "No. Technically security is high and they know this is going down and the threats made, but it is all just talk. I have to be there and then maybe after that I can get another position and go do something." My frustration leaked out at that. I was so damn bored and nothing had clicked with the research James had done. I still didn't know what Japan might want. What did a country that wanted to be left alone need?

"Then if you think we would let you go and not be there with you, you need to have your brains checked." Sable pushed herself off the wall and draped her arms around me from the back, dropping a kiss on my head. "We love you and that means being there to help and protect, just like you try to do for us." She overrode my protests. "Hush. That is why Jo is so mad. We will always be there for you, because we know you will always be there for us. Now, we have other important stuff to discuss." She dropped one more kiss on my head and I sighed as she pulled away. Jo was still glowering at me, but had lost the stiffness in her body.

"And what is that?" I asked, trying to ignore Carelian laughing in my mind.

"Shopping, of course. We all need dresses fit for a New Year's Eve party." The smiles on their faces made me groan.

"Fine. I've got dinner with Indira and Steven this weekend, so next?" I gave in to the inevitable. I knew they would never let me just wear something simple.

"Ooh, yes. Ask Indira if she would like to come with us. She knows the best places."

I gave Sable a doubtful look. "You know she is out in Virginia near Quantico, right?"

"So? Sidestep her here." Sable gave me a look, and I nodded.

"Fine. Though I don't think they really realize how easy sidestepping is for me."

Jo rolled her eyes and got up, her anger fading. "No, they are well aware of it. They just know how to keep their mouths shut. But I'm still annoyed with you. I'm almost tempted to get Sable and me dates just to prove how annoyed I am."

"Ooh! Charles could come as our plus one," Sable blurted, a wide smile on her face.

I dropped my head in my hands and groaned. "I apologize. I should have known better. And..." I trailed off. "Yes, he's on the list but the secondary invitees depend on acceptance." This time I paused and with an evil grin. "Jo, you should ask Shay. I bet he'd show up if you did."

The two of them exchanged glances, wide smiles crossing their faces. "Deal. I'll twist Shay's arm to come and you'll have six mages at your back you know are on your side."

"When will I learn to keep my mouth shut and why do you think Shay will come?"

Jo shrugged. "He's always been kinda nice and if I present it as a prank, I bet he'll come. If nothing else to see what trouble you attract."

I narrowed my eyes at her, wanting to refute that, but I knew deep down in my bones that would happen.

~You know, I am surprised they did not specifically ask you to invite other denizens,~ Carelian said mildly. He'd quit laughing and was stretched out on the floor, looking like he was an inch away from melting into it.

"Why? I wasn't really the one that was supposed to do that. And the list came...from... the Chinese." I said the last part, thinking slowly. "They had a few sections about criteria, but us, Jo, Indira, Sable, Steven, were all specifically listed. The others were every merlin and archmage that had made a name for themselves. Nah, it can't be that. There were also ambassadors, political people, directors. It's a big list. I think the list is approaching a thousand people and of that at least half of them are mages."

~Ah. Oh well. Though I think we should do dinner and invite others over.~

I gave him a long look. "Are you saying Esmere and others want to come over for dinner?"

~I do not believe I said that,~ he replied primly. ~Though it would be nice to have civilized conversation.~

The three of us snickered and looked at the calendar. "What about Thanksgiving?" asked Sable. Would Hamiada be willing to let us have dinner in her grove? Perfect weather, we can bring food from the kitchen, everyone can come and Dad and your family can come, Jo? We can even invite Indira and Steven, and Charles and Arachena?"

I thought about that. "That would be fun. I think I can open a door to Hamiada's grove anywhere if she lets me, though it won't last long, and we can just walk in. Do we include Marco and Paulo's family?"

Jo looked at Carelian, whose tail lashed for a moment, then settled. ~Yes. Baneyarl loves children. I would invite Tiantang.~

I flinched a bit. "Fine, but just him. I am not sure I could take Zmaug, too, or Onyx, much less feed them." I was still annoyed at her.

~Oh, you are starting to get into the game. That will be a wonderful amount of subtle insult. Invite her son, and not her. Esmere would be proud of you.~

"Wait, that wasn't what..." I trailed off as the three of them started planning food and I just shook my head, staying out of the way.

Saturday I stepped out to my work step spot in D.C. and hailed a cab. Indira and Steven lived in Montclair, but we had agreed to meet at a restaurant near D.C. They thought I was renting an apartment in the area and they knew I avoided driving, if at all possible. I could drive, I still just worried about things going wonky and it was easier to take public transportation.

Carelian had decided to skip dinner in favor of going to talk to his mother and probably Tiantang. I got the feeling those two had struck up a friendship. I worried that I was stifling him from having his own life.

I stepped into the restaurant and spotted Indira and Steven near one of the windows. The hostess escorted me over, and they rose as I approached.

"Cori, you look exhausted." Indira gave me a tight hug, inspecting me closely.

Before I could say anything, Steven had pulled me into a hug as well. "I agree. What's going on that a cushy job in the State Department has you so exhausted?"

If you had told me five years ago the jerk FBI agent would become like a big brother, I would have called you an idiot. But it was true, and I'd learned he'd be there if I needed him.

I waited until the waiter had taken our order, then pulled on Air from Sable to create an auditory shield for the discussion. Then I told them everything. The draft camp, Bridget, Tirsane, the weird job, the pressure on me for my inheritance, and Tiantang and Zmaug.

I paused in the middle when they brought out our meals. This restaurant specialized in mage cooking. The chef, I assumed sous and not the head chef, brought our food to the table. His mage tattoo was clearly displayed, but I suspected he had a wealth of hair up under his white chef hat.

"And who had the broiled salmon salad?" Indira raised her hand.

The chef, a man in his early thirties, set a bowl of salad with cranberries, nuts, and goat cheese liberally sprinkled on it before her. He then brought out a portion of salmon.

"Seasoning request?" He waved his hand at the array of salts and spices on the tray.

"Mmm, lemon, mustard, and black salt please," Indira said, after pondering her options for a moment.

He nodded, seasoned the salmon, and then looked at it. It sizzled and bubbled sitting there on the plate. I couldn't help but grin. I'd have to tell Jo about this trick. She used fire to warm up coffee occasionally, but this was new.

"And you, miss?"

I had ordered sea bass, thinking to take the extra home for Carelian. With him in mind, I chose my seasonings. "Sea salt, lemon, and red peppers." He smiled at me and set it up. Then it started to bubble as he deftly put the salmon on Indira's salad.

"As for your filet, sir. What temperature and seasonings?"

Steven went with horseradish, butter, and smoked salt. In a few minutes his was sizzling away as my steamed vegetables were pulled out and the sea bass put on them with seasoned rice pulled out from the steamer.

When he left, our food had been perfectly prepared and I really needed to get Jo cooking guides for this. Maybe I could do this without screwing up. Maybe.

After moaning over the perfectly cooked food, I went back to my explanation. When I was all done they just looked at me. After a long moment, they glanced at each other and snickered. It sounded so funny to hear it from them, but it didn't surprise me.

Steven looked at me and laughed. "Cori, I have done twenty years now in government service, and I don't believe I have ever been involved in as much drama and incompetence as you managed to stumble into. Yes, people use favors and threats to get different mages under them sometimes. But I have no idea what Pearl did to get you, and it blew up so badly in her face. I think that everyone realizing familiars are people too is a good thing, but Merlin." He shook his head still laughing a little.

"And really, Cori," Indira chimed in. "Did you think Jo and Sable would stay home any more than we would? Trust me, we are going to be there prepared for war in every meaning of the word." She got a distant look in her eyes. "I would suggest two things."

"Oh?" I wanted to rail about them coming, but I knew I didn't have a chance of talking them out of it. So why waste the energy?

"See if you can get the specs on the virus so we can know what it looks like. If the Chinese are planning on using it at the party, we might be able to stop it if we know what it looks like."

I felt my eyes widen as I looked at her.

"You don't really think they would. Do you?" I didn't know what to think about that, but the idea made me shudder. Breaking molecular bonds like Jo had done with the nicotine was magnitudes easier compared to hunting out a virus. You had to mutate the virus or break it apart. And you needed to know the shape of it intimately because viruses were tiny lifeforms, too complex for any specific identification like a nicotine molecule.

Indira shrugged. Today she had on a royal blue silk blouse that made her look like she would be on a runway. I'd managed to put on nice slacks instead of jeans. The shrug caused the material to ripple, and I spared a moment of envy to just ever be that elegant.

"I don't know. But it seems a simple thing to prepare for. But really, Cori..." She paused, uncharacteristically hesitant as she pushed food around her plate.

"What?"

"Do you really think they will be that crazy to attack?"

I shrugged helplessly. "I don't know. But I've decided governments aren't sane. I still don't know what Japan wanted from James' research and neither do they. Who kills someone over something when you don't even know if it exists?"

Steven laughed. "Governments have been doing that since the beginning of time. I don't see it changing anytime soon."

I sighed; my life had been easier before I knew all this. "And the other thing?"

Indira gave me a wintery smile. "Make sure you can run in the outfit you wear to the celebration."

We all fell silent. Dinner ended in a quiet camaraderie and they promised to be at the party.

Carelian didn't get any sea bass. It was too good.

Chapter 43

Section 2.45.5

All interactions between mages, if not related to draft duties, shall be regarded as private conversations, and prying by the OMO or the Draft is frowned upon. Engendering resentment outside of the draft is guaranteed to send mages to other countries.

SPIRIT

Thanksgiving had been wonderful, if stressful. But in the end the laughter and love made it one of the best Thanksgivings, and the largest, I'd ever had. Christmas had been much more low key, with John Lancet, Sable's dad, staying with us and going to the Guzman's for Christmas dinner the mundane way—driving.

But since then it had been a non-stop whirlwind. While this department wasn't actually in charge of managing the party itself, we were the key point as to figuring out what the Chinese and Japanese wanted, exactly how the treaty was being celebrated, and a hundred other details that made no sense to me.

It was a mix of a New Year's Eve and an early Lunar celebration plus the treaty. It would be a huge party for everyone, and there was almost nothing competing with it.

I was kept busy with crap that while I'm sure was important to someone, to me it came across as stupid stuff. I'd turned in the list well before Halloween, after removing all the mages that Tirsane had unmagicked. There were only four on the list. Apparently most of the mages she had affected were not merlins or archmages.

The report I'd pulled from the OMO made me blink. Over three million mages had been set in an "Under Review" status. The American Indian Nation and North Korea didn't participate with the OMO oversight, and a country or two in Africa, but to know that many people around the globe had their magic pulled away was stunning. And there were probably some that hadn't reported their magic that had been removed, especially if they were hedgemages.

It was simply more information for me and data that didn't point to anything. Japan was still a mystery, though I knew Hishatio was staying at the embassy until the party, but I didn't have an answer for him.

The last week was a rush of people freaking out and me trying not to roll my eyes. Even Jo and Sable seem caught up in the drama. I'd gotten a dress that looked elegant in a rich russet red shading to gold. It was a simple sheath, but it had slits and let me move and since it went to the floor, I could wear flats and be somewhat comfortable. Carelian had consented to wear a black vest with a bowtie the color of my dress. He was ostensibly my date. Charles was coming as the plus one for Jo, but escorting both of them. While they had no issues showing up anywhere as a married couple, it was nice to have someone to dance with, and oddly, Charles enjoyed dancing and was good at it. I just hoped he realized they'd drag him to every event just to have another dance partner.

I planned on staying alert. Every nerve I had vibrated with hyperawareness, and I didn't know what else I could do. I saw the guards everywhere. Though they did blend in better than I expected, they were still obviously present.

The party was being held in the Ronald Reagan Hall. It had been dedicated to him after he was assassinated, the fifth president killed in office. The event space was huge, with the Atrium being where the main gathering was, but they had also grabbed the Atrium Hall and the ballrooms to lay out the food and provide areas to sit and talk. It was beautiful, complicated, and I was very glad I had done nothing but the guest list.

Watching guests come down the Oculus into the Atrium was as impressive as it sounded, and I could have spent the entire night doing nothing but people watching. The clothes, the attitudes, the mages were fascinating. So many merlins, but no one else had the number of filled in branches as I did. It made me feel like an outsider as eyes drifted up to my temple and did a double take. If hiding my tattoos hadn't been a crime, I would have applied make up over them completely.

Pearl had promised to talk to me next week about my new assignment. Just the fact that I had one gave me a feeling of hope. I was so ready to NOT be here. If I was lucky, I wouldn't be in Washington D.C. at all.

Jo and Sable were checking out the food, and Carelian had followed them over to the tables. There was a table full of food for the familiars. I'd seen at least five others, but that didn't mean he was going to pass up what might be on the human side. Besides, he said he wanted to smell the food, make sure it was okay, but there was so much perfume and other odors he was sneezing a lot.

Everywhere I looked, people were smiling. I'd seen Pearl moving through the crowd, talking to people and being a social butterfly. For a rotund woman she moved with deceptive lightness, and I had never seen her glow like this. Scott Yang was here, and almost sported a smile on his face, but not enough that he looked creepy. And I was tight as a wire waiting for it to all go wrong.

Maybe I'm just paranoid and need to let it go?

Shay had declined Jo's offer. She said he had a prior commitment this month, and part of me had been relieved. I'd rarely seen him since I started college, but he still had a way of unnerving me.

I turned at the sound of a throat being cleared. Standing behind me was Hishatio and a woman. He looked calm and unruffled. She looked a bit more nervous. The tattoo on her face told me she would be one of the Handmaidens. The crease between her brow told me more.

I nodded to them both, offering a slight smile. "Maiyutsu-Shi. I did not expect to see you here," I said when he did not introduce his companion. From what I could see, she acted like he was talking to a wall or something. I let it be.

"I had come to see if you had made any progress in your research?"

He sounded hopeful, and I almost felt bad as I shook my head. "I still have found nothing that James would have left for you. Mostly it is boxes upon boxes of notes."

His hands tightened into fists. "If the world would just leave us alone, this need would not be so great. A decade of isolation. Is that so much to ask?"

He said that part in Japanese, but Carelian, even though he was on the other side of the room, translated it for me.

I blinked, tilting my head. "Mr. Yamato, did you mean you are looking for a way to cut Japan off from the rest of the world?"

He froze mid turn and glanced back at me. "Looking? That is a wish. It is more what we need. Time and isolation. James said he had the answer. Now I shall never find it out."

The water wall flashed into my mind. "I think I know

what you're looking for, but the price will be high for your mages, and I do not know if it can make you fully impervious. It should make it much more difficult for the rest of the world to reach you."

His eyes lit up, then became wary. "And what do you ask for this?"

I wanted to say I would just give it to him, but I paused. "I would like to think on it and discuss it with you and whomever else after this event is over."

He nodded; his eyes shuttered. "That seems wise. I look forward to meeting with you at that time." He spun and took the woman by the elbow and they strode off as if someone on the other side was calling to them.

I watched for a long time, unable to imagine the fear and need they had to cut themselves off from the rest of the world. It would eat up most of the offerings of an archmage in a month or two, depending on their power. If they had familiars or merlins they could support it for longer, but it would lock most of their mages into supporting that wall.

"Nice party. Can't say I'd want to do these all the time, but it isn't bad. Food is good." Charles' voice by my shoulder had me jerking a bit and the glass of water I held in my hand sloshed on my shoe.

"Don't do that," I hissed, trying to get my heart rate under control. With the music and chatter of people, I hadn't heard him approach. He grabbed a glass of champagne from a waiter who was walking by offering them to everyone, and handed it to me.

"Talk to you? Offer you champagne?" he asked, giving me a look. "Deep breath and relax. None of this is your responsibility, so just enjoy it."

"And if something goes wrong?" I muttered, wishing my hair was down so I could hide behind it. I fiddled with the glass, but champagne didn't even sound good.

Mostly I just wanted to be out of these clothes.

"You let all the very competent people handle it. You know the people that are paid to deal with things like this?"

The event seemed so bright and bubbly and I felt like I was being an idiot, jumping at shadows.

"Would you like to dance?"

I blinked and looked up at Charles, who smiled. "I was dragged here so the three of you would have a dance partner. And I don't mind dancing."

"I'd like to point out those two did the dragging. And I'm not the best dancer," I commented, looking out at the dancers. "But yes?" I set the glass of bubbly down on a small table, glad to have a reason to move. Maybe I would burn off some of my nervous energy.

He gave me one of his rare smiles and took my hand. The dancing area wasn't huge, and it definitely wasn't rock, but a nice box step that he led me through, not even wincing when I stepped on his feet occasionally. It was more fun than I expected. We went through two sets, nothing fancy. I knew Jo had claimed him if the musicians played a waltz. I had no idea how she even knew how to waltz.

Carelian had found a corner where he and another familiar were talking. I didn't know what the denizen was, other than maybe canine, which struck me as odd. Carelian had little patience for dogs in general.

~You okay?~ I asked, as Charles led me off the floor. Arachena had declined to come. Saying instead she had some art to work on and a quiet evening would be nice.

~Why would I not be? Excellent food, the appropriate amount of fear and awe at my presence, and my queans looking glorious.~

I didn't know if I should blush or roll my eyes. ~It just looked like you were talking to a dog.~

He hissed in my mind and I rocked my head a bit with the pain. ~Do not call an Aralez a dog. That is an insult to them. They are intelligent creatures that only roughly share the shape of your poor creatures.~ They were both staring at me, and I swore the being he spoke to looked like a laughing dog, about half Carelian's size.

~Okay, I'm sorry. Have fun.~ I bowed out of the conversation to his mental humph and tried not to giggle.

"Everything okay?" Charles asked as we drifted back to the wall, out of the way of all the other attendees. If it hadn't been made very clear I needed to stay, I'd have already gone home. My own panic levels were slowly fading. All this stress over nothing.

Or never come.

"Yeah, I'm just insulting beings right and left. I would have preferred to stay home." I mentally castigated myself for the whine. I had nothing to whine about.

"I get it. You'd prefer the jeans and low-key existence all the time." He sounded understanding, and I glanced up at him.

"You like this?"

He shrugged. "If I'd needed to find a date to bring here, I would have loathed it. Being invited by three gorgeous women who like me as a person? That makes it much more fun. Besides, dancing is a good way to get some exercise."

I gave him a sharp look. Over the years, he had lost weight and slimmed down. "Is that what you've been doing? Taking dance lessons?"

Charles laughed, a true laugh. "No. My grandmother taught dance way back when, and when I was a pre-teen to teen, I would be her escort after my grandfather died. It started out as feeling sorry for her, I guess. But the women at her get-togethers loved to dance. They were happy when I came to dance with them." He shrugged, a hint of red on his cheeks. "I think this is the first time I've danced since she died. It's been nice."

I slipped my arm into his and squeezed it. "You're a good man, Charles."

The flush faded at that. "Not as much as you might think. All of us have dark things we hide, Cori. Never forget that."

Surprised by the sudden darkness in his voice, I looked up at him. He forced a smile and shook his head. "You keep on believing the best in people, Cori. It's what makes you special."

I slid my eyes sideways, huffing a laugh. "I believe everyone is trying to kill me. I'd be happier if I wasn't so accurate."

~Cori?~ Carelian shot a question into my brain and I turned to look at him. He had risen to his feet and his fur along his body and tail was rising up to a full bristle. The creature next to him was weaving through the crowd of people toward his mage, I assumed.

"What?" I said, looking around. People were still mingling, a few dancing, mostly in little groups waiting for the ceremony scheduled in thirty minutes. Maybe after that I could leave.

~Something is wrong. Tiantang is coming.~

"What?" This time my voice was much louder and a few people looked at me, curious. I spun trying to figure out what might be going on.

In front of us a rip formed with the accompanying slash of pain. My heart raced as I backed up. Most rips you could only see if you were looking at the right place, and then they looked like a ripple in the air. But this one gaped wide open about ten feet from me starting at about a foot above the floor to halfway to the ceiling. The lights and shadows in it hinted as to the realm inside. I had to remember not to lean in and try to see what was in there. People backed up from it, as it gave off a feeling of static electricity that was uncomfortable.

When Carelian brought people from one place to another, he always went through glades or locations that he knew were safe, like Baneyarl's or Hamiada's spaces. This was a path through the unformed regions. Only denizens could move through that safely, humans didn't do well in raw magic.

People were scattering back and the mood changed from festive and excited to something darker and worried. I saw people filtering into groups, but I didn't have time to analyze what sort of grouping was being created as Tiantang came charging out of the rip.

Tiantang shouted in my mind. ~Cori, they have attacked you!~ I flinched, resisting the urge to cover my ears. It never did any good. Multiple people around us, all with color on their temples, were staring at us and I wondered if they had heard what he said.

"Tiantang, what are you talking about?" I squeezed out the words, my body vibrating.

~They have poisoned everyone!~

Chapter 44

Section 2.20.6

Infractions are treated the same as the general populace with an eye toward using a mage in a way beneficial to the current jurisdiction. But a pattern of behavior will be treated much more harshly for mages.

ORDER

The room came to a screeching halt, even the music skittered to a stop, and everyone stared at the dragon.

Tiantang for his part was undulating back and forth, making me dizzy.

"What do you mean poisoned everyone?" I asked, trying to stay calm. I was pretty sure I hadn't been poisoned, as I'd been too nervous to eat or drink anything.

~I've been listening. They said they needed to occupy you and the poison would fill that.~ He all but wriggled in place, and I shook my head.

"Tiantang, do you know the poison?" Everything hinged on that. I couldn't do anything if I didn't know what it was.

He curled up tight. ~They mentioned a fish and that Japan would be the obvious source,~ he murmured. At this point, people had started to creep closer, their eyes flicking between me and the dragon. Carelian's warmth pressed to my side and I let my hand stroke his back, not caring about fur on my dress.

I'd taken Indira's warning to heart and pulled out my phone. That and lipstick were the only things I had in my purse. I'd downloaded an app on it that was a detailed compendium of poisons, bacteria, and viruses. It was a searchable database, and it had cost a decent chunk of money. Since I had just used it for work I would be filling it on an expense report. The government could repay me.

~Jo, Sable, better get over here.~ I knew they'd heard me, but the odds were they'd started this way as soon as Tiantang appeared.

I typed in fish and Japan and poison and waited, staring at the screen and ignoring the others around me.

"We're here." Jo wrapped her arm around my waist in a brief hug and I closed my eyes, feeling immeasurably better.

Three things popped up and one grabbed my attention. "Tiantang, was it Fugu?" I used the name of the poison and he stiffened, raising his head.

~Yes that!~ He whipped his head around and he went from a frantic puppy to a deadly creature in the blink of an eye. I don't know how to explain it but where there had been frantic energy and movement, waving whiskers and rippling scales, now there was stillness, sleek power, and anger. ~They dare? They attack my mage. They seek to hurt all and succeed in a coup. That shall not happen.~

Before I could react he had streaked through the rip like a spear of red and it sealed behind him with a crack.

That's different.

I shook my head and looked back at the poison, and everything suddenly got worse. "Merlin," I hissed, and people started to step closer to me.

"Cori, what is it?" I looked up to see Steven striding through the crowd, Indira following behind him. They both looked elegant, but what caught me was the worry on their faces.

"Tetrodotoxin," I said. Most people looked at me blankly so I expanded. "Puffer fish poison."

The ripple of curses that went through the area had me freaking out as I read faster. It looked bad as I read through the symptoms.

"Any idea how they got it to us?" someone asked, and I just shook my head. I didn't have a clue, but I did know how to deal with a poison.

"It says the symptoms are tingling, numbness of the lips, and then difficulty breathing." I looked up and blinked at the crowd of mages surrounding me. "Umm.. that describe anyone?"

I could see gazes turn inward and then people started raising hands. Crying or panicking wouldn't help. "Okay, how many Transform or Entropy mages do we have?"

People raised their hands, and Indira waved them over. "You should be able to find this molecule structure and break the bonds." I looked around for something to write with and sighed. I moved over to one wall and with my lipstick wrote out the formula. I was charging them for this as well. I liked this lipstick.

$C_{11}H_{17}N_3O_8$

"Find it and break it," I said.

"Who are you to be telling us what to do?" a woman said, striding out of the crowd.

"If you can think of something better, for Merlin's sake, do it. But I figure neutralizing the poison is the best first response," I growled out, more than happy for anyone else to do this.

Charles stepped up behind me, looming a bit. "She is one of the saviors of the SEC. You know? She and her family here shattered the nicotine structure for an entire stadium?"

The woman looked like she was about to say something else. Anger flashed in her eyes, though she jerked her head down in a short nod that might have indicated respect. The man next to her started to gasp.

"Babe, I think I have a... problem." His lips had an odd tinge of blue on them and his knees buckled as he started to go down.

She lost her arrogance and caught him, lowering him down. "Robert, you don't get to die on me, not like this."

Around us people were starting to gasp and choke. Others stared at their fingers with worry.

Security was sprinting to me. "Ma'am?"

"Call 911. Mass casualty event. Tetrodotoxin. They'll need respirators." They looked at me, eyes grim. One of them made the call on the radio while the other kept scanning. For what, I wasn't sure.

I looked around, wondering what food or drink had poisoned people and then if it mattered. No one else was going to eat or drink anything. Mostly I was confused and tried to stay out of the way. A few people—okay, a few dozen—were seriously ill and had collapsed, but the poison had only really started to kick in and the transform mages were knocking it out fast. There were at least two medical doctors here, and everyone was spending offerings recklessly to help repair the damage it had caused.

Why had they done this? Surely they had to know my history. That meant they knew I had experience dealing with poisons, and this place was crawling with educated mages.

It made no sense. I spun looking at the scattered people. Most were focused on the downed attendees, mages, politicians, famous people. The undercurrent of others sobbing and yelling for attention as first responders streamed in made it organized chaos.

Frustrated and ready to run away, I backed into a

corner, trying to stay out of the way. I was strong, but this was better done with finesse. Movement caught my eye a split second before I heard the crack of multiple rifles. From the upper Oculus and the 14th street entrance, about twenty people in dark jumpsuits appeared and they were shooting at us.

We're easy targets!

Frantic, I pulled dust and food and formed it into a shield but there was so much area that I couldn't cover it all.

"Shooters, shield!" I screamed.

Someday I'd have to figure out who to thank for the draft, because at least half the mages there reacted. Not by screaming or yelling, but by grabbing tables and putting them over the wounded, others sent lightning toward the shooters, still others set air whirling like a tornado around us.

"No Time Bubbles," Steven boomed as he frowned and a gun fell apart in a shooter's hand. "Grab your target, take them down. I'll get clearance, I'm FBI."

It was like his words had removed a safety, and if I hadn't been so frantic to find Jo and Sable and make sure they were okay, I would have watched with awe.

I know if there had been a filmmaker there, he would have filmed all of it, and been muttering about winning an Oscar. I saw mini-fireballs, ice shards, wind, and things that had never occurred to me. A woman peeked around a table, eyes narrowed, and glared at three of the shooters on the walkway around us, and they began to scream. I could see the water pouring out of their bodies as they seemed to crumple in on themselves.

"Amateurs," she muttered, then dove behind the table as a hail of bullets hit.

Others were just as lethal and I wanted to be sick as I saw eyes rupture, bodies age, and at least two men drop like they'd been knocked out, which they probably had. I thought about doing a KO wave, but there were so many people that I couldn't do it as a wide band. People might die if I knocked out their caregivers. There was more than one person using Air to keep people breathing as their lungs locked up from the paralysis of the drug.

I flinched as a bullet impacted by my head and I started to move. I was acting like an idiot. I spotted Jo scrambling from one person to another, Carelian by her side as she focused and I assumed shattered the molecular bonds to stop the poison.

"Sweep your air along the top, and then remove it from their lungs there," Steven barked. I kept my head down and kept moving toward Sable, who leaned over a man.

"Don't worry, I have the air going in and out, and I'm forcing your lungs to contract. I'll keep you breathing until help arrives." She talked to the man, who had started to get color back in his face and he closed his eyes.

"You got this?" I asked Sable, not that I could do anything without my kit. I was starting to think I should just wheel it everywhere with me.

"Yes. But I can only do one person at a time. It requires too much concentration to risk doing multiples." She didn't look at me, still watching him. "I can't move air in too hard or I'll rupture his lungs, too soft and he won't get his lungs to pull in the oxygen."

That made sense. I knew how respirators worked, and she was simply using magic to act as one. Which meant she didn't need me to hover. I looked around for anyone who needed my help and spotted Pearl huddling near an overturned table, lips turning blue and blood streaming down her arm.

I scurried over to her side, inspecting her. "Can you still breathe?"

"Barely," she gasped, and I cussed. I looked at the wound. A bullet had passed through the fleshy part of her arm, painful and bloody, but not life threatening.

"Lay down. I'm going to get your arm taken care of and see if I can help you breathe." In theory, oxygen would be better than air with all its other gasses, but trying to separate out the O2 only right now wasn't something I could do and keep my eyes on the rest of the stuff. I tore a long strip off a tablecloth, using entropy to get it going, as I worked on moving the air into her lungs nice and steady.

Color started coming back into her face as I tied the pressure bandage on and I looked around. The gunfire had stopped and from what I could see all the attackers were down, either dead or restrained. Alixant and a few others had taken charge and more paramedics and firefighters were streaming in with equipment and meds to help those that had been attacked.

"Thank you, Cori. I'm sorry we didn't listen," Pearl gasped out, in between an EMT bagging her.

"My life. Go, get better." I stood and looked around. To my relief, Jo and Sable were headed toward me, a tired Carelian between them. All three of them looked disheveled, exhausted, and their hair a bit ragged from offerings, but none looked damaged.

I turned and saw Indira headed my way while Steven was directing the people streaming in to different places. I didn't know how many of our attackers were still alive, and I didn't ask.

"Are you okay?" I asked Indira. She'd fought like everyone else, and more than one mage had stared at her stunned. When I had time I needed to figure out how to wield my magic the way she did.

"I'm fine." She looked down at her dress and sighed. "So much for my dress though." It had a melted spot or two, some singeing, dirt, and what looked like blood on it. None of us looked much better.

"Merlin Munroe," came a voice from behind me and I turned to see Chun Wen walking up. Dressed in a tuxedo, he looked more elegant than in his normal suit.

"Chun Wen," I said nodding and started to turn back around.

"It is too bad you came through this unpleasantness so well. Huilang won't let you mess up her plans. Fortunately that is easily remedied."

"Huh?" I twisted to look at him, wondering if the English hadn't translated correctly.

He smiled at me as he slammed a knife into my stomach.

Chapter 45

Section 2.20.2

If a mage is convicted for a Class D or E felony, the jurisdiction may weigh the risks and the violence of the crime and choose to raise felony level.

CHAOS

The world stopped for that instant as he looked me in the eyes, the knife in my stomach. Then he pulled it out and went to slam it in again.

~Cori!~ Carelian screamed in my mind. There was a blur of red and Chun screamed, a brutal, pain filled sound, that cut off with finality. I had to blink to see Carelian standing over the limp body of Chun, whose throat was gone, his blood staining Carelian's muzzle.

"Cori?" multiple voices said, and I pressed my hands against the spreading red on my dress.

"Shit," I muttered. "This is not good."

"Over here, now," I heard someone screaming as I stared at my stomach. The red spread across my dress and I stared at it dumbly. Shouldn't this be hurting?

~Cori!~ I looked at Carelian standing over me, his panicked voice ringing in my ears.

"Hey. It's okay. I'll be fine." I tried to smile at him, but the world titled and Jo's face appeared in front of me.

"We are laying you down," she said, her face pale and eyes wide.

I nodded as I turned over the problem in my mind. Why had Chun stabbed me? It made no sense. In the scheme of things I was a no one. Huilang wanted to prevent me from stopping something? What? I was in America. If she was running a coup in China, what could she think I could or would do?

"Let me look," a new voice said, and I blinked again to see faces I knew hovering around me and a growling Carelian draped over my legs. No wonder I felt trapped. The person speaking I didn't recognize, but he had a uniform on.

I noted all that, but went back to trying to figure out the puzzle in my head.

"We need to get her to the hospital. The knife definitely perforated her bowel. I can smell it."

"Carelian?" I felt slightly outside myself, everything focused on the enigma in my mind.

~Yes Cori?~ He replied instantly and I could hear both fear and rage like I'd never felt.

"Can you see if Tiantang is okay?" There was pain starting to radiate out from my pelvic area and part of my mind checked what they were doing to take care of me. There were other yelling people moving around. I kept my attention on Carelian, though I did want to wipe his face. He had streaks of blood all over his beautiful fur.

They were moving me to a gurney, and more people were streaming in, but I knew something was wrong.

What plans? How could I be involved in anything?

As my attention was riveted on Carelian, I saw his reaction. His eyes already dilated, went full black, not a hint of the green remaining. I lifted my hand, and those around me froze.

"What?"

His eyes locked on mine; eyes dark. ~My quean, she has ordered two of her most trusted mages to teleport here with nuclear weapons. She called them suitcase nukes?~ He spoke only to me, and I didn't know if anyone else could hear him.

My heart stopped, and I stared at him. "She what? Is she trying to replicate the..." I trailed off and closed my eyes as it all hit me. "The ultimate coup. She destroys our country and everyone will think the Japanese are responsible."

How could I stop it?

"When?" I demanded, my mind racing.

He closed his eyes, and I brushed away people talking at me. I needed to think. It was so important. After my public fights with Japan, the slap in the face of me being at the treaty, everything, them bringing nukes here would be obvious, logical even.

~Minutes. Tiantang says he's trying to protect his chosen. The mages are attacking her under Huilang's command.~ Another pause. ~Huilang has mages with her and Tiantang and those loyal to Cixi are fighting. It is a glorious fight, but she is talking about making sure Japan and the US will never interfere again.~

"Is there a way to direct a sidestep?" I'd never asked because it had never mattered.

He titled his head, then nodded. ~They will do brute force. You can redirect, especially if they don't know their destination perfectly.~

Chun's assistant, everything fit. He could teleport, the brute force that would let him get here with a warhead that would take out all of Washington and only people that could step could get out. I could never get anyone out in time.

But...

I gritted my teeth. "Help me up." My eyes locked on Jo's.

"Cori, no. You need to get to the hospital," Jo protested, her face tear streaked.

"It doesn't matter. Help me up."

"Lady, if they don't operate on you in the next hour, you're dead," the EMT argued, and I smiled at him.

"And if I can't stop the nukes, DC will be gone in the next five minutes. Tape me up. Give me a shot. And then hope I put all the pieces together correctly."

The area around me had fallen silent at the word nukes, and Steven pushed to the front. "Cori, what the fuck is going on?"

"I don't have time. Hope I'm right, or Tiantang is very wrong. Jo, Sable, are you with me?" I turned my face to them, wanting them to say no, to tell Carelian to take them to Baneyarl's, or Atlanta, or anywhere but here.

Instead, they reached down and pulled me up, Jo wrapping a bandage tight around my waist. "Always. We will never leave you. What do you need?"

I smiled, though it felt like my heart was breaking. "A miracle. Jeorgaz, I need you." I yelled the words out. If he didn't hear me, we were all dead.

Around me people stared at me, faces white if they believed me, confused and angry if they didn't. A flash of flame and heat washed in front of me, then he hovered there. I saw Hishatio out of the corner of my eye glaring at the bird but I had no time or energy to waste.

"Jeorgaz, can you grant your assistance to someone as if you were their familiar?"

He tilted his head. ~If I chose.~ He sounded wary and looked around, then at me. ~Why are you hurt? Why are there dead around? Has Carelian been eating humans?~ His eyes lingered on the dead Wen and Carelian's bloody mouth.

I ignored all of that. "Will you grant me your assistance to create a pocket realm? I need to dump two nuclear weapons into it. Will it hold? Will magic hold the radiation?"

His wings flapped faster, blue flames licking out from them, washing over people who stepped back. ~If I create one in Chaos, one that will eat the radiation, but I warn you it will be deadly to anyone that goes there.~

"Will it harm magic or leak out to harm others?" I demanded as strength seeped out of me.

His flames changed to orange and red. ~Not in the way that you mean. It will be a very long time, but eventually the realm will be absorbed into Chaos.~ I got the feeling he was about to say something else, and the mages gathered around us all looked very interested. But if we didn't survive the next five minutes, then it wouldn't matter.

"Then do it. We need that realm now or we all die and this area becomes a wasteland."

He flapped his wings, hard, and they seemed to grow. Whereas before he'd reminded me vaguely of a red, orange, blue, and purple peacock, he grew, and sharpened, and where there had been a beautiful if frivolous bird, a predator now flapped in our midst. I was aware of people swallowing and taking steps back, but I didn't pay any attention. I was torn between focusing on Jeorgaz and trying not to pass out. Cold and heat washed through me and I felt lightheaded, but I didn't dare even take time to breathe. I could feel time slipping through my fingers, and no matter how strong I was, I couldn't pause the Earth to give us more time.

~Corisande Munroe, I grant you my focus.~ His voice boomed through my mind and my hand sank into Carelian's fur, leaning on him.

"Jo, Sable, may I pull on you?" I might have begged, but I was going to need to figure out how to create a realm and pull everything into it in the next ninety seconds. I had no pride, just fear.

They stepped up, each one of them taking a hand. "For always and eternity," Sable whispered in my ear as she wrapped her arm around my waist. Jo matched her, both of them holding me up. Carelian sat in front of me, his back preventing my knees from buckling.

"Jeorgaz?"

~Go, pull on me and imagine creating your own world. Normally I'd say decide what you want, but for now, just imagine something huge, empty, and impervious.~

I had no time, so I just grabbed the image of a huge gaping abyss, hungry for everything and anything. Immense, untouchable, and beyond the predations of man. Magic poured out of me, the three of us, the five of us, and I wanted to scream at the sensation of so much magic pulling at me.

~Hurry, Cori. They are coming here!~ Carelian's voice was frantic, and I felt something about to appear near us.

I wanted to demand why here, but the body of Chun Wen gave me that answer.

~It exists, it is enough. You must grab the path they are forging and pull it there, to the place you created.~ Jeorgaz spoke urgently in my mind and I wanted to sob. I didn't have the knowledge, the ability to do any of this.

"Cori, use us. We're here," Jo whispered in my ear and my magic reached. The asterine in my ring sparked, then my magic surged up matching with Jo and Sable. My entire being sung with power, filling all the branches as they held me in their arms. Our magic multiplied from what it was. Carelian was a part of it, supporting and making us more than we had been. Then Jeorgaz added to it and for a moment I felt invincible. I squeezed tight. They squeezed back.

I waited, the newly formed realm empty, and I trembled at the power beckoning me to use it. We had enough offerings we could have done anything with two familiars. We could have stopped the Earth.

~Now,~ murmured Jeorgaz, and I focused on the incoming weapons and the pocket realm I'd created. I'd always felt the place I was stepping to before I arrived, a second or two, then I would appear. This time I felt them coming. I'd never looked before, but now I could feel them coming. Teleporting was more like jumping than sidestepping. I needed to change where they were landing.

My head spun and cold wracked me, but I leaned into Jo and Sable, and I kept the space I'd created and I pulled the rug of reality to my space. I felt power, anger, hunger flowing through that tunnel, the radiation was a wave of need and desire. Fire, Air, and more writhed in that wave of destruction.

Magic swaddled me as I dropped the connection to the realm, locking it away for all existence. I hoped.

My eyes opened, not that I'd realized I had closed them, and I looked at Jeorgaz. "Did it work, did we do it?" The fact that I was alive to ask answered a lot of it, but what if I'd dumped them someplace else? A place where others were hurt?

~I believe so. The realm is sealed and unless you gave someone access, it cannot be reached.~ He beat his wings and looked around.

I followed his gaze and everyone was staring at the three of us and I saw a pink light coming from the asterine. It surrounded us, and I looked up into the faces of Jo and Sable. They glowed, both from the light and with joy.

"You did it, Cori." Sable squeezed my hand as she said that.

"We did it." I dropped my gaze to see Steven and Indira staring at me. Then the world went away.

Our society has many laws for mages, some realistic, others punitive. But one thing that any arbitrator of the law should remember, mages are weapons. I urge this august body not to make the laws that protect us so onerous that those they are meant to control, revolt. Our history tells us that when there is enough rage, numbers mean very little. ~ Speech on the Senate floor in 1898.

CHAOS   ORDER   SPIRIT

It was the beeping that pulled me out of the peaceful darkness. It wouldn't shut up. I had to fight to open my eyes as they seemed to be stuck together, but soon enough a bland white ceiling revealed itself.

The last few minutes unspooled in my mind and I closed my eyes again. Obviously I was alive. Last thing I remembered Jo, Sable, and Carelian were alive. As long as that remained true, I could handle anything else.

"You going to say something, or just lay there waiting for a kiss from your true love?" Jo asked, a note of humor in her voice.

I puckered my lips, expecting a light kiss. Instead, Carelian licked them.

"Ewww, cat breath. What have you been eating? Rotten tuna?" I gagged and stuck out my tongue, needing a glass of water.

~Ha, that is your own breath you smell. I have sweet salmon on mine. Would you like some?~

That had me opening my eyes again. "Am I dying? You're offering to share salmon?" I turned my head to see him braced on the handrail of my bed with Jo giggling behind him.

Mel Todd

"I always knew you loved him more than me," she said between giggles. Sable walked in, and her face lit up as she saw me talking.

"Well, if he's sharing salmon, I'm dying. So I shall say my final goodbyes now." I would have cast my hand dramatically over my forehead, but given the IVs attached to it, I figured that wasn't a good move.

"I think the doctors might be annoyed at losing you after spending four hours patching you up," Sable said as the door closed behind her.

"Ooh. Okay, I need to sit up, have some water, and you need to spill. What happened?" The need to know burned, but first they got me water, raised the bed, had the doctor come in and look at me, and Carelian moved over to the window bench, his purring loud enough I could hear it over the beeping.

The doctor told me the knife had pierced my right lumbar region, but while it had cut two loops of my intestines, it hadn't hit any other organs. I'd need to stay overnight to make sure they flushed everything out fully, but he was certain I would have a full recovery and would need to do some physical therapy to strengthen the cut abdominal muscles. But otherwise I should be safe to go home tomorrow.

"Steven and Indira are on their way. You are going to have to wait until they show up, as they have all the details. Heck, even we aren't sure what the outcome is or was." Jo sat next to Carelian, after lifting up his head and dropping it back down on her lap. Sable was in the chair in the room.

"You two are okay? Nothing happened to you?" There had been so much blood, then with the bullets flying around, I wasn't positive they had not been hurt.

"Other than being exhausted and losing a good ten inches of hair," Jo said, holding up her hair that had taken a major hit. "Sable figured out how to move the air for multiple people at once, and there was a Water merlin who showed me how to use Water to start flushing people's bodies. It was a variation of what I do at my job, but through their blood vessels and organs instead. It was very cool."

I sighed in relief and sagged back a bit. Already I felt like I could gladly take another nap.

A knock sounded at the door before I could ready my next question. Lifting my eyes took effort, but I smiled when I saw Steven and Indira slip in. They almost looked as exhausted as I felt.

"I'm really glad you look like shit," I slurred out. They looked at me, then burst out laughing.

"It may be a good or a bad thing, but I know how you feel." Indira slid over and kissed my forehead. "It sucked knowing you looked like death warmed over and everyone coming in to see you looked marvelous. How are you?" She scanned me up and down.

"Meh, I'll live. Tell me what happened," I demanded, forcing my eyelids to stay open. I had to know.

"You look like you've been beaten up one side and down the other. You sure you're up for this?" Indira asked as she sat down in the last chair while Steven settled against the wall behind her.

I tried to sit up a little straighter, but the protest from my abdomen changed my mind. "No. I need to know what happened and why? It's driving me crazy. I knew they were trying something, but poison? It seems so lame, not to mention they knew I'd dealt with a poison situation before." I glanced over at Jo, who was busy paying attention to Carelian. "Though the fact that Jo saved everyone doesn't get near enough airtime."

Jo let her hair, noticeably shorter and uneven, fall to hide her face.

"Ignore her, she's being coy," Sable said with a grin, and Jo jerked her face up to glare at Sable, her cheeks flushed with color.

I snickered as she avoided all our gazes.

"Spill, why in the world did all that happen? The poison, the stabbing, and then nukes? Are they insane? Why?" I was so tired I wanted to cry, but instead I moved again, letting the jolt of pain help chase away some of my exhaustion.

Steven heaved a sigh. "Besides the fact that you seem to have a Murphy's Cloak that is draped about you and everyone in your world?"

I glared at him. "Yes. Because I dispel the blasted thing every time I sense it."

Everyone in the room snorted. "I have days where I think being Magic's Herald makes you a permanent lightning rod for the odd. Because really, Cori—the stuff you get into." Jo stuck her tongue out at me and I made a face. I didn't ask for this, I just tried to deal with it.

"There are still a few details that are being nailed down," said Steven, "but here is what we've figured out so far. Keep in mind the general aspect is probably accurate even if some of the details aren't exactly."

I let out my breath in an exasperated sigh and circled my finger, urging him to get to the point.

He rubbed his nose, but I think he was hiding a smile.

"Very well, Merlin Impatient. China had the virus for a few years and they were getting ready to release it targeted to the exact enzyme combination you presented in your doctoral research. But your little display with the SEC football game had them worried. They still think you were the one that broke the molecule. We think they figured they needed a treaty so more people than just us had the virus. It would shift attention away and if they spread it far enough, it would take mages giving their lives to break it down, as a virus will replicate, a basic poison won't. Either way, no one would be able to point fingers at them and we would be short of mages."

Indira piped in here. "And by China, we mean it was mostly Huilang working with the previous emperor Qixiang. The rest of the cabinet members say they didn't know what was planned and they have all been truth sensed."

I nodded slowly, though I knew with careful words you could trick truth sensing and no one at those levels of government would ever be forced to speak. At least by outsiders.

"But the rest?" I prompted, still not sure what I was missing.

"When you showed up at the treaty negotiations, they freaked and it made it worse when Tiantang disappeared with Carelian. They were sure you were a plant to get them to force their hands. It was part of the reason they threw such a fit, hoping the State Department would sit on you."

"Which they did," I muttered. It had been a very boring three months.

"Yeah. Well with Qixiang deposed and Cixi coming across as a very different sort of leader, Huilang decided to make her move. Remember this is China. Long multi-layered plans are the norm." I nodded at Steven's reminder.

It made sense when the familiar for the empress of China was over one-hundred-fifty and still regarded as a child. Just how old was Zmaug?

"They had planned on the party for a while, which was why they dragged their feet so much. Once they felt New Year would be selected, they made the treaty so good that Japan and the US couldn't resist. Then Huilang kicked everything off for her plan."

"What was her plan?" I couldn't keep the question in, even if it was followed up by a huge yawn and a whimper.

"Her next round of meds is due in a bit," Jo said. "Don't take too much longer. She'll have a week at home to get all the details."

Steven nodded, though he frowned as he looked at me.

"Tell me. I can handle it a bit longer," I demanded. Not knowing might drive me insane. They all gave me skeptical looks, even Carelian, but I ignored them. "Go on."

Steven shook his head, but started speaking. "Japan's issues with the US and you are relatively well known. So the best guess is Huilang decided to solve all her problems at the same time and throw the suspicion on Japan."

That made no sense to me. Why would people think it was Japan? It clicked even as I fought through the drug cloud.

"The poison is a very Japanese-based one, and the bombs. It would look like payback from World War II. The fact that I would be killed in the same incident only increases the impression Japan was behind it." I shook my head. "But what was the stuff with Chun?" I waved at my belly. "What brought this on?"

"This is strictly a suspicion, and only because of Carelian and Tiantang do I have any info at all." I motioned at Steven to get on with it. I didn't want to fall asleep before I got all my answers. Steven huffed at me, but I saw his lips twitch. "Chun was devoted to Huilang. He wanted to make sure you wouldn't ruin any more of her plans. He had no idea she was sending nukes. The two she sent would have taken out most of DC and further."

I frowned. "Then how did they know where to sid-, I mean teleport to? I thought they were coming to Chun."

Steven shrugged. "No clue. But the Regan building is really well known. Getting pictures and studying them or even Chun sending pictures back would have been easy enough to do."

"Oh." I rubbed my nose. "They were going to kill all those people? I mean, I don't think the President would have been killed, would he?"

Steven sighed. "Yes. They were giving a party at the White House. Those bombs would have removed most of the Washington elite and thrown us into a power struggle that would have taken years to get out of. But her biggest advantage would have been taking out most of the OMO that were also at a local party and a large segment of our active merlins. So our mage base would be severely impacted, our leadership would be in shambles, and Japan would be blamed for everything because there would be no survivors."

"Tiantang?" I suggested, but my heart wasn't in it. No one would believe him and there would be a war.

"She is still trying to take control of China but from what I've been told, Cixi is winning people to her side right and left. If she holds on, it will be interesting to see what China is like with a female ruler."

I nodded but my eyes kept closing of their own free will. "Why the poison? The nukes would have killed everyone."

"Mostly a distraction. They knew you would be able to solve it, but since they spiked the champagne, they figured you would have a lot of people panicking and it would distract everyone as the nukes were coming in. And even if you knew, no one thought you'd be able to do what you did." He paused. "What did you do?"

I opened my mouth, stopped, and shook my head. "I really don't know how to explain it. What about Chun?"

Indira snorted. "As near as anyone can figure, he was devoted to the world that Huilang planned on creating and thought you were in the way. He also was behind the attack on your house in Albany. The money wired to the idiots was traced back to him."

"We don't know for sure what he planned or why, because someone," Steven stopped to glare at Carelian, who just purred louder, "ripped out his throat. But it looks like a crime of opportunity. Not anything else. The house had been intended to distract you, as most people get upset when their house burns down."

"If I hadn't been there?" I'm not sure I wanted to know, and from the looks on everyone's faces I had my answer.

"You were. The president wants to give you the Medal of Freedom," Steven said. His words made me roll my eyes even as Jo and Sable perked up.

They started to talk about medals and China, all the flowers people were sending me, and how I was trending on social media though almost no one realized what I did. There were cards and balloons all over the room. I'd have to look at them later.

My eyes caught on a white origami crane nestled in a vase of flowers, and I just knew somehow it was from Hishatio. I smiled. I needed to find the water wall notes for him. There was no reason to keep them and if his people wanted their isolation so desperately, I would not stop them.

I let my eyes close, and the sound of my friends and family talking lulled me to sleep. Secure in the knowledge they would be there if I needed them, just as I would always be there if they needed me.

Drafted Luck

Appendix: Magic Symbols

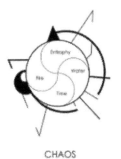

CHAOS

Chaos:

- Entropy
- Fire
- Water
- Time

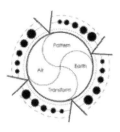

ORDER

Order:

- Pattern
- Air
- Earth
- Transform

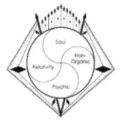

SPIRIT

Spirit:

- Soul
- Relativity
- Non-Organic
- Psychic

Author Notes:

Book 5 has arrived and I hope it lived up to what you were expecting. I'm already writing the next book called Faded Luck and it will be different yet again.

If you loved this novel, please take the time to leave a review, you will be amazed at the difference it makes.

You can follow me on social media at the following places:

Website: https://badashpublishing.com/
Facebook: https://www.facebook.com/badashbooks/
Twitter: https://twitter.com/badashbooks
Instagram: https://www.instagram.com/badashbooks/

There is a Twisted Luck Fan Group. I hope I see you there -
https://www.facebook.com/groups/150012450367159
9

If you're interested in free books, keeping up with what is going on in my life, as well as sales and launch announcements, you can sign up for my newsletter at my website. You never know what freebies might be in it.

Take care!

Mel Todd

Mel Todd

Mel Todd has over 29 stories out, her urban science fiction Kaylid Chronicles, the Blood War series, and the new Twisted Luck series. Owner of Bad Ash Publishing, she is working to create a place for excellent stories and great authors. With over a million words published, she is aiming for another million in the next two years. Bad Ash Publishing specializes in stories that will grab you and make you hunger for more. With one co-author, and more books in the works, her stories can be found on Amazon and other retailers.

Made in United States
Orlando, FL
09 June 2022

18646468R00217